Dark Southern Sun
LOVE, FRIENDSHIP, AND HONOR
IN
THE GOLDFIELDS OF OLD
AUSTRALIA
(v2)

I0525819

By Shaun J. McLaughlin

ISBN 978-0-9879035-6-3

Published by Raiders and Rebels Press

http://www.raidersandrebelspress.com

Front cover art, *Wathaurung Gathering*, 2012 by Wathaurung elder
and artist Marlene Gilson

*This novel I dedicate to my wife, Amélia Ah You, for her years of
support, good advice and affection.*

Table of Contents

What the Tide Brought In

March 1845

«Is he dead?»

The boy nods towards the shirtless, white man lying face down on the pale sand. Each gurgling wavelet races up to tickle the stranger's bare feet.

The boy and his younger sister gaze from the cool shade of a gum tree thicket to the beach below. The pungent fragrance of eucalyptus permeates the languid air. Shadows cast by the spear-like leaves dapple their dark bodies. Immobile beside the multi-toned bark of the trunks, they are invisible. Curious and patient, they study the body for signs of life.

«He is alive,» the girl counters. «I know it.»

Her brother points to the sky.

Overhead, a scavenging gull glides in wide circles, descending. The gray-backed bird swoops in low on billowed wings and alights a yard from its intended snack. It cocks its head several times at the inert form. Certain the body is indeed carrion, the gull hops forward and nips one extended hand with its massive yellow beak.

Fingers twitch. The gull squawks and leaps into the air. Heavy wing beats scatter powdery sand.

Mystery solved, the two children slip from their copse, worm through scrubby cedars, slide down a dune, and stalk towards the prostrate figure. The boy kneels, reaches for the man's furthest shoulder and rolls him over.

Hot, raspy sand jolts the stranger's sunburned back like a whip. His breath hisses out.

*****

Ryan forces his sea-salt-caked eyelids open. Two naked children, black silhouettes against the cloudless Australian sky, scrutinize him with detached curiosity. He wills his mouth to form words. Chapped lips, dusty gums and a swollen tongue struggle to eject two syllables. "Wa—ter."

The boy understands. He scampers to the nearby freshwater creek. The younger child smiles. Ryan finds the grin comforting. It promises help.

The oldest child, a lad showing his first traces of body hair and muscles, returns with a water-filled wooden bowl. He hands it to the younger and trots away. The girl kneels, slips her fingers behind Ryan's head, raises his chin and dribbles water into his mouth. Ryan's stiff throat rebels. He chokes and coughs. The child chatters soothing words and keeps the life-giving drips flowing.

The boy returns with an armload of cut poles. He constructs a lean-to of sticks. The young builder applies sheets of bark on the hut's sunward side, shading Ryan from the punishing sun.

After a brief animated discussion between the young natives in a language that mystifies Ryan, the lad again disappears. Ryan drifts to sleep.

Later, a creeping chill nudges him awake. The southern autumn sun is setting and the sand begins to surrender its warmth. Despite the cold, sleep returns.

*****

The man shivers in slumber. The girl knows he needs warmth but she has not yet mastered the magic of fire-starting. With muscles strong for her age, she pulls the man onto his side and wiggles her way next to his torso. She curls up into a fetal position, pulls one of his red-haired arms over her and lends the sick outsider her body heat. Stroking his hand, she waits, and watches the moon rise.

A sharp bird-chirp jolts her from half slumber. Her brother is returning. She whistles a response. She senses the presence of many bare feet padding across the night beach. The adults are coming.

*****

Ryan awakes to the sensation of gentle fingers applying salve to his tender back. He swivels his head and recognizes the girl from the beach. She hides a giggle with her hand, leaving a dab of oily paste on her nose.

Beneath him, animal skins cushion his damaged body against the hard ground. A bark ceiling arches overhead in a pole-hoop hutch with one wide opening. Bird squawks and the windy flutter of leaves tell him the hut is in a forest. Morning heat wafts in through the open doorway. Outside, people tread in and out of view and speak in a language full of long vowels sounds. He detects a pungent aroma. He sniffs to detect the source. His armpits are the culprits.

Behind the girl, a woman beats a slurry of water and vegetable paste. A shawl of animal skins adorns the shoulders of her otherwise unclothed body. Her nakedness startles Ryan. Middle-aged, she has weathered features and a wide nose. Gray and black hair spirals from her scalp like bundles of braided rope. Collapsed breasts dangle almost to the bowl she clutches.

The woman acknowledges Ryan's sky-colored irises with a smile, showing two tooth gaps. Ryan grins in return, though the effort stings his cracked lips.

She kneels beside Ryan. In tiny portions, she feeds him wet mush. He concentrates on the wooden spoon to avoid acknowledging the coal-pebble nipples inches from his face. With her steady help, Ryan eats the entire meal. The girl wipes off food globs dribbling down his chin. He smiles his gratitude and returns to soothing sleep.

Each time he stirs, the girl is there, ready with water or bits of food. She twirls her slim fingers in Ryan's ginger curls, tugs at his auburn whiskers, and strokes the half finger on his left hand. Ryan indulges the charming waif and accepts the role of a child's plaything. Always, her doe-like eyes twinkle with light. Her perpetual smile and bone-white teeth illuminate the shelter.

Ryan returns her smiles, happy to be in her company, glad to be alive. Days earlier, a saltwater grave seemed his certain fate.

After two days of convalescence, Ryan forces himself to crawl from the hutch. He pulls himself to his feet using a sapling and examines this new country. He counts six pole-and-bark huts beside a slow-flowing stream in a glade of towering gum trees. People go about their duties with an occasional peek in his direction. He estimates there are thirty-five adults and children.

The boy from the beach and the girl emerge from the forest shadows into the encampment. The boy carries a dead creature resembling a small, blunt-quilled porcupine. Ryan recognizes the fluid gait of a skilled tracker in the lad. His thin lips and a sharp jaw line add seriousness to his youthful face. Dark orbs probe the world from beneath bushy eyebrows. His pleasure at seeing Ryan flips the boy's features from stern to welcoming.

The girl grabs Ryan's wrist and waves her brother over. The girl chatters at her sibling and points to Ryan.

"My sister ask what your name?" states the boy in decent English.

"Ryan. What are yer names?"

"I Weeyn. Mean fire," the boy replies. "My sister Alinga. Mean sun. What mean your name?"

"Naught, as far as I know. 'Tis just a name."

Alinga shakes her head, not happy with Weeyn's translation. She argues with her brother and questions her mother until Weeyn shrugs and says, "We say your name now Warrain. Mean belongs to the sea."

"'Tis a fine name, thank ye."

"The name keep my sister happy and quiet; so, is good," Weeyn says, winking.

"Who is the woman taking care of me?" Ryan says, pointing.

"Our mother. Her name Mokborree. Mean peace. My father name Laarr. Mean stone."

Alinga asks another question.

"My sister say how you come to beach where we find you?"

"There is a big island to the south called Van Diemen's Land. A storm smashed my boat when I crossed the strait. I clung to the wreckage and washed up on shore."

"Is big island your home?" Weeyn says.

"No. My home is far across the ocean. I'll tell ye stories some day."

Alinga latches onto Ryan's partial finger and speaks.

"My sister ask how you lose finger."

Ryan hesitates. Can he explain frostbite to children who may not have seen snow or ice? He gives half the truth. "'Twas infected. I had to cut off the top half."

Weeyn translates. Alinga smiles in acceptance and speaks again.

"My sister ask how many summers you live?"

"Twenty-seven," Ryan says.

Weeyn conveys Ryan's age to Alinga by opening and closing the fingers of both hands several times. Ryan recognizes confusion—she cannot yet count well.

"How many summers have ye and yer sister?"

"Thirteen me. Nine her."

"Where did ye learn yer English and numbers?" Ryan says.

"I go school for black boys and work for white man in his stable," Weeyn says, looking down. Ryan senses the boy's memories of the stable are not happy ones.

Alinga pokes Weeyn and whispers a question. "Alinga ask if you stay with us."

"If ye'll let me stay. 'Twill be grand."

Weeyn answers his sister. She whoops and clamps her arms around Ryan's waist. He tousles her thick mop of straight hair.

"Alinga and I found you," Weeyn says. "We want you here. Father let you stay maybe. He is *arweat*—the headman."

"I see ye and the men hunting everyday," Ryan says. "Can I help hunt food?"

"Is Warrain strong now?"

"I'm a tad wobbly but better every minute."

"Can Warrain throw spear?"

"No," Ryan says. "But, I used a weapon like that afore." He points to a stone-bladed tomahawk leaning on a tree. "Can I go with ye tomorrow? I've lain too long eating yer food. I must contribute."

Weeyn points to Ryan's pale, shirtless chest. "You need wear something. It cold season here. Morning hard before sun come."

Weeyn speaks to his mother in their language. She replies with a single word Ryan does not understand, but the meaning soon becomes obvious. Mokborree extracts a long string of flexible sinew from a jumble of personal belongings and uses it to measure Ryan, first across the shoulders, then from chin to navel. She ties knots to indicate length.

Mokborree sorts through a pile of brown possum pelts and selects one. She holds it to Ryan's body, squinting and frowning. She arranges selected skins on the ground and murmurs a command to her daughter. Alinga threads a bone needle with thin strips of sinew and begins sewing the sections together.

By nightfall, the seamstress and her apprentice complete the possum wrap. Smiling, Mokborree pulls the navel-length garment across Ryan's wide shoulders. He bends, letting Alinga tie the single clasp at the front. She admires the man and her handiwork.

"Pretty!" she blurts, using the one English word she knows so far.

*****

Next morning in darkness, Weeyn nudges Ryan awake. His new garment keeps his upper torso warm in the predawn chill but rasps his healing back. He ignores the irritation and his cold-numbed bare feet.

Weeyn leads him to a fire in the camp's center. Ten naked men and youths examine Ryan when he arrives. They say nothing.

A middle-aged man sitting by himself on a log stands at Ryan's approach. Thick legged and broad shouldered, he wears a fur loincloth and a possum shawl. Unlike the other hunters who range close to Ryan's height of five-foot-eight, this man is a six-footer. He sports thick waves of graying hair. A grizzled beard hides his neck. Ryan notices parallel puffy scars on the man's belly. Ryan had seen similar scarification on Tasmanian natives and assumes they are self-inflicted, perhaps in a native ritual. He notes random scars he guesses are old wounds.

"Warrain," Weeyn says, "this is our *arweat*, and my father, Laarr."

"Pleased to meet ye, Laarr," Ryan says. He resists the cultural habit of extending his hand to shake.

Laarr sits and points to the log beside him. "Here!"

Laarr pats Ryan's knee with a chubby-fingered hand. "You one lucky *amadeat*."

Ryan glances to Weeyn for an explanation.

"Amadeat is our word for white man. My father's English is small. He means you lucky we found you. Most clans kill you. My father forbids killing whites except in defense."

Weeyn picks at his baked fish and continues. "All families in our clan—we are Wathaurung—once welcomed strangers as friends. It a duty. Many now angry and mean since the amadeat came to take our land."

Laarr pulls a stone-bladed knife from a pouch, stabs a fish baking in the coals, and passes it blade and all to Ryan.

"Eat friend."

Ryan picks the flesh from the bones and eats in silence following the others' example. The end of Laarr's meal signals the end for all. The men scatter and return with hunting weapons. Laarr seizes Ryan's upper arm in a near-bruising grip and leads him towards Weeyn. He exchanges words with his son, and leads the hunters upstream.

"Father says you prove yourself. He worry you scare game. Today, you and I hunt alone."

"What game do ye expect to find in this dark?"

"Most animals in our land sleep in day," Weeyn says. "Best time hunt is first light. We follow river and wait."

Weeyn offers Ryan a tomahawk, and takes the same and a spear for himself. He leads the way downstream on a riverside trail. Ryan strives to keep one stride behind his young friend. Any further apart and Ryan is certain his guide would disappear into the darkness.

After several hundred yards, Weeyn halts. "Make no noise. Listen!"

Ryan tunes his aural sense using a technique taught to him years earlier in colonial Canada. He isolates and identifies each sound, and blocks those that are nature's chatter: the gurgling hiss of the river on rocks; the flutter of wind-tickled leaves; dew dripping from trees to the ground. A bird call—likely an owl—he ignores. It's not game. A faint chewing and an occasional scratching above emerge from the background racket. He cups his palms behind his ears to amplify the sounds.

"What you hear?" Weeyn whispers.

"An animal overhead is eating leaves or seeds. It changes position often and climbs with sharp claws. There is another twenty paces to our left."

"Another? I not hear it before…but now, yes. Very good, for an amadeat."

"What are they?"

"*Walert*. Possum in your tongue."

"I need to repay yer mother for my garment. How do we get them?"

"Wait for light. I show." Weeyn squats on the sandy ground and hugs his knees to his chest for warmth.

Ryan remains erect. His shivers abrade his peeling back against the new cloak. He grits his teeth and seeks distractions. He sends his ears into the forest scouting for further animal signatures. Small creatures, too numerous to count, rustle amid the forest debris of cast-off leaves and twigs. He picks out a scuffling noise downstream, something to investigate later.

Ryan peers eastward through the trees. A blush of blue hems the horizon. Early-rising birds begin a sleepy twitter. Another twenty minutes will bring sufficient light to hunt. Ryan sniffs the air, memorizing alien scents he will attempt to identify later.

Right on schedule, Weeyn rises and tiptoes to a clump of gum trunks.

Ryan stares into the canopy. The shadows under the foliage are too murky to determine which tree holds their quarry. "Which is it?" Ryan asks.

"Watch. Learn," Weeyn says. He steps to the nearest trunk, brings his mouth an inch from the bark and exhales a lungful of hot air. At the fourth trunk, he waves to Ryan. "Come close. See."

Ryan squints at the patch of bark where Weeyn targets a stream of warm breath. Several minuscule brown hairs flutter. "What see?"

"An animal has left strands of fur when climbing the tree. 'Tis what ye mean?"

"Yes. Possum fur. It lives in this tree."

Ryan steps backward to where he has a wider view of the lower branches. The gum is young, six inches in diameter and twenty-five feet high. They wait as darkness retreats from the tree's canopy.

Ryan spots the possum half way up, an unnatural lump in the fork of a branch. Ryan signals Weeyn with a soft, three-note whistle, then, in one swift action, heaves his tomahawk. The weapon spins blade over handle and wallops the cat-sized marsupial, knocking it from the tree. Dazed, it falls at Weeyn's feet. The boy pierces its skull with the spear tip.

All smiles, Weeyn joins Ryan, holding the possum by its bushy tail. "Warrain no ordinary amadeat."

"Years ago and far away," Ryan says, "a native lad like yerself and his grandfather taught me to hunt and track. Later, I lived in the forest as a trapper. The only difference here is the animals."

"Were the natives black?"

"No. They have lighter skin, darker and redder than us whites."

"Did amadeat steal their land?"

"Aye!"

After an uncomfortable silence, Ryan says, "Let's find the other walert."

When the humans approach, the second possum slips into a hole thirty feet up a large gum tree.

"Watch and learn, white man," Weeyn teases.

With his tomahawk, the boy cuts notches in the trunk two feet and four feet from the ground. He holds the tomahawk in his mouth, slips bare toes into the lowest cutout, and hoists himself up. Standing in the first foothold, he chops a third cleft and steps into the second notch.

Ryan follows Weeyn's progress while he carves and ascends his crude ladder. When Weeyn pulls up even with the possum's hole, he hollers down, "Be ready."

His arm darts into the hole up to his elbow and emerges with a fistful of squealing fur. He flings the beast to Ryan's feet. He clubs it once with the blunt end of his tomahawk.

The two hunters follow the river valley. They investigate the scuffling sound Ryan detected earlier. A foraging wombat dashes into a burrow at their approach.

"Come see dumb wombat," Weeyn says.

The bear-cub-shaped marsupial is headfirst in its refuge with its rear end visible.

"'Tis not much of a burrow," Ryan remarks.

"*Ngoorr-ngoorr* has hard hide on back end. Other animal cannot kill wombat. But hunter can." Weeyn dispatches the beast with his spear.

At a river pool lined with reeds and rushes near the sea, Weeyn and Ryan alternate spearing eels, trying to out-do the other in the size of their catch. Weeyn wins. Ryan pokes under stream rocks to catch crayfish, a trick he learned as a hungry convict in Van Diemen's Land.

On the seaside beach, Weeyn builds a fire by rubbing sticks together—a feat Ryan had heard men speak of but not witnessed. They roast eels and crayfish for lunch.

Ryan can now appreciate the scenery he missed the day he washed ashore. A river ten paces wide at the mouth penetrates the land without rapids or obstacle as far as he can see from the beach. Behind the row of dunes, a narrow tableland abuts a wall of precipitous hills. Row upon row of gum trees cover the slopes. Ryan catches glimpses of nearby thick trunks through which parrots of green, red and blue dart with noisy squawks. The conglomeration of treetops over the hills reminds Ryan of a green, woolen sweater draped across broad shoulders.

In the afternoon, they return to camp with the fifty-pound wombat, three possums, one bandicoot and six fat eels hanging from a pole slung on their shoulders. Alinga runs to Ryan, clapping. Mokborree, beaming with pride in her son and houseguest, accepts the food. Without a pause, she begins skinning the animals using a stone knife and the sharp edge of a mussel shell.

Ryan and Weeyn relax by the campfire and snack on wattle seeds roasted in their pods on the coals. They sip cool water sweetened with crushed flowers from a plant Mokborree called *woorrak*. Ryan picks slivers from his feet, wishing he had the natives' leathery soles.

They both rise when Laarr leads his hunters into the cluster of huts with their catch of wallabies. Alinga speeds across the compound and clamps herself to her father's thick leg. She relates the great success of Warrain's hunt. Laarr lifts his daughter into his brawny arms and strides towards Ryan and Weeyn.

"Warrain," the arweat says, "good hunter. Laarr happy."

"Can Warrain hunt with men tomorrow?" Weeyn asks.

Laarr shakes his head no, replies in his language, and walks to his shelter carrying Alinga.

"What did he say?" Ryan says.

"He say no hunt tomorrow. Time to leave. Cold rains come soon. In morning we start long journey."

"Where are we going?"

"A place we call *balla arat*."

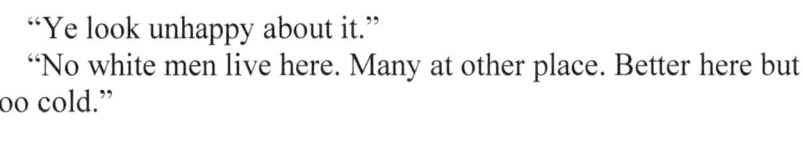

"Ye look unhappy about it."

"No white men live here. Many at other place. Better here but too cold."

Allow Me to Introduce Myself

April 1845

Walter Fraser hears the screech of a cockatoo. He halts his horse and holds up his hand. His two companions rein in their mounts. From his vantage point on the ridge, Fraser spots a pair of black legs framed by a gap in the foliage below, visible for an instant in the gum tree shade.

"Did you see him, Billy?" Fraser asks his Aboriginal tracker.

"I did, boss."

"Are they Djadjawurung?" asks Scott Healey. "I didn't see anythin'."

"It never fails to amaze me," Fraser begins, "how a man born to this country can be so senseless in the bush." Ignoring the audible sound of Healey gnashing his teeth, Fraser continues. "I was born abroad but my bush sense matches any black. Is that not so, Billy?"

"Yes, boss."

"Scott, look betwixt gaps in the canopy to the forest floor where the sun is probing. Relax your focus to better see movement on your periphery. Be ready for moments when wind creates openings in the branches. I bet you can spot them if you try."

Healey's single bushy eyebrow arches. Fraser has hit the nerve he aimed for. He grins.

"There. Two others," says Billy, pointing.

Fraser passes Billy a collapsible telescope. "What clan are they?"

Billy sweeps the forest with the scope. "Hard to tell, boss. Here the Djadjawurung and Wathaurung lands meet and customs are similar."

"Let's shoot 'em and check later," Healey says, pulling a rifle from his saddle scabbard. "It's easier to tell the buggers apart when they're lyin' still."

The chuckles from Fraser and Billy counter the tension caused by Fraser's badgering. Healey's shoulders and jaw relax.

"Wait, boss," Billy interjects.

"What do you see?"

"They be Wathaurung, boss. I recognize one." He leans in his saddle and returns the telescope to Fraser.

"Who is it?"

"The boy from your stable, boss."

"Which boy? There have been legions," Fraser says, turning to scowl at Healey.

"Weeyn, boss."

Fraser smiles. "Put the gun away Scott. Let us pay them a friendly visit."

"If we ride down the gully on our right, we can get in front, boss."

"Lead the way, Billy."

*****

Laarr's family group slips through the shadowy forest striving for invisibility. Footfalls make no sound on the rain-sodden soil and leafy debris. Moisture rising at the sun's beckoning fills the glades with mist and aids in concealment. The damp air is thick with the camphoric aroma of gum trees.

They follow a wooded creek valley and avoid the open plain. Quiet and stealth are essential where uncertainties lie. They are approaching the fluid border of Djadjawurung territory and must be wary—sometimes their ancient kin are not friendly. And white people now claim much of their old lands.

The group plods at the pace of the slowest—the elders wrapped in rain-soaked kangaroo robes. No one speaks. After seven days of abuse by showers and chill winds from dawn to dusk, and subsisting on slim rations, none waste energy on needless talk. Even the sun's appearance this morning brings no cheer.

Laarr had painted seven white stripes on his left arm the first day. Each morning he washed off one. Today, a single line remains. Soon they can rest.

A cockatoo spies them from the canopy and calls a warning. Thirty-five people cannot avoid all avian detection.

Three youths, Weeyn included, scout ahead: one in the center and another on his flanks. Behind, Laarr and eight warriors march with of a knot of women, children and elderly carrying their belongings. Ryan and a youth guard the rear.

Ryan shuffles, head drooping, a spear resting on his shoulder. Each footfall is delicate. Bruises and nicks mark his feet. His gut gurgles. For six days he has eaten uncooked roots and raw meat. No one can start a fire in the wet woods.

His thoughts drift back to the two years he spent on a chain gang in the Van Diemen's Land penal colony. He endured poor food, inclement weather, and inadequate clothing and footwear. If he must, he can tough it out, but he wishes he had a proper pair of boots and a chance to dry out.

He shifts the spear to his other shoulder to give his arm a rest. Laarr gave him the crude lance—nothing more than a long, sharpened pole. In brief breaks in the march, Weeyn taught Ryan spear-throwing basics. Ryan realizes he is no threat to man or beast unless close to his target. The tomahawk hanging on his waist in a leather loop remains his weapon of choice.

*****

Weeyn catches the glint of morning sunlight reflecting off a brassy, polished object—a color not part of nature. He freezes and scans the nearby forest clearing.

Three men on horses study him. Weeyn's stomach tightens when he recognizes the two white men he prayed never to see again. The one called Scott has a carbine resting across his saddle. Years ago, Weeyn witnessed the man's speed and accuracy with firearms—he cannot escape.

Weeyn issues a sharp whistle, imitating a parrot's distress call. The two youths on his flanks understand the signal and run to warn Laarr.

"Well, well Weeyn, how handsomely you have grown," says Fraser.

Weeyn remains mute. He gulps air to calm his trembling limbs.

"You remember Scott, do you not," Fraser continues, waving a hand towards his white companion. "And this black fellow is Billy. He works for me now to punish those sheep-stealing Djadjawurung."

"Punish mean kill!" Weeyn's adolescent voice breaks and he squeaks in a boy's soprano.

Fraser smiles. "Such a quick mind, Weeyn. You were always my best black student. Such a shame you ran away." His faux affection fades. "Perhaps, you should return."

Healey picks up the tone in Fraser's voice and swings the gun muzzle towards Weeyn. Billy spurs his mount forward to help encircle Weeyn.

Weeyn's pulse races. He wipes clammy palms on his thighs. His eyes dart beside him and behind. Fight or flight both mean death, but he will not surrender to these men.

*****

Ryan trudges forward and almost collides with the main group. "Why did ye stop?"

Laarr points ahead, "Bad amadeat."

Weeyn! Ryan bolts into the forest. He weaves among tree trunks and denser brush, using all his tracker skills to be soundless and unseen. He chooses a path part way up the side of a gentle ridge, hoping the extra height may provide an advantage.

A glint of sun on a rifle barrel brings him to a stop. Downhill, he spots three men on horseback in a semi-circle around Weeyn.

Like a dingo stalking a wary bandicoot, Ryan moves silent and unseen. He selects a route with the least undergrowth and fallen branches that could make a sound if stepped on. Focusing forward, he reads the ground's rough contours through his bare soles.

Ryan edges to within five yards above and behind the horsemen. His spear in his left hand, Ryan raises his tomahawk in his right and concentrates on the nearest man with the rifle.

"Lower yer gun or I'll brain ye!" Ryan yells.

The riders swing their heads towards Ryan but show no surprise or worry. Such a subdued reaction alerts Ryan—these men are experienced fighters, not the type he can spook or bluff. Weeyn fades into the forest's dark safety. Ryan's distraction has paid off. Now is time to back away from confrontation.

"Gents. I mean ye no harm. I believed ye were a threat to my friend. Sorry."

The shorter white man motions the rifle bearer to drop his weapon. Ryan welcomes the good faith gesture. He leans his spear on a tree and rests his tomahawk blade sideways on his shoulder. That way, the weapon is non-threatening but available.

"Good day to you," says the leader. "Please allow me to introduce myself. My name is Walter Fraser. What brings an Irishman to these woods in the company of blacks?" Fraser's tone would suit a man chatting to a new acquaintance at a social gathering.

Fraser appears to be thirty. He has a sandy mustache and piercing, cobalt eyes. Strands of golden hair poke from the edges of his black derby. His prominent hooked nose resembles the beak of a predatory bird. While it's difficult to size up a man on horseback, Ryan guesses he and Fraser share the same height and build.

"I was shipwrecked last month, sir," Ryan says. "The Wathaurung saved my life."

"I do not recall news of a recent wreck. What ship were you on?"

"Not a ship, sir. 'Twas a rowboat I built in Van Diemen's Land."

"You rowed across the unpredictable Bass Strait and lived. Remarkable! Allow me to introduce my companions. This is my foreman Scott Healey."

The age of the foreman is hard to pin down—maybe twenty-five, Ryan thinks. Slim, long in the torso, and clean-shaven, his dung-colored irises squint from a sallow face. Wavy, chestnut hair protrudes from under a faded, white slouch hat.

"Over here is my native tracker, Officer Billy, formerly of the Native Police Corps."

The bulky clansman in a faded blue uniform with polished brass buttons is a younger and shorter version of Laarr. Ritual scars etch his shaven cheeks. Hatless, his hair is cut in white man fashion.

"Pleased to meet ye all. My name is Ryan."

"No surname?"

"Naught I care to recall," Ryan says.

"I assume from your previous residence that you were a transported convict?" Fraser says.

"Yes, sir, but pardoned now."

"What was your crime? Petty thievery? Bad debts?"

When Ryan fails to answer, Fraser continues. "Come, come, Ryan. No need to be ashamed. Unlike me, most people in this country are convicts or their spawn. Is that not so, Scott?"

Healey shifts in his saddle but does not answer.

"My man Scott is the illegitimate child of two convicts, a clumsy pickpocket and a Billingsgate prostitute. Your pedigree could not be worse."

Healey clamps shut his eyelids and grits his teeth.

Ryan answers Fraser's question. "Naught of the men on the transport ship with me were common criminals, sir. We were political prisoners caught on the losing side of a fight for liberty."

"That sounds familiar!" Fraser says, stroking his mustache. "Were you with those Americans who attacked a Canadian colony years ago to drive out the British?"

"'Tis correct."

"As a man with Scottish roots, I too have no love for the English. I applaud your effort," Fraser says. "And I take it you consider yourself a man of honor."

"I like to believe so, sir."

"And Weeyn is a friend worth defending?"

"'Tis so, sir."

"Then, our business is done. Do you care to accompany us to civilization, such as it is? Buninyong is a few hours east."

"No sir. I thank ye. I have much to learn about this land. These people are the best teachers."

"Fair enough. Is there anything I can provide to make you comfortable?"

"Well, I could use a pair of boots, sir. I lack the natural leather soles of my mates."

Fraser leans from his saddle to examine Billy's footwear and then Healey's. "Scott, give him your boots."

Healey glowers at Fraser.

"Dear boy," Fraser almost whispers, "take off your boots. I will buy you a fancy pair in town. Even those American boots you always covet in that shop window."

Healey's dour features soften. He unlaces his high-topped leather boots, pulls them free and tosses them towards Ryan with a grunt.

"Take care, Mister Ryan no-last-name," says Fraser. "We will meet again."

Seconds after the riders disappear into the trees, Weeyn steps up to Ryan. "Did he hurt you?"

"Nay. He was a gentleman, to my surprise. Do ye know him?"

"I work in his stable when boy."

"Oh, he's the one who taught ye English. He and his quiet friend seem like decent fellows."

Weeyn staggers like a man slapped.

"What is wrong?" Ryan asks.

"No trust them. They devils."

Alinga's Wish

April 1845

That afternoon, Laarr washes off the last stripe on his arm and signals the trek is finished. He chooses a campsite in a spacious glade of massive gum trees. On one side, a narrow creek tumbles in a steep-sided gully of square-edged stone.

Ryan's choice to not leave with Fraser pays off in new bush knowledge as Laarr's family transforms the shady dell. While parrots and magpies scream protests from treetops, the women clear the ground of live vegetation, withered leaves, strips of old gum tree bark and branches. The men scavenge the surrounding forest and return with bundles of greenwood poles sharpened at both ends. They jam one end in the ground, bend the pole and stick in the other end, forming a hoop. A crisscrossing pattern of hoops forms a skeletal dome. At overlapping points, the men tie the poles together using flexible roots. Next, men and women stack or tie great sheets of peeled bark to the domes.

Ryan almost claps in admiration at their productivity. The group erects a new mia-mia every half hour. Within three hours, everyone has shelter. The women crawl in and arrange fur rugs over the sandy ground.

The branches and bark cleared by the women become fuel for a fire. Two wallabies become the first cooked meal in a week. Rendered fat sputters and sparks on the coals as hungry children learn a lesson in patience.

The group, rejuvenated by warmth and food, sheds their weary posture and stoic silence. Firelight reflecting from the leafy canopy creates an illuminated sphere in the dark, primal forest, a confined world alive with animated chatter and laughter.

Ryan sits on a log, enjoying the spectacle of happy people. Alinga kneels beside him, untying and retying his boots. The laces fascinate her. Weeyn lounges against a tree to Ryan's left, sharpening a bone spear point with a stone.

"In the brief time with ye," Ryan says, "I've not seen such joyful activity."

"Many families live near here in winter. Soon they visit or we go them," Weeyn says.

"How many Wathaurung family groups like yers are there?"

Weeyn wiggles his fingers while he counts. "I think, twenty-five."

"Do they live in peace?"

"Sometimes men jealous about women. Sometimes keep old grudge and fight. Most time peace. Much war with other clans."

"Are all groups small like this one?" Ryan sweeps his arm towards the crowded fire area.

"Some more. Some less. Each family has arweat and his brothers, wives and children." Weeyn answers Ryan's questions, all the while working the bone to fine point.

"So, if everyone in the group is related, where do the wives come from?"

"Girls come from other family groups. Best way. Makes our clan big family. Less fight."

"What age do men and women marry?" Ryan asks.

"Girls go live with husband family after ten summers. Become real wife after first blood."

Ryan blushes at the casual mention of menstruation. His color does not show in the orange firelight. "When do men take wives?"

"When become good hunters. Maybe twenty summers. Listen," Weeyn points to a knot of giggling matrons. "Many women this night tease my older cousin Tomboko because wife coming soon."

"Where is his betrothed?" Ryan asks.

"She come soon at *caribberie*."

"What is a corroboree?"

Weeyn cringes at Ryan's pronunciation but lets it be. "It when people eat and dance and marry and celebrate. We tell Dreamtime story."

"What is that?"

"Dreamtime long ago when spirits created the sun, earth, trees, animals, and people. Dreamtime set all living things in proper place and made rules how we live on land. Visions come from Dreamtime. It place our spirits go when we die."

"'Tis much like parts in the white man's bible."

"Dreamtime not for amadeat." Weeyn scowls. "You know nothing of our laws."

Ryan clears his throat, preparing to defend himself, but hesitates. How can he defend himself given the history of whites in new lands? He has witnessed dispossessed original inhabitants in North America and Van Diemen's Land. He pats Weeyn on the back and contemplates the amber sparks rising into the night air.

*****

The next morning, Ryan joins the men and youths for the dawn hunt. They trot from the forest at first light into the expansive, rainy-season grasslands. Raindrops on the thigh-high blades soon slather their bodies from toes to waist. Ryan luxuriates in the body warmth generated by exercise on a chilly morning, even as he fights the weight of dew-drenched trousers.

The hunters, except Ryan, carry three weapons: a *koorr*, a wooden club; a *karnweel*, a slender, twelve-foot spear with a notched tip to make it harder to extract; and a thicker, six-foot spear they call a *daar*. All spears have wooden points. Ryan makes a mental note to obtain metal spear points for them when he can.

Laarr guides the hunters up a shallow valley and locates a troop of *goeem*, gray kangaroos. All the men, except two youths, form two lines and arrange themselves along the valley's two summits. The sun rises.

Shouting and the dull crack of wooden clubs clunking together grows in strength. A dozen kangaroos bound along the valley floor fleeing two noisy young hunters. With the other men, Ryan begins to jog through the high grass, staying on the troop's flanks, their presence preventing the roos from mounting the valley's sides.

The valley ends in a steep gulch. Trapped, the beasts wheel around to confront their pursuers. For a moment the goeem have the advantage with their greater numbers and superior weight. Two bucks that Ryan estimates are close to seven feet tall guard the front. But hunters employ weapons and tactics. Laarr points to two juvenile males. The hunters close in. Ten karnweel hiss through the air. The victims squirm and squeal in the dust. The hunters allow the survivors to escape. No point, Laarr explains, to kill beyond your needs.

After returning from the hunt, Ryan hurries to the creek to wash smeared roo blood off his arms. He removes his boots and soaks his feet, savoring the cool water swirling around his ankles. While the new boots protect his soles, trapped sweat makes walking uncomfortable. He has heel blisters. He needs socks.

Weeyn and Alinga locate him. From the ravine edge above, the girl commences an excited banter.

"Yer sister is always a cheerful, chattering bird," Ryan says.

"She happy," Weeyn says. "Mokborree say we can show you our land and how find food."

"Find food," Alinga repeats. To illustrate her growing English vocabulary, she mimics putting food in her mouth and chewing.

The three companions hike upstream. Ryan imagines how odd they would appear if seen by whites. Two naked black children leading a pale-skinned white man dressed in laced boots, tattered breeches, a wide brimmed hat of kangaroo skin and a possum shoulder wrap.

Weeyn carries his weapons. Few mammals are active at midday, but his hunter instinct never rests. Alinga holds a woven basket containing a simple bone knife. She inspects the ground passing by her feet.

Ancient trees with mottled trunks, hungry for sunlight, permit little space between interlaced leaves for sunbeams to find the ground. Ryan follows the flight of a cockatoo across the thin forest gap created by the creek bed. Flowers add splashes of color to the greenish-gray monotony.

Alinga shouts in Wadawurrung. She drops to her knees by the base of a rotting trunk of a stubby tree, a variety unlike the ubiquitous and endless varieties of gum trees. She borrows her brother's tomahawk and starts knocking off chunks of the porous, punky wood. With her knife she pokes into crevasses at soil level and extracts thumb-sized grubs. Each one she discovers elicits a coo of delight.

"Is that food, Weeyn?"

"Yes, Warrain. Good. You see."

Weeyn points to a nearby shrub, a woody stump sprouting a thick crown of long grass-like leaves. Ryan recognizes it as a live version of the dead one Alinga just excavated. "Good food inside,"

Weeyn says. He retrieves his tomahawk from his sister and slits open the truck to expose a starchy, white pulp. "Try eat."

Ryan scoops a morsel with his tomahawk and pops it into his mouth. It has the consistency of an uncooked potato. He recognizes the taste. "'Tis what Mokborree fed me when I first arrived."

"Yes. Name *yakka*."

A hundred yards further, Alinga signals a new discovery. She leads Ryan by the hand to a cluster of low plants with leaves that remind Ryan of carrot tops. She uses her knife like a garden trowel to pry long, white roots from the pebbly soil.

"'Tis some kind of parsnip," Ryan exclaims.

Alinga half fills her basket with roots before they continue.

They emerge from the last tendril of forest into a sward of thigh-high grass. Warmth caresses their shade-cooled bodies. Weeyn follows a faint path. The ground rises in stages from a flat plain towards a round hill a mile to the north.

Weeyn raises his spear to halt their march. "Come. Slow," Weeyn says. "*Kadak*."

Ahead on a rocky outcrop, a snake resembling loops of coiled rope glowers at them.

"Is that one poisonous?" Ryan asks.

"Yes."

"What do we do now?"

"You watch and learn," Weeyn says.

Alinga gathers two fist-sized rocks. Weeyn inches closer to the big reptile. His sister tosses one stone overhand. The rock lands, bounces once and brushes the snake. It coils into an angry bundle. Keeping her distance, Alinga tosses the second rock with precision. It rolls and hits the serpent. It hisses and raises its murderous head skyward on its scaly body until it peers at Alinga from two feet off the ground. Weeyn flings his spear with impressive accuracy. The blade pierces the snake's neck. The reptile collapses, writhes for half a minute and goes still.

"I'll nary be that fine a spear thrower," says Ryan. "I can barely hit a tree."

Weeyn decapitates the snake and lifts the arm-width, five-foot body into the air. "Dinner," he says with a grin.

Weeyn leads the way up the slope to a shady glade of gum trees at the hill's summit. Alinga scrapes away the surface leaf litter to create a fire pit and buries her parsnip roots in the sand. Weeyn deposits a bundle of wood and starts a fire. Ryan guts the snake.

When the new fire ceases the initial flare-up and subsides to flickers and even heat, Weeyn drapes the snake carcass over the fire on a tripod of greenwood sticks. Alinga picks the white grubs from her basket and lays them in a row on a flat rock next to the flames.

While the meal cooks under Alinga's management, Weeyn and Ryan stroll to the glade's edge and scan the rolling plain to the east. The scene spans at least ten miles. In the distance, a plume of wood smoke rises. Much closer, a white smudge flows across the plain.

"What's that?" Ryan asks.

"Is big herd *boolgana*, sheep," Weeyn explains. "Every winter we come here, more boolgana. Less land for Wathaurung. When we hunt, stay far from sheep. If close, white men think we steal."

"What makes that smoke way beyond?"

"White man town."

Ryan stares at the distant sign of colonial habitation. He knows from experience that, no matter how long he stays in the bush, eventually he will return to his own kind.

Alinga bounds over to Ryan. Her grin wide, she says, "Eat!"

Ryan lets the exuberant youngster tug him along. To Weeyn, he says, "Have ye been teaching her English?"

"She not let me rest. All time teach, teach, teach."

Alinga pushes Ryan to a log near the fire. She points to another log and barks a command at her brother. He sits. The two men exchange smiles and shrugs.

Alinga places two roasted grubs on a thin sheet of bark and passes it to Ryan. "Eat! Good." Hands on her hips, she waits for his reaction to her meal starter.

Ryan pops one toasted bug into his mouth and chews. The taste reminds him of nuts. "Very nice. Thank ye," he says.

Alinga claps her hands and smiles.

Weeyn fakes a cough and points to his open mouth.

Alinga laughs and serves him two grubs. The last grub, she pops in her mouth and retrieves her guests' bark platters. Raking apart the fire embers with a stick, she exposes the parsnip tubers. She spears two with her knife, arranges them on Ryan's bark, slices them lengthwise and passes the platter to Ryan. After serving her brother his share, she sits cross-legged in the sand and picks at her own root.

A vision of years ago in Ireland flashes in Ryan's mind. His sister and he, both children, sit at a play table made by their grandfather. His sister pretends to serve tea and crumpets. Girls everywhere thus prepare for their future roles like Alinga today. Ryan sighs at the memory of his long dead sibling.

"Careful, Warrain. Food hot," Weeyn says.

Alinga steps close to Ryan and blows on the parsnips. She raises her ebony-in-ivory eyes to Ryan and says, "Better!"

With the parsnips consumed, Alinga serves the last course, snake. She shows Ryan how to peel the hide off the meat. It reminds him of eating fish cooked in its skin. The flavor is much like chicken.

To Weeyn, he says, "She's taking fine care of us."

"Is Wathaurung way."

All three stop eating. Breathing pauses. A sound, a mere whisper of something different from the forest's natural tone, triggers their primal instincts. Though brief, like a single flat note in a string ensemble, they cannot ignore it. Only their eyes move, first to ensure weapons are within reach, and then to explore the bush around them.

Leaves rustle from behind where no wind exists to create such movement. To the left, an unseen weight fractures a twig. A spiny echidna flees from the shadows to the right. Weapons ready, Ryan, Weeyn and Alinga survey the forest in three directions from which something or somebody is approaching.

From the fourth direction, laughter.

A warrior, who Ryan guesses is twenty, poises at the glade edge, a spear in hand. Taller by several inches than Ryan, his arms and torso are sculpted with muscles. His chest is etched with ritual scars.

To Weeyn, he speaks words in Wadawurrung that sound like teasing. The youth leaps to his feet and jams the butt of his spear into the dirt. The warrior reacts with hoots of joy and flashes a wide mouth of white teeth.

"Loklok," Weeyn blurts in English. "I no like this game."

To Ryan's relief, Loklok responds in English. "Weeyn, dear boy, is it not better for a friend than an enemy to test your skills? You have improved. Last year I came within a stride before you heard me."

In a heartbeat, Ryan concludes Loklok is a bully. Growing up Irish in world run by the English taught him that survival sense by the time he could walk. Ryan strides to within two paces of the visitor.

"I'm Warrain, Weeyn's friend." Ryan rises on his toes, giving him extra height before the warrior.

"My name is Loklok. It means eagle," the warrior says.

"'Tis a curious phrase ye used for a Wathaurung."

Loklok raises his brows in a silent question. Ryan continues. "When speaking to Weeyn, ye said 'dear boy.' Ye are another pupil of Walter Fraser, I reckon."

Several sounds follow, so close in sequence they seem to be one chord: Weeyn sucking in a startled breath; a shriek from Alinga; and, wump when a spear embeds in the sand at Ryan's feet.

Ryan does not budge, except to touch the tomahawk hanging on his belt. He squints at the young warrior's anger-twisted face.

Three warriors step into view and raise their spears. Loklok waves them off and walks towards Ryan.

"Are you a friend of that *bunyip*?" Loklok asks.

"Nay," Ryan says.

Alinga darts in front of Loklok threatening him with her knife in Ryan's defense. Loklok flicks her blade aside, his features now showing mirth, not anger. He lifts Alinga under the armpits and raises her aloft. He speaks to her in soft, affectionate tones. She thrashes and kicks the air.

Ryan shifts his weight to his rear foot in preparation for a lunge. In the microsecond between Ryan's impulse to attack and the actual step, Weeyn's spear shaft slaps a stinging blow across Ryan's chest.

"Stay, amadeat. None your business."

Ryan thrusts the spear away and glares at the boy. "Yer letting him hurt yer sister."

"He not hurt her. They play. Loklok her betrothed."

Ryan taps the toe of his right foot, making a rapid beat on the sand. He strokes his half finger and sucks in several deep breathes before he speaks. "Instead of hitting me, Weeyn, couldn't ye've said something sooner?"

*****

Ryan's longer legs outdistance his young companions on the hike back. Arriving at the encampment, he borrows a steel-bladed tomahawk and struts into the bush. By the time Weeyn and Alinga arrive, Ryan has harvested poles to build his own shelter.

Weeyn sits by the campfire, ignoring Ryan.

With a child's uncomplicated empathy, Alinga comprehends Ryan's intent. She helps gather sheets of bark. Together they finish his mia-mia before nightfall. Alinga carries Ryan's one belonging, a fur blanket, from her family shelter into his.

Her lower lip trembling, Alinga says, "Angry at me?"

Ryan lifts her chin with his index fingers until he can look in her eyes. "I'll nary be angry with ye, wee lass."

Alinga jumps forward, beaming. She wraps her thin arms around his waist and presses her check to his ribs. Ryan pets her thick hair, until a sharp call from Mokborree summons Alinga to evening chores.

*****

Without Weeyn to wake him, Ryan misses the morning hunt. The maniacal call of a kookaburra jars him awake at sunrise. He emerges from his low shelter on hands and knees. The camp's remaining occupants seem busier than usual. Mokborree tosses him a slice of cold kangaroo for breakfast and departs into the forest.

While he chews the gamey meat, Ryan observes camp activities. Women and girls, in tight gossiping knots, skin and carve game, pound roots into mush, and wash fruit. Pairs of older men carry in bundles of dry firewood and stack it near the central fire pit and two secondary pits.

"Must be a corroboree coming," Ryan mutters. Finishing his sparse meal, he joins the elders in gathering wood.

By noon, the hunters return with a kangaroo, two wallabies and several woven baskets packed with white clay. The women take possession of the carcasses. The hunt complete, the men crouch beside the supply of clay.

Laarr remains on his feet. He commences speaking in formal tones to the circle of men. Ryan cannot decipher the words but the waving arms and foot stomping tell a story.

When Laarr finishes his recital, he dabs a stick in the gooey clay and begins to paint himself. Starting with his left shoulder, he draws a diagonal line across his chest down the right side of his torso. At his pelvis he curves the lines in towards his groin and down to his right thigh. He draws another line parallel an inch from the first line. He draws a second pair of parallel white lines from his navel past his groin to his left thigh. Finished his art, Laarr lifts his palms to the sky and chants. The chalky lines vibrate on his raven skin.

Laarr sits and the oldest man in the group rises to recite his story. Finished, he paints his body. He creates a circle four inches in diameter on both shoulders, followed by two others close together on his chest, and a fifth above his navel. From the lowest circle, he paints a snaking line across his belly, past his groin, to his left knee. He chants to the sky and sits.

Each man in order of age recites a story and decorates his body. No two patterns are the same. Ryan guesses the painted shapes represent the storyteller's life. The younger men tell shorter stories and draw smaller pictographs. Weeyn, the youngest hunter, scribes his chest with two modest circles.

While the men embellish their bodies, the women and female children adorn themselves with headbands and necklaces of leather from which dangle feathers and shiny bits of shells.

In a heartbeat, all chatter ceases. The dull thump of wood on wood filters through the leafy soundproofing. Thirty-five people peer into the forest. The sound, rhythmic and faint, grows in volume. No one's demeanor indicates worry, so Ryan assumes guests are coming.

A cortège of Wathaurung warriors from another family enters the compound, pounding two-foot-long wooden clubs together in a martial beat. Every male's body sports a unique symbolic pattern, including lines and circles on their cheeks and foreheads.

Ryan pats the tomahawk on his belt when he spots Loklok.

Behind the warriors come the women, wearing their finest shell and feather jewelry. Shy children creep in at the procession's rear. The visitors outnumber Laarr's group.

The adornments of one girl exceed those of other women: extra necklaces, plus bracelets and anklets. About five feet tall, her slim body lies on the cusp between child and young woman—hips beginning to curve outwards, breast buds adding faint contours to her chest. The girl's skin color is mahogany, unlike the typical Wathaurung ebony.

A visiting matron marches the maiden—Ryan assumes she is her daughter—over to Laarr. The girl balances on trembling legs close to her mother and gawks at her feet. Next to Laarr looms his eldest brother, Murrangurk, and his son, Tomboko. The latter passes the girl's mother a bundle of possum skins, knives and stone tools. In response, the woman leads her daughter by the wrist to Tomboko. Ryan recognizes the word *lanapoon*, which he has learned means wife. The simple marriage ceremony lasts a minute.

Loklok strides over to Mokborree. In his words to her, Ryan hears Alinga's name. Mokborree crosses her arms and shows her back, refusing to talk to her future son-in-law.

"I guess ye dislike him too," Ryan mutters to himself.

Loklok paces the camp's perimeter searching for his fiancé. Ryan spots Alinga scampering along the shady edges of the encampment like a wary bandicoot, hiding from her pursuer.

The mingling groups exchange greetings and gifts. Ryan leans on a tree near his hut, reading the universal human stories that require no translation. Relatives embrace family members after the long separation. Joyful wailing and happy tears pour from parents and their married daughters. Other than brief peeps at him, everyone ignores Ryan.

The young bucks from both families gather at the main fire pit and compete to be the first to produce flames using rubbing sticks. Loklok gets his tinder smoking, coaxes the flimsy ember into a tongue of flame with puffs of breath, and ignites the waiting kindling on one side of the fire. Weeyn, in second place, applies his flame to the fire's far side. Soon, the new flames engulf the dry branches. Loklok carries a burning branch and ignites a second campfire. Weeyn ignites the third fire pit.

The edge of sunlight creeps across the forest canopy. Darkness soon reduces distance until no world exists beyond the fires' glow.

While the women prepare the feast, the men gather beside the central bonfire. Loklok monopolizes the conversation. He points to old wounds on his body, each is a lighter shade of black and encircled in white clay like a battle medal. He pantomimes the thrusting of a spear and slamming of a club. He tells the story of every fight, his audience stone-faced to his bragging. Other warriors recount similar tales with less bravado.

The feasting begins. Girls pass out helpings on bark platters. Mokborree makes sure Ryan gets his share of parsnips, yakka mush, fruit and roasted wallaby.

The meal ends near midnight when the last morsel of food disappears. Children gather the now greasy bark platters and toss them in the fires, which roar up in response.

The older women form a cross-legged row at the firelight's rim. Across their knees, each stretches a skin, fur side down, forming a sort of drum. These they beat with their hands, keeping time. The tempo set, they commence a chanting, singsong a cappella.

A tight column of men, women, boys and girls—Alinga and Weeyn included—emerge from the darkness, pounding their feet to the beat. The hunters bang wooden clubs together, matching the rhythm set by the seated women. The dancers encircle the central fire, singing and chanting.

Seated, Laarr leads the dancers with a staff, like a maestro before an orchestra. He marches the mob of sixty dancers clockwise and counter-clockwise at his pleasure, with the greatest air of authority.

Loklok waves to Alinga ahead of him in the dance formation, trying to get her attention. She ignores him and concentrates on her dance steps. When she does glance up, she smiles to Ryan seated near Laarr. Ryan smiles back. Loklok, his hunter's senses tuned to every nuance, notices the exchange. Even at a distance, Ryan spots

Loklok's flared nostrils and clamped teeth. The young warrior fidgets but remains in the dance position Laarr assigned him.

Ryan applauds the stamina of the revelers. The sweating dancers dip and sway to Laarr's commands. They shuffle and stomp. Arms wave. Bodies bend and crouch. Dancers rise to full height, fingers tickling the sky. After two hours, Laarr offers his baton to Boort, the elderly leader of the guest group, and he directs the performance for another hour.

Laarr barks a command. The long dance ends. Women and girls move deeper into the shadows. The body-painted hunters remain. Young boys fetch spears and pass them to the warriors.

The women drummers start a new beat, strident and quick. Men begin a dance that imitates war. Feet pound. Spears thrust. Voices grunt. Dark skin melds with the shadows, while the white clay patterns catch and reflect the amber firelight. Their human forms dissolve. Spectral lines and pulsating circles dance among the fire sparks. Ryan shudders.

The Wathaurung expose their innate feral savagery, the product of innumerable years surviving despite hunger, weather, poisonous creatures, warring clans or marauding white settlers. By the dancer's ferocity, the men promise their lives in defense of their families and clan.

Every time Loklok mimes a spear thrust, his unblinking glare locks onto the object of Alinga's attention. Ryan answers Loklok's threats with a stony stare.

The enacted battle continues for at least an hour, until, in finale, the warriors roar two great shouts, jam spear points at the sky, and stop as one. In the unfamiliar silence, Ryan can hear their ragged breathing.

*****

No one arises for the dawn hunt the next day. Weeyn, who slept outside, lies between two fur rugs, observing visitors roll up sleeping skins and stretch their limbs. Smoke curls from multiple cooking fires. The murmur of dozens of disconnected conversations drifts past his ears.

Loklok strides to Weeyn. He barks a question in Wadawurrung. «Where is your sister?»

«I know not, Eagle.» Rising to his feet, he adds, «I will search for her. Wait here, please.»

Weeyn trots to the closest hut, whispers pleasantries to the occupants and scurries to the next hut to deliver a brief weather report. He visits every hut. In no case does he mention Alinga. At Ryan's mia-mia, his true predetermined destination, he whistles to awaken the red-haired sleeper. Ryan rises on his elbow with an inquiring look.

"Stay in. Loklok want fight. Maybe kill you. I come when safe."

"Thank ye, friend."

Weeyn visits the last two huts to mutter a cheerful good morning. He returns to Loklok, shaking his head. «I am sorry, Eagle my future brother, my sister Sun must be gathering roots in the forest.»

«Why does my betrothed always smile at that white dog?» Loklok asks.

«She is amused at his pink skin and ocher hair. Her actions are childish, nothing to concern a great warrior like you,» Weeyn answers.

Loklok puffs out his chest, peers about the hut area again and trots off to catch up with his departing family. Weeyn follows at a discreet distance to ensure Loklok does not change his mind and return.

Weeyn whistles across the creek gorge to the thicket beyond. Alinga emerges from hiding. She scampers down one rocky slope, up the other and takes her brother's hand.

«Thank you. I love you, Fire.»

«Sun my sister. You cannot run from Eagle forever. You are promised.»

«I never promised!» Alinga says.

«You are too young to understand such things. But you must obey our father.»

«Eagle scares me. Does our father understand that?»

«Eagle is the best hunter and fighter in our clan,» Weeyn says. «He is the first son of the arweat. There is no better husband. Our father does what is best for you.»

Alinga frowns but says no more.

*****

Alinga parts her brother's company and meanders between tree trunks to her parent's mia-mia. Mokborree pounds yakka in a wooden bowl with a short club.

«Can I help, mother?» asks Alinga.

Mokborree ignores the question. Her pounding of the starchy plant's innards intensifies.

«You are angry. Why, mother?»

Mokborree slams the club to a halt in the mush and turns on Alinga. «I am angry because I have a fool for a daughter.»

Mokborree renews her punishment of the yakka. «I should send you to Eagle's family today and end your dishonorable behavior.»

Alinga feels her lower lip tremble and sockets begin to sting with tears. «But I hate him,» she says.

Mokborree pauses, smiles and strokes Alinga's cheek. «You are my only living daughter. It is my duty to help you attract the best husband. I was lucky to love your father from the start. Eagle has good in him. You will love him in time. You will have beautiful children together.»

«I see adults making children,» Alinga begins. «He can never touch me like that.»

«You are young. This thing will not seem so strange when you are older.»

«I will go hunt roots now,» Alinga says, to avoid further talk of babies. She spots the new girl, her cousin Tomboko's wife-to-be coming her way. Her name, Tarrarrapeel, means white.

«Are you Sun, daughter of Peace and Stone?» she inquires of Alinga.

Alinga nods twice.

«I am Tarrarrapeel, but everyone calls me Tarra. My new mother sent me to find food in this forest. She says you will show me.»

Alinga scrutinizes the older and taller girl. Besides her lighter skin, Alinga spots other anomalies: hair less dark and irises with a hint of blue. «Does illness make you light skinned?» Alinga asks.

«I am not sick, silly,» she replies. «My father was a white man.» Her tone belies any negative concern for her differences. «That is how I got my name.»

Alinga gasps at the revelation. She has never conceived of a Wathaurung woman marrying a white. «Does your father live with your family?»

«No. He took my mother when she was young. I was born away. We came home four winters later.»

«Why?»

«I know not. Mother does not speak of it.»

Other questions about the ways of white men tickle Alinga's tongue but she decides to wait. «Come. I will show you where the best food hides.»

Alinga leads her new companion downstream from the huts. She reveals the locations of parsnips and other tuberous plants. She escorts her to where the nut and fruit trees grow. Together they forage and fill their baskets.

«How many summers have you?» Tarra says. «I have ten.»

«I have nine,» Alinga answers.

«Soon you will be the age to join the family of Eagle,» Tarra remarks. Squatting, she hacks into a rotting yakka stump searching for maggots.

Alinga shudders at the casual remark and is glad Tarra does not notice. «Is he a nice man?» she asks.

«My cousin is handsome and a great warrior.»

«But is he kind?»

«He is the best hunter. He already has one wife and can afford another.»

Alinga stomps her foot.

«I am sorry little Sun to tell you this,» says Tarra. «Eagle desires many sons. So he will marry many wives.»

«I am a chief's daughter. I should be a first wife. The only wife.»

«We are girls. It is not for us to choose,» Tarra says, looking away.

Tarra's casual and confident veneer fades. For a second, Alinga sees the frightened girl from yesterday.

«White, do you love your betrothed?» Alinga says.

«No. I met him yesterday,» she whispers.

«When will you make babies?»

Tarra shrugs. «When my new mother tells me I am ready. Not soon, I hope.»

Alinga ponders a heretical concept. «If I tell you something, do you promise not to speak of it to others?»

Tarra rallies her spirits at her friend's conspiratorial tone. «I so pledge. Tell me.»

«I want to choose my husband.»

Tarra's eyes enlarge. «Never! This law comes from the Dreaming.»

Alinga settles cross-legged beside Tarra, and pokes her knee. «If you could choose, who would it be?»

Tarra blushes.

«You love another boy, not my cousin,» Alinga chortles. She claps her hands in glee. «I knew it to be so. Who is it?»

«I will not say. That would be sinful.» On the defensive, Tarra asks a question of her own. «Who would you choose? Tell me!»

Alinga ponders the question, then replies, «There is no one.»

The girls stroll home holding hands. They tell happy stories of summer days, good food and friends. They avoid further talk of husbands and babies.

Alinga skips for joy when she spies Warrain and Weeyn near the fire conversing as friends. She tugs Tarra. «Come with me. I must ask Belongs-to-the-sea a question.»

«Is that the white man's name?»

«Yes.»

«Is he mean? My first mother says white men are all bad,» Tarra says.

«No. He is a good man. Come.»

*****

Ryan detects movement on his periphery. Alinga and the new girl enter the encampment.

Ryan nudges Weeyn. "Yer sister has found a friend."

Weeyn straightens his spine. The gesture is not lost on Ryan. "Ye know this lass?"

"Yes. She Tarra. We met when last visit Boort's family."

"She's a pretty one. Do ye fancy her?"

"She is Tomboko's wife. No more question."

Alinga approaches, her smile wide for Ryan. She chatters a flurry of Wadawurrung at Weeyn. He cocks his head. Alinga speaks again. They argue. Weeyn shrugs and turns to Ryan. "She say to ask you funny question."

"'Tis fine. Ask."

"In your clan, do fathers choose husband for daughter, or can daughter find own husband?"

"In the past, parents in my country and other white lands always chose the husband. Times are changing. Most daughters can refuse now."

Weeyn translates. Alinga bounces in a circle mimicking a frolicking joey. Tarra laughs at a private joke the men do not get.

"What's going on?" Ryan says.

"My sister be more crazy every day," Weeyn replies.

Kangaroo Fighter

May-June 1845

Sleep eludes Alinga. Today's revelations have knocked her preordained, no-options fate askew like a hut tipped by the wind. First she learned women can marry outside the clan, even another race. Then Warrain told her white clans do not force girls to marry against their will. Boundaries that once formed cages shrink to obstacles. The alien concept of self-determination takes root, expressed in a child's terms. *I can do what I want.*

While her parents snore and her brother twitches in his sleep, a hazy dream she has repressed for weeks seizes advantage of the weakened world order and pops into her mind in perfect clarity. *Warrain can be mine.* Alinga emits a startled whimper.

Her mother stirs. «Bad dream, daughter?»

«It is nothing.»

It is far from nothing. Her heart thumps in her chest. Youthful naïveté assures her the goal is noble and possible. Yet, at nine she has the wisdom to comprehend that pouting and tantrums are useless tactics in this case. Ideas and schemes jumble and flip while the hours of night pass. Her juvenile optimism tells her a hidden path exists, but finding it eludes her young intellect. When sleeplessness exhausts her higher cognitive abilities, the primitive part of her mind that speaks in pictures, not words, connects her with the Dreaming.

Alinga is a young dingo, alone on the parched summer plain. She is desperate for water, but several aggressive dingoes guard the water hole. Knowing she cannot fight or outrun them, she kills a plump rat and carries it in her jaws. Dropping the meal before the big canines, she says: «The best one of you take this offering.» While the others fight over the meal, she drinks her fill.

*****

As is his custom after a hunt on a warm morning, Ryan sets out for a private pool to bathe. Delicate ferns grow from earth-filled pockets between the moss-coated rocks of the creek wall. Their green fans droop over the watercourse. Trickles of groundwater flow from cracks and plunge in miniature cataracts to ripple the basin. A shaft of sunlight streams in through a break in the tree canopy.

Ryan is scrubbing his chest when Alinga pops her face through the fronds of a tree fern and calls, "Warrain!"

He reaches for his trousers to cover up but the girl scampers to his side before he can jam a foot down a pant leg. Instead, he sits on a boulder and drapes his trousers across his lap. Alinga is blind to his nakedness. To her and other Wathaurung, clothes are for warmth, not modesty.

Face-to-face with Ryan, Alinga pokes a slender finger at his shoulder. "Warrain teach speak." The same finger now touches her chest.

"Ye want me to teach ye to speak English?"

Her features scrunch in puzzlement while she tries to parse the verbs, nouns and pronouns in Ryan's words. Like anyone new to a language, she responds to the words she recognizes, "Speak me English."

"Does Weeyn teach ye English?"

"Not more," she says, her brow furrowed with seriousness. "Warrain teach!"

"I'll ask Laarr."

Alinga recognizes her father's name and nods in understanding.

"After I finish my bath," Ryan says. Struggling against the culture rules that make nudity shameful or prurient, Ryan tosses aside his concealing pants and slips into the pool.

Ryan and Alinga locate Laarr squatting outside his hut, wrapped in a fur robe, talking to Weeyn.

"Weeyn, 'tis good ye are here. I may need translation," Ryan says, as he hunches down by the patriarch's feet. "Laarr, my friend. Alinga wants me to teach her English. I will if ye agree to it."

Laarr exchanges words with Weeyn, and replies, "Warrain teach Laarr, Weeyn and Alinga."

"Aye."

*****

Most days after the morning hunt, the three students sit beside Ryan's hut to learn the white man's language. On rainy days, lessons adjourn to Laarr's large hut.

Ryan starts by teaching his pupils related pairs of nouns and present-tense verbs: spear and throw, tomahawk and chop, knife and cut, legs and run. He discusses English words for colors, tools and accouterments of camp life—hut, spoon, pot, basket—the parts of the human body, relative time—yesterday, today, tomorrow—the names of natural features—tree, river, cloud—and words related to weather and temperature. In the second half of each lesson, he grills them on the words taught at previous lessons.

Over time, Ryan adds articles, prepositions, personal pronouns and conjunctions. He instructs them on how to create a simple future tense by adding 'going to' with a verb, and a simple past tense by adding 'did' to a verb. Refined verb tenses can wait.

After ten days, Ryan insists all conversation during lessons be in English—he prohibits Weeyn from translating.

In the second month, Ryan gathers pebbles in a basket, and with those simple props, he teaches them to count to one hundred. By adding or removing groups of pebbles, he explains the concepts of addition and subtraction.

Laarr absorbs words explaining life in a hunter-gatherer society—terms for weapons, animals and hunting. He falters where words lack a physical manifestation: articles, prepositions, and conjunctions. Numbers beyond twenty confuse him.

The problems evident in Weeyn's English begin to disappear. He expands his tenses, and incorporates articles and prepositions.

Alinga's unfaltering concentration during lessons and rapid progress astounds her family and instructor. Her young mind drinks up knowledge like rain on dry ground.

At Alinga's insistence, Tarra joins the lessons after the first month. "If my friend not speak English, how I talk to her?" she asks her father.

"Other girl not need speak English," Laarr answers.

"Father," Weeyn says, glancing at Tarra, "the white man is here to stay. It is better if more Wathaurung speak English. Women can teach their children."

Laarr waves his hand in agreement. Tarra rewards Weeyn with a smile.

After another week of lessons, Alinga makes two announcements. First, she proposes to sleep in her own mia-mia because her parents snore too much. Ryan is astounded when Mokborree and Laarr agree. No parent in his culture would permit a female child to overnight in the bush on her own. But, he remembers, Alinga has foraged for food alone for years. She is safe.

Alinga next states she will speak English exclusively.

Within a day, Mokborree's frustration at her unintelligible daughter erupts into high-pitched scolding that Ryan can hear across the camp. Still, Alinga refuses to use her birth language.

Fed up after several days, the elders complain to Laarr of Alinga's lack of respect. After stern words from the arweat, his daughter amends her language policy to use Wadawurrung with Mokborree and old people. For all her younger cousins and their families, she speaks only English.

*****

On a cloudless mid-winter day, the sun blankets the land with a welcome hint of heat. Ryan departs to his secluded fern-fringed pool to wash. While he strives for a daily cleansing, stinking is often preferable to shivering from cold water and frigid air. Clean and refreshed after six grubby days, he follows a familiar creek-side path to the encampment.

From the high bank, he spots Tarra and Alinga squatting in shallow water, rinsing yams and parsnips. Close together, they chat in confidential tones. Ryan steps down the slope.

"So what are ye two talking about?"

Both girls giggle. Alinga loosely closes her left hand around the index finger of her right, and slides the finger in and out of the hole formed by the hand. She makes mocking grunts. Ryan's jaw drops and his cheeks blaze. Both girls point at Ryan and screech with laughter. Parrots launch off trees with fearful squawks.

Ryan's impulse is to flee. His sex education came from the procreative antics of farm animals, followed by vague and terse explanations from his parents. Nothing in his European upbringing prepared him for girls of nine and ten miming fornication. His limited Catholic training suggests the simple act of seeing Alinga's rude gesture verges on carnal sin.

He blinks and draws in deep breaths to compose himself. His rational mind fights to accept the cultural difference. Sex is not secretive or furtive among the Wathaurung. Children see parents copulate in family huts and witness trysts in the undergrowth.

He is their teacher now, and that notion steadies his nerves. Ryan takes a seat on a boulder a yard from the girls. "Any questions?"

"Tarra has big question," Alinga says. "Ask him," she insists to her friend.

Her expression inquisitive, Tarra asks Ryan in a clinical tone, "Does hurt girl when husband first make baby?"

Ryan gasps and blushes. He rises on wobbly legs and steadies himself on a tree. Not only has his limited sexual experience left him without an answer, the image of himself discussing details of intercourse with two naked children overloads his cultural adaptability. "Ask yer mother." He pivots and strides up the slope.

Back at his hut, Ryan senses heightened activity among the women. He locates Weeyn next to the fire.

"What's happening? Another corroboree?"

"Yes. In two days. Loklok's father, Boort, did invite us."

"I'd prefer not to be near Loklok," Ryan remarks.

"You no need to come," Weeyn says.

"May I stay and guard this place?"

"Yes."

*****

Alinga has known for two months a reciprocal corroboree was inevitable. She has planned for that inescapable event since the previous celebration. With the date now close for the visit to Loklok's encampment—a place where she realizes she cannot hide from him—she puts her scheme in motion.

In the dark hours, she crawls from her lean-to and orients herself by the creek's gurgle. Aided by feeble moonlight peeking between occasional gaps in the tree canopy, Alinga follows a route rehearsed a dozen times in the previous weeks.

She crab-walks down the darkened creek bank, clutching well-worn and familiar root and rock handholds. After sipping the cool creek water, she gropes her way up the far bank. At the top, Alinga counts four strides in the pitch dark to where habit tells her the path lies. Her bare feet sense the difference—the earth compact, cooler and debris free.

Going right, she walks thirty-three strides using the English counting Warrain has taught her. Shifting a quarter turn left, she takes nine paces. Stretching out her arm, her fingers contact the bark of a hut wall. The scent of Warrain—a tad more peppery than her people— confirms her destination. Crouching, she slips into the hut with all the cautious quiet of a mouse. Her keen hearing picks up his gentle breathing. She curls up like a sleeping canine and falls asleep.

Alinga stirs when Weeyn whistles to his white friend to arise for the dawn hunt. Ryan pushes up on one elbow and spots her at his feet.

"What are ye doing here?"

"I hear strange noise in forest. I scared. I sleep here. Feel safe."

Ryan pulls on his possum wrap, pats Alinga's noggin, and crawls out to join the hunters. Alinga lies by the hut entrance in plain view and drifts to sleep, smiling.

She awakens after dawn to the rustle and banging of women at their choirs. She feigns sleep and waits for the dramatic discovery she is certain is her gateway to happiness.

Female feet tread across the ground. Alinga's bush-trained ears can distinguish one woman from another by the weight and meter of their steps. Mokborree is coming.

After an interval, which stretches Alinga's patience to near eruption, a shriek of horror from her mother rewards her restraint. Mokborree drags her from the hut and cuffs her ear. Alinga dodges a second blow by scampering up a gum tree.

*****

Weeyn, weighed down by a buck wallaby draped across his young shoulders, returns to camp behind the others. He finds the group in argumentative turmoil, with Warrain at the center of the drama.

Weeyn drops his burden and worms his way through the mass of spectators. Laarr, his hefty hands under Warrain's armpits, has the white man pinned to a tree, his feet dangling. The arweat berates Warrain with cacophony of Wadawurrung curses and threats.

"Help me," Ryan calls to Weeyn.

Weeyn asks Tomboko what has happened. He explains that Mokborree found Alinga sleeping in Warrain's hut like a betrothed wife. A long observer of his sister's crafty ways, Weeyn deduces the mischief she has wrought.

«Father,» Weeyn begins in his native tongue, «Belongs-to-the-sea did not dishonor Sun. He could not appreciate what it means for a child-woman to sleep at a man's feet.»

Laarr drops Warrain onto his ass among the fallen gum leaves. «Explain,» Laarr asks Weeyn.

«My sister is dingo clever. She wants Belongs-to-the-sea and Eagle to fight for her.»

Laarr stands over Ryan. "Did Warrain invite daughter sleep your bed?"

"No. She came in saying she heard a noise in the forest. I dunno yer customs. I'm sorry."

Laarr extends a hand to Ryan and pulls him to his feet. Laarr shrugs an apology and stalks off searching for Alinga. The family members disperse to their huts, muttering.

Weeyn spots his sister thirty feet up in the shadowy forks of a gum tree. He throws up his arms in frustration. Alinga laughs.

*****

Alinga descends from her tree haven and seeks out her father for the required public scolding. Contrite tears will soften her father's big koala heart. He will not beat her, nor will Mokborree hit her in his presence.

On quivering legs and with her chin on her chest, she sniffles while Laarr, his voice audible throughout the glade, vilifies her for the potential damage she has caused. «Daughter Sun, why do you dishonor Eagle in this way? He is a chief's eldest son and surely a chief himself in time.»

«He is mean, my father, and already has a wife,» she replies, trying to sound humble.

«Being the second wife to a great man is better than the only wife to a lesser man.»

«Not for me. I hate him,» she mutters.

«Your mother is my second wife. Do you think less of her?» Laarr says quietly.

Alinga blinks at the revelation. Doubt creases her lips.

«My first was Orana. She could not bear me children, so I married your mother.»

«But I know I can make babies. That is not the same,» she pouts.

Laarr crosses his arms. «Eagle's father is our closest ally. If he discovers your indiscretion, it could sever the bonds binding our two families. And Eagle has the right to break his marriage promise or fight Belongs-to-the-sea.»

Alinga's heart leaps with joy.

«News of your foolishness must not go beyond our group,» Laarr roars. «Go to your little hut and stay until we leave for the corroboree tomorrow. Fast and contemplate your misdeeds.»

Alinga retreats to her private hutch but she has anticipated her father's punishment. Tarra makes prearranged visits, bringing bits of meat and roots.

«White my friend,» Alinga says, «when we visit your old family tomorrow, please tell your cousins of my dishonor.»

Tarra gasps, shocked by the request. «Eagle will kill Belongs-to-the-sea.»

«No. Belongs-to-the-sea is a great warrior. He will defeat Eagle and take me for his wife.»

«Why?»

«Because he loves me.»

Tarra arches her brow in doubt and waves a dismissive hand.

«He does!» Alinga insists. «My heart tells me. Help me.»

«I will not do this thing,» Tarra says. «It brings danger.»

«Remember, when we talked of marrying a man we love. Help me now and I will help you be with the man you love someday.»

Tarra averts her sight. She chews absentmindedly on a parsnip meant for Alinga. «I am promised to another. That cannot be undone.»

«Yes it can, if the spirits will it.»

*****

Laarr's encampment empties the next day at noon. Ryan walks downstream to spearfish, returning with five members of an unknown perch species. He bathes in the creek. With the glade to himself, he warms himself before a roaring fire and cooks fish impaled on a stick.

Four armed warriors emerge from the forest as soundless as evaporating dew and surround him. Two Ryan recognizes from the day he met Loklok.

"What do ye want?"

The men say nothing. One points to a forest path and signals for Ryan to follow. Ryan is unarmed and outnumbered. He has no choice.

After an hour walk, Ryan's escorts deliver him to the camp of Boort, father of Loklok. In the lines of onlookers, Ryan spots Laarr and his family. Alinga alone among her family exhibits no apprehension.

Boort, whose name means smoke, is shorter than Ryan, stout and elderly. His long locks and beard are white and he leans on a staff for support. Beside him, his brother Dyeelaga, whose name means spark, holds his brother's arm in support. He has the same stout build, but shows no gray hairs and no sagging posture.

The old chieftain, his glare directed at Ryan, begins a solemn speech in Wadawurrung. Loklok steps to his father's side to translate. "My father says you corrupted the mind of an innocent child to satisfy your evil white man's lust. You dishonored the families of Boort and his long-time friend Laarr."

Boort continues his sonorous speech. Loklok translates. "This great dishonor must be avenged and the evil cast out. You will die and the girl must join us this day."

"Do I get a chance to defend agin this charge?" Ryan asks.

Loklok answers with a mocking grin. Ryan realizes Loklok does not want Boort to hear the question. Ryan turns at the murmur of low voices in the crowd behind him. Laarr is striding towards them with Weeyn in tow.

Boort shakes his staff at Laarr and bellows ancient insults. Laarr waves a fist under Boort's nose and barks his own invective. Men from both family groups clench spears and grumble. The chiefs notice subtle movement towards battle and cease their blustering. Neither condones needless bloodshed. Their voices fade to whispers. They negotiate a compromise.

Stone-faced, Laarr delivers the verdict to Weeyn and points to Ryan. The boy's forehead furrows with the weight of the news. He ambles to Ryan.

"My father did tell Boort you mean no harm to my sister. Boort agree now. Loklok told lies. But the dishonor to Loklok remains. He did demand you fight."

"Have I a choice?" Ryan asks.

"If you no battle Loklok, the long peace between our families ends."

"Then, I will."

"Fight must be to death of one," Weeyn imparts in a whisper.

Tremors begin in Ryan's gut and spread up his torso and across his shoulders. Perspiration seeps from his pores. He recognizes the symptoms of fear. It has visited before. He knows his only recourse is to banish such a useless emotion and face the threat clinically.

Ryan sucks in a calming breath and exhales. He appraises Loklok like a boxer at the first match against a new opponent. The young warrior has a height and weight advantage. Loklok has an array of weapons to choose from and experience using them in battle. Ryan has never tangled with a man in armed combat; however, a life growing up among taunting English schoolboys in Ireland has honed his street-fighter skills. Scuffles with hardened criminals in the penal colony advanced his fisticuff abilities. Ryan sees one slim chance to win.

"Weeyn," Ryan says. "Please translate my words so everyone can hear."

Weeyn nods.

"Loklok," Ryan hollers, "I'll fight ye but I choose the weapons."

Weeyn translates. Boort and Laarr nod to each other. It is agreed.

"What weapons does the white dog want?" Loklok responds, and points to a cache of spears, clubs, boomerangs and tomahawks.

Ryan treads in a wide circle, parading before the assembled families. He removes his possum shawl and leather hat. He holds his fists to the sky, and says, "My weapons of choice are my fists and my feet."

Weeyn translates.

"You mean to fight like a kangaroo instead of a warrior?" Loklok says in both English and Wadawurrung.

"I fight with the weapons our creators gave us, afore men created weapons of wood, bone and stone."

Weeyn translates. Ryan watches the crowd's reaction. He sees no obvious display of disapproval.

Boort speaks. Weeyn translates. "The white man did choose his weapons. It is settled."

Loklok unties the leather thong holding his knife and tomahawk. He removes every ornament and apparel. With not a visible ounce of body fat to pad him, parallel bars of muscle ripple across his abdomen. His biceps bulge. His pectorals quiver at each flex of an arm. The muscle definition on his legs provides an easy study in anatomy.

By Ryan's assessment, Loklok is his better in most attributes of a fighter. Ryan hinges his slim hope for victory on his belief that Loklok has never fought without a weapon. The way Loklok holds his hands open and low are signs of a man intending to wrestle, not box. Ryan must stay out of Loklok's crushing grasp and trust that his wiry muscles will react a tad faster than Loklok's brawny limbs.

Ryan removes his boots to lighten the weight on his feet. People push in closer, forming a fighting ring forty feet in diameter. The two fighters stalk each other around the perimeter, their eyes connected in mutual malice. Ryan holds his fists tight and arms high, guarding his face and chest.

"I will kill you with my bare hands," Loklok boasts.

"Well dear boy," Ryan mocks, "prepare to meet yer first Irish street fighter."

Loklok snarls and lunges, his arms held out like a wrestler reaching for someone's neck.

Ryan pushes off with his rear foot bringing his left knee high and forward. To Loklok it appears Ryan will deliver a kick with his left leg. As Ryan expected, the warrior drops his hands to protect that side from the anticipated blow.

Momentum from Ryan's initial leap carries him closer to Loklok. Without first placing his left foot down, Ryan springs with his right leg and snaps his foot forward aiming for Loklok's now exposed left ribs. In the split second when both feet are off the ground, Ryan turns his right hip into the kick to add force. He grounds his left foot for balance and counterforce at the moment of contact. The simultaneous sounds of his sole smacking flesh, Loklok's sharp exhalation, and the twig-snapping pop of fracturing ribs startle the observers.

Ryan dances backwards and settles into a fighting stance, while his opponent struggles for breath. A less experienced fighter would have pressed the attack and not waited for Loklok's traumatized diaphragm to relax. But Ryan respects Loklok's abilities and wagers the young warrior can dig deep for lethal resources if necessary. Time is on Ryan's side. A broken rib hurts little initially—it is the swelling to soon follow that makes movement painful.

Loklok begins a tentative approach. He has changed his arm position from wrestler-style to a boxer's stance. Ryan steps in towards Loklok and darts aside. Loklok pursues the redheaded fighter. Ryan's feet dance an Irish jig, carrying him in and out, clockwise and counterclockwise—never close enough for Loklok to strike a blow. Ryan knows he cannot exhaust Loklok by making the big warrior chase him around the ring but the warrior's pounding feet jar his cracked ribs. The pain is now evident on his chiseled features.

Ryan darts in and fakes a high jab. When Loklok's hands rise to guard his face, Ryan lands a body blow to Loklok's exposed broken rib. Loklok coughs and drops an arm to cover his rib, exposing his head. Ryan lands a left uppercut as he rises on his feet.

Loklok's jaw snaps shut with an audible crunch. He staggers and throws his arms wide to break his fall. Ryan leaps across the distance and lands a merciless front kick on Loklok's unguarded torso, further punishing his damaged ribs. The young warrior lands on his back with a jarring thud, sending bolts of searing pain into his inflamed ribcage.

Ryan steps back, unwilling to hit a man on the ground.

The onlookers are silent. Even the birds seem to have gone mute. Loklok's raspy breathing punctuates the silence. To the amazement of most, Loklok pushes himself upright. The warrior picks a knife from his weapons pile and raises his dark gaze to Ryan.

Ryan tenses. Has Loklok broken his word and now intends to fight with weapons? But the Wathaurung man surprises Ryan. Loklok pulls the razor-sharp blade across his middle from below the broken rib to the opposite side. The incision swells with blood.

He drops his knife and speaks to Ryan. "To a true warrior, pain is like a mosquito. A mere nuisance."

Loklok surges across the ring at Ryan, who dodges left and right. Loklok anticipates both movements and lands his massive fist on the side of Ryan's skull.

Ryan loses his balance and staggers. He tucks and converts his fall into a backwards roll. He springs to his feet beyond Loklok's immediate reach. His ear rings and his head throbs but the hit has done little damage.

Ryan back-steps from Loklok and waits for the next attack. Loklok's ragged breathing tells the true state of his health. Despite the bloody theatrics, he hurts. But, Ryan is certain Loklok will not quit until dead, unconscious or disabled.

Ryan fights off a growing respect for Loklok. He will not let sympathy weaken him. "Ye are a bully needing a whipping," Ryan mutters to refocus himself.

On cue, Loklok advances. Ryan shifts his stance and attacks in a rapid, side-stepping motion. Without interrupting the flow of the move, Ryan jerks his right knee up even with his chest and unwinds like a coiled snake. Ryan's right leg snaps out. The heel slams down on Loklok's right knee while the warrior has full weight on that leg. Ryan twists his hip into the blow, doubling the kick's effective mass.

The support structure of Loklok's leg blows apart. Cartilage snaps. The patella crumbles. Tendons and ligaments stretch near to snapping. The femur, tibia and fibula jerk out of alignment. Loklok collapses forward onto his chin, groans and passes out.

The Wathaurung are in shock. No one expected Loklok to lose. And none had ever witnessed Ryan's style of combat. The one exception to the stony silence is Alinga. She bounces up and down, clapping.

The rules say he must now kill Loklok. Ryan has no experience in murder, and doubts the wisdom of executing the chief's son. Ryan waves over Weeyn and approaches Boort.

"Great chief," he says. "'Tis with sadness I accept this victory."
Weeyn translates each time Ryan pauses.

"Yer son is the toughest man I've met."

Boort lessens his funereal expression at the compliment to his son.

"I ask ye to not force me to kill him. In my land, dishonor comes to the man who strikes an unconscious opponent."

Weeyn translates. Boort places his right hand on his heart.

"I don't want to cause bad feelings among old friends," Ryan continues.

Weeyn translates. Alinga ceases her victory dance.

"We all want peace among the families of Boort and Laarr. Peace can't exist if I stay. Loklok'll die afore he gives up," Ryan says.

Weeyn translates. People in the crowd nod. They catch the direction of Ryan's monologue. Alinga begins to weep.

"I'll gather my kit and go live with white men, if that suits ye."

Boort listens to Weeyn and replies.

Weeyn translates. "Your words are wise and fair, kangaroo warrior. Go in peace."

Ryan bows to the old chief and steps away. He notices Alinga sobbing in her father's brawny arms. Ryan salutes Laarr and begins the return trek.

"Walk with me, Weeyn," Ryan says.

They remain silent until beyond Boort's encampment.

Ryan stops. "This is far enough. I need to say a few things."

"Speak, my friend."

"I owe ye, yer sister, and yer family my life. I can never repay that debt."

"Nice words, amadeat; but our worlds and gods are different. We not see you again, I think."

"Here is my promise to ye. I'll visit every winter if I can and locate yer camp."

"I hope true."

"Say farewell to yer sister for me. She seems sad to see me go."

"She crazy child," Weeyn says, grinning.

"Go back to the corroboree. See ye next year."

Ryan overnights in his mia-mia and hikes east the next morning. He stops at the first ranch house he encounters and asks for work. The owner requires another shepherd at one of his distant sheep stations. He hires Ryan on the spot and sends him north to help guard a herd of five thousand sheep. Fellow shepherds lend him clothes until he can buy his own.

Old Friends, New Roads

January 1846

Ryan trudges into Ballarat, dodging wagons and buggies that raise dust from parched soil. As he trekked across the sunburned country, Ryan imagined the town as having tidy streets of wood and brick buildings. Instead, he finds rows of tents along a meandering dirt road, lying beside the narrow Yarrowee River.

A church and police station boast low wooden walls around their tents. A scattering of wooden facades serve as fronts for tent stores. Ryan estimates the entire village houses fewer than one hundred residents. In a valley surrounded by forest-denuded hills, Ballarat has an ethereal quality, suggesting it might not be there a week hence.

Ryan buys a two-day-old copy of *The Melbourne Daily News*. Its date, January 21, 1846, reminds Ryan his twenty-eighth birthday has slipped past without notice. He sighs and settles on the bench of a rough-hewn wooden table in a tent tavern. The owner has rolled up the tent's front to air out the stuffy and hot interior.

The newspaper is the first publication he has read since washing up on Australia's shores ten months earlier. The sheep station, his abode for the last seven months, had nothing to read, and no one to talk to once he and the two uneducated shepherds exhausted all topics of conversation.

Ryan, his back to the street, reads, sips tea and devours a lunch of eggs, potatoes and toast. With seven months wages in his pockets, he spends money with a clear conscience on simple luxuries, the first since he departed Van Diemen's Land.

A shadow falls across Ryan's open newspaper. Walter Fraser smiles and saunters into the tent. "Mind if I join you Mr. Ryan no-last-name?" Fraser removes his derby and runs a hand through his blond hair.

"Aye," Ryan says, folding his paper. "I use Warrain for my surname now."

Fraser perches across from Ryan facing the street and opens a button on his black coat. "Ah yes. Warrain is a legendary name now among the Wathaurung."

"'Tis so?"

"Yes, dear boy. Billy tells me your fight with Loklok is the biggest yarn recounted around black campfires. I have since heard it told by whites in bars. Warrain, the white man who fights like a kangaroo, who barehanded defeats the best warrior the Wathaurung had to offer. It reaffirms white superiority for those who have any doubt."

"'Tis naught. I tricked him into fighting on my terms."

"You are modest," Fraser says, pausing for a second. "Have you employment at present?"

"Nay. The rancher closed his station and had no requirement for my services."

"Is that so?" Fraser says. "I could use a tough and resourceful man like you."

"What business are ye in, Mr. Fraser?"

"I operate a large sheep station south of here and a freight line running merchandise and materials from Ballarat and Buninyong to the harbor at Geelong."

"What do ye need me to do?"

"Whatever I require." Fraser's voice drops a halftone down the scale. Like a song switching from a major to minor key, it primes the listener for sadness or trouble to come. For Ryan, it reminds him that Weeyn and Loklok both called Fraser a devil.

Ryan gropes for a graceful way to decline without insult. Fraser's attention switches to something in the street over Ryan's shoulder.

"Ryan. A rough fellow is gawking at you. Do you owe anyone money or have you dallied with someone's wife of late?"

"Nay," Ryan replies, turning to face the street.

A man with a sandy beard and thinning flaxen hair eyeballs Ryan from his seat on a freight wagon hitched to six large horses.

"Is that you, Lone Pine?" the man calls.

Ryan's mouth hangs open. The name belongs to another time, another continent.

"Aye. 'Tis me."

"You carry many monikers," Fraser remarks.

The man, in his early thirties, climbs from the wagon and walks closer. Shorter than Ryan, he carries more bulk. Ryan recognizes the confident American stride. "Gates! I heard ye had returned to New York."

"No such luck. I need to earn money for passage."

Ryan turns to Fraser. "Mr. Fraser, this is William Gates. He's one of my fellow political prisoners. And William, this is Walter Fraser, a local businessman."

Gates peruses Fraser with narrowed eyes. "Your name is familiar. Are you the fellow with the vendetta agin the Djadjawurung blacks?"

Fraser squints. His brow wrinkles. He pushes his derby on his head, and without a word to either man, he rises and exits the tent.

"I trust you have no truck with that bugger?" Gates asks.

"Nay. We've met on two occasions. What is this vendetta ye mention?"

Gates hollers to the tent's rear, "Does this hovel serve beer?" The proprietor dips his head for yes. "Then bring me one," he calls out. To Ryan, he adds, "I take it you still don't imbibe spirits?"

"Aye."

"You buy me a beer and I'll tell you about Fraser. Deal?"

"Aye. When did ye arrive?"

Gates settles on the bench. "I arrived ten months ago. A few from our group worked for our passage on ship out of Hobart Town. I now work for a big sheep rancher north of here. What's your story?"

"I lived in a remote area of Van Diemen's Land where no ships anchored," Ryan begins. "I built a boat and tried to row across last March, ran into a storm, and nearly died. A family of Wathaurung saved me. I stayed with them for three months and then worked at a sheep station. Tell me about Fraser."

Gates indulges in a long guzzle of beer. "People tell me that rascal has murdered over fifty blacks out of revenge. Years back, a party of warriors, who Fraser assumes were Djadjawurung, massacred his parents and siblings. He has vowed to wipe out the entire clan."

"Is there no law in this country?"

"No one goes to jail in this land for harming a black. I'm told whites on juries won't convict a white for killing a black. I hear Fraser is a real contradiction, though. He acts friendly to other clans and funds a school in Buninyong for black boys."

"I met two lads who attended Fraser's school and neither is glad for it," Ryan says.

"No doubt he is up to mischief."

"Or his lead hand, Scott Healey." Ryan glances at the street to ensure Fraser has gone. "Ye showed up at a perfect moment. He was trying to hire me."

"If you want a job, come with me. I work for the Willis brothers. They run seventy-thousand sheep north of here and need men. I dropped off a few tons of wool in Geelong and am heading back." Gates detects uncertainty on Ryan. "Do it. I'd like a familiar face around. We can chat about old times."

Ryan recalls Gates. The gregarious American never showed a second of fear or doubt during or after the four-day battle in November of 1838 along the New York-Canada border that ended in their defeat, the hanging of eleven and the exile of sixty. Ryan can trust him.

"Aye, I need a bit of time to buy books to take with me."

"No need. Willis has a room full."

"How can I say no?"

*****

Five hot and cloudless days later on an arid, upland plain, Gates pulls the wagon into the paddock area by a wooden barn. The lanolin scent of wool lies heavy in a breezeless day. The bleating of sheep and bawling of lambs is constant.

Gates climbs from the high wagon and waves over a stable hand to unhitch the horses.

"Walk with me. I'll show you this place." Gates leads Ryan across a dusty compound surrounded by a village of wood-sided barns and shacks. "This is the center of the Willis brothers' main station. They have five smaller stations on fifty-thousand acres, each with ten to twelve-thousand sheep. Over there are the stables and the two bunkhouses for the whites and the blacks." Gates continues, pointing as he speaks. "Here are shearing sheds. And in those yonder, we dry the fleece and bale it for transport. The Willis brothers ship two hundred and fifty tons of wool to Geelong a year. We have a herd of draft horses and four big wagons to haul bales of wool and bring back supplies."

"Who sees to all those wagons?" Ryan asks. "These hard roads and long miles wear them down fast, especially the wheels."

"We fix what we can here and bring in wheels from the south."

"'Tis costly." Ryan points to a wool wagon, its wheels the height of his chest. "One wheel must be worth a month's wages."

"More," Gates replies. "Here comes the boss," he says.

An average-sized man in his early thirties dressed in standard working clothes ambles towards them from the ranch house. In every way but his expensive imported boots, he'd pass for a shepherd.

"So, Gates," Willis says, his English West Country accent assaulting Ryan's ears, "any problems?"

"No. Mr. Willis. I got the load to your broker in Geelong and he credited your account the price you expected."

"Good. I can always rely on you. Who's this then?" Willis adds, tilting his head towards Ryan.

"This is Ryan, a mate from America. I found him in Ballarat and brought him in case you needed another man, sir."

"Was he with you in that wretched penal colony?"

"Yes sir. We were convicted together, shipped together, and shackled at times together."

Willis steps up to Ryan, hand extended. "We are all former convicts here. I'll not hold that against you. I'm William Willis. A friend of Gates is all the reference I need. I can always use another man ta mind sheep and handle wool."

"Any honest work suits me, but I wager I can be better use to ye."

"I'm listenin'."

"The wagon we arrived on will not go far with its next load. The right rear hub will fail soon."

"Show me."

The men return to the wagon.

Ryan points to several small radial cracks in the wheel hub. "Whoever built this hub used poor wood. 'Twas likely a bit flaky. Any hard jolt fully loaded and I expect she'll start to fall apart."

"I appreciate this information but I do not require a wagon inspector."

"No, sir. But ye need me."

Willis' cocks an eyebrow.

Ryan continues. "Wherever I look, there is wood: barns, bunkhouses, buggies, wagons, barrels. I can do any manner of working with wood. I've been a carpenter, shipwright, cooper and wheelwright. I can keep yer wagons rolling."

Willis smiles. "We have little use for a shipwright in this region, but I can use a carpenter and wheelwright. I like a man who says what he wants. I came ta this land a convict and decided ta be a rancher when my pardon came. I walked out past the last station I found and squatted on a region the size of a minor English city—because I wanted it. I'll hire you startin' at shepherd's wages. If you have the skill you claim, I'll increase your pay. Deal?"

"Deal, sir." They shake hands.

"What do you require?"

"I'll need tools for shaping hubs, spokes and rims, and a supply of the proper wood."

Willis points to a large barn. "We keep many carpentry tools in there. Make a list of what you lack and I'll see it is delivered. Do not expect imported oak. Native trees will have to do. Anything else?"

"'Is there a smithy? I can reuse the old iron tyres for new wheels if ye've a forge."

"Yes. Gates can show you all our facilities," Willis says, patting Gates' shoulder.

"Do yer facilities include a library, sir?"

"Why, yes they do. The family collection is open ta any literate employee in his off hours."

"Thank ye, Mr. Willis. I look forward to working with ye."

"Come with me," Gates says. "I'll show you the bunkhouse and mess hall. I hope you like mutton."

Ryan smiles. He loves mutton. "Is there any chance of getting pen and paper? I promised a friend back home to write when I had an address."

"Yah. Mail goes out anytime we send a wagon to Buninyong or Geelong."

Ellen

February 1847

Ryan guides the loaded wool wagon through rounded, red earth hills after a seven-day journey in gentle, late summer weather. In the foreground, the Barwon River flows by farms and stumpy former forests. Beyond he can see the church spires of Geelong and the bay.

He muses on his recent past. For thirteen months he has labored for the Willis brothers repairing the precious wagon wheels and mending anything made of wood. He is now the highest paid employee on the station. His only regret—his duties and the long distance prevented him from visiting Weeyn and Alinga as he promised.

Today is his inaugural trip to Geelong. Willis mustered all other employees for the peak shearing season. Ryan, who has never sheared a sheep, became a teamster out of need. Ryan had no experience driving a team of six, but the big Clydesdales proved gentle, strong and easy to manage.

Geelong is a proper town in Ryan's estimation, with a grid of streets, and shops and houses of permanent construction. Ryan locates the post office on Barwon Terrace, following the directions Willis gave him. He picks up the Willis family mail and pockets the one letter addressed to him. In the harbor area, he locates the Willis' wool broker. Stevedores unload the twelve compressed bales of wool. Ryan secures several packages ordered by the Willis brothers onto the empty wagon. With his list of tasks complete, he guides the team into the scrum of wagons and buggies choking the afternoon waterfront.

Progress is mere inches a minute at times. Most traffic consists of nimble buggies and box wagons. His big rig demands plenty of room to pass or turn.

Noise assaults his ears used to the empty plains. People holler at each other and their horses. Along the quays, industrious men pound wood with hammers, tighten the metal rings on barrels with whacks from mallets, and load and unload ships with squeaking cranes and cussing instructions. A hot breeze off the bay mixes hints of rotting fish with the stench of horse dung, acrid foundry smoke and unwashed humanity.

Ryan pulls his wagon up to the foot of a wharf on Corio Bay and sets the brake. He clutches a cowbell and an iron rod, stands on the wagon and begins banging. A lull in the cacophony rewards his attention-getting effort.

"I've a freight wagon headed to Buninyong and Ballarat and beyond on the morrow," he shouts. "Five shillings per hundredweight." Willis gave him permission to accept any return cargo he can arrange and keep half the proceeds.

People continue their errands. Ryan waits several minutes. No takers. He guides the team to the next wharf and repeats the bell clanging and call for customers. No one accepts his offer. He reaches to release the hand brake to move on, when a voice from behind rises above the ubiquitous clangor.

"Do you take passengers?"

Ryan swivels in his seat. A young woman has a white-gloved hand on the side of his wagon. Her emerald irises hook him like a fish. Orange curls burst from her modest gray bonnet like an erupted milkweed pod. Ringlets drape the shoulders of her mauve, full-length dress. Her oval face is symmetrical and her features delicate. Only her almost invisible blond lashes and eyebrows detract from perfection. Ryan has not seen such a freckled Celtic beauty since leaving home.

"So what part of Ireland are ye from?" he asks.

"The Australian part," she quips.

"Ye were born here? Ye seem fresh from Dublin."

"Is that where you originate?"

"I hail from the south, nigh Wexford. Been away nine years now."

"I presume you have interesting tales to relate. They will surely make for fine conversation on the road to Buninyong. I assume you will accept me as a passenger."

"Aye. For ten shillings I'll transport ye and any luggage." Ryan halves his rate without a second thought. "I should warn ye, this wagon was not made for comfort."

"There is no regular stage going north. Your conveyance will suffice. Pick me up tomorrow morning at Mrs. Sampson's boarding house on Church Street. Can you locate it?"

"Aye. I'll meet ye at sunrise."

She holds out her gloved right hand. "Ellen O'Sullivan. Pleased to meet you."

"Ryan Warrain, at yer service," he replies, meeting her gesture with a light grip.

"That is an unusual surname," she responds, "though vaguely familiar."

"An explanation will be part of tomorrow's conversation."

*****

Ryan rises two hours before sunrise at a humble teamsters' inn, eats two slices of buttered bread, and belts back a mug of warm tea. He packs food and water for the trip in a canvas sack, and heads to the boarding stable. He dresses the six Clydesdales in their complicated tack of collars, traces and harnesses. The stable hands load and secure a full barrel of water on the wagon—drink for the horses in dry areas ahead. Ryan pays for boarding and feed from the expense fund Willis gave him, and steers the team out along slumbering roads towards Church Street. The sun rises from a pink easterly glow and spills golden light the length of the empty roadway.

Ellen is waiting on the boarding house steps. She hefts a suitcase and satchel onto the wagon before Ryan can do his gentlemanly duties.

"Good morning Mr. Warrain. A splendid day for travel," Ellen says, climbing aboard with no assistance and sitting to Ryan's right.

"Morning to ye, Miss O'Sullivan. A grand day it looks to be."

A brief smirk creases Ellen's jaw. "How long is our journey to Buninyong?"

Ryan releases the brake and whistles a note to the team. The six horses step in unison. "'Tis nearly fifty miles or about ten hours in this season with an empty wagon," Ryan says, "including halts to water the horses and stretch our legs."

The wagon soon passes the town's outskirts and rumbles over the rutted rural road. Springs under the wagon platform and beneath the seat smooth the jolts somewhat. Ryan ignores it. Ellen does not complain. A gentle breeze keeps the plume of dust to their rear.

"I do love a journey into unknown country." She leans forward at each bend in the road and cranes her neck, eager to observe what new wonder may expose itself next.

"Ye nary mentioned what takes ye to Buninyong."

"I am to be employed as a teacher at a school for native boys," she says.

Ryan makes the logical connection. "Is yer employer Walter Fraser?"

"Why yes. Have you made his acquaintance?"

"Aye. Twice."

"Your tone suggests you have misgivings. Am I in any peril?"

"Fraser has a dark reputation, as ye will hear, but I believe a white woman is safe."

"Can you enlighten me as to his alleged darkness?" she says.

Ryan retells Ellen what Gates told him, facts confirmed many times since by others.

"That horrid little man," she exclaims. "I should halt here and walk back."

"I'll return ye, if 'tis yer wish. But…maybe ye can do some good. Two lads I know went to Fraser's school and had a hard time of it. Maybe ye can reduce whatever harm he causes."

Ellen stares at distant hills and speaks no further of returning to Geelong. The team crests a hill and the port town disappears behind them.

"Thank God we are now beyond the prying eyes of the respectable burghers of Geelong and their prissy spouses. The heat will soon be oppressive." Ellen removes her bonnet. An avalanche of orange curls envelopes her shoulders. She gathers the unruly locks into a ponytail and ties them with a ribbon. Her delicate fingers unfasten the top two buttons on her high-collared Victorian dress, exposing a triangle of pale skin. She removes her gloves and unfurls her parasol to block the sun.

Ryan averts his eyes while she adjusts her clothes. His peripheral vision catches a glint of gold from Ellen's left hand.

"I see," Ryan says, "'twas wrong to call ye miss."

Ellen smiles. "I was flattered I could still pass as a miss." She twists the ring on her finger and continues. "I have been married five years but have not seen my husband in four, nor received a letter. Here I am at twenty-five not knowing if I am a widow or an abandoned wife."

"Did he tell ye where he was going?"

"We were living in Sydney. Seamus secured a position as first mate on a whaler bound for Antarctic waters. The job promised him a generous percentage of any profits. He departed for Geelong to catch the ship. His last letter came from New Zealand where they stopped for stores."

She tilts her parasol to stay in its shade as the wagon rounds a turn.

"I took employment as a teacher because Seamus provided no income. My parents both died of cholera years ago. I am an only child. A married woman without family to fall back on has three choices: shopkeeper, teacher, or prostitute."

She laughs at Ryan's blush. "While I am sure I could excel at any of those, teaching is my preference."

Again Ryan blushes.

"I assume by your countenance and lack of bawdy retorts that I travel with a gentleman, despite what your rough attire suggests."

Ryan smiles and nods, uncertain of a better response.

"Continuing my story. After four years, I traveled to Geelong to make inquiries. The harbormaster said no one has heard from the ship that Seamus embarked on, but he confirmed whaling ships often disappear for years. I decided to stay, finding the town preferable to dwelling in Sydney. I have given up waiting for him. So, now I am relocating to a frontier town to start a new life."

"But unless ye've evidence he is dead, ye'll nary be free of him," Ryan says.

"True. The law and our church will insist I am bound to him for life. Pity. I hoped to have children."

A mile passes in silence.

"So tell me your story," Ellen says.

"'Tis difficult to know where to begin," Ryan replies. "My family set out from Dublin for the Canadian colonies in 1837. My mother and a brother died on the voyage. My father, older brother and sister died at a pestilent quarantine station."

Ellen pats his forearm. "I am so sorry. I comprehend the magnitude of such loss. Please continue."

"Instead of farming, like we planned, I spent a summer living with the natives. That autumn, I moved to a town called Kingston in what was then Upper Canada. A rebellion broke out. I had no interest in serving in the bloody British militia; so, I hid in the islands of the St. Lawrence River. I became entangled with the rebels and found myself in a pitched battle. I escaped capture, but by a long string of circumstances, I ended up in prison. The British shipped me to the penal colony in Van Diemen's Land. After my pardon in 1845, I built a boat to row across. A storm wrecked it and I almost drowned. Two Wathaurung children saved me. They gave me the name Warrain. I lived with their family for a spell and now I work for a rancher up north in New South Wales."

"Now I recognize your name. I am in the presence of the famous Warrain who fights like a kangaroo."

"Don't tell me that yarn has made its way to Geelong."

"Astounding. Please recount details of your life with the Wathaurung, especially the two children."

"'Twill take most of the day."

"I am a captive and willing audience."

*****

At dusk, Ryan brings the wagon to a halt in the center of Buninyong. While a majority of village dwellings are tents like nearby Ballarat, several one and two-story wooden shops line the street. The town boasts a post office.

"I have arranged board in an establishment run by the Presbyterian minister's wife. I hope I succeed in hiding that sin from my priest." Ellen laughs. "I am so wicked."

"Aye. There be a bit of angel and devil in ye, for sure."

Ellen retrieves ten shillings from her satchel. Ryan hesitates to accept. She pushes the coins on him.

"While we have become friends, business is business. Please!"

"Aye." He jumps to the ground to help Ellen dismount. She waves him off. He places her luggage on the wooden sidewalk and asks, "May I carry these to yer rooming house?"

"No need. It is steps away."

Their eyes connect.

"I quite enjoyed your company today," Ellen says. "Will you kindly look me up when you pass this way?"

"Is that proper, Ellen?"

"This is the bloody frontier. Here, I decide what is proper for me. Discretion is required, but I am allowed friends."

Ryan smiles at her profanity. "Then, I'll pass this way whenever I can. Until then, I'll write, if it suits ye."

"I expect no less."

Ryan's Return

June 1847

Ryan tours the new wagon works in the Willis compound, admiring the progress made in four months. On his return from Geelong, he'd made the elder Willis brother a proposition. Half the cost of any wagon is the wheels, he said. Wheels for the wool wagons cost four pounds each and need replacing every few months. Instead of having the constant expense to maintain the station's wagons, Ryan promised to make it a source of revenue if the Willis brothers granted the upfront capital. He and assistants would keep all the Willis wagons and buggies in top shape and build wagons and spare wagon wheels to sell to other stations. William Willis heartily agreed.

Since March, wagons returning from Geelong hauled loads of prime logs. Of the hundreds of gum tree species, Ryan found four varieties with the strength and durability necessary for wagons and wheels. He hired two men with carpentry and sawyer experience as apprentices. Gates and other ranch hands, while hauling wool to Geelong, drop off new wagon wheels at Ballarat to be fitted with iron tyres for pick-up on the return trip.

Yesterday, Willis Wagon Works sold its first two wagons to local ranchers. In addition, half a dozen spare wheels are ready to roll, and a pile of hubs is curing for future wheels.

Leaving the shop, certain his apprentices can manage in his absence, Ryan crosses to the stable, carrying saddlebags stuffed with provisions and a rolled blanket. Under the terms of his deal with Willis in March, Ryan purchased a riding horse with an advance on his salary and extracted a promise he could take time off. His mount, a six-year-old roan gelding Ryan named Dan, is saddled and waiting, his reins held by Gates.

"How long will you be gone, lad?" Gates asks, while he wraps the blanket roll in canvas and secures it to the saddle's rear.

"A month, I wager," Ryan replies. "The apprentices can manage my duties for that long."

"Off to see your black friends?"

"Yes. If I can locate them, I'll stay a couple of weeks." Ryan checks to make sure the saddle cinch is tight, and mounts.

"Here's hoping you get good weather," Gates says, giving a thumbs-up salute.

"Thank ye."

Ryan is aware Gates thinks him eccentric for traveling at the start of the southern winter. Nights are cold and rain is frequent. But, winter is the quietest month on the station and the one season his Wathaurung friends visit the plains west of Buninyong and Ballarat.

The trip begins well. In a clear sky, the weak sun provides warmth to counter the chill in the south wind. Dan's hooves make a comforting rhythm on the dirt track. Ryan senses the young horse's eagerness to leave the paddock's confines.

The rolling plain, with scattered groves of gum trees, unfolds before Ryan. The lea—a vibrant green now, thanks to the seasonal rain—is devoid of human settlement. Waves of sheep flow over hills and often block his passage. Troops of gray kangaroos and packs of slinking dingoes keep their distance. Except for high-soaring ravens, the winter plain is empty of birds.

Ryan counts on game to supplement his slim rations. A new .36-caliber, five-shot Paterson Colt revolver—his latest purchase with his generous wages—rests in a holster under his knee-length oilskin jacket. While not as accurate as a rifle, the pistol is an effective hunting tool when combined with Ryan's native-trained stalking skills. Gates also insisted he carry a weapon for protection from bushrangers. While not numerous, such outlaws are a fact on the frontier.

Dan's pace exceeds that of a wagon team and the horse expects fewer rests. Ryan calculates he will reach Ballarat in three days of travel.

*****

Ryan rides westward from Buninyong an hour ahead of sunrise in a light drizzle. His wide leather hat and oilskin coat keep him dry. The temperature is seasonally mild; so the rain carries little chill. Dan high-steps through the sodden kangaroo grass.

Ryan is unsure of Laarr's location but does not expect to search widely. He is certain they will detect him first—a lone white man on a horse.

By midday, Ryan locates the forest-topped hill where he encountered Loklok two years earlier. He sets up camp. The clouds break apart. A streamer of sunlight, hazy with water vapor, illuminates the glade. He cooks a lunch of bacon and eggs over a fire. He sets the billy near the flames to boil water for tea and opens *Nicholas Nickleby* by Charles Dickens. Ryan tosses green twigs and branches on the flames to increase the smoke. Dan chomps grass at the forest edge.

Ryan finishes his first cup of tea and prepares to pour a second. Dan raises his head and perks up his ears. Ryan closes his book and rises with his right hand on the gun inside his coat. Someone has come, but friend or foe?

"Only a white man makes so much smoke," says a voice in the underbrush.

"'Tis on purpose, so even a blind Wathaurung can find me."

A warrior carrying two spears slips from the concealing forest into the shadows. Ryan's pulse surges—*Loklok*. Ryan's fingers tighten on the pistol grip.

The warrior paces towards him, showing no hostile body language, saying nothing. The mystery man's path intersects the shaft of sunlight—not Loklok but a muscled younger man bearing a striking resemblance.

"Weeyn! Ye've grown a foot since we last talked. I feared ye were Loklok."

"Loklok easy to name at distance. He limps from your fight, Mr. Kangaroo Fighter." Ryan winces at the new name. Weeyn grins.

"How is yer family, well I hope?" Ryan asks.

"Yes. Well. The spirits good to our family."

"And Tarra. Is she still there?"

"Yes. She twelve now. Becomes a real wife soon."

Ryan notes the off-tone of Weeyn's remark, and drops the topic. Ryan suffered a broken heart of his own before his deportation and sympathizes.

"Can I stay with yer family for a spell? I miss the bush life."

"You go soft from white man living," Weeyn says. "Good you come here. Make you strong."

Ryan marvels at how Weeyn can see through his layers of clothes. Ryan raises a palm in protest, but stays quiet. The life of a wheelwright is not strenuous when you have apprentices. A lack of exercise and the camp cooking has put a few pounds on him.

"I've tea if ye'd like a mug."

"No. Fraser did make me drink it. I hate."

"Let me pack up and we'll go to yer camp."

With Dan on a lead, Ryan ambles beside Weeyn. Rain droplets clinging to the winter grass soon soak Ryan's boots and pant legs. He ignores the discomfort. Approaching his thirtieth birthday, Ryan knows he needs to toughen up. He sweats with the effort to match his young friend's pace. At fifteen, Weeyn is close to Ryan in height. His chest and arms are beginning to show his father's brawn. A trace of beard smudges his chin.

They both relate highlights of the last two years. Ryan talks of his growing wheelwright enterprise. Weeyn remarks, without boasting, his skills in hunting and fighting have earned him the option to take a wife soon. So far, he has no interest. "I not ready to care for wife and babies," he explains.

Ryan puts an arm over Weeyn's wide shoulders. "Glad I am to see ye agin, friend."

Weeyn throws his arm across Ryan's upper back. "Weeyn happy Warrain keep promise to visit."

After two hours of hiking, Weeyn enters the forest and follows the familiar creek. In ten minutes, they reach the camp. The location is different but the setting—an open glade beneath towering gum trees—is the same.

Ryan greets the group in Wadawurrung. Laarr and Mokborree jostle aside their relatives to be close to the guest.

"Warrain, mighty fighter, honors us," Laarr says.

"'Tis my honor to be agin with the family of Laarr."

Pulling a canvas bag off his saddle, Ryan exclaims, "I've presents for my family."

To the arweat, Ryan gives a long-bladed, steel knife—a much-coveted tool and weapon among the clans. For Mokborree, Ryan has lugged an iron cooking pot from Ballarat, perfect for a hearty kangaroo stew. She squeals like an excited girl and pats Ryan's cheeks. Weeyn receives a steel-bladed ax. Ryan passes out steel spear tips to the hunters.

His last item is for Alinga. He spots Tarra at the rear of the onlookers. Half hiding behind her is Alinga. Ryan crosses the compound to his young friend.

Like her brother, she has grown—five feet tall now, Ryan guesses. Wider than before, she still reminds Ryan of a young tree—the same girth from armpits to thighs. Tarra, now several inches taller, has developed further towards womanhood: her lack of clothing reveals her new curves.

"Alinga my friend and savior, I've brought ye this." He pulls a book-sized, wooden case from his pocket. Opening it reveals a mirror. "I always said ye've beautiful eyes and a smile that lights up the world. I wanted ye to see what I mean."

She gapes at him, trembling and aphonic.

*****

Alinga interrupts her chores when Weeyn enters the camp with a white man and his horse. She watches as the stranger distributes presents. The man begins walking towards her. He is clothed and shaven, at first unfamiliar. An old sorrow tickles her consciousness. Closer now, his smile, his sea-blue irises, and the ocher curls poking from under his hat all identify him. A wave of emotion teases her belly. Remorse like nausea rises up her throat. Breathing is difficult. Her heartbeats quicken and grow shallow. The old feelings return and threaten to smother her. Lightheaded, she leans on Tarra.

Two years ago—an eon for one so young—she grieved his departure. Weeks of sorrow rolled past, in time replaced by dull, endless emptiness. And now, when she has almost forgotten him, here he is, talking to her, saying she is beautiful, giving her a gift.

She glances at the looking glass. A somber girl reflects back. Alinga knows the image is her—past reflections in water gave her a general idea of her appearance. The mirror's clarity is like flowers in sunlight instead of twilight. She does not feel beautiful.

"'Tis yer face, Alinga," Ryan says. "Pretty."

She thrusts the gift at Ryan and runs as fast as her long legs will carry her. In the comforting bosom of the forest, she crumples in a secluded grove and cries for hours. Weak and exhausted by the effort, she slips into slumber and dreams.

Alinga is a young dingo, alone on the parched summer plain. She waits concealed, viewing a lone adult dingo drink from the water hole. His fur is an odd color, far redder than usual. Four dark dingoes rush the red one. He fights for his life. Outnumbered, he is disemboweled.

Alinga's scream awakens her. Her breath comes in gasps. She understands the meaning of her dream.

*****

"Me see me?" asks Tarra. She seizes the mirror from Ryan without waiting for a reply. She smiles at her reflection and pulls stray strands of her wavy brown hair into place.

"Is Alinga unwell?" Ryan says. Concern creases his brow.

Tarra returns the looking glass. "Are all white men dumb like wombat?" she calls over her shoulder as she strolls to her family hut.

Ryan blinks and tilts his head at the remark. He seeks out Weeyn and locates him on the camp's edge. He's chopping firewood with his new ax.

"This good," the youth exclaims. "I thank Warrain."

Weeyn cuts a fallen tree into sections and splits them into manageable pieces.

"Yer sister spake nary a word. Has she forgotten me?"

"She remember," Weeyn replies without pausing. At each chop, wood chips leap skyward and fall to mingle with the forest debris.

"Has she forgotten her English?"

"Speak English good." Chop! Chop!

"She acts…I dunno…sad."

"I say before—" Chop! "—just crazy kid." Chop! "No got smart yet." Chop! "Dream too much."

"What dreams?"

Weeyn stops, leans on his ax handle and replies, "You dumb like wombat."

"Damn it. 'Tis what Tarra said. What do ye mean?"

"Wombat sticks head in burrow, but rump show. Not see world, but world see wombat."

"I know wombats. 'Tis naught to do with me." Ryan's right boot toe taps the ground at a steady beat.

Weeyn recognizes the meaning of Ryan's twitchy toe. "Warrain not be angry. Ignore my sister. We hunt tomorrow. Have fun like before." He pauses, smiling. "Maybe find wombat." Weeyn snickers at his own joke.

Ryan grins. "'Tis grand to be here again."

*****

Days pass in the old, welcome routine. At dawn, Ryan and the hunters scour the forest and plain for game. In the afternoons, the men eat, talk and do light camp duties. Twice a day, Ryan leads Dan to the grasslands to eat his fill.

Ryan has built his own mia-mia and a corral nearby for Dan. In the hut, he stores his saddle and most of his clothes. He wears a hat, light breeches and a cotton shirt. He acclimates to the chill in a few days. The rigors of climate, hiking or trotting for miles, carrying game or firewood, and eating bush food suit him. He sheds pounds.

He misses Alinga and her smile. During his stay two years earlier, she followed him like a puppy and made excuses to be near him. This time, she avoids him. She does not greet the hunters' return. She has ignored his offer to teach her additional English.

*****

Alone in the forest, in a cluster of low bushes near the creek, Alinga studies her reflection in the gift mirror. Warrain often said she is pretty. Why? she wonders. Her eyes are large, yes. She forces a smile. Her teeth are white and even. Is that beauty? Her nose is wide and flat, like those of her people, but less so than most. Does Warrain like her smaller nose? The skin on her cheeks and forehead is soft and smooth. Dense hair frames her face. She identifies nothing unsightly in her appearance.

«If Belongs-to-the-sea says I am pretty,» she muses in her ancient language, «why does he not want me?»

Alinga often spies Warrain's furtive peeks at young women in the camp. His expression of longing is common among young men. But when he looks at her, his features show only friendship. She wonders why. She tilts the mirror to inspect her chest. *Like a boy*. She answers her own question. *To Warrain, I am a child*. She finds solace in her emerging patch of fine-grained pubic hairs—a new addition to her body that she knows from observation heralds change.

«He cannot imagine the woman I will be. When I am older, he will love me,» she says to her reflection.

She notices movement across the swallow creek gorge. Warrain descends the far bank to his favorite bathing pool. Every second or third day, he comes to this waterhole. And each time, she waits and guards him from above.

He piles his white man's clothes and boots on rock. Alinga notices the ridges of his abdominal muscles show more definition. His buttocks, thighs and biceps have lost their softness. Naked is how she enjoys him the most—only then can she relish the red hairs on his chest, legs and groin. And the little brown spots on his shoulders he calls freckles. *Adorable*!

He slips into the cold water up to his chest. He grunts with the temperature shock. With a thing he calls soap, he makes white foam and rubs it on his body.

She spots an unnatural shadow slinking amid gum trees upstream. Others follow. Four men creep along the watercourse. No one in her family would employ such stealth so close to camp.

The expected danger she dreamed has arrived. She must warn Warrain. She picks up a thumb-sized rock.

*****

Ryan, fully soaped, slips into the pool to rinse, growling from the cold jolt. A stone plops into the water a yard ahead. Pebbles do not fall from the sky. He scrambles to shore, gathers his clothes and probes the forest for the thrower.

Alinga pops above low shrubbery on the far bank. With hand signs, she motions him to be quiet and come to her. Ryan never questions her bush sense. With his bundle of clothes held to his chest, he leaps up the hill and slips into her green warren. He crouches beside Alinga. She points through a gap in the brush. Ryan reconnoiters the forest upstream. Four armed warriors stalk the watercourse, searching for something.

They're looking for me!

One man he recognizes from his first meeting with Loklok. The assassins stop at the pool he vacated. One kneels to investigate

Ryan's footprints in the wet sand. He points towards Laarr's camp. Another warrior slaps his thigh in disappointment. The men return the way they came—their ambush a failure. Ryan pulls on his breeches and boots, to be ready in case they return. His pistol is in his hut—a mistake he vows not to repeat.

With a finger, Ryan lifts Alinga's chin until her pupils meet his. "Ye saved my life agin." She doesn't answer. "But how did ye find me?"

"I search here for roots," she lies.

"I'm lucky to know ye." Ryan bends and kisses her forehead—a Platonic peck fitting for a sibling or an aunt.

Alinga's mouth opens but no words emerge. Water wells in the corners of her big eyes and dribbles down her cheeks. She flings her arms around Ryan's neck, curls up in his lap and buries her face in his chest. At first baffled, Ryan deduces the narrow escape with the warriors has unnerved her.

He strokes her back. "'Tis alright now. The danger is gone." He rocks her until the sobs abate.

*****

Phony sniffles soon replace Alinga's real tears. She did not expect this closeness and is in no hurry to leave his strong arms. She has not cuddled with him since the night on the beach.

"Are ye better?" Ryan says.

She unravels from his arms. "Yes. We go now." She holds his hand during the short trek to camp.

"I should tell yer father what happened." Ryan seeks out Laarr and Weeyn, with Alinga still in tow.

"We should take our warriors and hide by pool," Weeyn says when Ryan finishes his story. "If they return, we attack."

Laarr listens to his son's youthful advice, and frowns. "I not kill family of Boort. Much trouble already." He places a paw on Ryan's shoulder. "Warrain like son, but must go."

"I'll leave tomorrow. May I return next year?"

Laarr smiles. "Tomorrow go. Tonight all feast. Wish our brother safe journey. Come next winter."

Ryan's departure does not devastate Alinga this time. She is confident he will return and she accepts seasons must pass before she can make him hers.

Fraser's Station

July 1847

In the late afternoon, Ryan rides into Buninyong. He boards Dan at a stable and takes a room at the nearest hotel. He washes, shaves and departs on a mission.

Ryan saunters along the row of dwellings—mostly tents—on the town's main residential street. He stops at the school sponsored by Fraser. Standing in the road, Ryan begins to sing a popular Irish ballad, based on the 1798 Irish rebellion, taught to him by his late grandfather.

Come all ye warriors and renowned nobles
Who once commanded brave warlike bands
Throw down yer plumes and yer golden trophies
Give up yer arms with a trembling hand.

Attracted by his untrained but passable tenor, people emerge from tents into the street.

For Father Murphy of the County Wexford
Lately roused from his sleepy dream
To cut down cruel Saxon persecution
And wash it away in a crimson stream.

A middle-aged man joins in with a fiddle. Two boys in the school stick their heads out the tent flap, giggle and dart inside. Midway into the third verse, Ellen steps out and, to Ryan's surprise, adds the high, clear notes of a tin whistle to the ensemble.

By the fourth verse, the mass of people closes the street to buggy traffic. Many clap in time to the music. Others sing in step but not always in tune. Though awed by the reaction, Ryan keeps singing. Before the final verse's last notes leave his lips, the revelers begin clapping and hooting. Jugs of rum make the rounds.

Her cheeks creased with a wide smile, Ellen steps forward and speaks words only Ryan can hear, "Did we not agree to keep our friendship discreet?"

"'Twas not my intention to start a ceilidh. I felt like singing and…" He ends with a shrug.

"You had no idea half this street claims roots in Ireland?" Ellen says. "Nor that you might awaken the intense love of the distant homeland common throughout the great Irish diaspora, whose numbers were well represented on the convict ships that populated this continent?"

"Nay," Ryan replies, flashing an impish grin.

"Did you visit me for a purpose other than a serenade?"

"Aye. Can ye ride a horse?"

"Certainly," Ellen says.

"If ye be willing, I'll come by tomorrow at dawn and take ye for a ride."

"Where will we go?"

"'Tis a surprise. And don't eat. I'll make breakfast."

"I shall happily join you on condition you bring a regular saddle. This lady does not ride sidesaddle."

Ryan glances up the street. Couples caper to the fiddler's reel. "Let's join the festivities."

"Can you dance?" she asks.

"I can move around without stepping on yer toes."

*****

When Ryan reins in Dan by Ellen's school tent, the sun has not yet cleared the horizon to warm the cold morning air. Tied behind is a bay mare he'd hired from the stable. Alerted by the clop-clop of shod hooves, Ellen meets him by the door.

"Let us be off before you break into song," she says, with a toss of her hair. She mounts the horse and arranges her loose skirt over the saddle.

"Are ye comfortable riding at a trot? Our destination is ten miles down this bush road."

"Proceed at a gallop if you wish. I can keep pace."

Ryan and Ellen ride east, side-by-side on a dirt track. Mist hovers in horizontal strata above the dew-soaked sward. The land is void of humans except for the occasional shepherd. Sheep dominate the landscape and co-exist with kangaroos and wallabies.

The rising sun spills blood over the eastern hills, setting the top layer of mist glowing like iron in a forge. They speak little and communicate with smiles.

Within twenty minutes, the destination is evident to Ellen. "Is that mountain ahead our breakfast reservation?"

"Aye. 'Tis an old volcano, I'm told, with a grand lookout at the top."

By riding at a steady trot, they reach the volcano's base in another hour. Ryan stops at a pond to rest and water the horses. When next they dismount, they are two hundred yards above the plain on the treed summit. Ryan unties two duffle bags attached to his saddle.

"Can ye cool the horses while I build a fire?"

"Certainly," she says.

Ellen leads their mounts in a wide circle through the glade of gum trees, admiring the expanse of sheep range and forests. Ryan clears a patch of ground for a fire pit. He gathers dry wood by cutting the dead lower branches from living trees. In the rainy season, wood lying on the ground is too wet to burn. With years of practice at fire starting with flint and steel, Ryan soon has robust flames licking the fuel. He puts a pot of water on to boil.

From one duffle, Ryan extracts three bundles wrapped in clean cotton cloth. The first, when untied, yields six scones, already sliced and buttered. These he places on a flat rock by the fire to warm.

The horses now cooled, Ellen secures them to a tree with long leads and joins Ryan. "Did you bring marmalade for those?" Ellen asks.

"I did." Ryan points to one duffle bag. "'Tis in there. Fetch the two folding camp chairs while ye're at it. Make yerself comfortable, lass."

Smiling, Ellen sets up the chairs. "I cannot recall when a man last prepared breakfast for me."

"Get ready to be pampered and delighted," he answers.

He puts four scoops of ground coffee into the now boiling water. From the second packet, Ryan removes several strips of dark meat and places them in a frying pan with two strips of bacon.

"What manner of meat is that?" Ellen inquires.

"Walert. 'Tis a native delicacy. I boiled it several days ago to remove the natural grease and gamey taste. Then I dried it. The bacon grease adds to the flavor and softens the dried meat." He stirs the strips of meat, making sure all sides are cooked.

The third bundle he disassembles like someone unpacking delicate china. Inside the wrapping is a wad of straw. Curious, Ellen watches over his shoulder. Ryan picks away the golden stalks a pinch at a time until he reveals four white oval objects.

"Eggs! You dear man."

Ryan cracks the eggs into the frying pan. They sizzle and pucker in the liquid bacon fat. He pulls the boiling coffee off the heat to let the grounds settle.

"That coffee smells divine," Ellen says.

From the packs, Ryan retrieves a ceramic sugar jar, plates, tin cups, cutlery and cloth napkins. He serves Ellen her coffee and breakfast, then his. Ryan observes her refined manners—her fork and knife ever in the proper hand and held at the correct angle.

Over breakfast, Ryan recounts his recent visit with Laarr's group. Ellen listens and eats.

"Is another coffee possible?" Ellen asks at the end of her meal.

"Aye. Pass yer cup. One and half sugars?"

"How observant," she replies with a smile.

"Come walk with me to the crater rim. Carry yer coffee. 'Tis not far."

Side-by-side, Ryan and Ellen peer into the ancient volcano's dormant heart. Gum trees fill the space wall to wall. Parrots adorn the forest canopy, adding color to the uniform gray-green leaves.

"I can nary get used to most trees being the same color," Ryan remarks.

"How is it different where you lived?"

"In both Ireland and the part of North America where I lived, there are easily fifteen or twenty big tree types. Their leaves have different shapes and shades of green. Along the St. Lawrence River in autumn, broadleaf trees change color: many shades of yellow, orange, and red. For a time, the forest looks like a living sunset."

"I'd love to see that someday," Ellen replies, turning to Ryan.

Ryan slips his hand around hers. She returns a light squeeze and a smile.

Ryan leans towards her, noticing tiny flecks of brown in her green irises. On an impulse, he bends closer, his lips aimed at hers. Ellen presses her coffee mug to his chest. "Let us mount the horses and ride the crater rim."

"I hope I did not—"

She places a finger on his lips. "I'm flattered, not annoyed. But, this setting is too romantic for me to let down my guard. Besides, I must return soon. I told my students to attend after midday."

Relieved he did not insult her, Ryan bows with a theatrical flourish. "Your steed awaits."

During the ride to town, he asks, "How many students are ye teaching?"

"I have four bright Wathaurung boys under ten. They live with a local black family. Mr. Fraser pays their board. I had one ten-year-old but Fraser transferred him to his station."

"Any girls?"

"Alas, no," she says, with an edge to her voice. "Mr. Fraser says *lubras* are just baby makers and not worth educating."

"'Tis harsh," Ryan replies. "Do ye know yet what harm comes to the boys at Fraser's station?"

"I am uncertain," Ellen says. "To my queries, Mr. Fraser merely replies there is more to a boy's education than reading and writing."

Ryan glances at Ellen. "'Tis an odd answer."

"Yes, and suspiciously cryptic."

*****

Walter Fraser sips tea on a bench and reclines in the sun against the front plank wall of the Buninyong Hotel. He scrutinizes the residents, travelers and ranch hands going about their affairs. Officer Billy works his way through the crowd, his polished boots and brass buttons a contrast to the faded uniform he refuses to discard.

"Any news for me Billy?" Fraser says, twisting the end of his blond mustache.

"Yes, boss. Kangaroo Fighter is back. He comes this way now," he says, pointing.

"Please flag him down," Fraser says.

"Yes, boss."

Billy waits until Dan and Ryan are within ten paces, and barges into the street. Ryan reins in Dan to avoid a collision.

"What are ye doing?"

"Boss wants talk to you," Billy says pointing to Fraser. "I hold horse." Billy snatches the bridle without waiting for Ryan's consent.

Fraser notices that Ryan offers no protest to Billy's impudence and dismounts without any hint of annoyance. *As if he meant to find me. Odd!*

"Would you care for a nice cup of tea, Ryan? The innkeeper has a small supply of honey if you wish a sweetener."

"I'd prefer maple syrup but honey will do, thank ye."

Fraser motions Billy to fetch tea. With no hesitation, Billy ties off the horse and enters the hotel. His status as Fraser's man and a former policeman gives him privileges denied most other members of his race.

"Maple syrup is a rare commodity under the Southern Cross," Fraser begins. "I gather you acquired that taste in eastern North America."

"Aye. Syrup is one thing I miss."

"Sit, please." Fraser points to the long bench. "I trust you had a pleasant morning with Mrs. O'Sullivan?"

Ryan frowns. Fraser expected that. No one likes their little secrets exposed.

"Do not worry. I am pleased she has such an honorable man for a companion. A woman like her, alone and attractive, should have a man someplace to discourage philanderers and other male riff-raff."

"What did ye've to say to me?" Ryan says.

"Straight to the point. Fine with me." Fraser sets down his teacup. "Billy tells me our mutual friend Loklok has put a price on your head."

"How'd ye find out?"

"Billy has many friends in the black community from his years in the Native Police Corps."

"Friends?" Ryan says, his eyebrows drawing together.

"I understand your skepticism," Fraser says, smiling. "Friend is a turn of phrase only. Billy was a fearsome officer and many respect his violent capabilities. The blacks do what he asks."

"Why is my enemy yer concern?" Ryan says.

"We whites should be allies when the blacks get murderous," Fraser answers. "A word from me and Scott and Billy will track Loklok and kill him for you."

Fraser detects shock playing across Ryan's features, followed by squinty-eyed indecision. Fraser assumes Ryan is considering the offer.

"Um…if any killing is required on my behalf," Ryan says, "I'll do it myself."

"Well said, but…have you any experience with that deed?"

Ryan chews his lower lip. "Nay."

"Loklok has sworn a blood oath against you. My advice is to always carry a gun and use it if necessary. Do not think. Point and pull the trigger."

"Ye seem quick to wish a former pupil dead," Ryan says.

"Loklok was a failure," Fraser says. He sips his tea and continues. "He has a keen mind but lacks the ability to be stoic when presented with difficulties and challenges. His aggressive outbursts compensate for a lack of a backbone."

"Is that what ye do at yer farm, present boys with difficulties and challenges?" Ryan says.

"In a manner of speaking. Please visit," Fraser says. "I would welcome an opportunity to show you my operation. I still harbor the wish to have you working for me."

Ryan fidgets with his teacup.

"Come with me. It is just east of here."

"Aye."

*****

Fraser's compound is a flat area one hundred yards wide covered with close-cropped grass and patches of bare sandy soil. Arranged in a square are the main house, a bunkhouse, a crew kitchen, stables, a shearing shed and a long open-sided pole barn. Fraser's arrangement is similar to the Willis compound but something is out of place. Ryan cannot fix upon the difference.

"Come. Let me show you my wagons." Fraser says, gripping Ryan's shoulder. "Billy," he calls, "take the horses to the stable. Have the new boy give them oats."

"Yes, boss."

"This is the heart of my enterprise." He stops at the pole barn. "I have fifteen wagons, ten on the road and five before you."

Ryan's examination uncovers no flaws in the wagons, fittings or wheels. Dark burgundy paint covers each wagon body. The name Fraser Haulage Company in white block lettering adorns the wagons' sides.

"I have rethought your role in my enterprise," Fraser begins. "Your reputation as a wheelwright increases your value. I will offer whatever Willis pays plus twenty-five percent."

"I dunno. I like working for Willis."

"You would be closer to the lovely Ellen," Fraser says with a wink.

"I'll think on it."

"When can I expect an answer?" Fraser says, his voice dropping a halftone.

Ryan stares at Fraser, annoyed at his insistence, cognizant he could never work for him. Before he is obliged to answer, Scott Healey saunters over from the stable.

"Did the boy feed our horses?" Fraser says.

"He is now. I had 'im assigned to…er…other duties."

Fraser frowns. His eyebrows knit together.

Ryan shares Fraser's annoyance at Healey's smug manner. "What duties?" he asks.

A flash of guilt crosses the tall foreman's expression, but his composure returns. "Whatever I tell 'im needs doin'."

"Go fetch him," Fraser orders. "I bet he would be pleased to meet Ryan."

Healey scowls but does Fraser's bidding. A minute later he herds out a skinny, barefooted, native boy dressed in oversized clothes. His narrow skull is shorn to near baldness. Ryan notices the lad shuffles like he has a cramp.

"Nalong. Say hello to Warrain, the famous Kangaroo Fighter."

The boy's downcast eyes flit up and widen, but he remains silent.

Ryan gambles Healey and Fraser do not understand Wadawurrung and speaks to Nalong in his native tongue. «Do they treat you well here?»

The boy smiles for Fraser's benefit. His words tell the truth. «I pray everyday for the spirits to return me to Dreamtime.»

Healey cuffs the boy on his ear, knocking him to the ground. "Don't speak that damned gibberish."

Expecting a further beating, the boy curls up with his arms covering his head.

Ryan steps between Nalong and Healey. He rises on his toes close to the tall white man's face. "I asked him a formal question about his family. By custom he had no choice but to answer as he did," Ryan lies.

Healey snarls at Ryan. Fraser intervenes and pushes the two potential pugilists apart. "Scott, dear boy, Ryan could not have known we demand only English be spoken. And," he says, lowering his voice, "it is bad manners to discipline the help in front of guests."

Healey's jaw stiffens at Fraser's criticism. He scowls at Ryan and strides to the barn.

"What family group is Nalong from?" Ryan asks.

"The same as Loklok."

"Loklok had nary a nice thing to say about ye," Ryan says, crossing his arms. "Why would Boort allow it?"

"Obviously, what Loklok told you is not what he told Boort." Fraser rubs the back of his neck. "The old chief wants his people educated in the white man's ways. Why do you ask?"

Ryan drops the pitch of his voice and takes a half step closer to Fraser. "I'm escorting Nalong home to his people." Fraser stiffens in protest. Ryan continues. "Mr. Fraser. I don't want trouble with ye, but this lad is frightened and is being harmed by Healey and perhaps others." Ryan chooses not to accuse Fraser directly. "On my honor, I can't leave him here."

Ryan notices Fraser's brow furrow and his nostrils flare.

"I have five armed men I can assemble in one minute." Fraser growls. He parts his black coat to show a holstered pistol.

In a flash, Ryan fathoms what is different at Fraser's station—there are no blacks, other than the boy, and no women or signs of women. All occupants of the compound are burly white men, no doubt slaves to any of Fraser's whims.

Ryan holds his ground to maintain respect. "No doubt, Mr. Fraser. But let's not shoot each other today over this boy." Ryan nudges aside his oilskin coat to reveal the butt of his Colt.

"Agreed," Fraser replies, exhaling tension. "No point in shedding white blood for such a poor pupil. He tends to sniffle and whine."

Speaking to Nalong in Wadawurrung, Ryan says: «I will take you to Smoke. Please fetch my horse and your belongings.»

The boy leaps up like a startled wallaby and bounds into the stable.

Fraser points to Ryan's pistol. "Is that a Paterson Colt?"

"Aye."

"A very fine weapon…when it works," Fraser says, in his former jovial tone. "It has a reputation for fouling or breaking down at the most inopportune moments."

"I keep it clean and oiled. Nary worry."

Fraser's forced smile vanishes. "One word of warning Ryan," he says, his voice husky, "I like you but do not meddle in my affairs again."

"I'll try not to."

"If you do," Fraser adds, "you will have more than Loklok to worry about."

*****

Several hours after dawn the next day, Ryan halts Dan on a hilltop west of Buninyong. He and Nalong had camped outside town overnight. The boy said little.

"'Tis as far as I can take ye, lad. Yer cousin will kill me if he spots me."

Nalong slides off the saddle from where he'd clung to Ryan like a limpet to a rock.

Ryan points to a distant mound. "See that big hill. Boort's camp is to the north. Ye can find it easily."

Nalong regards Ryan with an expression of shy affection. The boy struggles to select words. "Thank you mighty Warrain," is all he manages.

"Ye are welcome brave Nalong. Please tell Boort that Warrain says Fraser is a bunyip."

Nalong nods.

"And ye must tell Boort the truth of what happened at his station."

Nalong's eyes widen with fear.

"Do ye know Loklok also suffered abuse?"

"No," Nalong murmurs.

"He was also a stable boy for Fraser. But he did not tell the truth. If he had, maybe Boort would not have sent ye to Fraser. Ye can stop it happening agin to another boy."

Comprehension softens Nalong's features.

Ryan pulls a steel-bladed tomahawk from a saddlebag. "Give this to Boort as a sign of respect from me, when ye tell him what Healey and Fraser did. He'll believe ye, even if Loklok denies it."

"I tell this thing you ask." Nalong begins undressing. "I do not need these rags."

Ryan spots a trace of dried blood inside the discarded trousers. Red welts streak the boy's boney back. Even though Ryan knew Healey abused the boy, he winces at the evidence.

"All white men are not bad like Healey and Fraser," Ryan says.

"Warrain only white man I not pray killed." Switching into Wadawurrung, Nalong adds, «May the spirits of Dreamtime protect you and your family.»

Ryan observes Nalong's progress until the boy becomes one with the grassland.

Going Solo

January 1848

A dry summer wind whips sand granules and dried grass across the Willis compound. Desiccated gum leaves gather in nervous piles in the lee of buildings. Acrid dust creeps even into noses covered by bandannas. The parched ground has not felt a drop of rain in two months.

Ryan and two helpers work inside the main wagon shed, replacing a wheel on the largest wool wagon. The natural light illuminating the interior is hazy with dust seeping between cracks in the shed's planks. Wind gusts rattle the window glass.

Ryan supervises the men while they jack up the wagon. He helps remove the defective wheel to ensure it suffers no further damage. A close inspection of the hub and wooden rim confirms his earlier diagnosis. The repair is a minor one his helpers can manage. A new section of rim and two spokes will get the wheel rolling.

William Gates enters the shed and waits while Ryan's helpers install a replacement wheel. "How is my wagon coming?" he says.

"'Twill be fit for yer journey to Geelong tomorrow," Ryan replies, without glancing at his friend. "We need to fit a new tongue. The old one is showing cracks."

"You can still come with me," Gates says in a soft voice. "We'll find a ship and return to America together."

"I've no family there like ye, and no reason to leave," Ryan answers.

"Weren't you betrothed to Johnston's daughter?"

Ryan delays his response. Kate has not entered his mind for months and he has not spoken of her for two years. "She could not wait for my return. She married another."

"Oh! Sorry. Another sacrifice to our lost cause," Gates says, trying to sound philosophical.

Ryan ignores the topic and looks at his friend. "Have ye money for ship passage?"

"I've saved almost every pound I've earned. Yes, but little to spare."

*****

The next day is already hot by sunup. The languid air permits haze-free views for miles. Ryan oversees the men loading wheels onto a wagon bulging with wool bales. The driver will drop off the incomplete wheels at the blacksmith in Buninyong.

His bag over his shoulder, Gates comes up to Ryan. "It was grand to work with you. It made Australia less lonely."

Ryan shakes the offered hand and says, "Make sure ye write to me when ye arrive home."

"I will."

"And say hello for me to any of the old lads ye run across."

"I sure will."

Ryan pulls twenty pounds in notes from a pocket. "Take this. I bet ye are tighter for money than ye are telling."

Gates smiles. "Thanks. I could use it." He climbs on the passenger seat next to the driver and waves at the Willis family.

Ryan's eyes follow the wagon in the sparkling morning air until it disappears into its own dust fog. That evening, he has an extra helping of desert in silent celebration of his thirtieth birthday. He reads the latest letter from his friend Ada in Canada. She updates Ryan on the lives of people once close to him. He blows out the lantern.

*****

The passing of a significant milestone and the departure of Gates unsettles Ryan's comfortable life at the Willis station. With no other employees he counts as friends, he spends his free time alone, often reading a book, riding on the open range or target shooting with his revolver. Ryan cannot deny the obvious—at his age he must soon make hard decisions concerning his future or be someone's employee until his health fails through age, disease or misfortune. *After that—what—destitute final years?*

One day alone in the wagon shed, while planning and shaping a wheel spoke—an activity he can almost do in his sleep—an idea unfolds in his meditative mind. Clues to his future surround him.

That afternoon, he seeks a meeting with William Willis in the ranch house library.

"Well Ryan," Willis says, "what is it today—another business idea?"

"Yes, sir, in a manner of speaking." Ryan clears his throat. "I'm giving ye notice. I intend to set up a wheelwright shop in Ballarat or Buninyong. 'Tis time I was my own man."

Willis sighs. "I expected this. No man of your abilities stays forever. How much notice are you givin' me?"

"I'll stay 'til the end of May, ten weeks. That gives me time to train the lads better so ye suffer little at my leaving."

"That is generous and considerate, Ryan. I owe you much. As a token of my appreciation for your contributions ta this station, please use any materials ta build yourself a box wagon or buggy. You will find it essential in your new enterprise."

"Thank ye, sir. 'Tis been grand working for ye. I've nary met an Englishman I thought highly of afore."

"We were both transported here by high-handed British bastards. That erased any racial history separating us."

"Aye."

*****

June 1848

On a clear day, Ryan waves to Willis and departs. With Dan hitched to the box wagon, Ryan begins his new life. He counts his blessings: a fine horse, a new wagon, and nearly eighty pounds in savings—plenty to buy tools and materials for his new trade.

His plans for the next few weeks are simple. He will visit Laarr's family, meet Ellen in Buninyong and scout a location for his new business near Ballarat.

Miles of rolling green plateau pass. Ryan sings every old Irish folk tune his grandfather once taught him. At the loudest volume he can sustain, and with some notes missing the mark, his singing scatters herds of sheep in his path and sets kangaroos bounding away in terror.

After four days travel, Ryan guides the wagon west from Buninyong towards the familiar mount where he met Weeyn the previous year. He steers well south of it to avoid Boort's winter territory. He passes the last sheep herd. Two troops of kangaroos and a flock of emus scrutinize him from a distance.

He skirts the narrow band of gum forest that hugs the hidden creek, staying in the grassland. At midday, he stops to make lunch in an area he senses is close to Laarr's territory. Once again, he feeds wood to the campfire beyond what is necessary to cook, and piles green boughs on the flames to make smoke. He sips tea, reads and waits.

*****

Weeyn sits on a possum robe and leans on a gum trunk surrounded by a dense thicket of scrub brush. A clearing four paces wide is a private refuge to which he returns often for one purpose.

Eyes closed, he listens, waiting.

The warning squawk of a cockatoo announces his expected visitors are near. Faint sounds, no louder than a gum nut makes falling on sand, come to him over the windy rustle of leaves. The regularity of those minor noises signals footsteps.

Tarra's glowing face appears amid the shrubbery. Now thirteen summers, her hips are full and her breasts large and round. Her belly shows a bump where her first baby is growing. Weeyn smiles and stretches out his hands. She slips into his arms. He seeks her lips with his.

«Oh, Fire, I miss you,» she whispers in his ear. He caresses her breast. «And I miss your soft touch.»

«I long for you every day, my beloved, and curse fate that my cousin claimed you instead of me,» Weeyn says, his nose buried in her wavy hair.

She slips her fingers between his legs. «I pray the child inside me is yours.»

*****

Through gaps in the brush, Alinga observes the lovers. Her brother clasps Tarra's face with two hands and kisses her. Their bodies entwine on the possum rug. Alinga justifies her spying as a way to learn the ways of intercourse, to be ready. Sometimes her body tingles in a strange, pleasurable way when she imagines herself in the arms of her own lover.

Alinga plays an integral role in the secret affair. She and Tarra leave daily together to scavenge for roots. Some days, on Weeyn's request to his sister, they detour to his refuge. Alinga, hides, waits and stays alert for interlopers.

A drifting scent distracts her. The unmistakable odor of burning gum wood taints the breeze. She decides to investigate, to make sure no one stumbles upon the two lovers whose senses are too engaged in carnal pleasures to notice the world beyond.

Alinga sniffs the air and follows the smoke trace west towards the forest edge. She stays in the shadows and flits from one tree trunk to the next. She spots a smoky fire. Nearby are a horse and wagon—and Warrain.

She studies him, absorbing his physical details. His hat is off, showing his long curly hair. A line of hair like a red caterpillar smears his upper lip. He looks her way.

*****

Ryan senses a presence. A snort from Dan confirms it.

He probes the deepest forest shadows. There! Two spheres of equal size and inches apart glow in the false dusk of tree shade, white beacons in a dark visage.

"I see yer eyes Alinga. Why are ye hiding? Come out," he calls, without rising from his seat.

A dark form slips from the gloom. In a slow, uncertain pace, she pads towards him, stopping a yard away. Taller now, her waist curves inwards and hips out. Her upper legs are no longer boney limbs. Her chest is in transition from girl to woman.

Too bad. She'll have to go to Boort's family soon.

"Can ye guide me to yer father's camp?" he asks her.

She hesitates. "Not now." She points into the forest. "Tarra—"

"Is she in trouble?"

Alinga ponders her feet and scratches her ear. "No."

"Is she needing yer help?"

A faint smile touches her lips. "No-o."

"Is there anything I can do?"

Her body tenses like a dingo poised to leap. She fidgets. Her mouth twitches. Her doe-like eyes shimmer with surface moisture—dilated black pupils in black irises focus on him. Ryan sets down his book and sits upright.

"Are ye unwell?"

Alinga steps forward. A tentative finger reaches out and pets his mustache. Ryan smiles at the gesture, mistaking it for curiosity.

Just as a hummingbird can go from a hover to a speeding blur in a blink, Alinga shoots out her arms, grabs both his cheeks and plants her full lips on his.

His eyelids close on reflex. His arms fly up but quiver in the air next to her hips, not sure what to do next. Though mushy, wet and brief, there is no mistaking Alinga's unpracticed embrace for anything but a kiss, and not the kind meant for a sibling or maiden aunt.

She releases him and flees into the forest.

Ryan falls off the log onto his back, gawks at the clouds and replays what just happened. He canvasses his memory for all past encounters with Alinga over the last three years. A pattern emerges. *'Tis a child's crush she has.*

Ryan is into the dregs of his second mug of tea when Weeyn emerges from the forest. The youth's height now surpasses Ryan's by an inch. He is thickly muscled. Ryan notices a hint of rooster swagger in his gait.

"Ye look chipper, friend Weeyn."

He grins. "Welcome friend Warrain. My sister say you here."

"Is Tarra having troubles?"

"No," Weeyn replies, his eyes widening. "What did sister tell?"

"Naught," he says. "Alinga was acting strange and mentioned Tarra's name."

"They hunt for roots. Must stay together, Laarr say so," Weeyn lies.

"I guess that explains part of it," Ryan says, now the one bearing the grin.

"What she do?" Weeyn asks.

"Let's just say I'm no longer dumb like wombat."

"Ah-h."

An hour later, Ryan guides the wagon into the camp with the help of a dozen people to cut brush. He distributes offerings from his wagon. To each elder, he gives a woolen blanket. He passes out metal spear points to Laarr, Weeyn and every hunter. In addition, he gives Laarr a file and whetstone for sharpening his knife. Mokborree gets her wish—another metal cooking utensil: a frying pan. For the children, he brought hard candy.

With formal greetings complete and Ryan's charity almost exhausted, the group disperses. Alinga sidles up to Ryan, her expression both shy and expectant.

"Did ye think I forgot yer present?" he says.

She lowers her chin and raises her eyes like she has seen Tarra do with Weeyn. She answers with a coquettish shake of her head that hides her eyes behind strands of hair.

Ryan passes her a slim, hinged wooden box. Fingers trembling, she undoes the brass clasp and opens the lid. Inside, a dozen sewing needles of various gauges lie embedded in red felt next to several spools of stout colored thread.

She eases the lid shut and holds the box to her chest. Eyelids fluttering, she says in a soft voice, "Warrain very kind to Alinga."

She touches his upper lip. He tenses, expecting another amorous assault.

"What is that called?"

"'Tis a mustache."

"I no like. It prickles," she whispers. She holds the box behind her. That position pulls her shoulders back and thrusts out her nascent breasts. A coy smile dimples her beaming face.

Again, Ryan is mesmerized, unable to move or say anything to set her straight. Ryan spots Tarra watching them, smiling. She is one year older and already married and pregnant. In his world Alinga is a child, but here she has adult status.

His stomach feels tight and queasy. It is nerves, the fear of steering the wrong moral course between his prudish Victorian upbringing—where how to reason with a naked maiden never enters polite conversation—and the simpler societal rules of the Wathaurung.

Before he can muster a response, Alinga twirls and departs to show her gift to Tarra. The young women glance back at Ryan and laugh.

"Hard to believe ye are only twelve," he mutters, as she saunters away with the gait of a cat.

*****

The next day, Ryan convinces Weeyn to hunt emus with him instead of joining Laarr and the other hunters. "I can only stay a few days. 'Twill give us a chance to talk."

They exit the leafy, forest sanctuary, treading northwest. Ryan wears shorts to avoid dew soaked pant legs while they stride through the high grasslands. Boots, hat, a pale cotton shirt, and his holstered Colt complete his attire. Weeyn is naked. A tomahawk hangs from his waist on a leather thong. He carries four long feathers and two spears tipped with the new metal points.

"What are the feathers for?" Ryan asked.

"You wait. You see."

Ryan tromps beside Weeyn considering his next question. "Is Loklok still meaning to kill me?"

"When you win fight, Loklok lose much honor," Weeyn says. "Much happen since. Loklok now more mean."

"What else have I done?" Ryan asks, as he rubs his half finger.

"The boy, Nalong, told Boort what did happen to boys who did work for Fraser. Boort angry at Loklok for not tell truth. He lose more honor. He did beat his wife so hard, she almost dead. Boort say Loklok not be arweat now. Loklok blame Warrain. You must be careful—many warriors follow Loklok."

Ryan stops walking and faces Weeyn. "When ye came home from Fraser's station, did ye tell Laarr the truth?"

Weeyn grimaces. "I wait many days, then I tell."

"How did yer father respond?"

"He thank me. He say no more boys go to school of bunyip."

Ryan reaches for Weeyn's shoulder. "Yer a brave lad. Ye will make a wise arweat some day."

Weeyn shrugs off the complement and renews their trek.

"I live closer now," Ryan says. "I can visit regular."

"My sister be happy," Weeyn teases.

Two miles further, Weeyn slips behind an isolated copse of gum trees and motions Ryan to be still. He looks in the direction Weeyn points. The unmistakable long-legged silhouettes of emus line the nearest hill summit, five hundred yards ahead.

"How do we get close?" Ryan asks.

"*Kaweerr* see good. Hear good. We not hunt in open. They run. We make emu come to us."

"How?"

"Watch and learn, white man."

Weeyn cuts a long, narrow branch from a gum tree. To the end, he ties the leather thong that held his tomahawk.

"Give me shirt," Weeyn orders, pointing to Ryan.

Ryan tosses it. Weeyn rolls the garment into a loose ball and ties it to the thong. He tucks the feather quills into the ball with the vanes sticking out. Weeyn's contraption resembles a fishing pole with baited line.

Weeyn dangles the balled-up shirt in the open beyond his shady tree cover. He sets the pale cloth ball swaying in a narrow arch. Weeyn adds an occasional jerk to make the ball seem alive.

To Ryan's surprise, the far-off emus raise their heads from grazing. A large one takes tentative steps towards the bait. "Curious creatures," Ryan whispers.

"No talk," Weeyn answers. "Get gun ready. Shoot two when close."

Ryan pulls the Colt from the holster, cocks the hammer and waits in the shadows.

With cautious, long strides, the flightless birds step forward to investigate the pale twitching blob. Several times they seem to lose interest, stop and graze. Each time, Weeyn's jittery bait catches the attention of one adult and they all restart their advance.

When the lead bird struts to within twenty-five yards, Ryan raises and aims the pistol. He can easily hit the rotund target at that range but waits, to be assured of two clean shots before they flee.

Twenty yards. Fifteen yards. At twelve yards, the flock hesitates. Ryan squeezes the trigger, cocks the hammer, and fires again. Two emus drop dead. The survivors retreat through the grass at speeds to rival a horse.

Weeyn deconstructs his bait and returns the shirt.

Ryan notices a mischievous smirk. "I know that look. What are ye thinking?"

"My sister favorite meat is emu. She have more reason to be crazy for Warrain."

Ryan ignores the jest and points to the birds. "Do we dress these here?"

"No. Wathaurung use all parts: meat, feathers, bones. Carry to camp," says Weeyn. He heaves the larger bird onto his broad shoulders.

Ryan has lost ten pounds since his last visit and added muscle to his chest and biceps; yet, he struggles to lift the smaller emu, a fifty-pounder. The limp corpse tends to slide off his shoulders. With his burden balanced, he follows Weeyn and catches up after a few minutes.

"I am surprised Alinga lives with ye," Ryan says. "I expected she'd be with Boort's family by now."

"Father waits. Tell Boort Alinga not ready. Truth, Laarr not like Loklok."

"Good for him."

"And Mokborree no like Loklok. Worry he hurt Alinga."

"I saw yer mother turn her back on Loklok once when he came to speak to her. I knew she didn't care for him."

Weeyn hoots in amusement. "What Mokborree did is custom. When daughter marry, mother feel old—so mother never talk to betrothed."

Ryan smirks. "That is not uncommon in my culture, but for different reasons."

Another wry smile crosses Weeyn's face.

"What be on yer mind now?" Ryan asks.

"Maybe Mokborree soon turn back on you."

"I'm not Alinga's betrothed!"

"In our custom, betrothed man gives a gift each year to mother of girl," Weeyn says, chuckling.

Ryan stumbles with his load but checks his fall. "And I've brought Mokborree a present these last two years is what ye're saying."

"Maybe we soon be brothers." Weeyn drops his load, laughter weakened, and flops to the ground holding his belly, his head on the emu like a feathered pillow.

Ryan does not share his mirth. Alinga's infatuation is a road to heartbreak. She is not his future. Peripheral movement catches Ryan's eye. The long grass sways as if ruffled by a breeze. The day is windless.

"Get up Weeyn. Trouble's here." Ryan pulls out his gun, counts the full chambers—three—and cocks the hammer. "They must have heard my shots earlier."

The Wathaurung youth springs to his feet, a spear in either hand, and studies the faint shifts in the long-stemmed grass. "Five men crawl."

"We can take them but let's talk first. If they are Boort's people, we should avoid bloodshed."

Weeyn yells to the grass in his native tongue. Five embarrassed warriors rise from hiding, their faces painted with white lines and circles. Loklok is not among them. They begin treading forward, the pace cautious but determined. Ryan holds his Colt in the air. The men halt.

"Ask why they came," Ryan says.

Weeyn shouts the question. Ryan recognizes the answer. "Warrain."

"Are they doing Loklok's bidding?"

Weeyn relays the question. One man briefly replies. "He say yes."

"Say, if Loklok wants to talk, come in person. And then tell them to leave."

Weeyn passes on the message. One man shakes a tomahawk at Ryan. The Colt barks a response. The weapon's stone blade shatters. Its owner recoils like a man from a poisonous snake. The five retreat into the grassland.

"Will Loklok ever stop hunting me?"

"Not until one of you dead."

*****

July 1848

Ryan steers his wagon into the Buninyong street to Ellen's school. Its door flaps in the winter breeze. He dismounts and steps inside. The piles of wind blown leaves caught in the canvas corners suggest a long absence. He exits and scans the street.

"If ya's lookin' fer that teacher lady, she's up at the boardin' school now," says a passerby. "Too bad, we'll miss yer singin'."

Ryan laughs. "Thank ye." He remounts Dan.

Ellen is indeed now teaching in a new wooden dormitory and classroom on the edge of town. Ryan pokes his head inside the door. Eight white boys, segregated by age, line two long benches. Each has a handheld chalkboard and chalk. Ellen is teaching them how to print the word 'Australia.'

She spots him. "Class. Print the word ten times. I shall return in a minute." She hustles him out the door. "I am thankful for the lack of a serenade this visit."

"I can sing for ye later if ye bring yer tin whistle," he replies, grinning.

She rolls her eyes. "I will dismiss class in one hour. Please return and get me away from this town's dusty streets."

"Aye. Bring a shawl. 'Tis brisk today."

For the next hour, Ryan scours the bakery and grocery stores for the best bread, cheese and fresh fruit. He arrives at the school on schedule.

Ellen mounts the wagon bench and points into Ryan's picnic basket. "What are those lovely red fruits?"

"Quandong. They grow in the wild here and taste like apricots and rhubarb."

"I adore how you never fail to bring something exotic to the table." She pats his knee.

Ryan concentrates on maneuvering through the heavy horse and buggy traffic. "I don't recall such crowds afore," he remarks.

"Did you not hear the news? Someone found traces of gold west of here in the Pyrenees. It precipitated a minor prospecting rush."

"I chose a good year to start a wagon business," he says.

"Indeed. Have you commenced operations yet?"

"Nay. I need to buy material and tools in Geelong and then set up my shop."

Breaking free of town traffic, Ryan drives northwest on the road to Ballarat. Grazing land adheres to the road edges. Wooded hills loom in the distance both east and west.

"Where are yer other students?" Ryan asks.

"The headmen began pulling the boys out. Mr. Fraser could not replace them. I was puzzled as to why."

"And do ye know the reason?"

"I do. You put me out of a job and I applaud you for it." Ellen loops her left arm through Ryan's right arm, and leans her head on his shoulder.

Ryan welcomes the weight of her against him. "And now ye teach white children."

"Yes. But now the natives have no school."

"Won't one of the churches open a school for them?"

"Some Protestant denominations approached arweats about schooling without success."

"What happened?"

"The church insists the children abandon their native gods and accept Christ. The arweats refuse."

"Reminds me when the English in Ireland made our religion illegal."

"It is comparable but not identical. All churches are exclusive. The native gods are not illegal, just not accepted."

"Ye make a point. Still, 'tis not fair to deny them education when so many have a keen mind for it."

"The world is not fair."

They ride in silence until Ellen says, "Describe the recent visit to your Wathaurung friends."

Ryan recounts the gift giving, the emu hunt with Weeyn, the general health and activities of his closest friends, and long evenings by the fire listening to stories.

"How is the girl, the one who found you on the beach? Does she reside with her family?"

"Aye." Ryan swallows, trying to unglue his tongue.

"I sense you have an intrigue to impart."

"Aye."

"Well! Out with it!" She jabs an elbow in his ribs.

"The wee girl is becoming a young woman and has strong feelings for me. She kissed me when 'twas most unexpected."

Ellen laughs at Ryan's stricken expression. "Infatuation for an older man is natural in girls nearing womanhood. No doubt your red hair has exotic appeal. It will soon pass and her fancy will shift to a man from her clan and closer to her age."

"Her family has already chosen her mate. Her affections can't go to another."

"Has she confided her feelings concerning her future husband?"

"Aye. She hates him, and for good reason. He's a bully and a brute," Ryan says. "We fought once. 'Tis how I became Kangaroo Fighter."

"Ah-h. I suspect her feelings go beyond infatuation. You became her rescuer, her white knight—no pun intended."

"What do I do?"

"You could avoid contact with her."

"Aye, but I'd nary see Weeyn and his family. He and Alinga saved my life."

"In that case, I can offer no advice." After several minutes of silence, she says, "Did you enjoy the girl's kiss?"

"Nay!"

"Did you dislike it?"

He hesitates, his mind retraces the previous few days. "Nay!" He gathers his words. "'Twas a child's kiss, too soft and wet. But it had passion. I'd be lying if I said I found no joy in it." He turns to Ellen. "'Tis been eleven years since last I was kissed proper."

She leans and graces him with a faint kiss on his cheek, an ethereal peck, a mere brush of a butterfly wing. "Where are you taking me today?"

"Wait and see," he answers, glad for a change of subject.

Two miles down the road, Ryan directs Dan onto a rough, rural lane. Ryan halts the wagon four hundred yards from the main road at the base of a slope. A shanty, a stable and a corral rise from the wild grasses. Rows of gum trees follow a creek into the distance.

"This wee station is for sale."

"How is the water supply?" Ellen asks.

"The creek runs most of the year and there is a shallow dug well behind the house. What do ye think?"

"I suggest it requires a hard working and talented man to fix the obvious flaws but it seems well suited and well positioned for a wheelwright. It is also within an hour's travel if you want to visit me on Sunday afternoons...if that is your intention."

"'Tis."

"Then please, let us eat and after escort me around the grounds."

Opportunities

April 1849

The directions to the remote ranch near Ballarat are sketchy but, after two false turns, Ryan locates it nestled in a valley. As the new wagon pulled by Dan approaches the cluster of farm buildings, Ryan frowns at the lack of activity. No horses pace in the corral, no sheep graze the pastures and no chickens scratch in the yard.

Ryan stops near the wind-worn farmhouse and hops onto the rain-soaked ground. His plan is to deliver the wagon ordered two months earlier, collect his money and return on Dan using the saddle in the wagon.

"Hello," he calls. "Are ye here, McTeague?"

The door creaks on leather hinges. A man Ryan does not recognize steps out, ducking his head to clear the door's top casing. "He went to the new goldfields near Smythesdale," the stranger says with a Scots accent.

"Who are ye?"

"Stephen McNichol."

Ryan waits for additional information. The man stays mute.

"Are ye the new operator of this ranch?"

"No."

Frustrated by the rain and the man's brevity, Ryan loses his temper. "What the hell are ye doing here, and who's to pay for this new wagon?"

"I worked for McTeague. He sacked me. He paid me an extra two schillings to wait, to say he be sorry."

"How long have ye waited?"

"Four weeks."

"Ye waited four weeks for two schillings." Ryan can't hide his surprise. "Why for God's sake?"

"Because I promised."

If not for the Scottish accent, Ryan would have guessed Viking lineage. Ryan estimates he's six-feet-six in height and well beyond two hundred and fifty pounds. The fit of his clothes suggests the bulk is muscle not fat. In his mid-twenties, his yellow, close-cropped hair and whiskers fit the Norse motif.

Ryan shakes his head in frustration. "Damn gold rush. It should be bringing me business, not t'other."

Stephen returns a questioning lift of an eyebrow.

"'Tis the second time. Last week a rancher canceled a wagon I'd half finished and departed for the diggings. What do I do with these extra wagons?"

Without a pause, Stephen replies, "Start a haulage company."

"H-m-m-m," Ryan mutters, "Fraser handles the haulage in these parts."

"Mr. Fraser charges too much and can be unreliable. Economic growth means room for another company."

"What do ye reckon are the best products to haul?" Ryan asks, rubbing his chin.

"Wool and hides go south to Geelong. Supplies for diggers, stations and merchants come north. Hard goods, like textiles, cookery and tools, and non-perishable food items like sugar, flour and salt. You might ferry a few diggers north with their supplies if they do not mind a rough ride, but avoid fancy coach service. Too costly."

Ryan steps closer and peers into Stephen's gray eyes, uncertain if this oracle is real. "How'd ye get yer business sense?"

"Through my employment as assistant factor for a shipping firm in Edinburgh."

"What brought ye to Australia?"

"A convict ship."

Ryan chuckles at the familiar answer. "Tell me yer story."

"My immediate superior pilfered from the firm. He placed evidence to implicate me. The son of a crofter's word be no match for accusations from minor English gentry."

"'Tis always the way," Ryan says, shrugging his shoulders.

"Can I beg a ride to town? Any town."

"I'll do better than that. I'll give ye a job, Stephen."

"What job?"

"Running my new haulage firm. I'll keep the wagons in shape to roll. Ye keep them full of cargo."

"Am I an employee or a partner?"

Ryan laughs at Stephen's directness. "A true Scotsman ye are for sure. Ye start as an employee. If ye are as good as ye think, I'll make ye a partner, but I retain the major share. Deal?"

"Aye." Stephen envelops the proffered hand with his. "We may require other teamsters. I can drive a team but I need time to line up customers and do the books."

"We'll hire men—mostly blacks, when I can. Is that a problem for ye?"

"I care for the quality of a man's work, naught else," Stephen says.

"I must build a better corral and purchase horses and tack. I can manage the cost of one team for now," Ryan adds, "and get others when profits permit."

"I will manage the stable work for now," Stephen offers.

"One more thing," Ryan says. "Do ye mind working for a non-practicing Catholic?"

"Not unless you mind working with a devout Presbyterian."

Ryan smiles at the retort. "Gather yer stuff. I'll tell ye stories of my time living rough with the Wathaurung on the way."

*****

July 1849

Within three months, the fruits of Stephen's idea exceeds Ryan's modest expectations. His two new wagons and his older box wagon are on the road at least five days a week servicing eager customers in the Ballarat and Buninyong area. They buy four pairs of draft horses plus all their harness gear.

Ryan's shanty now has a new bedroom and office for Stephen. Their two newest hands, Gellibrand and Polligerry, middle-aged men from of the Wurundjeri clan, are busy expanding the stable and constructing a bunkhouse. Three local Irish teamsters do much of the driving—Ryan could not find qualified native drivers and vows to train some.

The workload demands long days. Their only respite is Sunday. On the Sabbath, they ride into Buninyong together. Stephen spends the day at church services or Presbyterian charity work. Ryan shops for supplies among the merchants who open on Sunday, and he visits Ellen. To avoid judgmental townsfolk, they always picnic in the countryside or the bush. On rainy days, they stop at an inn south of Buninyong. The Irish proprietor greets them like old friends and asks no questions.

Despite their regular rendezvous, Ellen maintains a romantic distance. To Ryan, their relationship is akin to gentleman accompanying a sister on her outings. A kiss is out of the question. While Ryan grows impatient, Ellen seems content with the arrangement.

On a cool mid-winter day in July, Ryan struggles alone in the wagon shop's limited shelter—a roof on four poles with no walls—trying to pry a damaged wheel off his box wagon. This repair is the last obstacle to clear before he leaves for a week. Every time he gets sufficient leverage on the wheel to slide it off the axle, the wagon slips from its jack.

Stephen spots Ryan's Sisyphean struggle, strides over and lifts up the wagon's back end. "Try now," he says.

Until that moment, Ryan doubted one man could support the end of a wagon: wheels, axle, deck and all. "Are ye sure ye can manage?"

"Aye, if you do not gab all day."

In thirty seconds, Ryan rolls the recalcitrant wheel to the workbench. "Ye can let her down while I fetch the spare wheel."

"Get it. I will wait."

In under a minute, Ryan returns and roles the replacement into the shop and slides it onto the axle. "That'll do. Thank ye."

Stephen lowers his burden, showing not the least bit of strain. "I have news."

"Go ahead."

"It may be difficult to locate your friends," Stephen says. "The gold diggings to the west forced the blacks off their usual winter grounds."

"I nary find them. They find me. But thanks for yer warning."

*****

Hiring Stephen provides Ryan with a secondary benefit. The big Scot can manage the business alone for brief periods. Ryan can visit the Wathaurung when no wagons need repairing.

The new gold field Stephen mentioned is not as extensive as Ryan expects, but it centers near the valley where Laarr and his ancestors have camped for eons during winter. Ryan wanders south, following the general direction of the familiar creek. With the short winter day nearing a close, he sets up camp in the shelter of a gum grove.

After brushing and feeding Dan, Ryan builds his cooking fire and spreads canvas on a rope to give him a crude tent shelter from any rain. The clouds are low, dark and pregnant with moisture.

He sips tea and imagines how Alinga might appear now. He calculates she is thirteen. In Victorian culture, a girl her age, dressed in puffy layers of clothes, has the sexual attraction of a fence post. Not so in tribal culture with its indifference to nudity. She and Tarra live in a community where sexual intercourse is a common sight and girls prepare for marriage early in life. Wathaurung girls are more socially mature than any lass of European descent.

Ryan cares for Alinga and her future. He appreciates he must not trivialize her sensitive, romantic feelings. But neither can he encourage her further. He is poised in the center of a web—not yet entangled but unable to flee.

Musing about Alinga naturally reminds Ryan of his deadlocked relationship with Ellen. He smiles at the irony. With Alinga, he holds the suitor at bay. With Ellen the roles reverse.

"Damn it, Ellen. Forget that husband and save me," he whispers into the dark.

*****

Alinga is a young dingo crouched under cover near a pond. A pack of dingoes surrounds the water: drinking, sleeping, mating or playing. All is at peace until a large dingo with a limp enters the scene. He snarls at smaller dingoes. He searches for someone. Alinga comprehends it is she he seeks. If the limping dingo detects her, she must run into the desert, beyond the water, beyond hope. She explores the shore and scrub brush, searching for the rare red dingo. She sees him coming.

Alinga crawls from her lean-to. Moonbeams slip through the canopy of gum leaves. Alone, she stares at the night sky through the leaves. Her fingers caress her taut belly. She imagines Warrain. She senses he is near.

*****

Ryan emerges from his tent the next morning to sunshine. His campfire is burning, water is boiling, and a koala carcass roasts on sticks over the flames.

"Warrain sleep like old man," says a familiar voice.

Ryan spots Weeyn, Alinga and Tarra in the dabbled shade. The older girl holds her infant son Lakorra, which means sky, to her milk-enlarged breast. She glows with the self-confidence and social status of motherhood. Weeyn has grown and packs heavier muscles than last time—definitely a son of Laarr. Alinga is now an opening blossom: her body displaying new curves and contours.

Each wears garments to cover their groin area. Weeyn's is a loincloth. His muscled buttock flex in the clear air. The girls wear garments resembling short skirts.

"Yer wearing clothing. Why?"

"Missionary man did tell Laarr we all sinners because no wear clothes," Weeyn says. "We no go Heaven when die. We go bad place he called Hell. Laarr did bargain with missionary man. He did agree we cover man and women parts."

"Does yer father believe in Hell?"

"No. He make missionary man happy. Laarr not believe silly white man stories."

Alinga steps closer. "Do you like?" she says, pointing to her skirt. She has embroidered the hem with multicolored versions of the symbols people paint on their bodies at a corroboree.

"Beautiful," he replies.

She steps closer. Their eyes lock. She holds him captive in her deep ebony pools. She lays her long-boned fingers on his shoulder. A fingertip slids across his bicep and down his forearm to his fingers. She pauses and encircles his half-digit with her warm palm. "I dream you coming last night."

Ryan shuts his lids and breathes deeply to calm his racing heart. Alinga's power over him surpasses his expectations. Mirthful chuckling forces its way into his addled brain. To his right, Weeyn and Tarra beam with stifled laughter. Alinga wears a siren's smile.

"What're ye laughing at?"

"You squirm like snared bandicoot," Weeyn answers.

*****

After his arrival at Laarr's camp and the distribution of new blankets, tools and candies, Ryan pulls Laarr and Weeyn aside.

"Laarr. I have started making and fixing wagons. I use wagons to carry white men's products. I need Wathaurung men to work for me as the business grows." He tries and fails to read Laarr's expressionless face. "Do ye understand what I'm asking?"

Laarr exchanges a few sentences in Wadawurrung with Weeyn and responds. "You want my people work in white men's world. Yes?"

"Aye."

"Why good for my people?"

"Look to the years to come, wise Laarr," Ryan begins. "The Wathaurung lands grow smaller while the white world grows bigger. Can the land feed all yer clan while the white men steal more and more? Is it not better if Wathaurung learn our ways, earn money, and get an education?"

Laarr studies the ground and scuffs a toe in the dirt. Ryan knows to wait.

"Your words bring truth to my ears and sadness to my heart. I answer later." Without another word, Laarr walks alone into the forest.

"Many clansmen labor on farms," Ryan says to Weeyn. "The pay is poor. Ye witnessed it yerself. I want Wathaurung men willing to learn skills that will pay better, men who can be carpenters, wheelwrights and teamsters. Men can work part time with me; so they can visit home."

"I know Warrain offers this in kindness." Weeyn steps closer and clasps Ryan's shoulders. "Is there a place for black men in white world?"

"I wish I could say aye. But, my people nary share the land fairly, even with other whites. Yer only chance is to fit in as best ye can." Ryan looks across the camp and the free and contented people. "'Tis a shame that someday the great Wathaurung will no longer tread these lands as free men and women."

Weeyn scuffs the grounds with his toes before replying. "Yes. We last free Wathaurung. I will help Warrain."

"Come to my station and work."

"I stay here," Weeyn answers. "I get men work for you. How many?"

"Five to start. I'll find jobs that suit them and train them."

"You pay blacks same as whites for same job?"

"Aye. Ye have my word."

"Weeyn trust Warrain."

Ryan lays an arm over Weeyn's shoulders. "Ye saved my life. Ye've taught me many things. I'm like yer elder brother, yer *wardoong*."

A mischievous smile sneaks across Weeyn's dark features.

"I recognize that look of yers. Ye are conjuring up something to mock me with."

"No mock," Weeyn says, with a toothy grin. "Time my wardoong take a Wathaurung wife."

Ryan steps backwards and bangs into a gum trunk. "Ye mean yer sister?"

"She best Wathaurung girl not married."

"She's promised to Loklok. Ye told me to mind my own business afore. I remember ye whacked me with a spear shaft."

Weeyn shrugs. "Laarr no like Loklok. He may talk Boort to end agreement."

"I can't marry Alinga," Ryan blurts.

"Why? Black girl no good?"

Ryan's mouth hangs open in shock. He'd never consciously reject Alinga for her race—or would he? "Her color is naught," Ryan mutters.

"Why then?"

Ryan struggles for words. A vision fills his mind. He is strolling arm-and-arm through Ballarat with Alinga. People step off the sidewalk to avoid them. Louts yell insults. His customers go to Fraser. For once, he considers the social disaster having a native wife would cause. And, what would Ellen say?

"Ah-h...she's too young for a wife in my culture." The half-truth gives Ryan a temporary excuse and satisfies Weeyn.

"We wait," Weeyn says. "Must end Loklok betrothal first."

*****

By the communal fire, Ryan inspects Alinga. She shares a log with Tarra on the opposite side. Ryan tries to ignore her undeniable allure and her growing seductiveness. He focuses on the ground at his feet and pretends he has not met Alinga before tonight. He forces his mind to imagine that scenario and raises his head.

She slouches while she eats a shank of meat with bare hands. Legs spread open, her new clothing hides nothing. She chatters with Tarra as she chews, while scratching her abdomen with greasy fingers. Ryan's mind flips to his last visit with Ellen— elegant, well mannered, and not out of place if at tea with Queen Victoria.

Savage versus sophisticate.

Ryan understands Alinga's manners and bearing are normal for her society, but in his world she'd fit in like kangaroo at high mass. *But can she change? Can she learn our ways? Aye, if she had a mind to. She is bright.*

Alinga glances his way and smiles, and continues talking to Tarra.

*****

Alinga peeks at Ryan across the fire. She discovers him studying her with an unfamiliar expression. A breath catches in her throat at the intensity in his gaze.

She nudges Tarra. «See the way Belongs-to-the-sea beholds me with hungry eyes. What does it mean?»

Tarra scrutinizes Ryan. «It means he now sees you like a woman, not a child.»

Alinga pokes her friend's knee. «Would he make a good husband?»

Tarra shrugs. «Belongs-to-the-sea is not one of us. He tries to fit in but will not succeed. He is a fine warrior and hunter. And he is handsome. In those ways, a wife would be lucky.»

Alinga pulls Tarra from the fire into the night shadows to avoid being overheard. «My brother says our ways are passing. He says we will finish our days living in the white man's world. I could leave here and live with Belongs-to-the-sea.»

Tarra hugs herself and frowns. «In the white world, you cover your skin with itchy clothing. Do you want to sleep in their stuffy houses and never move with the seasons and walk their filthy towns?»

«Life with him in his world sounds better than a life here with Eagle.»

«But, what if Eagle was not your betrothed? What if a kind and gentle Wathaurung warrior wanted you for his wife? What if you had that choice?»

Alinga sighs and glances at Ryan. To Tarra she whispers, «I made my choice many seasons ago like you did yours.» With her lips an inch from Tarra's ear, Alinga says, «Imagine I lived with him and you and Fire lived with us.»

«That is child's talk. I belong to another.»

«Only our ways bind you to him. In the white world you could—»

«No,» Tarra hisses. «My honor and the honor of my family do not allow it. Speak no more of it.»

«Your honor never stops you making babies with my brother,» Alinga snaps.

Tarra has no response.

*****

August 1849

On a late morning Sunday, Ryan and Ellen ride into the countryside west of Buninyong. Under a cloudless azure sky, the air is motionless and near the freezing point. The white fuzz of hoarfrost coats leaves and twigs in the shadows where the low winter sun has not yet driven away the shade. Despite the chill, Ellen wears no bonnet or scarf. Her orange curls bounce with the rhythm of her mount. Ryan admires how competently she handles a horse.

In casual trail conversation, Ryan relates his week with the Wathaurung to the gentle squeak of saddle leather and clomp of shod hooves on soft ground. Ellen listens, tossing in an occasional question, showing an acute interest in how the family prepares food, makes clothing and raises children.

"On the last night, they held a feast in my honor with dancing until almost dawn," Ryan says, finishing his account.

Ellen rides in silence for a minute. Her gaze follows the progress of a troop of kangaroos retreating into the bush.

"I can nary get used to how they carry those big joeys in those pouches," Ryan says.

"What happened this time with Alinga?" Ellen blurts.

"Naught."

"You did not mention her name in your entire recounting of events." She swivels in the saddle to address her next question. "Is she still with her family or married off now?"

"Aye. She was there."

"Has her infatuation passed?"

"Nay."

Ellen frowns. "Is your interest in her heightened?"

"Nay." He ponders trees on a nearby ridge.

"What occurred that is too embarrassing to discuss?" Ellen demands.

Ryan shifts in the saddle. "'Tis hard to put into words."

"Is she attractive? Do you harbor strong feelings for her?"

"Aye, she's a looker." He mulls his next words. "I care for her but not the way I care for ye." He returns his attention to Ellen.

"Poor Ryan," Ellen says, a sad smile deepening her frown lines, "caught in the web of two women who are pledged irrevocably to other men."

"I'm not in Alinga's web," Ryan protests.

"You certainly are. You care for her and feel beholden to her for saving your life. And, you now see the woman emerging."

"'Tis partly true."

"The very fact you cannot talk casually concerning her as you do Weeyn and his family tells me she has set your desires and emotions churning."

Ryan leans sideways in his saddle and touches Ellen's hand. "How long do ye mean to wait until ye admit yer husband is dead or nary coming back?"

"I have given it no thought," she replies, looking away.

Ryan spots the evasion. "Ye can ask the church for a separation. Say ye were abandoned."

"That would still not let me remarry."

"Aye, but we could be husband and wife in everything but law. 'Tis Australia. Old rules don't matter as much."

She contemplates his hand on hers and probes his face for clues. "That sounds vaguely like a proposal," she says in a voice so soft Ryan leans closer to hear.

"Ah-h-h, Ellen, me lass. Ye know where my heart's desire lies."

Ellen turns in her saddle. Ryan makes out a stifled sniffle.

"Ellen. Are ye crying?"

She whirls to glare at him. "We are friends. It cannot be any other way. I made vows. Take me home. I demand no further talk of this."

*****

Ryan rides Dan home at a trot through the late winter chill. Clouds cover the sun. The day's mood now matches his own. His tensions dissipate the closer he gets to his station. Hard work yields predictable results and rewards, with no mystery or heartache.

Stephen walks out to greet him and holds Dan's bridle while Ryan dismounts. "How did your visit go? Will we be getting workers?"

"Aye. Laarr'll send two lads who've driven wagons afore. If they speak well of us, others'll come."

"Do they speak English?"

"Aye and with less accent than ye do, Scotsman."

Stephen laughs. "And was your rendezvous with Ellen pleasant?"

Ryan throws up his palms in frustration. "Have ye much experience with women, Stephen?"

"Enough to know to be careful."

"I wish I'd taken better care," Ryan mumbles.

"There be supper inside," Stephen says. "Go. I will take care of the horse."

Ryan accepts the offer. He is mopping up the last dregs of lamb stew with fresh bread when Stephen returns. "Who taught ye to cook?" Ryan asks.

Stephen pours hot water into a ceramic teapot. "My Mam," he answers. "I be the youngest of nine sons, with no sisters. Mam taught me to cook when I be a wee lad because Da had more sons than needed to work our poor farm."

"How'd ye go from a farm to assistant factor?"

"There be no future in farming for the youngest son. So, I became assistant cook for a boarding school. I accepted half my wages in classroom lessons, despite the taunts of the rich lads. It so happened I be handy with numbers. My size got me a job in a shipping firm's warehouse. My schooling got me a position in the office."

"And bad luck got ye here."

"Maybe it be good luck," Stephen philosophizes. "A low-born man can rise higher in this land than back home."

"Aye. 'Tis a land of opportunities, except for finding a wife."

"Aye. There be just a smattering of white women on this frontier," Stephen says, "and they all be married." He places two mugs of steaming tea on the table and sits opposite. "Save that topic for later. We have a problem."

"Tell me."

"Mr. Fraser visited four days ago. He asked for you. I told him I be your partner—a small lie I trust the Lord will forgive—and he could speak to me. His brain be near to exploding with anger because of our competition for haulage. He called you an arrogant upstart and vowed to kill your business. Next day, he cut all his rates in half. I matched those cuts and he lowered his again by half."

"So, he's charging a quarter of his old rate?"

"Aye. And I matched that too," Stephen says.

Ryan taps his fingers on the wooden table while he makes quick mental calculations. "We can win this war."

"What be your plan?" Stephen responds.

"I can make and fix wagons cheaper than Fraser pays for his. That's an advantage. We've a better reputation. 'Tis another advantage. Still, I wager he can run at a loss for months."

"So we keep our customers happy and reduce costs to survive," Stephen says.

"Aye. Gather the lads tomorrow. I will explain we must cut their wages by half until this fight is won. When we can, we will restore the wages and reimburse each man for money lost."

"And I will work for no wage at all until then."

"Thank ye, Stephen."

*****

The next day, Ryan and Stephen scowl while their Irish teamsters walk out to head for Fraser's compound. Ryan's demand for a wage concession fell the day before the teamsters received job offers at full wages from Ryan's rival. His two Wurundjeri hands, Gellibrand and Polligerry, pledge to stay with Kangaroo Fighter, and they insist no clansmen will work for Fraser. Miraculously, the two promised men from Laarr's group, the young brothers Benboo and Corrain, arrive that week. Ryan greets them in Wadawurrung, introduces the brothers to Stephen and the others.

"Now what?" asks Stephen.

"Ye and I'll ride with the new lads until they learn our routes, and meet our customers and suppliers. Once Benboo and Corrain can drive without us, we send Gellibrand and Polligerry with them to train as drivers. Ye and I can alternate driving the third wagon, but my time is better spent in the shop making wheels. That may be our only source of profits. Can we do it?"

"Aye. It means longer hours but I be no stranger to that. I still expect Sunday morn free for church."

"I'd not ask ye to give up church," Ryan says. "The extra work load gives me a reason to avoid Ellen for a few weeks."

"Be that wise?"

"If we are mere friends as she insists, it can't hurt."

Price Feud

October 1849

Ryan retains little optimism after three months into the price feud with Fraser. Stephen frowns each time he examines the accounts. "The only joy these numbers bring me," he says one day," is how much Fraser must be losing with ten wagons on the road."

"Like foes drowning in the same lake and rejoicing in t'other's misfortune," Ryan mumbles.

Ryan's plan to train all his native workers as teamsters has succeeded. They learn quickly, they work hard, and most customers accept them. A month earlier, everyone agreed to zero wages—only a room and meals. Even then, Ryan's store of funds continues to dwindle despite money coming in for wagon wheels and repairs. The cost of feeding people and horses, buying raw materials, keeping harnesses and tack repaired and all the little costs exceed the firm's earnings.

"Pardon. I missed that. What did you say about misfortune?" Stephen asks.

The rhythmic beat of horse hooves galloping into his compound saves Ryan from replying. "I'd better see who it is." Ryan crosses the room and opens the door.

"Hello, Ellen."

Ellen stares at him from her mount with an expression Ryan cannot comprehend—part anger, part sadness. "This is not a social call. One of your drivers was shot. He is resting at the school."

"It must be Polligerry. What happened?" Ryan steps outside.

"That makebate who passes as Fraser's foreman confronted your driver," Ellen says. "He said you were stealing Fraser's customers. He said it takes two hands to drive a team and he shot your man's hand."

"Where is Healey now?"

"In the Buninyong Saloon."

"I'll hitch a wagon and follow ye."

"I will not wait. Come to the school." She whirls her horse and gallops up the lane.

Stephen calls through the open door. "One of us should fetch Polligerry. The other must settle accounts with Healey. This is a direct assault on our business meant to intimidate our customers and employees."

"Aye. Ye see to Polligerry."

*****

Ryan ties Dan in front of Buninyong's largest saloon and slips into the dusky interior. Drawn shades keep out the spring heat. Twelve men occupy the thirty-by-fifty-foot public space. All but one scurry to the exits at Ryan's arrival. A lanky man leans on the bar sipping a whisky. When his vision adjusts to the low light, Ryan confirms his guess—it is Healey.

"I s'pose you're lookin' for me," Healey murmurs through a crooked smile.

"No fighting in here," barks the proprietor.

"Step outside," Ryan says.

"Not when you're wearin' a pistol. I've just a knife." He touches the long blade on his belt.

Ryan removes the Colt and delivers it to the proprietor. "Keep this for me." The man slips the weapon onto a shelf below the bar. Ryan follows his opponent outside.

News travels fast. Men and a few women already crowd the sidewalk and street. Ryan can see people hurrying from shops and dwellings.

Good, I want witnesses.

Healey's grin stretches his sallow mug into a caricature of mirth. "I knew shootin' your darkie would bring you out." He pulls a straight razor from his pocket and snaps it open. The blade reflects the midday sun. With his other hand, he slips a Bowie knife from its sheath.

Without a word of reply, Ryan tugs the tomahawk from his belt and holds it low and behind his right hip. He begins slow, methodical steps towards Healey. Ryan assesses every detail of his opponent's expressions. Experience taught him most fighters betray themselves if pressed.

Healey is no exception. A frown replaces his jauntiness. Ryan expects his uncertainty—by holding his weapon behind him, it appears less threatening. It nudges Healey's suspicions. A bully is easy to intimidate.

Healey stalks sideways in a circle to keep Ryan at a distance. Ryan follows at a steady pace waiting for an opening. He never underestimates an opponent—at least not any more. In a fight, he acknowledges his weaknesses and stresses his advantages.

Ryan knows he is no match in a knife fight against a taller, long-armed mauler like at Healey. The razor is lethal—even a nick in the right place could bleed a man to death. Ryan cannot prevail if he engages Healey on his terms. His one hope is for Healey to become rattled and leave an opportunity for Ryan's speed and trickery.

Healey continues shuffling sideways, squinting and licking his upper lip. People in the congregation of the curious begin to boo. A few shout 'coward.' Healey growls through clamped teeth. Ryan smiles. He concentrates on Healey's mask of anger—it is where the signal will come from.

The sideways circular dance continues. The onlookers rain insults on Healey. Ryan hears "Hurrah for Kangaroo Fighter." That catcall ignites Healey's rage. He bares his teeth. The signal! He lunges, both weapons aimed at Ryan's head.

Ryan shifts his weight to his right foot. Healey falls for the feint and directs both his weapons to where he calculates his target will be. Ryan shifts left and throws himself to the ground beside Healey's right leg, well under his malevolent blades. Ryan breaks his fall with his left arm and swipes his tomahawk at the ankle of Healey's fancy cowboy boot. The keen metal blade slits the leather and severs Healey's Achilles tendon.

Healey howls with excruciating pain and topples. His hat slips off, exposing his hidden bald patch. Ryan leaps to his feet. He kicks away the knife and razor to a wall of applause and shouts of hurrah. Ryan is not finished. An example must be made.

Healey, his energy spent, weeps on the road in agony. Ryan knocks the man onto his stomach with a kick to the ribs. He tugs Healey's right arm and yanks it straight out. He steps on the wrist to hold the hand steady and splay the fingers out.

Ryan sweeps his gaze along the wall of now silent men, so everyone can read his expression. "No one hurts my people," he yells. With a swift chop of his blade, Ryan amputates Healey's trigger finger at the first knuckle.

"Try shooting someone now, ye bastard," he shouts at the whimpering form squirming in the road dust. Restrained applause ripples the crowd. Ryan may have gone too far but has no regrets. No one will forget his message. He retrieves his Colt and rides to Ellen's school.

Stephen has already arrived with the wagon. Ellen is helping Polligerry, his hand bandaged, climb up to the seat.

"How badly is he hurt?" Ryan says.

"The bullet went through his palm," Ellen replies. "He will mend."

"Be your dealings concluded with Fraser's man?" Stephen asks.

"Aye. Healey will cause no trouble for a few months."

"Polligerry," Ryan says, "Mr. McNichol will take ye home. Ye are off duty until better. The job is yers for as long as ye want it."

The slim, weathered, fiftyish man smiles his gratitude. "I be better soon. Have many-many wounds more bad in old battles."

"Thank you, Mrs. O'Sullivan," Stephen says. He shakes the reins and the matched Percheron pair begins their plodding pace to the station.

"Do you know much of Polligerry's people?" Ellen asks Ryan.

"Nay. He's not much of a talker."

"He talked freely with me. His people had the misfortune to inhabit the lands where Melbourne exists today. Between disease, displacement and battles, the Wurundjeri dwindled. Just twenty of his clan remain scattered throughout the territories of rivals. He and Gellibrand are both *ngurungaeta*, headmen of vanished groups."

"I thank ye Ellen for that story and all ye did for him." Ryan reaches out to clasp her hand. She steps back.

"I must prepare classes for tomorrow."

"Shall I call on ye this Sunday?"

She reads his expression for a second and looks at her hands. "I cannot. I made plans to escort the children to a performance by a traveling troupe. They are staging *Hamlet*."

"Then maybe next—"

"No!" Her green eyes flicker with intensity. "I desire time. Do not rush me."

Ryan chokes down an exasperated sigh. He fights an impulse to sweep her into his arms and blurt his true feelings, but has the insight to know 'I love you' are the last words she wants to hear right now.

"Gidday to ye, Ellen," is all he can manage.

*****

"I have an idea," Stephen says the next week, when he and Ryan review the firm's finances. "Fraser has lowered his rate again out of spite for you thrashing Healey. It be one-tenth of his rate before this price feud started. As I see it, we have two choices."

"Quick bankruptcy or slow bankruptcy?" Ryan mutters. Elbows on the table, he holds his head in his hands.

"That be our certain fate if we match his new rates," Stephen says in dour Scots style. "We have been playing his game and it be time to stop. I propose we raise our prices to above the break-even point—say..." he makes a quick calculation "...three pounds per ton from Geelong to Buninyong and two shillings extra to Ballarat."

"Are ye mad?"

"Trust my experience. Price does not always motivate customers. They will pay a premium price for quality service."

Ryan sits up. "Go on."

"Rumors of gold be everywhere," Stephen says, closing his ledger. "People speculate men have found deposits already but no one wants to admit it for fear of bringing government interference. Those rumors attracted newcomers. Demand for haulage be growing even while we struggle to stay afloat. Ironic, do you agree?"

"Aye."

Stephen taps the table with his index fingertip. "Shipping costs be now so low and demand so high that a wee pound or two extra per ton hardly matters. Our reputation as quality haulers matters. So does your reputation as an honorable man. I wager people will pay to keep you in business. No one wants the return of a Fraser monopoly."

"'Tis worth a try."

"To sweeten the pie, offer our regular customers priority service. If there be a lineup for haulage, they move up the queue. Are you with me?"

"Aye."

*****

Walter Fraser steps out the front door of his five-room ranch house onto the covered porch. Scott Healey dozes in a stuffed chair in the shade. A sickly lamb snuggles on his lap. Fraser smiles at his friend. No matter that nine in ten abandoned lambs die, Scott always fetches the baby bottle and tries his best. Such a contrast to the man's scant respect for human life.

Fraser notices the bottle of laudanum on the side table is empty again. He knows no lecture on the medicine's addictive qualities will lower Scott's intake until the pain in his ankle subsidies.

Fraser tiptoes closer and crouches to sniff the bandage. The fresh scent of washed fabric wafts to his nostrils. *Good, no gangrene*. He kisses Scott's bald spot.

Billy rides into the compound. Fraser checks his pocket watch. *Right on time as usual. How can a man with no timepiece do that?*

Fraser crosses the compound to make sure conversation does not disturb his sleeping friend. "Billy. Is it true what I heard?"

"Yes, boss. Kangaroo Fighter raised rates."

"Damn you. Do not glorify him with that bloody name."

"Sorry boss. I forget."

"By how much did he raise his price?"

"To three pounds, boss."

"Excellent. He is finished in a matter of days."

Billy exhibits no emotion.

"Are you not overjoyed at our victory, Billy?"

Billy looks at the clouds. "We no win, boss."

"What!"

"Kang…I mean Ryan no lose customers. All wagons working."

"Why in God's name?"

"People need wagons. They tell Billy cost not important."

Fraser shakes his fists and roars at the sky, "Someone please deliver me from this marauder!"

A hacking cough from the porch answers Fraser. Scott stirs. "I'll kill him for you," he says in a narcotic drawl.

118

"Shut up, you fool," Fraser bellows. "You tried and failed miserably. Next time it will be you who is dead." Addressing the former constable, he asks, "Billy. Who in your clan will kill him for me? I'll pay fifty pounds."

Billy shakes his head. "No black man will touch him. Not for any money. They say he walks with the spirits."

"You do it. I'll give you seventy pounds. Bigger money than you have ever had."

"No, boss. Billy do anything you ask, not that."

"You are a Christian now. You do not adhere to that spirit claptrap, do you?"

"Jesus come. Spirits not go."

Fraser growls and spits in Billy's face. "Leave my sight, you insufferable shite sack."

*****

Polligerry returns from his first trip to Geelong since his hand healed. He convinces Gellibrand to unhitch the team for him while he gives important news to the boss men.

Stephen answers the soft knock on his office door. "Come in Polligerry. How was the run to Geelong?"

"Good-good, mister. All customer get cargo on time. They happy-happy. Here is money." Polligerry pulls notes and coins from various pockets. "Polligerry also carry big news for boss men." His gray locks sway as he swivels his head, searching for Ryan.

"Ryan," Stephen shouts through the open door into the shanty's main room. "Can you come here a minute. Polligerry has news so great he be near to wetting his breeches."

Ryan enters the office and smiles at his driver, who is shuffling his weight foot-to-foot. "What news have ye?"

"Bad man charge six pounds for ton starting today."

"That means the price feud be finished," Stephen says, cracking a rare smile.

"Polligerry have more news," the euphoric man says. "Bad man sack five drivers. Say no has money. Has empty wagons now."

"Polligerry my friend," Ryan says, "tell the men, we'll soon pay full wages and all money we owe them."

"Money nice. Beat bad man better." Polligerry graces them with a toothy laugh and hurries from the room with his message to the staff.

"How much must we charge per ton to cover expenses and give full wages to everyone, including ye?" Ryan asks.

His sight fixed on the ceiling beams, Stephen makes mental calculations. "Four pounds two from Geelong to Buninyong. Three shillings extra to Ballarat."

"Then that's what we charge for now."

"You mean to continue the feud, I assume?" Stephen asks.

"I propose to drive that evil bastard out of business. We can survive at four pounds a ton. He can't."

"I advise against that course of action."

"What?" Ryan asks. "We have a perfect opportunity."

"If Fraser goes under, we cannot meet the demand for haulage soon enough. A new operator will fill the gap. Better the devil you know than the bunyip you don't."

"Aye. I grant yer point. But I want to gain some advantage while I can."

"I will agree to a moderate approach. Do you have an idea?" Stephen says.

Ryan ponders a plan for half a minute. "For every haulage rate Fraser offers, we beat it by ten percent. We can make a decent profit and pay our employees well. Right?"

"Of course."

"That way, we can bleed him slowly and expand at a gradual pace."

"Aye, that may work."

"Can we obtain credit?" Ryan asks.

"I am acquainted with men in Geelong who will lend us money at usurious rates."

"No matter." Ryan waves his hand. "We'll repay the loan within a year."

"How much do we borrow?"

"Ask for at least five hundred pounds. One thousand is better. Engage a discrete third party to buy Fraser's surplus wagons. Hire someone who can tell a sound wagon from a derelict and who can haggle like a fishmonger's wife. I want the wagons at distress prices—not to exceed one hundred apiece. My goal is to match Fraser in wagons on the road. How's that sound to ye?"

"Brilliant. I will depart within the hour."

"Another thing. I made a drawing—a mere scribble—I want to show ye. It means another errand when yer in Geelong."

*****

December 1849

After breakfast on Christmas morning, Ryan and Stephen assemble their eight wagons, teams of horses in twos or fours, and all drivers. Their new wagons are ready to roll for the first time. Ryan and his men labored for six weeks to train new drivers, and to overhaul and repaint the stock purchased through a third party from Fraser.

Today, an Australian pine tree decorates the bed of every wagon. Each man wears his Christmas gifts—brown trousers, green shirts, and wide leather hats.

Every wagon and hat bears the new symbol of their haulage business in Kelly green—a kangaroo silhouette, its arms held in an obvious pugilist stance, inside a circle. Ryan painted it on the wagons using a stencil created by a draftsman in Geelong. A seamstress embroidered it on the hats. The design goes beyond a corporate brand. Ryan designed it as a message to every ill-minded bigot and ne'er-do-well: these wagons belong to Kangaroo Fighter and his employees are not to be harmed.

"This should get attention," Ryan remarks. His plan calls for Stephen to lead half the wagons to Buninyong while Ryan guides the remainder to Ballarat. In both towns, they will offer free wagon rides to children until sundown or until the summer heat chases people in doors. By the end of the day, everyone should see the new kangaroo design.

"I hope so," Stephen replies. "We have loans to pay."

"Stop fretting. Business has been steady and 'twill improve."

"You seem certain," Stephen says.

"'Tis a fact. I wish women were as predictable and manageable as business."

"Have you changed your mind yet? I can lead my wagon group to Ballarat and you do Buninyong, if you want a chance to visit Ellen."

"Nay. Not yet. Stick to the plan." He climbs on the lead wagon of his group. "Another thing. Stop by the lawyer fellow's office."

"On Christmas Day?"

"He promised to watch for ye. His clerk will let ye in the rear door. I drew up a paper for ye to sign."

"What paper be so important?" Stephen says.

"I split the enterprise into two companies: wagonwright and haulage. When ye sign the paper, ye become an equal partner in the haulage company on January 1. That is, if ye agree," he adds, a smile wrinkling his cheeks.

"Half be better than I expected."

"There is one condition. The haulage company directs all its wagon repair and replacement requirements to the wheelwright company. Does that suit ye?"

"It is sound business planning. I heartily agree."

Fork in the Road

June 1850

Stephen saunters into the shanty's kitchen area, pours two mugs of tea and steps outside onto the covered porch. Tucked under his arm is their mail.

"Here," he says, passing a mug and a letter to Ryan. "I added honey to yours." He reclines in a porch chair.

"Thank ye." Ryan cups the tea in both hands, enjoying the warmth on the chilly night. He sips the brew tentatively to test its temperature. He notes the envelope beside Stephen. "Another letter from Scotland?"

"Aye. From my eldest brother." He points to Ryan's letter. "Who do you know in New York State?"

"'Tis my old mate William Gates I told ye about." Ryan opens the seal and holds the letter towards the lamp light. "It says here Gates is publishing his memoirs. I'd like to read that someday."

Stephen nods absently. "I finished our books for May," he says in his managerial voice. "It be the sixth month in a row with an increase in revenue and profits."

Ryan smiles his acknowledgment, and continues reading the pages of looping script.

Over the last six months, Ryan has built two new wagons to use as spares when other wagons need repairs. He has added a smithy to allow him to forge iron hoops. Placed around wheel hubs, they double hub lifespan. His system of scheduled wheel replacement has eliminated unexpected breakdowns. Hard work has brought prosperity.

Stephen adds, "It benefits us greatly when Fraser keeps adjusting his rates upwards."

"I don't see why we don't just cut our rates and finish him off quickly," Ryan says.

"We have been through this. Quick growth will weaken us. Be patient," Stephen says.

Ryan shrugs.

"So," Stephen says, switching to his deacon's voice. "You have been dreamy of late. Which woman be on your mind, my friend?"

The price Ryan has paid for success is long hours in the shop. Other than uneventful visits with Ellen on his thirty-second birthday in January and to Mass at Easter, he has not journeyed from his station. Consequently, the one person of his culture available for conversation has been Stephen, now a close friend and confidant.

Ryan folds the letter. "Most days, 'tis both. Today, Alinga be uppermost," he mumbles. "I am due to visit. I dunno what to expect." Talking to Stephen has a confessional quality to it.

"Do you mean what to expect from her or what to expect from yourself?" Stephen asks, his eyes fixed on the expanse of stars overhead.

Ryan chuckles at the astute question. "Both."

"It be a shame this frontier has so few eligible women," Stephen muses.

"Are ye saying my problem be a lack of opportunities?"

Stephen puckers in mouth in a sign of concurrence. "In an established society, handsome and well-to-do gents, like ourselves, would be deluged with marital choices. Yet, here I be facing a monk's existence and you are caught between the impossible and the unconventional."

"Aye. If Ellen would only—"

"But she will not. That is a pity. Her honor and loyalty are what every man should seek in a spouse."

Ryan sighs and concentrates on the dark loom of far hills. He scratches his cheek. An image of Ellen's smiling face, orange cascade of curls and green irises hovers before his inner vision. Sure, she has said no multiple times in voice, expression and action. But, Ryan believes she loves him and might change her mind. A thread of hope no matter how thin and tenuous is still hope. *How long can I wait at thirty-two to start a family? Maybe Stephen is correct and Ellen was nary the true path.*

"How old be Alinga now?" Stephen asks.

"Fourteen, or so."

"Laws in the United Kingdom and its colonies set twelve as the marrying age for girls. The main churches do not differ." Stephen sips tea to punctuate his words. He watches Ryan's expressions over the edge of his mug. "So, in the eyes of the law and God, you have nothing to stop you."

Ryan tilts his head methodically side-to-side. "'Tis all too fast. A year ago, I had no intention of taking her for my wife. Now I can't rid my mind of that notion."

"What be your biggest fear?" Stephen asks. "Is it the condemnation of our society?"

"Nay. If I choose a black wife, society can go to—"

"What is stopping you?" he interjects to fend off the impending profanity.

Ryan sips his tea without tasting. He has no perfect answer. "I dunno if I love her, Stephen. I dunno if she'll fit in."

"Love is not required, Ryan. You—we—each need a woman to count on in hard times as well as good, someone to warm our beds and bear our children. Can she measure up to that?"

"Aye. I reckon she could."

"From what you told me, she has a quick mind," Stephen says. "With the help of our native employees, she will adjust."

"Aye. If an old men like Polligerry can fit in, Alinga can," Ryan says, settling into a relaxed position in his chair.

"And do you want to be a father?"

"Aye."

"From a purely practical viewpoint, which woman be better suited to fecund motherhood: the one who be fourteen or the one who be twenty-eight?"

"Alinga, I suppose." He rummages for and finds another excuse. "But, she's betrothed to another man."

"From what I recall, bush girls her age are married with a wee bairn by now. Something be afoot." Stephen studies Ryan as he shifts restlessly in his chair.

"Her father has turned agin her suitor, I know that much," Ryan says.

"Tell me your true fear—the one I ken you be holding back."

Ryan pushes himself up and paces the porch, his hands clasped behind him. "I stand at a fork in the road. I fret that the very act of speaking about it forces me to forsake one way for t'other."

Stephen tilts his head. "If I follow you correctly, you fear by acknowledging Alinga as a possible wife, it kills any slim hope of a future with Ellen. Am I close?"

"'Tis that exactly."

"Let me disabuse you of that conceit," he growls.

Ryan stops pacing and waits for the sermon he sees gathering behind Stephen's lips.

"You do not choose the roads to travel. God leads you down the path. If He means for Ellen to be yours, He will make it so. He may have reasons for directing your path to Alinga. Go visit your Wathaurung friends with a clear conscience. Do what is honorable. That is all the Lord requires of you."

Stephen crosses the few paces to Ryan and grips his shoulders with his heavy paws. "Whatever happens, I will stand by you, like I ken you would do for me."

"We might lose customers if I marry a black."

"Nay. You may receive fewer invites to supper, but business is business."

"I get no social invites now."

"Then what do you have to lose?"

*****

On the third morning of Ryan's quest to locate Laarr's camp, Dan follows a familiar trail by a woodland creek. For once, his smoky campfire attracted no one. Ryan gave up waiting. He arrives at the last former campsite he has any knowledge of, the grove used the previous winter.

He rides among the tumbled remnants of decayed mia-mias. He pauses by a cold fire pit. He remembers his critical examination of Alinga the previous year at that spot. His old reservations return— can she adapt to the white world. A voice inside says, "Yes she can."

She might be married now. That possibility brings a flutter of relief, followed to his surprise by a wave of melancholy.

"Damn ye," he mutters to himself, "get a grip! Make up yer mind."

He detects an unnatural patch of white on a gum tree, a minor anomaly, something a person not tuned to the forest patterns would fail to notice. At head height, someone has used sap to glue a two-by-two-inch square of cotton to the trunk. On close inspection it reveals the shape of a kangaroo embroidered in green thread. One forearm points west. Two stitched vertical lines lie next to the outstretched paw—two days travel for a family of mixed ages. Five or six hours on a good horse.

Ryan shoves the cloth fragment into a jacket pocket and taps Dan's flanks with his heels. The big gelding trots west through the trees and into the wide lea beyond.

*****

The young dingo rests on a hillside above the water hole. She spots the rare, red dingo in the distance. He acts confused, unsure of the path. Further away, beyond the visible horizon, a black dingo slinks her way.

Alinga snaps awake. Slumber envelopes the camp. She crawls from her hutch. The mia-mia are scattered across a widely spaced grove of gum trees on a craggy-edged hilltop. Driven from their preferred camps, Laarr choose the location because it is far from whites and offers wide vistas in all directions—easy to spot an enemy.

Alinga scans the winter sky for Mirrabooka, the constellation whites call the Southern Cross. Thus oriented, she hikes east at a brisk pace. Two hours out from camp, she stops. The morning sun spills over the horizon and begins warming her chilled body. The long grass spreads to the horizon, rippled by wind like waves on the sea. The single significant break in the land's even texture is a clump of yakka on a minor rocky outcrop. Amidst the spiky leaves, she weaves a ribbon of cotton torn from clothing donated by the church people. Her work completed, she returns home.

When the sun reaches its zenith, Alinga eludes her mother's tyranny of chores and slips away to a pond. In water so cold it makes her teeth chatter, she bathes using soap given by the missionaries. On a sun-warmed rock, she studies her reflection in her gift mirror. She picks flecks of food from her teeth and wets stray hairs that refuse to fall into place. Satisfied with her appearance, she returns to camp.

Alinga spots Weeyn returning from the morning hunt. "Come with me," she says. "Warrain returns."

He shrugs and follows.

*****

After five hours of riding westward across unfamiliar landscape, Ryan admits he might be off course. The embroidered directions were not precise. A degree or two of difference over twenty miles can create quite a gap.

He halts Dan at the crest of a grassy rise and probes the distance for any grove of trees that suggests a suitable camp for the group. Nothing but miles of grass.

He spots a faint, unnatural movement to his left on the edge of his visual limits. To give Dan a rest, he dismounts and walks towards the object. The horse follows without Ryan needing to lead him.

Ryan closes in on a cluster of yakka, the plant white men call grass trees. A ribbon of cloth flutters in the breeze. He unwinds the fabric from the spiny leaves and compares it to the square of cotton in his pocket. They seem cut from the same garment. A guiding hand has confirmed the correct path. He steps up into the stirrup, points Dan into the lowering sun and continues his quest.

An hour later, the orange sun touches the western horizon at the summit of a crag. Two human shapes block a portion of the brilliant light. The silhouettes, a brawny male and a slim female form, wave arms in welcome.

Ryan smiles. They have found him. He dismounts and walks the last fifty feet, noting the changes in his two friends.

Weeyn, now eighteen, is no taller than before, but his bare chest, arm and thigh muscles are massive.

Alinga is stunning. Her cherubic face has slimmed with maturity, allowing emerging cheekbones to enhance her features. She wears her embroidered skirt and a possum wrap covering her from shoulders to navel.

"Well my friends, 'twas hard finding ye this time." He pulls the two cotton fragments from his pocket and says to Alinga, "I suppose I've ye to thank for these."

She dips her chin to confirm his guess, but says nothing. Ryan drinks in her radiant smile and warm gaze, features he has loved since he met her. A flicker of mischief in her expression draws him towards the bottomless wells of her black pupils.

128

Alinga waves her brother away. Weeyn grins and says to Ryan, "I see you later."

Ryan deciphers the clues—Alinga intends another physical advance.

She checks over her shoulder to make certain they are now alone. A demure smile puckers her lips. With delicate fingers, she unties the thongs holding her wrap closed. She lowers her shoulders and the garment drops onto the grass. The corners of her mouth curl up while Ryan appraises the gift she offers.

He strains to adjust to Alinga in a woman's body. For so long, she was a skinny kid in his mind. Even a year earlier, her physical development was girlish. The breasts she is so proud of now, Ryan has to admit, are magnificent. Though he has limited experience with naked women, he cannot imagine a female form exists anywhere to surpass hers.

With the grace of a black swan, she glides forward. Her fingers slide up his jacket, traverse his shoulders and lock behind his neck.

"I see mustache gone," she whispers.

Ryan begins to form a reply but no sound escapes. Her full lips cover his mouth. Unlike her juvenile kiss two years earlier, this one is not mushy, wet or brief. Ryan's hands waver in the air, uncertain of a proper place to rest on her sculpted obsidian body. Unleashed emotions set his blood pulsing and every extremity tingling. Against those primal forces, his calm inner voice advises him to be a gentleman but not a prude. His fingers seek and encounter the fabric of her skirt. His palms cover her buttocks and squeeze their firm roundness. Her throat emits a contented hum.

Countless seconds or minutes pass. She disengages and lays her cheek on his chest. His nose nudges her thick hair, fresh with the scent of soap.

"This time," she says, "Warrain not run from Alinga like scared bandicoot."

"Aye. Nary agin."

She returns her fur wrap to her shoulders. "Come. Much has changed."

"Tell me as we walk?"

"I not tell. Must wait for father."

*****

Ryan senses the anxiety and excitement within the group before they enter the camp. Dozens of overlapping conversations in Wadawurrung come in ascending waves of volume. The entire family crowds the central campfire. When Ryan and Alinga arrive holding hands, the group's conversation switches to a gossipy banter punctuated with titters and giggles.

Laarr raises his brawny arms. Talk and movement cease. Hard-edged designs and symbols decorate his torso and thighs. The white etchings catch the fire's glow. Ryan has a revelation—they are battle symbols.

Laarr begins talking in a tone both sad and defiant. After a sentence or two, he pauses and points to Alinga. She translates for Ryan.

"Ten days past, Boort told Loklok next arweat of their family be Dyeelaga."

Laarr continues, and pauses.

"Loklok broke away to start own group. Ten warriors and families go with him."

Laarr speaks again, glancing several times at Alinga.

"Boort and Laarr pledged brotherhood. I not promised to Loklok now." She squeezes Ryan's wrist but shows no outward emotion.

Laarr grabs two spears from a stack leaning on a tree. Holding both high, he continues. "Loklok come soon to claim what he wants—me," Alinga says with a shudder. "He make war. Boort cannot stop him."

Laarr tilts his chin towards Ryan, expecting a response. Ryan understands his role. Had he not interfered, no battle would now loom. He steps forward.

"This is my family," Ryan says, sweeping his arms wide to include everyone. "I pledge myself to Laarr." He holds his pistol and tomahawk above his head. "I'll stay until danger passes."

Weeyn translates for Ryan and adds his own remarks. Ryan recognizes the Wadawurrung word for brother. The men of fighting age—ten in all with Laarr and Weeyn—gather around Ryan. Each in turn places a palm on his chest and recites words he cannot translate but whose meaning is obvious—a warrior's oath of fidelity.

Laarr assigns overlapping guard shifts to every male from youth to elder, so pairs of men are on sentry duty night and day. He puts Weeyn in charge of ensuring the men meet their obligations. Laarr restricts food gathering parties to one group of two men and one youth to ensure sufficient men remain to defend against an attack.

The camp settles but no one sleeps. All lounge near the fire, engaged in whispered conversation. Young women bring food morsels and water to the elders. Boys feed wood to the fire. Men sharpen spear points with files and whetstones—previous tributes from Ryan. They assess the leather strips holding spear tips and tomahawk blades in place, checking for loose or frayed bindings. Laarr and his brother Murrangurk carve a *keerram,* a tapered, three-foot slab of wood used as a battle shield.

Ryan sits on a stump, his sight glued to the flames. He deliberates on the cascade of recent events. Alinga kneels beside him with her head on his lap. When he rode from his station days earlier, he had not expected her to be free of her betrothal to Loklok. Even when discussing her as a potential wife with Stephen, that possibility came with uncertainty. Her availability remained in doubt.

Ryan doubts that God selects our path, as Stephen insists. Ryan puts little value in religion, having witnessed how poorly faith served the starved and disposed of Ireland. He admits, though, letting human events follow their natural course is sound advice. Ellen he pursued to no avail, unable to breech her defenses. Alinga he avoided until she matured enough to overcome his excuses. Alinga perches on the doorstep of his future—with whatever blessings and curses she bears. His fingers caress her hair. She hugs his legs in response.

Ryan must ask Laarr's permission to marry her, but decides to wait until they thwart Loklok's threat. Ryan wishes for good fortune on the five stars of the Southern Cross blazing through a gap in the scattered tree canopy.

*****

On the second day waiting for Loklok's attack, Ryan inspects the camp. Stacks of karnweel, daar and koorr lean on trees. Every warrior has a keerram. The women carry foot-long clubs on leather straps at their waists. Underage boys practice throwing toy spears at trees.

Each morning he has ridden out at least a quarter mile onto the plain and circled the treed knoll that shelters the camp. On Dan's back, Ryan can see further, and the horse can outrun any man if Ryan is caught out beyond the protection of Laarr's warriors.

Today, on winter solstice eve, low-hanging clouds emit a cold drizzle. A thin fog hangs in the air, reducing visibility. A damp chill manages to creep inside his oilskin jacket and woolen sweater; so, to white man's logic, no attack is likely. But Ryan now thinks like Wathaurung. He is on alert. Rain provides no defense against Loklok and the fog gives his men extra cover.

On edge all the daylight hours, Ryan returns to camp, his mouth dry and lower back cramped. The clouds part at sunset. In windless air, the winter cold pours from the heavens. Frost fills the hollows in the land. Raindrops freeze on grass stems. Even Loklok will stay close to a fire on such a night.

While Ryan attends to Dan in the corral, Alinga visits, wrapped in a wool blanket. With the garment hiding her sculpted body, Ryan can focus on her face. Her relief and happiness at the canceled betrothal is obvious. A non-stop smile dimples her cheeks. Firelight dances in her pupils.

She slips her arms around his waist and presses her body against his. His hands caress her lower back. So close, for a moment forgetting Loklok, Ryan is at peace.

"Tonight," Alinga says, "I sleep in your hut."

Ryan holds her at arms length by her shoulders.

"Yer father may kill me. I've not asked his permission."

Puzzlement clouds her face, and then she begins to giggle. Her dark, angelic features convulse with merriment. Her mirth builds to a musical cascade of laughter, a joyful melody that brings a smile to Ryan's lips. His fondness for her swells in his chest. He pulls her close.

"Father not kill you," she says. "In our custom, I can sleep in hut of betrothed. It not sleep to make babies, you silly amadeat. Sleep to share heat. Like first night on beach."

"I can barely remember that night," Ryan says.

"I lie close to keep you warm that night," she whispers in his ear. "I feel your muscles and hear your heart. I chose you as future husband."

"Are ye certain 'tis me ye want? Ye are free now to wed a Wathaurung warrior."

Her brows furrows—an unanticipated possibility enters her innocent and romantic mind. "You no want be my betrothed?"

Here is the decisive moment, the point at which an honorable man must make a decision he will not—can never—abandon. She expects him to proclaim her to be his future wife. No middle ground exists. Yes or no.

Despite her being close to twenty years younger, a different race, and unfamiliar with a life beyond the bush, she—at that moment—is the right one. Ellen's emotions and life are too complicated. Alinga never restrains her affections, is honest with her feelings, and does not keep him guessing.

He gives her a reassuring squeeze. "Aye. I do."

"What you do?"

"I want to be yer betrothed."

"And my *nganaboon*, my husband? And father of my babies?"

Ryan holds his breath. For a second, an image from his teens flashes in his mind. He trembles on a ledge of rock, working up courage to dive into the cold Irish loch twenty feet below. Quieting his fear, he leans forward until he passes the tipping point. He relaxes and gives into gravity.

Exhaling, Ryan answers, "Aye. I do."

*****

The Australian winter is in full vigor. Brittle ice coats the surface of standing water at dawn. The sun shines unrestricted by clouds but barely warms the air. The land is barren of animal life. Even kangaroos are rare. Recent hunting parties returned empty-handed. The women have exhausted the local supply of roots. Rations are slim. Everyone has some food but hunger lingers.

After a meager breakfast, Ryan continues his solo patrol on horseback. His eyes sweep the empty plain. Overhead, two ravens dip and weave in a courtship flight. He smiles at the message. His scrutiny returns to the ground. Where grass waved in the wind unimpeded seconds ago, eleven naked warriors with painted bodies now bound and leap forward, each with a spear poised and ready to throw.

Ryan cocks the hammer of his Colt. Instead of the usual satisfying metallic click, he hears a thin ping. The hammer returns to the neutral position with a light thud. In the instant it takes for Ryan to acknowledge his weapon is now no more lethal than a rock, Loklok and his ten men close in. A boomerang clips the brim of Ryan's hat. He digs his heels hard into Dan's flanks and lets out a whoop. The horse responds with a plunging stride and gallops out of danger.

*****

From the ridge, Weeyn spots Ryan riding Dan hard towards the camp. Weeyn needs no explanation. He shrieks a throaty roar—a Wathaurung battle cry. Everyone in the camp reacts. Women and elders gather up infants and form a protective group deep in the trees. The fighters seize shields and weapons, and hurry to join Weeyn. Boys too young to fight collect spare spears and hustle towards the scene of battle.

Warrain pulls up his horse beside Weeyn. "There be eleven with Loklok—mostly young men," he says, dismounting. "I'm taking Dan to his corral. He is too big a target."

"Is not better for man with gun to be on horse?"

"My damn pistol is broken. I need a shield and a spear."

"Get new shield by father's hut."

Weeyn joins the line of warriors at the rocky edge of the hill. His father leans on his spear in calm anticipation. Like all warriors in camp, Laarr has painted every scar from past battles with white clay. He boasts many. Weeyn and his young cousins have no battle wounds yet. Their family has lived in peace for years.

Below, Loklok halts his men beyond spear range. They gather around him, listening as Loklok gives instructions. Weeyn wishes the two men off hunting had returned. Loklok has them outnumbered.

Laarr pulls his men together and speaks. «Eagle and his ten outnumber our nine. We are better fighters. Eagle is their only warrior with battle scars.» He glances at Loklok. «His young men do not know how to fight. We have five warriors with battle scars. We are high on a hill. They must climb up to us. Our spears have the metal. Theirs are wood. Ours cut deeper. We will defeat them. Now, spread out two paces apart and wait.»

Laarr waves Weeyn close. «Where is Belongs-to-the-sea?»

«He puts his horse in a safe place. He will be here soon.»

«With his gun?»

«No. His weapon broke.»

«H-m-m-m. Bad omen.» Laarr's locks flop as he shakes his head.

«Look father,» Weeyn says, pointing down slope.

Loklok has separated from his men. He strides towards Laarr, showing a slight limp. He carries two daar. A koorr hangs on his waist. He halts within hailing distance.

«Great wise Stone,» Loklok says. «Give me what is mine and I will leave in peace.»

«She is no longer yours. I will give her to another,» Laarr shouts.

«No man will wed her because I will surely slay him.»

Laarr bellows, «Where are your manners? You do not make threats to an arweat. I will have words with your father concerning your poor upbringing.»

Even from this distance, Weeyn can see Loklok grimace.

«Last chance, old man. Bring me Sun.»

«Come up here, boy. Let me teach you respect.»

Daar in hand, Loklok's right arm jerks skyward. He exhales a wild and bloodthirsty whoop. At his signal, Loklok's men begin the attack, but not as Laarr or Weeyn expected. Five men sprint left and five go right.

Too late, Laarr comprehends the flanking maneuver. With a quick series of commands and gestures, he sends two groups of three to guard the flanks. Both include a brother of Laarr, another seasoned warrior and a young man. Laarr commands Weeyn to stay with him.

Loklok's tactics succeed. By the time Laarr reacts and his men deploy, they are too late. Running a diagonal route, both attacking groups scale the slope and gain the hilltop before Laarr's men can stop them.

Weeyn detects worry on his father. The big man peruses his two groups, who now face foes who outnumber them five to three.

Laarr has fallen into a trap by splitting his men. Below, Loklok waits, grinning. If Laarr and Weeyn run to help their men, Loklok can scale the hill unmolested.

Loklok has so mesmerized Weeyn and his father, they fail to notice Warrain's arrival.

"Ye two go help yer men. I'll take care of Loklok."

«About time,» Laarr mutters and trots to the right flank.

"Be careful Warrain," Weeyn says. "He will use weapons this time."

"Go. I can handle him."

When Weeyn arrives on the opposite flank, Loklok's men have just flung the first volley of spears. The distance is long. His uncle Murrangurk, cousin Tomboko and the other warrior sidestep the incoming missiles or deflect them with shields. Weeyn assumes their attackers are fearful; otherwise, they would have come closer before throwing half their supply of spears.

«Follow me,» Murrangurk says. «Throw your karnweel when I throw. Then go in close and jab with daar and hit with koorr. We fight close enough to smell their blood.»

Murrangurk bellows his war cry. Weeyn's heart drums in his chest and his body tingles as he joins the sprint towards Loklok's men. *Finally, combat.*

The four rush their opponents in a solid line of black flesh bristling with pointy objects. The five hold their ground, brandishing short spears and shields. Murrangurk flings his long spear when so close Weeyn can see the whites of his enemy's eyes. Two of their karnweel miss. One man falls with a spear through his torso, squirms a second and lies still. Another man retreats with a shaft protruding through his bicep.

Weeyn shouts, «Now four to three.»

The two sides form facing lines. Again, Loklok's well-coached men do the unexpected. Instead of direct engagement, they dash to the last man in Murrangurk's line—Tomboko. For several deadly seconds, he faces three armed men alone.

Weeyn arrives to his aid first. He deflects an enemy spear with his shield and jabs his daar low into his opponent's exposed thigh. The wounded man stumbles and falls. Weeyn grins. He dwells on his victory a heartbeat too long. Tomboko screams. Two daar pierce his abdomen and neck. Blood gushes from an artery.

For an instant, time pauses for Weeyn. The part of a warrior's mind, which can step aside from fear and pain in the midst of battle, reviews the scene. Weeyn assumes he has failed his cousin. He wasted a moment to gloat and it proved fatal. His cousin is dead because of him—his cousin who married Tarra. Did he hesitate on purpose, he wonders.

One of Tomboko's killers bends to withdraw his spear from his victim's belly. Weeyn slams his koorr on the man's arm. The blow shatters his elbow. An instant later, a spear from Murrangurk enters the man's ear and exits out his neck. As Weeyn engages the last enemy warrior still standing, his bulky uncle pulls a spear from Tomboko's dead fist and jams it with all his might at the last attacker. The steel-tipped blade splits the man's wooden shield, plunges into his chest and severs his spine. He falls like a felled tree. Murrangurk has avenged his son. Three of Loklok's men lie dead. The two wounded survivors have vanished.

Murrangurk wastes no time on victory or mourning. «Come. Help Stone.»

By the time they reinforce Laarr's group, the fight is over. Two of Loklok's men on that flank retreated with wounds. Laarr and his men bear minor scrapes and bruises . Weeyn and Murrangurk move in behind Loklok's remaining fighters. Trapped and outnumbered seven to three, they drop their weapons. The eldest, a man of about twenty summers, steps forward.

«You have a right to kill us. You have authority to be merciful. We accept your decision.» The defeated warriors, their backs erect and features impassive, await the verdict and sentence.

Laarr searches for Tomboko. He passes a questioning look to his brother. Murrangurk replies, «My son has gone to Dreamtime. His death is avenged. Spare these men or not, as you see fit.»

Laarr glares at each of the vanquished men. «You came today with a renegade to steal my daughter. I should kill you now.» He pauses, not wanting to be hasty. «I knew you as boys. You are nephews of my friend Smoke. I will spare you on condition.»

«Tell us the condition, merciful Stone.»

«Return to Smoke, beg his forgiveness and pledge to never serve Eagle, and never harm my family and its descendants.» Laarr slams the butt of his spear on the rocky ground. «What is your answer?»

Each man nods. «We agree,» the eldest replies.

Laarr points his spear in the direction of Boort's camp. They depart.

«Where is Eagle?» Laarr asks.

«And what became of Belongs-to-the-sea?» Weeyn adds.

*****

Ryan rushes Dan into his corral ahead of the battle. Alinga hugs him from behind, her fingers meeting at his navel.

"You fight Loklok. My dreams tell me."

"In yer dreams, do I win?"

"Maybe, with help from a little dingo."

"I dunno what ye mean."

"No time explain. Go now."

Ryan approaches the battle site and assesses the disposition of Laarr's troops. His warriors are outnumbered and hold weak positions. Loklok has Laarr and Weeyn captive like puppets in a minstrel show. Ryan's next step is obvious. He must tackle Loklok alone and release Laarr and Weeyn.

"Ye lads go help yer men. I'll take care of him."

Laarr mutters something in Wadawurrung and trots to the right flank.

"Be careful Warrain," Weeyn says. "He will use weapons this time."

"Go. I can handle him."

Ryan positions himself on the rocky edge. Loklok waits fifty feet away and a dozen feet lower.

"Ah-h-h. The white dog returns," Loklok says, faking cheerfulness. "Why do you fight for blacks? You are better off with your own kind. Taking what is not yours. Hurting without feeling."

Ryan has no answer for Loklok's unexpected psychological tactic.

"Have you ever lived in a land," Loklok continues, "where another race stole that land and made your people slaves?"

Ryan gags, unable to answer. *How could he know?*

"I dislike fighting my own people," Loklok continues. "Laarr is a good man. Not too smart, but true in heart."

Internal conflicts weaken Ryan's resolve. Loklok may be an arrogant, mean-spirited bastard but what he says rings with a truth so pure it can blind a man. Ryan lives on Wathaurung land, helping in a small way to dispossess the first people, like the English did to the Irish.

The spear and shield grow heavy in Ryan's arms. *We should be brothers, not enemies.*

"Warrain," Loklok says in a low voice, "bring me Alinga, and I promise to call off my warriors. No one needs to die."

Like morning sun clearing a field of ephemeral night mists, Alinga's name jars Ryan to reality. Loklok is not here to commiserate on colonial oppression; he came to press his one-sided honor code at anyone's expense.

"Ye can't have Alinga. She's mine," Ryan bellows.

"Yours!" Loklok roars.

"Yes," Ryan responds, raising his spear. "My betrothed. Soon to be my wife."

"Never!" Loklok springs up the hill, boulder to boulder, like stepping-stones across a creek. On each rock he spits out a single word. "I... forbid... you... to... defile... her...with... your... filthy... white...flesh."

In a final magnificent display of athletic prowess, Loklok vaults up the last few feet. Ryan prepares to jab Loklok in mid-leap. The warrior has another idea. He flings both daar at once—left hand and right—in midair with uncanny accuracy. Ryan deflects one spear with the shield. The other pierces his left shoulder.

The force and pain of the blow knock Ryan off his feet. Rocks slam into his spine, knocking the air out of him. He struggles to breathe and to locate a weapon. Loklok stalks towards him, raising his koorr high in preparation for a deathblow.

Ryan's right hand crabwalks across the rock, searching for the daar he dropped. His blind fingers touch the shaft. Loklok's koorr is at its peak, ready to descend. Ryan tries to wrap his fingers around the spear. His digits are sluggish.

Loklok stumbles. A fist sized rock drops from his forehead to the ground at his feet.

In the second that passes while Loklok recovers from the mysterious blow to his noggin, Ryan's fingers gain a firm hold on his spear. By rolling his prone body, Ryan drives the sharpened metal point into the closest place on Loklok's torso.

Clasping his groin, Loklok screams in pain and anger. Blood pours through his fingers. He stumbles and tips over the ridge.

With effort, Ryan forces himself to his feet, using his spear shaft like a cane. He clamps his teeth and yanks Loklok's spear from his shoulder. A grunt escapes his lips.

Alinga races up to him, a second rock in her hand. They scrutinize the sea of long grass. Loklok has disappeared. Ryan points to the stony ledge. Parts of his opponent remain. Two bloody objects—parts of male anatomy—lie on a patch of rock lichen.

"What should we do with those?" Ryan says.

"Leave them for the ravens," Alinga replies with clinical coldness. "Come to fire. I fix my warrior's wound."

"Nay, I should help Laarr," he says, glancing at the two knots of fighting men.

"No. Warrain not needed. Laarr win soon. Come."

*****

Ryan removes all clothing on his upper body to expose his wound. Thanks to the oilskin coat and sweater, the spear point penetrated less than an inch. Alinga washes the shoulder gash with warm water in which the women steeped medicinal herbs. She uses a thin-bladed knife to dig out spear slivers. Ryan clamps his jaw and tries not to flinch. When Alinga completes her surgery, she pours the herbal infusion into the wound. Ryan cusses in Gaelic at the stinging. Alinga applies a paste of mashed roots and moss, and wraps the poultice in a strip of cotton.

Before Alinga is finished, the victorious warriors return to camp. Mothers and spouses hurry to clean and dress their wounds.

The subdued conversational tone in the camp conveys a sense of relief, but no one celebrates. The burial of young Tomboko is underway. No one can ignore the scraping thumps of ferocious digging and grunts of human effort. Using a flat-sided stick and wedge of bark, Murrangurk excavates a hole four feet across and deep. He refuses everyone's help. Ryan makes a mental note to bring shovels on his next visit.

Tomboko's mother, howling with anguish, folds the body into a fetal position with Tarra's aid and binds him with possum rugs. They line the burial plot with leafy boughs. Murrangurk and Laarr lower the fur-clad corpse. Murrangurk fills the grave. He tramps down the soil and circles the pit with rocks. He jams Tomboko's spear into the loose dirt to mark the grave. Ryan detects no formal words resembling a funeral service.

With Tomboko interred, men gather the slain attackers and arrange the bodies side-by-side on the rocky ground at the forest's edge. Every able person gathers bundles of wood—the children bring sticks and the men logs—and erect a great pile of fuel on the corpses. Laarr brings a flaming branch from the cooking fire and ignites the pyre.

Everyone attends the flames in silence and patience, until the fire leaves no signs of the bodies. Elders use green boughs to rake the coals into a glowing pile. Laarr drives three spears into the ground at the ash pile's edge. That signals an end to the funerals.

In the late afternoon, the absent hunters arrive, hauling in a sizable kangaroo. The women descend on the beast and soon hang hunks of meat on sticks to roast.

*****

"Everyone will have a full belly this night," Ryan whispers to Alinga.

She grunts an affirmative without absorbing the statement. Her attention is pinned to Tarra, analyzing her every movement and gesture. Her friend is in mourning but fails to exhibit the level of grief expected of a widow. Tomboko's mother rocks back and forth, wailing. Her upper arms drip with blood where she has sliced her skin to show she shares her dead son's pain. Tarra has coated her arms and face with gray ash, but neither wails nor inflicts ritual wounds. Alinga worries for her—already elders point in her direction and gossip in each other's ears.

Tarra ignores her howling mother-in-law and lets her vision rove around the fire. Her eyes alight a moment too long on Weeyn.

His hungry stare devours her. Alinga hopes no one else spies their visual exchange. It could bring terrible trouble.

"Ye seem distracted," Ryan says. "Be there something amiss?"

"I worry for Tarra."

"What's wrong?" Ryan asks.

"I tell later."

"Then, can ye tell me about yer dreams? I'm curious. Who is the little dingo?"

Alinga turns from Tarra and smiles at Ryan. "Some night when sleep, I visit Dreamtime. Always I am little dingo. Dreamtime shows little dingo danger or problem. When I wake, I try stop danger or fix problem."

"Did Dreamtime tell the little dingo to leave the kangaroo sign on a tree?"

"Yes. And Dreamtime tell me Warrain getting lost."

"'Tis why ye tied cloth to the yakka?"

"Yes."

"What else did Dreamtime tell ye about me?"

"Many things. It told me to find you lying on the beach."

Ryan pulls her close. "Yer dreams saved my life more than once. Do t'others know of yer wondrous ability?"

"Weeyn…and now you…my betrothed." She hugs his left arm and rests her chin on his shoulder. Her tongue tickles his earlobe.

"If ye be my wife, ye must live with me. Are ye certain ye can leave yer family and this bush life? 'Twill not be easy learning to live in the white world."

"I go with Warrain. I be happy with my chosen husband."

*****

After a feast of meat, everyone relaxes by the fire. The younger warriors point to raw wounds and recount their recent heroics.

Ryan monitors Laarr from a distance, waiting for an opportunity. The arweat converses with his brothers and elders. Ryan decides not to interrupt. He senses anger in the group. Murrangurk repeatedly jabs a spear into the soil.

Laarr rises and strolls beyond the firelight to relieve himself. Ryan follows him part way and waits near the edge of camp.

A voice calls from behind, "Warrain."

Ryan whirls.

"I see you watch me, and follow. You want talk?"

"Yes, Laarr. I came to ask yer permission to marry Alinga."

Laarr's face clouds. He sticks out his lower lip and scuffs the ground with his big toe. Ryan opens his mouth to speak but Laarr waves for silence. Ryan waits as ordered but cannot stop folding and unfolding his sweaty hands.

To Ryan, time drags. He recalls a day in Ireland when he misbehaved in school. The nun forced Ryan to stand for an hour in a corner awaiting punishment.

Laarr, his eyes still fixed on the ground, begins to speak in a low voice. "I long know Alinga want Warrain. I hope Wathaurung warrior ask for her. Always bad for black girl marry white man." His brow furrowed, he looks up at Ryan. "Mother of Tarra go with white man when young. White man no want when she older. She come home. No man want her now for wife."

Ryan grips the chief's big shoulder. "Laarr. Am I like other white men?"

"No."

"Do I behave like I want much and offer little?"

"No," Laarr says.

"I owe my life to this family. Have I shown my gratitude?"

"Yes."

"Have I ever treated Alinga without respect?"

Laarr shakes his head no.

Ryan contemplates the big bear of a man. His heavy black and gray curls cover his forehead and ears. His tangled, grizzled beard hides most of his face. Moisture shines in the corners of his crinkled eyes.

"Why are ye sad, my friend?"

"My world end soon. My daughter, my jewel, leave with you. Loklok's curse dooms her if she stays. My son, the pride of my life, also must go. In better time, Warrain and Laarr hunt together, grow old, tell story, play with grandchildren."

"Is it really so bad?"

He frowns. "Alinga believe only she dreams. I closer to spirits. I see more than Alinga." He rests a big, callused paw on the side of Ryan's head. "I see end of our people. When Alinga born, white men few. In her short life, white men now many. My family, my entire clan, soon disappear like fish in a dry pond."

Ryan shifts up on his toes and pulls the big man forward until their foreheads touch. "My friend. It saddens me," Ryan whispers.

Laarr clasps Ryan's hands in his. "I give you Alinga. You marry tomorrow and after, you go. Visit when can."

"Ye said Weeyn must leave also. Why?"

"Not tell now. Wait for answer."

*****

Weeyn sits on a log near Mokborree. Elbows on his knees, his cupped palms support his chin. He shrugs at each of Mokborree's remarks but says nothing. He has not eaten since the battle. The emotional clash of disappointment, guilt and worry roil his stomach. Weeyn frets. He is the sole warrior without a wound to show from the fight. Worse, he cannot absolve himself of a role in Tomboko's demise. And the growing hostility over Tarra's lackluster mourning makes him twitchy. She is in danger. *What can I do?*

He observes his father and Warrain return from the far grove. His friend hurries to his sister and whispers in her ear. She hugs him, her face beaming. A trace of a smile cracks Weeyn's grim countenance. *At least someone is happy.*

Laarr signals to his son and walks into the dark forest. Weeyn follows the arweat to the rocky ledge. They overlook the grassy plain. A crescent moon hangs in a clear sky.

«Fire, let us discuss matters of importance.»

Laarr's use of formal Wadawurrung grammar warns Weeyn the conversation is not father to son, but arweat to warrior.

«Today, in battle, you made your people proud. You showed no fear and beat your opponent. Do you share that pride?»

«No, arweat. I let down my cousin. I hesitated, maybe for selfish reasons, and he died.»

«Your lust and love for White did not cause his death. Do not be so arrogant.»

Weeyn's brow furrows and he stiffens.

«You are surprised?» Laarr barks. «You cannot keep secrets from me. I have long known of your trysts with White. I know Sun was your accomplice.»

«But you did not stop us.»

«No. Lust drove you to do this bad thing. I hoped it would fade like fog before sunshine.»

«I love her. I always have.»

«A strong man, an honorable man, can love and not betray his kinsman.»

«Who have you told of this?»

«I told my brothers and the elders this night. By now, all know.»

«What shall you have me do?» he asks in a supplicant's voice.

«I give my sentence tomorrow.»

Laarr's tone changes from arweat to father. «What I must do brings deep sadness. My greatest wish has been that you would follow me as arweat.»

«I am sorry to fail you, father.»

«You are a brave warrior and at heart an honest man. You will make me proud again, even if I am not in this life to see it.»

*****

The next day at the sun's zenith, Laarr calls the group together. Weeyn, with a fur-covered bundle tucked under his arm, leads Ryan to one side of the gathering. Alinga and Mokborree wait opposite. A new possum wrap covers his bride's slim shoulders. Shell adornment and feathers hang on strings of leather on her ankles, wrists and forehead.

Ryan grins at her from across the fifty-foot circle. She returns a confident smile.

Laarr, his brawny arms crossed on his fur-robed chest, is center stage between his two brothers. Laarr smiles to each elder.

The arweat raises his arms and all murmuring ceases. Laarr commences a speech in Wadawurrung. People nod in agreement. Ryan picks out several words and asks Weeyn for confirmation. "Is he saying they're moving?"

"Yes. In two suns, we go to place with better water and game."

Laarr next points to Ryan. People smile. Young women giggle.

"Is he speaking of me now?" Ryan asks.

"You and Alinga," Weeyn says.

"What's he saying?"

"Wait. He speak English for you."

On cue, Laarr speaks to Ryan.

"Today, Laarr give Alinga to Warrain, Kangaroo Fighter, our friend." With hand motions, he directs the bride and groom to a spot in front of him.

Ryan retrieves the marital bundle of possum furs and metal tools Weeyn holds for him and comes before his soon-to-be father-in-law. Unfamiliar with Wathaurung custom, he speaks what he feels. "Please accept these gifts as my pledge to honor yer daughter and her family and her clan for as long as I live."

The few men who understand English translate his words to others.

Mokborree leads her daughter to Ryan. Laarr places Ryan's hand on top of hers. "Daughter. Now, you no girl, you woman. From this day, Laarr no more protect you or hunt for you. Now, Warrain protect and care."

He pauses while Weeyn translates for those who do not understand English.

He continues. "Alinga, you now wife of Warrain. Warrain, my son, you now husband of Alinga. May good spirits always walk beside you."

Ryan smiles at his bride. Her expression is like none he can recall—parted lips, moist eyes and glowing complexion. The word rapture comes to his mind.

"Alinga," he coos, "in my custom, this be where the groom kisses the bride."

Their embrace, while not a Wathaurung wedding tradition, speaks of love and needs no translation. Happy chatter washes over the jubilant couple.

"Ahem!" Laarr coughs. Ryan and Alinga return to the earthly plain. Ryan blushes and Alinga giggles. Mokborree pulls them back into the circle of people.

Laarr's features mutate from a smile to a scowl. The camp goes silent.

«Fire,» Laarr barks. «Come.» He points to a spot with his spear.

Weeyn trots forward. He keeps his expression impassive and his posture straight.

«White,» Murrangurk calls. «Come.»

Shoved forward by her mother-in-law, the young widow inches forward to a position indicated by Murrangurk's spear. Tarra trembles but holds her head high.

«Fire and White, you betrayed the honor of my nephew. What say you?»

Alinga bends to Ryan's ear and translates.

"How long was the affair going on?" Ryan whispers.

"Many seasons."

"Did ye know?"

"Yes."

To answer Laarr's challenge, Weeyn strides to Tarra and drapes his arm across her shoulders. She leans into him. A gasp ripples through the group. «Wise and merciful Stone,» Weeyn says in formal Wadawurrung. «We are guilty. What we did was out of love for each other.»

Alinga translates for Ryan.

"He's a bold one, for sure," Ryan replies.

Laarr continues. «White, by rights my brother can kill you.»

Alinga gasps.

"What be wrong?" Ryan asks.

Alinga waves him silent and strains to listen.

Laarr glares at his son, awaiting a response. Weeyn does not disappoint him. «With your permission, I will marry White and we will leave. We will put right what is wrong.»

Laarr relaxes when he receives the answer he expects. «I agree. I now make you husband and wife. It is the only way. But there is a condition.» He motions to his brother.

Murrangurk jams his spear into the soil. «White I spare. She must go. My grandson Sky stays.»

Tarra emits a piercing wail and drops to her knees, her face buried in her hands. Weeyn crouches to comfort her. Alinga begins to sob on Ryan's shoulder.

*****

Ryan leaves Tarra and Alinga in a tearful huddle by his hut. He seeks out Weeyn and comes upon him stargazing by Tomboko's grave. Ryan places a hand on his friend's shoulder.

"Is Tarra's boy yers?" Ryan asks.

"No. He has ears and nose like Tomboko."

Ryan smiles to show relief, glad Weeyn will avoid additional grief. "Have ye decided where ye will go?"

"No. She can no return to Boort's family. Maybe we live alone."

"Too dangerous," Ryan says. "Come live with Alinga and me. I can teach ye how to handle a team of horses or make wagons. If yer world is truly disappearing, join mine."

"Tarra hates the white world."

"She was a baby when her mother brought her back. She has no real memory. 'Tis not so bad. We live on a station, not in a town."

Weeyn lifted his eyes from Tomboko's spear in the fresh dirt to the stars. "Warrain words good. We go. She my wife. She will come."

"I'm pleased. 'Twill be grand to see ye every day instead of a few weeks a year."

Weeyn smiles, warming to the idea.

"Do ye have missionary clothes for the three of ye?" Ryan asks.

Weeyn nods his head.

"Good! We'll need them."

Adjustments

July 1850

The four trekkers halt in the night-darkened compound of Ryan's station. A guard dog barks. Stephen, lantern in hand, steps onto the porch and raises his arm to cast the light further.

"Ack! It be Ryan and three black lads. Come on in. I'll put tea on."

For five days they traveled. Ryan and Weeyn hiked while their wives alternated rides on Dan. They followed a meandering route to stay under forest cover. Without his gun, Ryan wanted to avoid meeting any semi-lawless prospectors or Loklok's men.

The previous day, to great protest, Ryan's companions had donned men's shirts, trousers and canvas coats. With their hair tucked under wide brimmed hats, Tarra and Alinga passed for boys in the dark. Not so when they step into the shanty and pull off their hats.

"Oh my Lord," says Stephen.

In the main room's wood-heated warmth, the young Wathaurungs strip to the waist. Only Ryan's shout to stop prevents them from completely disrobing. "Until ye learn our ways, keep all yer clothes on except in privacy," he says.

Stephen, a glorious shade of crimson, blocks his vision with both palms. "If the young ladies will please put shirts on, we can be properly introduced."

Alinga buttons her shirt and motions Tarra to do the same.

"How can you wear these things," Tarra complains. "They itch me. I feel tied up."

When the newcomers have fastened all necessary buttons, Ryan gives the all clear. "'Tis safe to look, Stephen."

Stephen peeks through splayed fingers and smiles. "Much better. Too much lovely female flesh is hard on a bachelor."

"Stephen," Ryan says. "This lad is Weeyn. I mentioned him often."

"Welcome." Stephen extends his hand. Weeyn, remembering Fraser's training, performs the required duty.

"This is Tarra, Weeyn's wife," Ryan continues.

"Pleased to meet you," Stephen responds.

"And this is my wife, Alinga," Ryan adds.

"Wife?"

"Aye. We are wed by Wathaurung custom."

"Well, then! Welcome to your new home, Alinga. I have heard so much about you."

Alinga reaches up to touch Stephen's pale beard. "Why you have gray hair when face so young?"

"'Tis not gray," Ryan explains. "'Tis blond. White men's hair has many colors."

"Alinga," Stephen says, "there be much to learn about our people and culture. Feel free to ask me any question at any time."

"Do you have wife?" she asks.

"Not yet."

"What wrong with white men, they marry so old?"

Stephen laughs. "Only your second question and I have no answer."

Alinga steps close to Ryan. She fixes him with a coquettish smile. "Where we sleep?"

"My room…I mean, our room is through that door," he says, pointing.

"Is room privacy?"

"'Tis private, aye, if ye close the door behind ye."

Alinga inspects the doorknob, figures out how it works, smiles over her shoulder at Ryan and disappears.

"Weeyn and Tarra can have my room," Stephen says, "until we build extra accommodations. I'll be fine in the bunkhouse with the lads."

"That is generous, Stephen. Please show them the way."

Ryan paces the empty main room. In one week, sudden shifts in events and personal choices have changed the course of his life. A world of love and family awaits after decades on his own. Alinga is not the only person who will need to adjust.

Stephen returns. "I had to explain the dunny. They were none too pleased with the stink."

"Aye, fresh from the bush with much to learn," Ryan says. "The other blacks can help. They've been through it."

"Tarra didn't want to use the bed, preferring to sleep outside," Stephen says. "In the end, Weeyn convinced her to stay inside for at least tonight."

Ryan nods to indicate he heard. He believes Weeyn and Tarra will settle in. His major concern is Alinga's wellbeing. "If ye find an opportunity Stephen, can ye explain Christianity to Alinga? Maybe, we would be better to also wed in a church. Our marriage means nothing here. She'll be seen as a bush wife or worse."

"Aye, I will, with pleasure." Stephen tilts his head towards the closed bedroom door. "She is a real looker that one, a bit skinny for my taste, but I can see the attraction."

"'Tis more than her looks. She has a kind heart and a quick mind."

Stephen stretches his arms and yawns. "I be heading to bed. It be late. Much to do on the morrow."

Alone in the main room, Ryan imagines what waits for him in the bedroom. He envisions his fingers tracing the curves of Alinga's body from shoulder to thigh. She is now his wife. He can start the family he has longed for.

Ryan sucks in a deep breath and crosses the room. At the door, he exhales and enters. Alinga lies on her back in all her naked glory—sound asleep. Ryan eases onto the bed beside her, pulls a blanket over them, and holds her close.

*****

At dawn, Ryan shows Weeyn around the station's main compound. The eighteen-year-old is indifferent to horses and farm livestock. To the young Wathaurung, they are animals—nothing new. In the woodworking shop and cooperage, Weeyn points to various tools and asks Ryan to explain their use. In the wagon shop, he examines every apparatus. He praises the sharp edges of spoke shaves, drawknives and chisels. He marvels at the jigs Ryan uses to shape hubs and assemble wheels.

"And this last shack is the smithy," Ryan says. "I make horseshoes and the metal bands for the hubs."

"How?" Weeyn says.

"I'll show ye." Ryan adds fresh coals to the hot hearth. He shows Weeyn how to pump the bellows to increase the heat. Ryan inserts an iron bar into the fire's center.

"Keep the bellows pumping," Ryan says.

With metal tongs, Ryan extracts the rod—now glowing red at one end. He lays it across the anvil and pounds it into a U-shape with a hammer.

"'Tis more complicated than that to make tools or parts but it gives ye an idea."

"I want learn this," Weeyn says.

"Are ye sure? 'Tis the most difficult craft at this station."

"Yes."

"I can use help, since I'm the single smithy. Are ye certain?"

"Yes. Yes."

"I should've brought ye here first, since yer name is Fire."

"Yes. The spirits chose this for me."

"I'm glad to have ye here. Let's get breakfast."

Ryan and Weeyn interrupt a donnybrook in the kitchen. Tarra and Alinga are hollering at Stephen in Wadawurrung and threatening him with knives. Weeyn brings quiet with one sharp word in his native tongue.

"What is this falderal?" Ryan says.

Stephen replies, "I was making breakfast as always and these dear ladies became hostile."

"Food our work," Alinga says, pointing to her and Tarra.

"I see we have adjusting to do," Ryan says, as he tries to stifle a smile. "Alinga, ye can't use a stove, or make a decent pot of coffee, or bake bread. Ye have no knowledge of using plates and utensils, or where to wash up when yer done. Let Stephen show ye how. When yer ready, ye two lasses can do the cooking."

"But Ryan," Stephen sputters.

"Sorry Stephen. In their culture, woman pride themselves on cooking and food preparation. Let them stake their claim and find their place. Please."

"Aye. I guess there be plenty else to do."

"Alinga. Tarra. Can ye give Stephen a few days to show ye?" They both nod.

"How do we get meat?" Alinga says.

"We raise pigs, sheep, and chickens. Talk to yer cousin Benboo if ye need a beast to butcher. He is my livestock boss."

"No kangaroo or wombat!" Tarra exclaims.

"No emu," Alinga says, sulking.

"Sometimes the lads spear some bush tucker, but ye can't count on it." He gives the women a minute to calm themselves. "Right then, where's our breakfast?"

"Coming up," Stephen says. "Ladies, let me show you how to scramble eggs and toast bread."

"I'll brew the coffee," Ryan offers.

"What is coffee?" Weeyn asks.

"One thing yer fine world lacks," Ryan says with a grin.

At breakfast, Stephen insists all his guests eat with utensils, not fingers. Tarra leads the way, recalling table manners from early childhood in her father's house.

"It easy," she says, "hold fork like this." She delivers her finer instructions in Wadawurrung. "White men allow eat some food with fingers." She picks up a half-slice of toast. "See! You learn quick. It easy."

Alinga and Weeyn soon master the use of a fork, though how they hold it—clamped inside their fists—would not pass muster in good company. Ryan sees he has much work ahead.

After breakfast and dishwashing, Alinga explores the shanty's interior. The main room includes the cooking, dining and lounging area. In the latter, several stuffed chairs group around a reading lamp.

Alinga ponders a shelf of books trying to guess what they are. She cocks her head side-to-side. She pulls one off the shelf. It flops open. She drops it in surprise and points at it on the floor.

"Husband. What those little marks?"

"Those are words. We use words to tell stories or describe how to do something." Ryan picks up the book she dropped, *Robinson Crusoe*. "Here is the word for father. Look. And on the next page, this word is mother."

"Book talks to you?"

"No, not talking. We call this reading."

"How you make words?"

"We put those marks called letters on paper. We call it writing."

Awareness creeps across Alinga's face. "You save talking for later."

"Aye. 'Tis part of it."

"Teach me reading. Teach me writing. Like you teach me English."

"I can try, but 'twill be better if I can hire ye a proper teacher."

*****

Four days later, he finds himself with the luxury of spare time. He peruses his library books, unable to choose between Dickens and Trollope. The sound of a horse in the compound, followed by a knock on the door, cuts his reverie short.

"Nary a moment's peace," he mutters. He heaves himself from the comfortable chair and opens the door. "Ellen!"

A moment of silence passes while they drink in the sight of the other after months apart. A smile softens her face. Ryan's heart pounds harder. She places her hands on his chest, and whispers, "Sorry for dropping in unexpectedly, but I came to impart good news—"

A door behind Ryan creaks. Ellen's focus shifts to something over his shoulders. Her smile withers. She takes a half step backwards and folds her hands at her waist.

"Can you explain why that half-naked waif emerged from your boudoir?"

Ryan swivels towards the bedroom. Alinga fills the doorway wearing only a man's shirt. The white shirttails end at the upper thighs of her long, dark legs.

"Aye. That is Alinga...er...my wife."

"Your wife!" Ellen bares her teeth. For an instant, Ryan fears she is about to slap him. Ellen reins in her Irish temper, but her green eyes hide nothing. "Did you not repeatedly tell me she was promised to another?"

"Aye. But her father broke off the engagement."

"And you wasted no time in filling the void, I see."

For the first time since he met her, Ryan feels like shouting at Ellen. *How dare ye ridicule my marriage after rebuffing me so many times?* He swallows his rage. He finds strength and calm in the knowledge his actions were honorable and necessary. "I believed 'twas time I took a wife...as I discussed with ye many times."

Ellen's mouth opens in shock. For a few heartbeats, she is numbed by indecision.

Alinga glides to Ryan's side and slips her hand into his.

Ellen whirls and strides to the door. She snatches the doorknob. Her arm tenses like someone ready to slam the door with intent and vigor. Her movement freezes. From behind, her shoulders heave, either from self-calming breathes or sobs. She releases the door handle and walks calmly to her horse without looking back.

*****

Two days later, Ryan and Alinga sit on the porch, enjoying the weak heat from the midday sun. Alinga holds Ryan's hand and plans their family. She wants two daughters and four sons. The appearance of Ellen riding down their lane cuts short her fantasy.

Ellen reins in her steed and dismounts five paces from them. With her leather-gloved fingers, she smoothes creases in her floor-length, pale green dress. Folding her hands at her waist, she assumes the poised stance of a well-bred woman.

"Please excuse my regrettable outburst the other day," she says to Ryan. "I have no right to be critical, given my situation." She pauses for a restorative breath. "As your friend, I wish you both happiness." She shifts her remarks to Alinga. "It will be difficult for a girl brought up in the bush to fit in our society. How may I be of assistance?"

Ellen at her best—her most sophisticated and generous—hits Ryan in his solar plexus. All his feelings for her, subdued for months, well up and threaten to burst forth in a sob. He loves her and senses he always will. He loves Alinga too. Different women loved for different reasons.

"Ellen my dear friend," he says, standing, "if ye truly mean that…Alinga needs proper women's clothing for one. And better schooling for another."

Before Ellen can answer, Alinga steps up close to her. She studies Ellen, not with anger or jealousy; rather, like she would observe the behavior of a strange bird. She touches Ellen's orange hair with a tentative finger.

"Look like fire. Not hot like flame. Very pretty." After years of melting her parents' anger with puppy-dog eyes and a cherubic smile, she has mastered a charm few can resist. Her dazzling teeth and her luminous orbs melt the stiffness from the older woman.

"I shall return tomorrow with dresses for her," Ellen says to Ryan.

"Nothing too fancy, please. She and Tarra hate clothes. I can barely get them to keep their pants on."

"You have another wife?" Ellen says, attempting to be jovial. "I understand such is allowed among natives."

Ryan rolls his eyes. "Nay. She is Weeyn's wife. He lives here now too."

"I suggest we start the two young women with simple, loose-fitting, ankle-length dresses. We can eschew confining undergarments for now. They should find that to their liking—comfortable, yet modest."

"Can ye recommend footwear? Neither has ever worn a shoe."

"I want shoes with laces," Alinga says, giving Ryan a secret smile.

Ellen regards Alinga's calloused feet. "Let us start with sandals or something like a moccasin. Feet need to be trained to the restraints of leather and heels."

Alinga grasps Ellen's right hand in both of hers. "I hear Warrain say you teach."

"Yes, I teach at a school."

"Can black girls learn read and write?"

"Certainly. Skin color is no measure of ability."

Alinga pivots to Ryan. Her comely face crinkles with lines of joy and expectation. Ryan reads the message.

"Can I enroll Alinga, Tarra and Weeyn in yer classes a few days a week?"

"Yes. I shall arrange it. The school will expect payment, but the tuition is not onerous. I shall have an answer when I return tomorrow."

"'Tis grand of ye to do this for us," Ryan says. He escorts Ellen to her horse.

"Dear Ryan," she whispers, "I cannot love you the way we...you wanted, but I can demonstrate my affection through your child bride. I shall endeavor to make her the best she can be."

Ryan helps Ellen into the saddle stirrup. "Thank ye from the depths of my heart."

He follows Ellen's progress until she disappears up the lane.

Alinga clutches his wrist. "Come." In the bedroom, she closes the door.

"Fire hair woman loves you. True as sun in sky."

Ryan shrugs in agreement.

"Can white man have many wives?"

"Nay. Just one."

"Good. I not like share." She unbuttons her shirt. "We make baby now. Warrain must make me full wife."

"Are ye sure. I wanted to wait until I arrange a marriage in a church; so ye'd be my wife in my culture also."

Alinga pulls Ryan's right hand and places it between her upper thighs. "This now yours."

She fondles his crotch through his pants. "That now mine. Your church change nothing."

Warmth gushes through his arteries. Nerves tingle. Affection fills his heart. He removes his clothes and lies beside Alinga. He caresses her velvety curves with his fingers as he has so often before with his eyes. She purrs cat-like at his touch. To his surprise, she rolls over, pushes him onto his back and straddles him.

"I once see Tarra do this."

Good Times

February 1851

Weeyn guides the wagon from Buninyong for the hour ride home with Ellen. Ryan assigned Weeyn to fetch his teacher after church on Sundays and transport her to the formal midday Sabbath dinner.

"What a grand serotinal climate we are blessed with this week," Ellen says. "Blue sky every day without the curse of blistering heat."

"Yes, ma'am. The weather spirits smile upon us with generosity." Weeyn turns and flashes a show-off smile.

"I am elated by your progress in speaking English, though I wish you had more time for class, like your wife and sister. They have surpassed you in reading and writing."

"Yes, ma'am. My future success now depends on how well I learn a trade. I read and write well enough. My spare time is best spent in Mr. Hiscock's blacksmith shop."

"Speaking of your name, did you accept the surname Ryan suggested?" she asks.

"Since I seem to need a surname, Laarson is an honorable choice. I thank him—" Weeyn halts in mid-sentence. The silhouettes of three riders emerge from the mirage-like heat distortions on the road ahead.

Weeyn reaches under his seat, retrieves his pistol and lays it on his lap. Ryan bought half a dozen new .48-caliber, six-shot Colt Dragoon revolvers, and trained Weeyn and others in their use. The increase in gold prospecting in the region has had the side effect of encouraging banditry from bushrangers.

But Weeyn knows they are not robbers. He recognized them immediately.

"Who are they?" Ellen asks.

"It is the bunyip Fraser and his two hired devils."

The riders block the road. Weeyn has no choice but to halt the wagon. Walter Fraser has the middle position, with Scott Healey to Ellen's right and Billy to Weeyn's left. Fraser and Healey have pistols drawn and resting on their thighs. Weeyn notices Healey now holds his weapon in his left hand. Billy's tomahawk hangs on his saddle.

"How delightful to see you, Mrs. O'Sullivan," Fraser says with a smile. "How have you been?"

"Very well, thank you Mr. Fraser. And you—are you faring well?"

"We are getting by. Business is picking up thanks to the increase in prospecting, though we are below my expectations, thanks to a certain upstart company." Fraser touches his black chapeau and points at the fighting kangaroo symbol on Weeyn's hat.

"And Weeyn, you appear very manly with that trimmed beard of yours. But, it pains me to discover my old stable boy working for that rogue outfit." His voice drops a halftone.

Weeyn understands the subtleties of Fraser's voice. He raises his gun and aims midpoint between Fraser and Healey. In return, they point their pistols at Weeyn.

"Drop your weapon, Weeyn," Fraser demands. "It is two to one."

Weeyn hears a metallic click beside him and Ellen speaks. "Correction. Two to two." She pulls a small-caliber, five-round pocket Colt from her cloth handbag and points it at Fraser. Her pistol is the only gun with the hammer cocked and ready to fire.

Weeyn glimpses a flicker of doubt on Fraser. At that moment, Weeyn cocks his pistol. He and Ellen now have the advantage. In the half-second Fraser and Healey need to cock their pistols, he and Ellen could get shots off. Billy, while having no gun, is the unknown threat.

Billy belongs to the Taungurong clan, but Weeyn calculates the crafty ex-police officer speaks several local languages, including Wadawurrung. «Do you dare interfere with Belongs-to-the-sea?» Weeyn says.

Billy's startled look acknowledges Weeyn's assumption.

«If I must shoot, I will spare you if you stay out of the fight.»

«I mean no disrespect to Belongs-to-the-sea,» Billy mumbles.

"Stop that bloody monkey gibberish," Fraser hollers.

With Billy now sidelined, Weeyn likes the odds. Ellen's steady grip tells him she knows how to use her lady-sized pistol. But someone has to break the impasse and it cannot be him. Any strong words from a black might push Fraser to a rash response. Weeyn slips his foot to the right and taps Ellen's ankle. The buckboard at the wagon's front hides the movement from their three antagonists.

Ellen accepts the challenge. "Mr. Fraser, do you intend to shoot a white lady?"

Fraser frowns. Beside him, Healey's arms tremble and his jaw twitches as if chewing something tough.

"Walter," Ellen says in her stern teacher voice, "I asked you a question."

Fraser plays with his mustache, his eyes on Ellen's gun. He reaches to Healey and relieves him of his pistol. "Scott, dear boy," he coos to his companion, "your hand is a tad too shaky for a weapon. You might shoot yourself." To Ellen, Fraser adds, "Scott requires his medicine. I bid you adieu." Fraser slips both guns into his saddlebag, tips his hat to Ellen and rides around and behind the wagon followed by his companions.

Weeyn flicks the reins to set the horse in motion. He smiles at his companion. "I have not met a white woman warrior before."

"It comes with the red hair and Irish heritage—plus encouragement from a father who desired sons and sired one daughter."

"Do we tell Warrain of this encounter with Fraser?"

Ellen considers the question. "No. Considering Ryan's antagonistic sentiments towards Mr. Fraser, he might confront Fraser and put himself at risk."

*****

Ryan calls the family to dine. Tarra and Alinga deliver platters of food and slip into their chairs. Every Sunday meal includes two ranch workers on a rotating basis. The two Wurundjeri, Gellibrand and Polligerry, are the guests this day.

As usual, Stephen recites a multi-faith grace of his own authorship. He thanks Jesus, God and the Dreamtime spirits for the bounty before them: in this case, roast lamb, baked potatoes, carrots and green beans.

For Ryan, these Sabbath feasts recreate the familial warmth and camaraderie he once relished in Ireland as a youth. As he enjoys a meal supplied from his own station, pride in his accomplishments and his natural modesty jostle for position. While wary of indulging in smug self-satisfaction, he decides he can abandon steadfast humility for one day.

In the last month, Ryan's workers have built a shepherd's hut on the two thousand adjacent acres he and Stephen. They have finished a new cabin housing Stephen's residence and office. A new ranch house is nearing completion—the dwelling where Ryan will of raise his children. The original shanty will soon belong to Weeyn and Tarra.

Weeyn's blacksmith skills surpass Ryan's by a league. Weeyn now makes all necessary metal tools and equipment for the station, except the iron tyres. And that is just a matter of time. Tarra has mastered basic math. With her innate organizational skills, she assists Stephen in inventory management. Alinga supervises the food supply for the entire station and prepares all meals for the family. While not yet numbered among the rich, Ryan believes he is on that path. The wagonwright business continues to grow, as does the demand for haulage. The cooperage has become a minor but persistent moneymaker. Weeyn's smithy promises to be the next profit source.

While he listens to the table chatter on weather, Melbourne politics, the price of wool and economic issues, he counts his blessings. Alinga and Tarra are pregnant. Their bellies bulge under simple but flattering white cotton dresses. They and Weeyn have mastered Victorian table etiquette and manners, thanks to Ellen's tutelage. Stephen, his senior partner and friend, manages every financial aspect of their enterprises, which leaves Ryan free to oversee operations. And by some miracle, Ellen remains in his life—not as the lover and spouse he once desired, but as a friend and confidante. At that instant, her roving scan of table guests alights on him and pauses. He winks. She returns a faint signature smile conveying she is at peace with their relationship.

The main meal over, pots of tea and coffee replace supper dishes. This is the point in the weekly gathering where Ryan encourages news and discussion.

"So tell me, what news do ye bring this day?" he says.

Well," Ellen says. "I bear both good news and bad."

"Go on."

"The school administrators decided two visibly pregnant native girls, who are not blessed with a Christian marriage, are a poor example to other students. In brief, you may not return. Weeyn may attend, if he chooses."

"I do not," Weeyn barks.

"I expected this situation," she continues. "Once the newborns arrive in April, they will need breastfeeding—something impossible even to contemplate in a classroom."

"And yer good news?" Ryan says.

"I arranged for a young teacher, new to our town, to take my classes Monday and Tuesday. That allows me, if you so desire it, to teach my favorite students exclusively in their own home."

"Of course, we will compensate you for your loss of income," Stephen chimes in.

"I would be grateful," Ellen replies, making Stephen blush with the radiance of her smile. "Money is tight, what with the steady rise in prices these days."

"If ye think it proper, we can provide ye a room once my men complete the new house."

"Thank you, Ryan. With Stephen as my chaperone, I see no reason such an arrangement would insult propriety," she says with a wink to Stephen. "The convenience of arriving Sunday and returning Tuesday has merit."

Alinga jumps up from her chair and hugs Ellen from behind. "I love you like a sister, Mrs. Ellen."

From the opposite end of the table, Ryan admires the two loves of his life, their heads in a filial embrace: Alinga's dark hair enmeshed with Ellen's fiery curls; Alinga's midnight skin and Ellen's fair complexion on opposite ends of the human color spectrum.

Ryan says, "Who else has news?"

"I do," Weeyn says. "Prospectors made a big gold strike west of Sydney. It may draw men from here."

"I doubt many will leave," Ryan says. "I hear reports weekly of small discoveries, all within fifty miles of here."

"Any day, someone will hit a big lode," Stephen adds, as he tops up Ellen's teacup.

"Any news from ye lads?" Ryan says, turning to Gellibrand and Polligerry. The bearded men whisper several words in Woiwurrung, and shake their gray curls in the negative.

"Any other news? Anyone!"

"The minister of our church has finally responded to my entreaties regarding your marriage," Stephen explains. "He will not require you to change faiths but the ceremony will follow our tenets. Alinga must be baptized and attend Bible classes for at least four months before the ceremony."

"What do ye think, Alinga?" Ryan says.

She bites her lower lip. "Sorry my husband, I must say no." To Stephen, she adds, "Thank you, but if I do what you ask, I will not see Dreamtime again."

Stephen shifts back in his chair. His eyes dart to Ryan and Ellen for support. Ellen shrugs. Ryan pouts. Polligerry breaks the awkward silence. "Wife of Warrain follows the path written for her. She is wise beyond her years." His words settle it.

"I accept Alinga's decision," Ryan responds. "The Ballarat and Buninyong society must accept us the way we are."

"Given your stature and reputation, I expect they will do just that," Stephen concedes.

Ryan fishes a glittering object from his pocket. "Alinga, give me yer left hand." Alinga reaches to Ryan. He slips a gold band on the fourth finger. "I was saving this for our church wedding but 'tis yers by right. This tells the world ye are my wife."

Alinga leaps up and buries her head beside Ryan's neck and weeps.

Of all the smiles around the table, only Ellen's is forced.

*****

That afternoon, Weeyn prepares to hitch a wagon to drive Ellen home. Polligerry leads a Percheron from the stable.

"Polligerry, what are you and Gellibrand not telling Warrain?" Weeyn asks.

Polligerry ignores the question, as may a man of his station among the clans.

Weeyn switches to his limited Woiwurrung. «What are you hiding, please?»

«What I keep hidden is for his sake. Nothing good can come of revealing it.»

«Tell me, so I may help protect him,» Weeyn says.

«A new bushranger has appeared to the north. A black one dressed like a white. He murdered two shepherds at remote sheep stations. Both men had their man parts removed and placed in their mouths.»

«Eagle!»

Polligerry nods in agreement.

«You were wise not to tell Belongs-to-the-sea. He might do something foolish. We will watch and protect him.»

«On this, the Wurundjeri for once agree with the Wathaurung.»

On the journey to Buninyong with Ellen, Weeyn reruns the day's events and conversations. Has success and a soft life dulled the senses of his friend Warrain? His heart remains true but he is blind to the small, deadly perils lurking in the shadows—a child alone on the land with no knowledge of lethal spiders and poisonous snakes.

Weeyn worries Ellen is one such peril.

"Why do you not converse, Weeyn? It is unlike you to be so taciturn," Ellen remarks.

"I am cursed and blessed with the keen senses of a hunter. Signs invisible to ordinary men shout warnings to me."

"Weeyn, I rarely hear you so eloquent but I am at a loss as to what you mean."

"May I give you an example?"

"Please do."

"At our meal today, like many before, I saw the message you sent to Warrain with your eyes and smile."

"It was nothing, merely a friendly exchange."

"Not true. I once made the same signs across a campfire when Tarra was married to another."

"How dare you impugn my integrity?"

"You remind me of the Shakespeare play we read last month. 'The lady doth protest too much, me thinks.'"

"I am astounded you recall that. You seemed half asleep."

"I remember everything I am taught or shown. It is a gift from the spirits."

Ellen crosses her arms. "I see you recall my lectures on literature better than my instructions on manners."

"I have no use for manners to hide truth," Weeyn counters. "If I can see your love messages to Warrain, be certain Alinga and Tarra can also."

Weeyn looks directly at Ellen. "Do not come between them."

"It is not my intention, let me assure you."

Weeyn softens his tone. "Warrain told me you have a husband and are bound to him by vows."

Ellen folds her hands and speaks no further that night.

*****

August 1851

"Benboo returned from a family visit yesterday," Alinga says.

She and Tarra relax cross-legged on the kitchen floor of the new ranch house, practicing English and peeling potatoes. They manage the task even as they suckle their newborns. Alinga's son Yearn, which means moon, and Tarra's daughter Maya, which means wind, were born a day apart, on windy nights with a full moon, with the aid of a midwife Polligerry recommended. The pale skinned children are plump and healthy.

"What news did he bring?" Tarra asks.

"Your son Lakorra is doing well in the care of Murrangurk's wives, and my parents wish a visit with their grandchild."

Tarra shrugs and kisses Maya's brow.

"Benboo says he had to walk six days to locate them. And the camp was in a place with poor water."

"Did Benboo bring news of my family?" Tarra asks.

"They are a half-day walk further west. Boort is weak but alive. Your mother tends to him."

Tarra smiles at the news. "So much has changed in our lives."

"We may be the lucky ones, my sister friend," Alinga says. "We are well provided for here."

"Luck comes with a price," Tarra says. "We gave up freedom to roam for confinement in this place."

"That freedom you miss will soon be gone for all of our people," Alinga says. "We have a safe place in the future here with our husbands."

"Our fate belongs to Warrain," Tarra states. "Let us hope he has more honor than my white father."

"He loves me. He is kind. He will not leave." She twists her left hand in the air to flash her ring, the gold radiant against her jet skin.

"He also loves Mrs. Ellen," Tarra mentions.

Alinga sighs. "Poor Mrs. Ellen."

"You dumb like wombat! She shows him koala eyes at every dinner and you pity her?"

"I loved Warrain when all signs said he could never be mine," Alinga says. "Now he is mine and not hers. That is sad for her."

"Do you not worry she may steal him?"

Alinga laughs. She leans closer to Tarra and speaks in a conspiratorial whisper. "Two nights last, after Mrs. Ellen went home, I mated with Warrain until he was exhausted. I am the wild young dingo. No man would trade me for an old lap dog."

Tarra chews a lip. "Do not tempt the spirits."

Alinga cocks her head towards the door. "I hear a wagon coming fast."

"Yes. Let's go see," Tarra responds. She refastens her dress. "Maybe Weeyn is home."

*****

The clatter of arrivals draws Ryan from the wagon shop. Stephen gallops in. His half-Belgian crossbreed sweats even in the cool air. Behind him, Weeyn lashes a team of Percherons at high speed down the lane. The wheels churn up clods of wet earth. His wagon rolls to a harness-jangling halt. The commotion brings Alinga and Tarra onto the ranch house porch and draws half the company crew into the compound.

"What news do ye bring?" Ryan says.

"Gold!" each replies. Their expressions of surprise turn to chuckles.

"Stephen. Ye first," Ryan says.

"A couple of diggers named Reagan and Dunlop made a huge gold strike in a valley near Ballarat. They are washing out at least ten pounds of nuggets daily. Claims nearby promise to be as rich."

"Well, 'tis no surprise. We've been expecting it." Ryan nods to Weeyn. "Is yer news the same?"

"Thomas Hiscock found a big gold deposit outside Buninyong. He is closing his smithy and offered to sell me all his tools and forges."

"At what price?" Stephen asks.

"One hundred and fifty."

"Can ye make and fit iron tyres on wheels?"

"Yes."

"Then ye and Stephen go into town tomorrow. Settle the deal and load up Hiscock's equipment. If people need a blacksmith, they can come here."

"I predict thousands of new prospectors and fossickers will soon invade this region," Stephen says. "It will bring us new opportunities."

"Aye. We should start making kit items diggers require; like shovelheads and pickaxes. Can ye make those, Weeyn?"

"Yes."

"It's time Stephen and I made ye a partner. We'll share with ye equally any extra money the blacksmithing brings. Ye be arweat of the smithy. But, the company's work comes first. Do ye agree?"

"Warrain is generous."

"We can all make enviable fortunes from this gold rush without ever turning a shovel of dirt," Stephen says, "if we can hang onto our men."

"What do ye mean?" Ryan asks.

"I heard workers are deserting employers to hunt for gold: shop clerks, shepherds, teamsters and laborers."

"Weeyn," Ryan says, "will our black crew run off?"

"Working with Kangaroo Fighter has honor. Digging dirt has none."

"It is no good for a black to have big money," Tarra comments from the porch. "Whites will steal it. Our people will stay."

A grin spreads across Ryan's freckled face. "Fraser employees whites only. I wonder how his business will fare."

"It may be another opportunity for expansion," Stephen adds.

"Aye. Let's go after the rest of his business."

"Not yet," Stephen says. "We must not grow too quickly."

Ryan sighs. "Ye are always holding us back."

"Aye, for sound business reasons. Trust me."

Gold Rush

January 1852

Ryan steps out onto the wide porch of the new ranch house. Yearn tags along holding his father's thumb. Ryan arranged to hold the weekly Saturday afternoon management meeting outside to benefit from any cooling breeze. He is already edgy from months of continuous work and needs no further irritations from the summer heat. Cicadas scream from the gum grove behind the house.

Already seated, Stephen reviews a page in his ledger. Weeyn plays peek-a-boo with Maya on his lap. She laughs and tugs at his beard and long hair. Polligerry picks through a pile of roasted wattle pods, gleaning any seeds he may have missed.

Tarra and Alinga serve mugs of tea to Polligerry, Stephen and Ryan, and water to Weeyn. Ryan stirs maple syrup into his tea. The syrup is an indulgence from his brief stay in Canada. Six months earlier, he began importing the expensive luxury for his own table. With the gold fields now flooded with men from the Canadian colonies and Northern States, his syrup imports soon became a new profit source.

"Gents, let's start."

Weeyn transfers his daughter to Tarra. Alinga retrieves Yearn. Polligerry sweeps his wattle debris into his hat and dumps it in the compound for the chickens to pick through. Stephen adjusts the spectacles he has begun to wear when reading or writing.

"I'll begin," Ryan says. "Our wagon works completed a new dray today for a mining group nigh Ballarat. That makes four wagons in three weeks. My wheelwrights filled orders for six new wheels this week, with Weeyn's help, and fixed any damaged wheels on our wagons. I refused an order for a buggy. The wheels are too delicate for our roads and not worth the trouble. I'm willing to let another outfit have that business. This being the dry season, the cooperage is busy making barrels for water transport, though there is little profit in it." Ryan settles in his seat and gestures towards Weeyn with his tea mug.

Weeyn sips his water. "My smithy was very busy this past week. We added iron rims to the six new wheels and bands to twelve new hubs and eight barrels. We forged tool parts, and pots and pans to fill all orders from stores in the two towns, but…" He shrugs.

"Tell me what's on yer mind," Ryan says.

"We work long every day. My men and I cannot do more than now."

Ryan frowns and rubs his half finger.

"Polligerry, what be the state of our teamsters, wagons and horses?"

"Good-good. All ten wagon busy-busy. All driver work hard-hard. No rest. Today, I take one wagon off road, axle bad. I use spare wagon. Just one spare, now. I put two mare horse on pasture—their little horse come soon. Two horse old—need rest few days. Use all spare horse now."

"What do ye recommend, Polligerry?"

"If stay busy-busy, need one more big wagon and four big horse, two more driver."

"Stephen, can we manage that?"

"Well," Stephen says, "we certainly can afford horses and lumber."

"Should we expand agin?"

"Yes and no," Stephen replies. "There are over ten thousand licensed diggers in our region and several mines. The demands of stores and miners are a growing opportunity. Prices for all products and services have doubled in six months, meaning we now make embarrassing profits. Fraser's operation has diminished to two wagons. He relies on men who went bust mucking for gold, most who can barely handle a team. There are two new haulers with one wagon each. We are now the biggest hauler in the region and the newcomers are undercutting our rates. They may become a problem."

"How many wagons do ye figure we can add?"

"There be customers enough to keep four additional wagons on the road running daily. Our impediments to growth are skilled workers and wagon maintenance. With their duties, Weeyn and Polligerry have little time for recruiting new men. Our wheelwrights must build or repair an average of four wheels a week merely to keep our wagons rolling. That does not count time spent fixing axles, whiffletrees and other components. The smithy cannot produce additional goods and repair items. We employ one wagon simply to haul in feed for the horses."

"This gold rush will not last forever," Ryan argues. "We must take advantage now."

"If we grow too fast it endangers our reputation for quality," Stephen fires back. "We should diversify. We can earn the same revenue from making wagons and miner's gear as we do from running haulage. Remember, manufacturing requires less maintenance than haulage, so greater profits. And then there be importing luxury goods. We cannot expand that business if we fixate on haulage."

Ryan chews his lower lip. "Weeyn, is the new apprentice working out?"

"Yes. But I can spare no time to train him."

Ryan stands and slaps the table. "On Monday, I'll begin teaching yer new man what I know. That will help, aye?"

"Yes," Weeyn says.

"I'll get my men working on two new wagons for our use," Ryan continues. He points to Polligerry. "Send someone out to recruit Wurundjeri or Taungurong men."

"Yes, Warrain."

"Stephen, give every man a ten shilling bonus for their hard work. Cut our haulage rates by ten percent to squeeze out the newcomers. Visit the surrounding stations and buy horses. I want more wagons rolling."

Stephen frowns at Ryan. "Are you forgetting this be a partnership?" he asks.

"We can seize opportunity or let new operators profit from our timidity. Which will it be, Stephen?"

Stephen removes his glasses and points them at Ryan. "We be successful because you have listened to me so far. You be too hotheaded at times."

Weeyn and Polligerry exchange startled glances and attend to shoelaces that suddenly need retying.

"I want that evil bastard driven out of business," Ryan shouts.

"Dunnae make our company part of a personal vendetta," Stephen says.

Ryan begins to pace the porch. "Why not? We treat our workers and customers better. We'd be doing some good."

Stephen sits back in his chair and studies Ryan through squinted eyes. After an uncomfortable silence, he puts his glasses back on. "Go ahead, build your wagons, but nothing rolls out of here unless I say it and its crew be fit. Agreed?"

Ryan emits a barely audible, "Aye," and steps inside the ranch house.

He fusses with his half finger and taps the toes of his right foot. Alinga glides barefoot across the pine floor. She wears the short, embroidered skirt from her nomadic days, having now established her right to be bare-breasted inside their home. Ryan marvels at how well her figure has recovered from pregnancy. Tucked in her left arm, Yearn suckles. Though not yet sixteen, motherhood has driven the last child traces from Alinga.

Her right hand snakes behind Ryan's neck and she pulls his lips to hers. Ryan, swept up by her passion and affection, forgets his argument with Stephen.

"Now, my husband smiles," she says on releasing him.

"Aye. Thank ye."

Alinga places Yearn in Ryan's arms.

"Is my husband happy with his son?"

"Aye. Why do ye ask?"

"Is my husband happy with his wife?"

"Aye!"

"Has my husband good friends?"

Ryan nods.

"Does my husband eat well?"

"Aye. What are ye up to?"

"My husband cannot eat money or be loved by money or be friends with money. You must not argue with nice Mr. Stephen."

"Ye were listening."

"A good wife always watches her husband. Who else will tell him when he is wrong?"

"I'm not wrong. I want to make money now so we can live well later. This gold rush will not last forever."

Alinga slips her slim fingers inside his trousers and giggles at his instant tumescence. Her warm breath tickles his earlobe as she whispers. "Yes, not wrong, my husband. Sometimes you forget what matters most."

*****

"I highly recommend everyone read it," Ellen concludes, with a sip of tea. "*David Copperfield* is surely Mr. Dickens' most remarkable achievement thus far."

"Aye, young Copperfield's tale sounds much like my own struggle," Stephen replies.

"Will ye lend us yer copy?" Ryan says.

"I can do better than that. Your thirty-fourth birthday was midweek. I bought you a copy in celebration."

"Ellen, ye are so thoughtful."

"My husband and I can read it together," Alinga says, glancing at Ryan.

"We have begun reading to one another at night," Ryan says by way of explanation.

"How charming," Ellen says without looking at either Ryan or Alinga.

Tarra removes the plates and cutlery from the Sunday meal. Yearn wails from the nursery and Alinga answers the summons. Gellibrand and Polligerry excuse themselves and return to the bunkhouse.

Ryan glances at Stephen and clears his throat. "Ellen, Stephen and I could use yer advice on a business matter."

"Oh my! You may be the first men in Australia to seek business advice from a woman." She gives her head a brief toss, setting her orange curls in motion.

"Don't mock me, lass. I am serious."

She folds her hands on her lap, settles in her chair and composes herself. "Please continue."

"T'other day, Stephen said we should be importing more luxury goods. At present, we bring in maple syrup and bolts of cotton. We want to expand that enterprise. Stephen and I are too engaged elsewhere to run it. And since ye know all the merchants and business folk in Buninyong and Geelong, can ye suggest such a person."

"What would be your formal arrangement?" she asks Stephen.

"We would create a separate company stationed in Buninyong or Ballarat, provide the initial investment and offer a one-third partnership. The partner can expect a modest salary and a third of net profits. The partner would be required to use our haulage for all shipments and deliveries."

"Can ye recommend someone to fill the job?" Ryan says.

"Yes—me."

Ryan smiles.

Stephen slaps the table in glee, jarring the top off the teapot. "Ach! You would be perfect. You have the sophistication and intelligence such an enterprise craves. I admit, I had not considered you before, but now it is self-evident."

"Thank you for your hearty endorsement, dear Stephen. What is our first move?"

"I will accompany you to Buninyong and instruct our lawyer to draw up the papers," Stephen says. "Next, we go to Geelong by stage coach, take rooms in a hotel, and spend a few days investigating the shipping firms. Does that suit you?"

"Indeed. It sounds like a holiday."

"What things do we sell?" Tarra asks.

"Silk and fine linen," Ellen offers.

"Tobacco," Stephen adds. "The stuff they grow here is barely fit for making sheep dip."

"American and Scottish whisky," Ryan suggests. "And champagne. Only the finest."

"No bloody spirits," Stephen protests.

"I am afraid Ryan is correct, Stephen," Ellen says. "It may offend your Presbyterian values but it is sound business. And no one expects you to imbibe your merchandise."

Weeyn asks the obvious question. "You will no longer teach school?"

"A lone woman such as I should embrace opportunities. A teacher's wage does not allow one to save for old age. But be assured," she adds with a maternalistic smile, "I shall continue to instruct my three favorite students."

"Why do ye look so glum, my friend?" Ryan asks Weeyn.

Weeyn rises, touches his hat brim in respect and exits the house without answering.

*****

Weeyn hides in shadow beside the original ranch house—now his family's home—watching the fading summer twilight. He can make out four of the five stars of Mirrabooka in the blue-black sky.

Half way across the compound, Ryan steps out onto the porch of his house and rejoices in the cooling evening air. As Weeyn expects, Ellen slips out the front door and joins Ryan. Weeyn cups his palms behind his ears to pick up their conversation.

In the lamplight, Ellen stands inches from Ryan. The closeness speaks of intimacy.

"You expected me to ask for the partnership tonight, did you not?" she says.

"Aye."

"Many others could do justice to the offer. Why me?"

"Cause I trust ye. And 'cause...'tis a way I can take care of ye."

"And to keep me part of your life, perhaps?"

Across the darkness, Ryan shrugs in response. Weeyn notices a hint of forward movement in their torsos, like a couple contemplating a kiss.

Tarra bursts from the house and almost collides with Ellen. "So sorry, Mrs. Ellen. I must check on Maya."

"Quite all right, child. I shall accompany you. I have not seen the little darling today."

Ryan disappears inside. In the shadows beside the main house, the darkness moves. Someone else was listening. Weeyn whistles a sharp bird-chirp. From the shadows come the answering notes.

Weeyn joins his sister. «What did you see?»

«A possum in heat.»

«What should we do about her?»

«Nothing. She is harmless.»

«But, Belongs-to-the-sea has given her the status of a wife by sharing his fortune.»

«That is our custom, not his,» Alinga says. «By trying to care for her, he will set her free. When she becomes wealthy, she can leave.»

«You are too kind, my sister.»

«Any word of Eagle? My old betrothed is the true peril.»

«He is a ghost. He kills. He disappears. Some say he wears different clothes: sometimes a shepherd or a laborer or a clansman.»

«Is he coming closer?» Alinga whispers.

«All killings are two days walk from here in every direction.»

«A circle?»

«Yes.»

«It is a message,» she says.

«A warning. He waits, I do not know why. Have you not dreamed of him coming?»

Alinga looks at Mirrabooka for strength. «Dreamtime has not blessed me since we departed from our family.»

*****

The summer night retains the day's heat. Weeyn returns to his shanty to find Tarra sitting topless on the porch staring at the stars and fanning herself. She has hiked up her dress hem. She is not wearing undergarments. Her near nudity is how she expresses her defiance of white society rules.

He sits in the second chair and observes his wife, waiting for her to acknowledge his presence. He has learned to respect her moody silences. She refuses to accept their new surroundings. The loss of her old life and separation from Lakorra have left her with anger she cannot or will not shed. Now almost seventeen, Tarra is no longer the girl he fell in love with.

Yet, still he loves her, though he admits the overwhelming thrill of being with her has faded. Her large eyes, broad face and shapely body—even after two children—still inspire his lust. Sadly, she shows little interest in lovemaking; perhaps, he believes, as punishment for him bringing her here. He misses their impassioned trysts three years earlier and the simplicity of life's responsibilities then.

«I know about Eagle,» she says, without looking at Weeyn. Speaking in their clan tongue is another way she rejects the white world imposed on her.

"Everyone knows, except Warrain and Mr. Stephen," Weeyn replies, refusing to switch to Wadawurrung.

«We should return to our lands. We will be safer among our warriors.»

"You are unwelcome in Laarr's family as long as Murrangurk is alive. Boort will not accept you either."

«There are other groups. Many families would accept us just to have a warrior of your stature.»

"I will not leave Warrain. His way is the future."

«Despite your darker skin, you have become more white than I.»

Weeyn absorbs the intended insult without a flinch.

*****

November 1852

Breathless, Ryan whispers in Alinga's ear, "I need to visit Ballarat for a day or two." They lie in bed. She has exhausted him. They have been reading Romeo and Juliet together at night. Shakespeare's great romance feeds Alinga's passion like dry wood on a hot fire.

"My husband has business in town?"

"I haven't visited for nigh six months. Much has changed since the rush began. I want to see."

"Alinga will miss Warrain."

Ryan runs his fingers through her hair. His former doubts about Alinga fitting in to white society have vanished. She has absorbed the rules and customs, thanks to Ellen. Any flaws in etiquette or style the average person will shrug off—everyone in Australia is a bit eccentric. Ryan knows her skin color will always set her apart but he hopes her charm and his community stature can overcome that obstacle.

"Come with me to Ballarat," he offers. "Tarra can mind Yearn."

Alinga straddles Ryan in a joyful embrace and kisses his chest and neck. "My husband proud of his wife, yes?"

"Aye."

*****

The following Wednesday, Ryan helps Alinga up to the wagon seat. The normally agile teen laments the confining undergarments Ellen has forced her to wear. "Alinga will die today. Cannot breathe!"

"Ye'll live." Ryan loads their suitcases. "Ye look like a refined lady." Ryan adores how fetching she is in the off-white cotton dress with gay floral pattern Ellen provided. The neckline dips to reveal a hint of Alinga's corset-uplifted breasts. Thin straps flow over her shapely shoulders. The synched waist and flared hips accentuate her figure. The sleeves end above her elbows. A pale yellow silk shawl protects her neck and shoulders from the cool edge to the morning breeze. As the wagon rolls along the Geelong Road, its margins green with spring shoots, Alinga leans against Ryan and scans for game in the grasslands.

"Alinga," Ryan says, "'twill be the first time people will see us together in town. Folks will stare. Some may make insults 'cause of yer color. Prepare yerself."

"Alinga is the daughter of an arweat and wife of Kangaroo Fighter. I will not be shamed by any silly white person." Her smile shows no hint of trepidation.

Ryan squeezes her hand.

The town has transformed since his last visit. Most tent structures near the central crossroads of Main and Barkly are gone. New wooden buildings, most without their first coat of paint, rise above the dusty street. Covered wooden sidewalks shield shoppers and pedestrians from the day's growing heat. Horses, wagons and buggies fill the wide avenue with a bi-directional river of clanking and creaking activity. Ryan guides his box wagon amidst the throng.

Diggers, many in dirty and shabby clothes, trudge north towards the nearby gold fields. An unrelenting barrage, much like the roar of a distant cataract, forces every human conversation to greater volume.

"What makes that sound?" Alinga asks.

"'Tis the sound of ten thousand diggers washing gravel in various contraptions."

Ryan hitches Dan to a post near the two-story Duchess of Kent Hotel and its restaurant adjunct, Café de l'Europe. The wood-framed structures, with a curved balustrade railing on the rooftops, rightly claim to offer the most elegant accommodations in East Ballarat. Three doors open to the street: one each for the bar, the hotel and the restaurant. Ryan guides Alinga through the middle door. The dark wooden flooring and wainscoting give the interior a funereal feel: it encourages conversation in whispers.

"Gidday Mr. Robinson. I'd like yer best room, please."

The well-dressed thirtyish, proprietor pushes aside his paperwork behind the desk and smiles. His visage fades to businesslike blankness at the sight of Alinga.

"Ah, yes, Mr. Warrain. Welcome back." He picks up a pen to write in the register.

"I've my wife with me this time," Ryan adds in a casual tone. He observes William Robinson squirm.

"Your wife?" Robinson mutters.

Alinga steps forward and drapes her left hand on Robinson's wrist, exposing the gold band. "I asked my husband to bring me here because so many people praise this hotel and the hospitality of its owners," Alinga says in the same voice she once often used to wheedle favors from her father. "You must be very proud of your reputation, Mr. Robinson."

Robinson's dour expression softens. Alinga's manners and charm erase her skin color and the poor man can perceive nothing now but a sensuous, young woman of rare beauty and good diction. Her language skills exceed Ryan's expectations. Ellen's vocabulary flows from his wife's lips.

"How many nights will you being staying with us, Mrs. Warrain?"

"Just the one."

"I suggest the suite on the second floor at the rear. It offers relief from the street racket."

"How very considerate, Mr. Robinson," Alinga says, finishing with a pearly smile.

In their hotel room, Alinga is an explorer venturing onto an uncharted island. She appraises every piece of imported furniture—discovering unimagined luxuries. Her delicate fingers caress fancy chairs, a chest of drawers, a ceramic washbasin and water pitcher. She holds the oil lamp to the window. She gasps when sunlight streaming through the cut-glass lamp body spews blobs of amber light on the walls. Her expedition of discovery ends by the four-poster bed.

She fingers the sheets. "What is this?"

"'Tis linen."

"So soft and cool," she coos.

Her pupils dilate. The pink tip of her tongue rests between her ivory teeth in a feral smile. In seconds, Alinga slips off her dress. Ryan spies a knife strapped to her leg below her right knee. Before he can question it, she glares at him. "Alinga is stuck in Mrs. Ellen's underclothes. Help!"

"Aye. I have a wee bit of experience in such garments."

*****

Ryan laces up Alinga's corset, amused by her string of Wadawurrung oaths and curses.

"Are ye hungry? There is a cafe next door, with fancy china cups and other such finery."

"Alinga could eat a wallaby."

"'Tis likely the best ye'll get is lamb."

At the base of the stairs, a door leads from the hotel into the Café de l'Europe. Inside, Robinson's partner James Sayers polishes cutlery.

"Gidday," Ryan calls.

"Hello Mr. Warrain. William did say you and your new wife were staying with us. I expected you might choose to dine here."

"Is there a problem," Ryan growls.

"Yes, but not as you may be assuming," Sayers replies, with a glance at Alinga. "Mr. Fraser is dining with that ugsome colleague of his. He has ruined the appetites of my best customers with his gruesome tales of murdering hapless blacks in the name of a family vendetta. I fear if you enter, there will be trouble. Your bad blood is legendary."

"I apologize for jumping to a conclusion," Ryan says, with a slight bow of his head.

"I recommend the Bath Hotel. Go west a few blocks and turn at Lydiard."

"Thank you for your kindness," Alinga whispers.

Arm-in-arm, Ryan and Alinga step out into the midday sunlight, squinting in the dusty glare. A door opens behind their backs. The sound of boot heels thud on wood.

"Well if it ain't Ryan and his black whore."

Ryan whirls to face Scott Healey, his dour mask misshapen by mirth, and Fraser, silent and tense. Both men have their pistols drawn but pointed at the ground. Ryan's Colt is in the hotel room. His trusty tomahawk hangs on his belt. Ryan concludes it is better that he not have his gun given the two-to-one odds and Healey's gunman skills. Ryan has more chance with his small battleaxe.

Alinga slips from his arm and darts into the hotel. Ryan steps off the sidewalk and puts the sun at his back. Mute, he glowers at his foes, waiting for the witnesses he knows will arrive.

Word rumbles up the road like a summer thunderstorm—Ryan and Healey are facing each other again. People flow into the street with the speed of a flash flood.

Fraser and Healey assess the jostling crowd of store customers, residents and diggers. Their narrowed eyes flit along the looming wall of observers. Their impromptu plan of harassment and bullying has gone awry. This audience expects grand theater. Now, something must happen.

"Why don't ye repeat what ye said, so all can hear it?" Ryan shouts.

Healey cannot ignore the bait. "How dare you bring your black whore into a town of descent folk?"

A murmur of apprehension infuses the circle of spectators. Women on the far sidewalk frown at Healey's rough language. Ryan turns to address the viewers. "Ye are my witnesses," he yells. "He has insulted my wife—my wife—in front of everyone." He spreads his arms wide for emphasis.

Ryan faces his opponents. "Mr. Fraser, we've heard from yer barking dog. What have ye to say?"

"If you insist on polluting your body with dark flesh, keep it private."

"Ye mean like ye do with those black stable boys?"

Fraser and Healey hiss in unison and point their pistols at Ryan. Behind him, Ryan hears people scurrying out of the firing line.

"What slanderous rubbish," Fraser counters.

"I know three lads who were abused at yer station in a most foul manner."

"They are liars."

"No native lad would invent such a dishonor."

Fraser's cheeks flush. He cocks his pistol.

"Do ye plan to kill me Fraser? I'm not some black man. Ye can't shoot me unarmed in the street and get away with it. Ye'll hang." Ryan is confident he has more than bluff on his side—he can count on Australian men to prevent the blatant murder of their own kind.

Almost as if cued, two men accost Ryan's foes. One, a tall, dashing man in his early twenties places the tip of his gun barrel on Healey's ear. The other, a shorter and younger man, covers Fraser.

The taller of the two speaks in an accent Ryan recognizes. "Drop your weapons. Fight if you must, but fight fairly." The strangers relieve Fraser and Healey of their pistols.

Facing a hostile mass, Ryan's foes have no choice now but to fight, if only to salvage respect from the debacle. Fraser and Healey draw their knives and step off the sidewalk. Healey, still showing a limp, takes tentative steps parallel to the sidewalk. Fraser splits from his partner and circles around Ryan to attack from the opposite side.

Ryan slips his tomahawk from its sleeve. He begins to wiggle his toes inside his boots—a strategy to prime his muscles for quick footwork. His eyes dart between his two opponents. He has never fought two armed men at once.

Behind Healey, Ryan catches a glimpse of a white-gowned blur burst through the ring of people. In four great strides, Alinga erases the distance to her target. She leaps onto Healey's back like a dingo onto a wallaby. Her knees straddle his six-foot frame like someone shinnying up a tree trunk. Her left arm encircles his neck in a chokehold. Before Healey can use his knife to fend her off, Alinga slides her knife across his upper lip, bisecting his nasal septum. She pushes off from her wounded prey. Healey, howling in anger and blind with pain, slashes the air with his knife. He bumps the raised sidewalk and stumbles to his knees. Blood gushes around the fingers clamped to his nose.

"Ladies and gentlemen, let me introduce my wife Alinga," Ryan calls to the bystanders. "One hundred pounds of angry dingo."

A warm round of applause greets Ryan's bravado and Alinga's bravery. Ryan exhales softly. Alinga broke an unwritten code in black-white relations by wounding Healey. It appears to Ryan, the white horde is willing to overlook it.

Alinga smiles at Ryan and retreats to the shaded sidewalk. Drops of Healey's blood stain her left sleeve.

When the assemblage quiets, Ryan treads towards Fraser. "What'll it be Mr. Fraser—an apology or a fight?"

Fraser spits at Ryan's feet, a clear rejection of the first option.

"What's yer pleasure, Mr. Fraser, weapons or fists?"

Fraser glances at Ryan's tomahawk and tosses his six-inch blade in the dirt.

Ryan scours the rows of people for someone familiar and spots the glitter of polished brass buttons. He waves Billy over and offers him his tomahawk. "Billy, hold this for me would ye?"

Hesitant, Billy peeks at Fraser. He makes a quick decision. "Billy take good care, Warrain."

Ryan closes in on Fraser. A chant arises among the older residents. New arrivals soon join. "Kan-ga-roo! Kan-ga-roo! Kan-ga-roo!"

Fraser puts his right foot to his rear and raises his fists in a standard boxer's stance. Sweat beading on his forehead belies his show of resistance.

"Spent a few hours in boxing class, did ye Mr. Fraser?"

Hate for Ryan distorts Fraser's face.

"Well, I spent years on the streets fighting boarding school twits like ye," Ryan says. "And I don't follow rules."

Ryan step-hops in close to Fraser. With a snap of his front leg, Ryan drills his foot under Fraser's guard and into his midriff. His lungs empty of air. His diaphragm constricts.

"That is for making Loklok mean."

Ryan lands a right roundhouse punch on the gasping man's left ear.

"That is for hurting Nalong. And..."

Ryan finishes with a left uppercut that cracks Fraser's jaw. "...that is for Weeyn."

Fraser lands on his butt. Dust billows from the impact. Unlike blubbering Healey, Fraser is silent and stoic in his pain and defeat. For half a minute he scowls at Ryan, his eyes mere slits, either from the pain or the hate. He sputters, trying to speak without moving his jaw. The nearest bystander shushes the crowd.

"Quiet. Let him speak."

"My advice to you Ryan," Fraser whispers, "is kill me now. My revenge knows no bounds nor time limit."

"Keep yer advice," Ryan says. "I've killed none til now. I won't soil my soul with the likes of ye." An ethereal déjà vu memory forms on the edges of Ryan's conscious mind. Ere he can force a complete image into the open, James Sayers waves to Ryan and hurries into the street.

"A lady on my staff took your brave wife into the hotel to scrub that blood from her lovely dress before the stain sets. If you care to wait inside, be my guest. Anything you desire, it's on the house."

"Why, thank ye Mr. Sayers. Tea for three if ye please. I wish to thank my two benefactors."

"Very good, Mr. Warrain."

Ryan seeks out Billy as the onlookers disperse. The proud Taungurong returns Ryan's tomahawk, exhibiting a hint of a respectful bow. "Fraser right. You should kill him now."

"I can't. T'would not be honorable."

"Kangaroo Fighter has too much honor. Sometimes kill is best."

Ryan concedes Billy has a good point but the opportunity has passed. "Ye better take yer boss to a doctor."

"Not my boss now." Without explaining, he walks away.

Ryan strolls up to the two well-dressed strangers who earlier confiscated his opponents' pistols. To the taller of the two, Ryan says, "Ye are from Canada, I wager?"

"Yes. Henry Ross at your disposal. And this," Ross says, pointing to his companion, "is Alphonse Doudiet, though everyone calls him Charlie. We arrived yesterday."

"Ryan Warrain," he says, shaking both offered hands. "Come for the gold, did ye?"

"We came to earn our fortunes," replies Doudiet, with a trace of a French accent.

"Please join me in the café. I owe ye at least a cup of tea."

"Our pleasure," Doudiet replies.

Inside, Sayers takes their order for tea and scones. Ryan makes a closer examination of his guests. Both are dressed as gentlemen:

day jackets, tailored trousers, silk vests and puff ties. Their practical wide-brimmed slouch hats hang on the hat rack by the door. Ross sports a fob watch on a heavy gold chain. A six-footer, with broad-shoulders and a large chest, he fills his chair. He has aquamarine eyes, ivory skin, and lips feminine in shape and size. Doudiet is the same height as Ryan, but slimmer, with the thin-faced, dark, bookish aspect of an intellectual. Doudiet has tried to hide his youthful countenance with a mustache but the sparsity of brown whiskers defies him.

"You seem well established, Mr. Warrain," Ross says. "I assume you arrived years ago; what is your story?"

"Please call me Ryan, gentlemen," he says, pausing to pass Doudiet the sugar bowl. "I washed up on the south shore seven years past. I'd be dead if not for my wife and her Wathaurung family. When I returned to white society, my partner and I built up a haulage business. The hunt for gold has been a blessing for us."

"You were a shipwrecked sailor, then?" Ross inquires.

"Nay. I was a pardoned penal convict in Van Diemen's Land. I had no money to buy passage off that cursed island; so I built a rowboat. A storm hit me hard near the coast."

"I do not mean to pry. Please excuse my curiosity," Doudiet says. "Were you transported for some infraction in Ireland? Your accent implies your heritage."

"Nay. I was arrested in Canada for a part I played in the Battle of the Windmill in 1838. Ye may have heard of it."

"I vaguely recall that episode," Ross says. "My father was active in the Toronto militia and spoke often of the unrest."

"I was living in Switzerland," Doudiet says. "We came to Canada in 1844 when I was twelve. I can't recall the events of which you speak."

"'Tis perhaps better if people forget," Ryan replies, shrugging. "Did ye register a gold claim yet?" Ryan asks.

"Not yet," Ross says. "I have experience in prospecting from California. We must locate a promising spot to sink the first shovel."

"From our preliminary exploration, we found precious few alluvial plains near Ballarat not already claimed," Doudiet adds.

"If we do not unearth gold in short order, we may default on our monthly license fee obligations."

"We heard numerous complaints directed at the authorities and the gold commissioner," Ross says. "The sole purpose seems to be to extract as much gold from the diggers as possible."

"An eight-foot square claim costs sixty shillings per month," Doudiet explains, "the equivalent of an ounce of gold monthly. Anyone with a poor claim is driven out."

"I never encountered the level of discontent in California I witness daily here," Ross says.

"I didn't know 'twas so bad," Ryan replies. "We rarely deal directly with diggers."

Sayers interrupts their glum chatter, delivering a beaming Alinga to the table. The three men rise.

"Mr. Warrain. May I present your wife, with all evidence of her bloody encounter removed."

Alinga studies the two Canadians. They in turn seem captivated by her cheery smile and welcoming eyes.

"Alinga, let me introduce Henry Ross and Charlie Doudiet. They hail from Canada nigh where I once lived."

Alinga flits towards Ross and touches his elbow. "Henry a handsome man. Almost as pretty as my husband."

Ross blushes at Alinga's directness.

"Such an attractive man must have wife, yes?"

"Um…uh…no. Not yet."

Doudiet chuckles at his companion. "This is a first—Henry Ross tongue-tied by a woman."

"Everyone be seated. Let's order another pot of tea." Ryan pulls a chair out for Alinga, the way Ellen has coached him.

Doudiet fumbles in the interior of his duffle bag. He extracts a large pad and a pencil. He props the pad on the table edge and begins to sketch. Alinga, curious, observes the young man as one might a new species of mammal.

"Do ye and Charlie have all the kit ye need for prospecting?" Ryan asks.

"Yes. We are well provisioned with gear and work clothes. We undertake daily excursions on hired horses to scout the land. I am tempted by a creek valley north of Ballarat. We shall commence digging presently."

Doudiet flips his sketch to show his work. Alinga gasps and claps her hands. Charlie's likeness captures her innocent smile, alluring eyes, long lashes and dimples. He removes the sketch from the pad, rises, and with a bow offers it to Alinga.

"For the comely, dark southern sun, with my compliments."

"Please excuse my friend," Ross says, "he is a poet and a romantic."

"And an artist, I reckon," Ryan counters.

"What comely mean?" Alinga whispers to her husband.

"It means nice to look at."

Alinga addresses Doudiet. "Charlie also comely."

The men chuckle at her use of the word. Undeterred she continues. "Charlie must be the son of creator spirits to make this magic on paper."

"Hardly. Just a man."

"Then how did you know Alinga means sun?"

Doudiet shrugs. "A lucky pun, I assume."

Alinga tosses her head, causing hair to sway across her face. "Charlie is closer to the spirits than he admits."

"Well, my father is a Protestant minister. Maybe it rubbed off," he adds with a grin.

Ross slaps his friend on the back. "Ask God to help us find gold, eh Charlie?"

Doudiet and Ryan laugh at the remark.

"Can you recommend a reliable gunsmith?" Ross asks.

"I buy mine from William Mumby on the Main Road a few hundred yards north. Are ye expecting trouble?"

"Several diggers alerted us to the danger of bushrangers in the areas outlaying the main goldfields."

"One particularly vile bandit is alleged to—" Doudiet begins to say.

"Please, do not speak of bushrangers," Alinga interrupts. The day-to-night change in her expression—from laugh lines to a furrowed brow—stops Doudiet.

"I apologize," he says. "Such talk is not for delicate ears."

Ryan hides his surprise at his dingo-fierce wife's unexpected squeamishness.

"Henry and Charlie must visit," Alinga insists to Ryan.

"Aye. We enjoy a special meal midday every Sunday. Come and meet my partners and family."

"We would be delighted," Ross replies.

"Ride three miles south on the Geelong Road and turn at the lane by the sign saying Weeyn's Smithy."

"We look forward to it," Doudiet says.

*****

Alinga and Ryan linger at the table after their guests depart. Ryan fidgets with his teacup. His gaze roves the dining room, now empty of patrons.

"Something worries my husband?" Alinga says.

Ryan presses his lips together while he forms his response. "A few winters ago on a visit to yer family…when I first considered ye as a possible wife," he pauses to clear his throat, "I imagined what might happen if ye and I walked down the streets of Ballarat as husband and wife."

Alinga leans towards Ryan and slips her hand over his. Ryan ponders the striking color contrast of dark flesh on pale.

"Not all white men are as accommodating as Mr. Sayers and Mr. Robinson," Ryan continues. "I worry people might step off the sidewalk to avoid us or louts might yell insults."

Alinga's reply is non-verbal. She lifts her eyelids to make her eyes appear larger. Her smile expands to reveal a hint of her ivory teeth. Her shoulders shift back to expose additional cleavage.

Ryan grins. "Aye, I admit ye can charm koalas from treetops, but we may encounter a few staunch bigots."

"My husband worries too much. I fought beside Kangaroo Fighter today. I risked injury for you. All white people will know by now. They may not like my color but they will respect me for who I am."

Ryan shrugs. "Ye may be too optimistic."

Alinga stands and adjusts her dress. "Come. Show me the shops."

She slips her left arm under Ryan's right arm. Before stepping into the sunlit street, she makes sure her gold wedding band is on display. Ryan sets a casual pace along the wooden sidewalk. Alinga reads the expressions of everyone they pass coming from the opposite direction.

Ryan tips his hat to every woman. Unescorted women smile at him in return but rarely acknowledge Alinga beyond a furtive glance. She expects that reaction. Her tomboyish defense of Ryan earlier in the day makes her a wild outlier in their opinion—a separation perhaps more unbridgeable than her color.

Women accompanied by husbands or male escorts are another matter. To the wary stares of the ladies, Alinga dips her chin and feigns shyness. As the men greet Ryan, Alinga makes eye contact and adds a coquettish tilt of her head. In every case, she observes the man's pupils dilate and as they surrender to an instinctive impulse.

Alinga flirts not for her own aggrandizement. She wants every red-blooded man to envy her husband. The more admiration and respect Ryan attains through her, the stronger will be her position in the white world, she calculates.

A group of boys whisper and elbow each other in the ribs as they pass by. Alinga aims her smile at the eldest in the group. The lad's face flushes with a rush of pubescent hormones. His friends tease him and duck as he tries to swipe them with his backhand.

Ryan stops when greeted by a rotund, thirty-something man standing by the main door of the Charlie Napier Hotel. The one-and-a-half-story English-style inn is so new Alinga can smell the sap in the wooden siding.

"Good day to you, Mr. Warrain."

"Greetings Mr. Gibbs. Allow me to introduce my wife. This is Alinga," he pauses, and continues, "and Alinga, this is John Gibbs, proprietor of this establishment."

Gibbs regards Alinga with an ambiguous expression, part frown and part smile. "Yes…I heard of your…um…adventures today."

The huntress in Alinga exploits Gibbs' uneasiness the way a dingo preys on a limping bandicoot. "You must be very successful in business, Mr. Gibbs, judging by the quality of your attire."

She brushes her index finger over the gold brocade of his vest. His eyes track her slim digit in its two seconds of travel. Alinga retracts her arm and touches the same finger to her chin. In the way a subject of hypnotism fixates on the movements of a dangling watch, Gibbs follows her finger. As she expects, his gaze drops into the black pit between her breasts.

Gibbs blinks twice and coughs. His attention flits between Ryan and Alinga. "I had no idea your wife was so well spoken and…um…charming."

Alinga perceives her race is no longer a significant concern for Gibbs.

"Thank ye, John," Ryan says. "Excuse us. We have household items to purchase."

"Good-day, Mrs. Warrain," Gibbs calls.

Ryan directs Alinga across the dusty street to the Criterion Store, the main source of textile products in the area. "Watch yerself," Ryan says. "David Jones is a harder case."

They step into the dimly illuminated store. Alinga sucks in a startled breath at the floor to ceiling shelves stacked with colorful fabrics.

A slim man of Alinga's height appears from the rear of the shop and scowls at Ryan. Not looking at Alinga, he says, "Mr. Warrain, while no notice is posted by the door, I expect everyone to know my preferences when it comes to customers."

Alinga senses Ryan's rising anger in the stiffening of his shoulders and narrowing of his lips. She straightens her spine to lift her breasts. She graces Jones with a demure smile and says, "I was told you have the finest shop north of Melbourne and—"

"Please leave," he says.

Alinga snags Ryan's forearm to prevent any violent impulse. Jones shows no interest in her physical charms. This is an unexpected circumstance—a puzzle to ponder later. She delves into her repertoire of tricks. *When a smile fails, try tears.*

Alinga imagines her parents scolding her as a child. Her lips begin to quiver. Tears stream from her sockets.

"Now see what ye've done," Ryan shouts. He reaches out to throttle Jones. Alinga intercepts his hand.

"Do not hurt Mr. Jones," she mutters through sniffles. She turns her wet cheeks to Jones and continues, "I apologize for not knowing your rules." She swallows and wipes tears with a finger.

Jones plucks a handkerchief off a counter. "Here, Mrs. Warrain."

"Thank you for your kindness, Mr. Jones." She dabs her eyes. "I wanted to add a woman's touch to our house; so, naturally I came here." She pauses to inhale. "I am just an ignorant lubra but hoped someone of your good taste might help me pick items suiting a man of my husband's stature."

Alinga observes Jones mien as the eloquence and modesty of her remarks melt his resistance.

"Very well. Just this once," Jones says with an apologetic smile. "What items do you require?"

"A few essentials: curtains, table clothes, table napkins, linen sheets—all of the best quality, of course," she says.

Jones licks his upper lip in anticipation of a rich sale. "Of course. Come this way."

*****

"Put this one on the mantle," Alinga instructs Tarra, using both hands to pass one of the new lamps with a cut-glass body. To her brother, she adds with a wave, "Take away those old things."

Weeyn gathers the reliable old metal lamps. "We can use these in the workshops."

"And put that old chair in the bunkhouse."

Weeyn chuckles at his sister's crazed exuberance.

Tarra frowns at the room's transformation.

"Why do you seem angry, my sister friend?" Alinga asks.

«White men destroy the living beauty of the forest and then fill their big houses with these dead things of color and glitter.»

Weeyn rolls his eyes and hurries away with an armload of old items.

Alinga kisses Tarra's forehead and hugs her. "I know you miss the forest. Tomorrow we will search for roots like the old days."

Tarra returns a weak smile. "I will check on the dinner."

Alinga evaluates every detail of the ranch house's main room and dining alcove. Yearn and Maya plod after her in their soft linen nappies, chattering in simple Wadawurrung. Six new lamps sparkle even without the wicks lit. She has placed them above a toddler's reach. The largest lamp hangs like a chandelier from a horizontal roof beam that spans the wide room.

Two brocaded stuffed chairs now perch near the fireplace. Embroidered linen adorns the dining table. Yearn snags a corner and for a moment threatens to topple Alinga's symmetrically laid table settings. Alinga scoops the boy and dangles him by his feet. He shrieks with joy. She swings him in front of the large, picture window, now framed with satin drapes in a rich burgundy shade. Ryan was generous to a point in Ballarat. He declined the four-poster bed but did agree to linen sheets and every other material desire.

"Sister," Alinga calls to Tarra through the door into the summer kitchen, "is the roast cooked?"

"It will be ready soon, sister."

"And potatoes?"

"Yes. Brown like Warrain likes."

Stephen enters through the rear door carrying a crock of flour towards the kitchen.

"Are your boots clean?" Alinga barks.

"Aye major. I brushed them off on the stoop."

"And no cooking."

"The mayor is overruled by the general. Ryan wants Yorkshire pudding for our guests and neither of you dark lovelies can make it."

Ellen enters through the front door. Maya waddles up to her, chanting in baby English, "Auntie, auntie." Holding the child in one arm, Ellen inspects the dining table. She tips her head in approval, setting her orange-gold curls swinging. Maya pulls one strand into her mouth and chews it with pearly teeth. Ellen refolds one linen napkin, oblivious to the cold glare from Alinga.

"One could imagine we are entertaining a head of state today," Ellen says. "Are our Canadian guests landed gentry?"

"I do not understand what is gentry. My husband needs more white friends," Alinga explains. "We will make them feel honored." She steps closer to the older woman. "Let Alinga see your face."

Alinga grabs Ellen's chin with her thumb and forefinger. Ignoring her teacher's startled expression, she examines every detail of Ellen's facial features.

"Your eyebrows are invisible," Alinga states.

"There is nothing wrong with my eyebrows, thank you."

"Mrs. Ellen must look her prettiest today. Come to the kitchen."

Ellen balks at the command but gives in to Alinga's tug on her wrist. In the kitchen, the teenage Wathaurung grinds and mixes beeswax and powdered ocher in a mortar.

"What concoction is that?" Ellen asks. "I am not another ornament to be polished."

"Do not worry, Mrs. Ellen. My people mastered the art of body painting. If you do not like, you can wash it. Stand still."

With a thin horsehair brush, Alinga applies the homemade makeup to Ellen's eyebrows, making the once invisible hairs a vibrant auburn to complement her hair color.

"Close your eyes. Keep them shut," Alinga commands.

She darkens Ellen's lashes with the same mixture and combs the fine hairs apart with the fibrous ends of a crushed twig. Tarra passes Ellen a folding mirror—Ryan's long-ago present to Alinga.

Ellen's expression relaxes. "Oh my!" She returns the mirror. "Why are you so concerned with my appearance?"

"A pretty man named Ross visits us today."

"Do not refer to a man as pretty unless he looks like a woman. Men are called handsome."

"You wait. You will see," Alinga says.

Weeyn sticks his head inside the door. "Two horses coming." He ducks out.

"Let us greet our guests of honor," Ellen says.

"Wait," Alinga calls. "Give Maya to Tarra. Do not look like a grandmother today."

"Thirty is not a grandmother's age!"

"It is with our people," Tarra says.

"Our handsome guest is young," Alinga adds. "You need to look younger."

"Alinga! Are you playing matchmaker?"

Alinga ignores Ellen's tone and replies with her usual innocent honesty. "You deserve a man other than my husband to dream about."

Ellen's already erect posture stiffens. Her lips twitch. She passes Maya to Tarra. She folds her empty hands and composes herself and her next remark. "Directness such as yours, while refreshing to some, is not always a welcome social grace. We will work on conversational subtlety at our next lesson."

Tarra intervenes. "You dingoes no growl. Smile. We must charm our visitors."

Outside, Ross and Doudiet dismount. While two of Alinga's young cousins lead the horses to the stable, Ryan introduces Weeyn.

The women sashay onto the porch. The four men, led by Ryan, amble over and halt at the porch steps.

"And here are my family and other partners," he says to the guests. "Alinga ye know. That is our son Yearn in her arms. To her left are Weeyn's wife and daughter, Tarra and Maya. On the right is my friend and partner in our import business, Mrs. Ellen O'Sullivan.

Alinga catches the hint of a reflexive twitch from Ellen at the word misses.

"Stephen!" Ryan shouts.

"I be coming," replies a muffled voice from the house. Stephen steps out, dipping his head as usual. He tries to rub a blotch of flour from his shirt.

"And this is my partner in all our enterprises, Stephen McNichol." Motioning to his two guests, Ryan continues. "And these Canadian lads are Charlie Doudiet and Henry Ross."

"I say, Ryan," Ross begins, "you seem to have surrounded yourself with the best-looking women in Australia."

Alinga observes Ross' vision sweep across all porch occupants and settle on Ellen.

"How soon to dinner?" Ryan says.

"Twenty minutes," Stephen replies. "As soon as I finish the pudding." He disappears into the house.

"Great! Time for a tour. Follow me."

When the men are beyond hearing range, Ellen says to Alinga, "You accurately described Mr. Ross as pretty."

"He thought the same of you," Alinga counters.

"You anticipated his reaction. How could you know?"

"No white woman is more beautiful than Mrs. Ellen. Mr. Ross is beautiful. Pretty always likes pretty best."

"Did you notice who the little one's eye could not resist?" Tarra says.

"I observed," Ellen responds, "Charlie is infatuated with our Alinga."

*****

At dinner, Ryan settles in his high-backed chair at the table head. He observes his guests and eavesdrops on their chatter. On his left are Tarra, Henry and Alinga. On his right are Weeyn, Ellen and Charlie. Stephen's bulk looms over the opposite end.

Weeyn and Tarra chat in Wadawurrung. The topics are domestic issues. Weeyn's hope for a son dominates his conversation. Tarra says little in response.

Charlie regales Stephen and Alinga with stories of his youth in Switzerland and grand descriptions of alpine meadows. The young man's attention rarely strays from Alinga. Ryan accepts that Doudiet finds Alinga, four years his junior, an object of adoration. What Charlie cannot fathom is Alinga's life experience puts her a decade past him in maturity. Knowing Alinga's fearsome loyalty, Ryan has no cause to worry.

Ellen is another matter. She follows Ross' every word. He talks of growing up the eleventh child of a dozen in Toronto. Despite limited means—his father being a tailor—he managed to get a solid education. Living on the edge of Canadian wilderness drew out his adventurous spirit. In 1849, he departed for California to prospect for gold. Hard work yielded dust and nuggets in quantities sufficient to cover expenses and no more. Now after three years, he is chasing the golden phantom in Australia. At twenty-three, he claims this is his last stab at prospecting.

Ross addresses most remarks to Ellen. She leans forward, creating a more intimate space. Ryan has not seen her this radiant since the day he sang for her in Buninyong. He admits to jealousy and knows he has no right.

Weeyn taps Ryan's foot under the table. «Belongs-to-the-sea must talk. You are arweat of this table. Keep the feast moving.»

Ryan acknowledges Weeyn's advice with a nod. "Ladies and gentlemen—anyone for another slice of beef or pudding?"

The response is as expected, no takers and all side conversations cease.

"Let's clear the plates and serve dessert. 'Tis a local favorite—quandong pie." Alinga and Tarra rise at Ryan's signal.

"Not for me, please Ryan," says Ellen, "but I recommend it to our guests." she glances at Ross. "It is a local fruit tasting much like apricots with a hint of rhubarb."

"Nary of us drink spirits," Ryan begins, "but Stephen and I keep a few bottles for guests, if Henry or Charlie would care for something stronger than tea."

"We have sherry and port," Stephen offers, "and whisky from America and Scotland."

Doudiet replies, "I'd fancy a drop of port, if you please."

"I developed a fondness for bourbon in California; so the American whisky would be grand," Ross says.

Ryan rises to fill the request.

"Bring me a scotch, please," Ellen says.

Ryan halts, puzzled. "Five years I've known ye and not a drop of liquor passed yer lips."

"I do not imbibe while here, dear Ryan, because a lady should not drink by herself. I have companions for compotation on this occasion."

"As the lady wishes." Ryan regrets the tone of his voice.

*****

After dessert, the hosts and guests adjourn to chairs on the porch. A spring wind wafts floral scents into the house through the open door. Ross and Doudiet go first. Alinga slips up behind Ellen and whispers, "Hold back a second."

Without acknowledging the command, Ellen dawdles until everyone else steps outside. She arches a questioning brow at Alinga.

"Does Mrs. Ellen desire time alone with Mr. Pretty?" asks the girl.

Ellen rolls her eyes in disbelief, all the while smiling. "You are perceptive beyond your years."

"Watch for a chance," Alinga says.

Outside Stephen, Henry and Ryan chat on the porch.

"You said you run wagons from Ballarat to Geelong," Ross says, "but is that the full extent of your routes?"

"Nay," Stephen replies. "We run the occasional load north to Bendigo when there be demand. In dry months, we make at least one weekly trip southeast to Melbourne."

"Could you accommodate passengers on the next freight wagon to Bendigo?"

"For ye and Charlie?"

"Yes. We intend to stake our claim a few miles south of there."

"Two days from now, Polligerry will drive to Bendigo with imported goods," Ryan explains. "Ye two can hitch a ride. I'll arrange for him to stop at yer hotel."

Alinga hooks Ryan's hand. "Come. Charlie says he will make a picture of us. We must stand in front of the house."

Doudiet reclines on a chair in the compound facing the house. His pad and pencil are at the ready. He directs Ryan and Alinga into position. Yearn rests in his father's arms.

"Now remain still," says Doudiet.

Weeyn watches over Doudiet's shoulder as he sketches. Alinga has her back to the house and cannot see if Ellen has taken her cue. Instead, she reads Weeyn's expressions to discern events behind her. The faint smirk on her brother's lips answers her question. Ellen and Ross have slipped into the house.

*****

Two hours before sunset, Ross and Doudiet depart after heaping lavish praise on their six hosts. Circumstance places Ryan and Ellen alone on the porch.

"Ye were taken with our new friend Henry, 'twas plain to see."

"Yes," Ellen says, with a tilt of her head. "I made no attempt to hide it. Pity I am not ten years younger."

"'Tis not yer age that impedes a grand beauty such as ye. It be yer husband."

Ellen replies with a wordless, nondescript humming.

"Ye did tell him?"

"Henry is aware of my marital status—not that it is any of your affair."

Weeyn's Test

June 1853

Weeyn shivers as his horse plods up the outlying grades of the pass leading into the rocky hills the white men call the Pyrenees. No other humans disturb the troops of kangaroos, flocks of emu and the occasional scurrying bandicoot. The cold wind tumbling from the snow-edged heights chills him in the saddle. He'd rather hike and generate some body heat, but by riding the big bay, he cuts his traveling time by several days. The demands of his smithy prevent a long visit.

By a meandering stream in a sheltered valley, he discovers his family's camp among widely spaced gum trees. His parents are alive and well, but have aged. Laarr's brawny chest muscles now sag and all his hair is gray. Mokborree walks with a noticeable stoop. The elders who formed the generational bridge when Weeyn grew up have passed on to Dreamtime. All young men and youths now work for whites and visit their wives and family on occasional furloughs.

Weeyn passes out the dozen wool blankets he brought and settles by the fire with his parents.

«You found a good camp this year,» Weeyn says.

«We are blessed that few whites covet this place yet,» Laarr replies. «The spirits provide much game for our stomachs but it is a cold place.»

«Has your sister forgotten us?» Mokborree asks.

«Sun speaks of you often, mother. She promises to visit soon with her son.»

«Have you a son yet?» Laarr asks.

«Only a daughter. White and I pray to the spirits for a son.»

«We miss the visits from Belongs-to-the sea,» Mokborree says. «Is he ashamed of his in-laws?»

«He honors us daily with his generosity and fair dealing. Wathaurung men learn skills that give them a place in the new world. My wealth now surpasses many white men.»

Laarr waves his right hand. «That is a wise path to the future.»

«A man of wealth can afford more wives,» Mokborree states. «I can find you a young maiden who will give you sons.»

Weeyn waves off the idea. He has no intention of adding to his marital tensions by insulting Tarra with a second wife. To Laarr, he says, «I look forward to a hunt tomorrow. It is too long since I walked the land as a Wathaurung hunter.»

«Because we are few, we hunt with the family of Spark.»

«You mean the brother of Smoke?»

«Yes.»

«Smoke has joined his ancestors?»

«Yes.»

*****

Restless dreams nudge Weeyn awake well before the tardy winter dawn. He rises and slips from his parents' mia-mia. For the first time in three years, starlight bathes his unclothed body. He trembles with cold. The soles of his boot-coddled feet have shed their calluses and he is now at the mercy of every thorn and sharp pebble.

He misses the simple pleasures of his former bush life and the oneness with his ancestors that comes from respecting the creator's seasons and cycles. But Weeyn has no illusions about the future or his place in it. The rapid pace of white expansion threatens to soon displace all the nomadic clans. Weeyn made this visit—this pilgrimage—to his family to renew his bond with the land while he still can.

He begins to jog along the rough path beside the creek. A half moon lights his way. The cold numbs his feet to the assault of sharp stones. He runs faster. The effort warms his flesh. He leaps over boulders in his path, pushing his leg muscles to a level they have not gone in years. He sprints up hills. His breath wheezes but he does not slow. Perspiration wets his brow and armpits.

Yet still he runs. He must pay a price for adopting the soft ways of the white world. Through pain he will rediscover his warrior spirit.

His lungs now burn with effort. Saliva thickens in his throat. He hacks and spits to clear it. The long muscles in his legs ache and beg him to stop. He continues his race.

He vaults a fallen gum tree. His trailing foot catches the protruding edge of a branch. He tumbles, tucking his chin to his chest. Arms forward, he guides his fall. He somersaults across a pile of branches and stones that nip and gouge his skin. He returns to his feet with barely a pause in the rhythm. Multiple pains speak of a sprained toe and lacerations.

The growing oxygen deficit distorts his senses. The night grows brighter and the shadows sharper and darker. Weeyn is no longer running alone. Beside him lopes a young Loklok. The apparition mocks Weeyn with laughter and surges ahead, opening up a lead.

Loklok's doppelganger glances over his shoulder at Weeyn and points ahead to a hill. Silhouetted against the setting moon, an old gum tree rises from the hill's summit. Loklok has chosen the finish line for the race.

Weeyn seeks in himself the untamed core that sets his people apart from the whites who have lived too long with creature comforts. The Wathaurung are like dingoes to the white man's pet hounds. He pushes his tapped-out body harder, closing inch-by-inch the gap with Loklok.

Like stepping from a darkened hut into bright sunshine, his world changes. Weeyn now gallops across the land on four legs. His front paws grip the ground first, his rear legs swing forward until they come even with his front paws, and then all four legs push off. He sails above the ground, his body stretching to his maximum, front claws reaching ahead, rear legs horizontal behind. In a cycle, the four limbs retract, come together, contact the ground and again fling his body into space.

Weeyn gallops past Loklok, who fades and vanishes. The dingo spirit bounds up the hill. At the tree base, the canine launches into the lower branches. His body morphs into a possum. The marsupial spirit clambers through the branches towards the leafy peak.

Weeyn clutches the slender upper tree trunk with his knees. His face to the sky, he raises his fists and emits a modulating howl.

High on the rocky shelves of adjacent hills, dingoes return the call of a brother.

*****

Weeyn returns to camp and joins the four hunters eating beside the fire. Laarr tilts his head to scrutinize the plethora of bruises, scrapes and cuts on his son, but says nothing. Sooner than Weeyn likes, the hunters rise and march upstream. His muscles beg for rest but he refuses to listen.

Dyeelaga and his men, six in all, cross the valley and join them. The two arweats arrange themselves and the other nine men in a long flushing line. While they march, they clank spear shafts together, setting a marching beat.

Weeyn's position is next to the only other young man in the hunting party. A lad he recognizes from a past corroboree as Dyeelaga's eldest son Nalong, now a brawny youth of sixteen. Weeyn eases closer. «Does Eagle know his father is dead?»

«The day after we buried Smoke, I found a dead raven impaled on a spear atop his grave.»

«Has anyone seen him?» says Weeyn.

«Only I.» An echidna darts across Nalong's path. He ignores it. They are after bigger game.

«Where is he?» Weeyn talks while his eyes rove the bush ahead.

«He hides in a cave nearby. Many white men hunt for him.»

«Will he leave to kill soon?»

«Yes. When the white men grow tired, they will go home. Then he will leave. And so will I.»

«Why?» Weeyn takes a quick glance at his companion.

«Eagle pledges to harm Belongs-to-the-sea. I do not know when. I will follow him and I *will* stop him.»

Weeyn frowns. «You cannot fight Eagle alone. There is no better Wathaurung warrior in this life.»

«It is my destiny. I must try,» Nalong insists.

A wombat breaks from cover. Both men chuck long spears. Weeyn's pierces a hind leg, wounding the beast. Nalong's weapon rips a mortal wound in its neck. Weeyn curses under his breath at his poor aim.

«You and I should stop Eagle now,» Weeyn says.

Nalong considers the idea. «Together we could defeat him, yes,» he exclaims.

«Tomorrow morning, we will hunt him down,» Weeyn says. By waiting a day, Weeyn can rest his muscles and practice throwing his spear.

*****

At the predawn meal the next day, Weeyn tells Laarr of his intention to hunt for Loklok. Laarr's brow furrows. «Eagle is a great warrior. He may defeat both of you.»

«Join us, father. Eagle is killing white men. He will bring down their wrath on all our people.»

Laarr stares into the fire's coals and replies, «Yes.»

Laarr discusses Weeyn's idea with his men. They listen, they nod, and they ask no questions. In the end, Laarr and his brother Murrangurk agree to help hunt Loklok, while the other two guard the camp.

An hour later, the four Wathaurung hunters wait in a thick grove of gum trees and shrubs. Up the slope is a narrow cave where Nalong last tracked Loklok. When the sun rises, light will flood the entrance. They plan to rush the opening with the sun at their backs and hope the glare distracts their quarry.

Each man carries a metal-tipped daar, a keerram carved from hard gum wood, and a koorr. Weeyn also has a steel-bladed tomahawk hanging at his waist.

Loklok steps from his cave and basks for a moment in the new sun's golden glow. «Is a troop of kangaroos making all that noise,» he calls, «or have some fools come to die?»

Loklok wears white man trousers, boots and a sheepskin coat. At Loklok's side, he dangles a thick koorr. He conceals his right hand inside his coat. Weeyn concludes by Loklok's attire he too has adapted to white living and may have softened. He grasps in a flash what Loklok is hiding.

«He has a gun! Throw now!»

Four daar arch across the sixty-foot span to Loklok. In the same blink of time, Loklok pulls his Colt and fires three shots. His first bullet hits Murrangurk and the second slams into Laarr. The third shot, meant for Nalong, misses. Weeyn's spear—the single lance to hit its target over the long distance—clips Loklok's right arm and dislodges the pistol from his grip. It slides down the slope.

Nalong and Weeyn sprint up the hill from two directions, their keerrams forward in defense and their koorrs held high for striking. In a maneuver designed to even the odds, Loklok ignores Weeyn and charges the less experienced youth. One strike with his koorr knocks aside Nalong's weapon. On the back swing, Loklok's koorr grazes Nalong's skull, knocking him prostrate in a swoon.

Loklok picks up a spent daar and holds it to Nalong's neck. Loklok's chest heaves from his efforts. It confirms Weeyn's earlier suspicion—the great warrior is out of shape, probably from long periods in hiding. His glorious reputation is a sham.

Loklok feigns a smile. "Weeyn, dear boy. How good to see you. Too bad we meet in such unfriendly circumstances."

"I will kill you and feed you to the dingoes."

Weeyn beholds a new expression on Loklok—worry. Weeyn's warrior skills have waned but working as a blacksmith has bulked up his arms and chest to a mass rivaling Laarr in his best days. In close combat, Weeyn believes he now has the advantage over Loklok.

"You have a choice," Loklok says. "You can fight me and perhaps best me, but I will kill this boy first. Or you can stand down. I give you my word as a warrior not to harm my foolish cousin if you promise to the spirits not to follow me."

A moan rises from behind Weeyn.

"Your father is alive. His life depends on help without delay. Make your choice, Weeyn."

"I give you until dawn tomorrow. After, I make no promises," Weeyn hisses.

"I accept." Loklok rests the spear on his shoulder. "Give my regards to Warrain." He jogs into the forest.

Weeyn attends to his fallen comrades. Nalong is woozy with a mild concussion. Blood trickles from his hair. A bullet has passed though Laarr below his shoulder. Murrangurk lies on his back, his pupils murky and unfocussed. A red hole above his nose oozes a trickle of blood.

"Nalong," Weeyn calls. "On your feet, warrior."

The youth pushes himself to his knees and rises on wobbly legs.

"Go to the camp and bring help. I will stay in case Loklok returns."

"Where is he?"

"I will explain in time. Go now. I order it!" Weeyn's command galvanizes the youth. He bows his head and trots down the valley trail.

Weeyn's family arrives when the sun reaches mid-sky. The thin line of people saddens him. The robust, multi-generational family he grew up with now consists of Laarr, two other middle-aged men, seven wives or widows, and six children.

Mokborree, now the most senior woman, cleans Laarr's wound and applies a poultice. She brags she has fixed worse wounds on her husband and he always recovered. Her optimism brings a moment of cheer.

Weeyn helps dig a grave. The women prepare Murrangurk's body. His two wives wail. Tarra's son Lakorra sheds silent tears for Murrangurk, the only father figure in his life. Weeyn does not reach out to comfort his young cousin. The memory of Lakorra's birth father holds Weeyn at bay.

The men lower Murrangurk into the earth. Dyeelaga arrives and places a tomahawk in the grave. His women folk pass out food they carried in bowls. Weeyn thanks Tarra's aging mother for the nourishment.

Nalong slips next to Weeyn. In English, he asks, "Where is Loklok?"

Weeyn explains his deal to save Nalong.

"He must be followed."

"I cannot help until sunrise."

"I made no such promise." He whirls to leave but teeters from dizziness.

"You are not fit to follow," Weeyn says, reaching to steady the youth. "Let him go. We will hunt him another time."

*****

Weeyn returns to the station sooner than expected, heavy with the messages he carries. Ryan, Alinga, Tarra and Stephen greet him on the porch. Their cheery expressions fade at the sight of their friend's dreary countenance.

"What has happened to ye?" Ryan says.

"We confronted Loklok. He wounded Laarr and killed Murrangurk," Weeyn says.

Alinga gasps. Tarra shows no emotion.

"There is more I must tell you about Loklok."

Alinga wiggles her fingers, a signal to her brother to not divulge their secret.

To Alinga, Weeyn says, "The stories must be told."

"Step inside, and let's hear it," Ryan says, holding the door for his friend.

*****

"I can't believe I nary heard about those killings," Ryan says, as he paces the room. "I best get into town more often."

"I heard about the killings," Stephen begins, "but I did not connect them to Loklok." Stephen fills a parlor chair, with his massive hands gripping the armrests.

"Ye all knew?" Ryan says, sweeping an arm past Weeyn, Tarra, and Alinga.

"Yes," Weeyn says. "So did all workers on this station. We kept it from you and Stephen because we did not want you to chase after him. You have businesses to run."

"Do not be angry, husband," Alinga says. "We hoped the soldiers or constables would get him."

"What should we do?" Ryan says, directing his question to Stephen.

"About Loklok or about our secretive friends?" Stephen replies, flexing his furrowed brow.

"We can't condemn friends for trying to protect us, even if they are wrong," Ryan answers. "We can post a bounty for Loklok. Maybe 'twill help."

"How much?"

"Two hundred pounds. That ought to get men's attention," Ryan says.

*****

When Weeyn escorts Tarra to their house, she balks at going inside. "I want to sit here," she points to a porch chair. "Tell me about your visit. How is my son? Is my mother well?"

"That news can be told by the fire inside instead of on this cold porch," he replies.

"I am closer to my family and ancestors outside. You know that," Tarra says. She drops into a chair and crosses her arms, daring Weeyn to argue.

Weeyn leans against a porch support column. "Lakorra is growing. He helps gather nuts and roots now and practices daily with a spear. Your mother has stiff joints but seems well. Dyeelaga cares for her. She said to say she thinks of you often."

Tarra nods her head, satisfied by the report.

"Now, can we go inside?"

"You go. I will sleep here to be closer to the spirits," she replies.

"Did you sleep outside while I was gone, even though I asked you not to?"

"It is not your place to separate me from the spirits," she says, crossing her legs.

Weeyn sighs. "Where have the spirits been for the last ten years when the clans fell before the white whirlwind?"

Tarra jumps up and slaps Weeyn on his chest. "Do not mock the spirits. They are all we have left."

Weeyn throws up his arms in resignation. "Stay here with your spirits. I am going to bed."

She grabs his shirt with both hands. "Now that Murrangurk is dead, we could return." She wraps her arms around Weeyn's waist and kisses his chin. "I want to make love again under the trees and frighten the cockatoos with our passion."

"We can visit," Weeyn says. Startled by her rare display of affection and desire, he will promise anything.

*****

August 1853

"Do any of ye have new ideas?" Ryan asks at the close of the Sunday meal.

"We could increase the reward," Stephen suggests. "Perhaps it will encourage a better class of bounty hunter."

Ryan does not reply. He doubts the idea's value but chooses not to argue. After two months, no one has claimed the generous reward promised for the capture or killing of Loklok. Hundreds of miners down on their luck accepted the challenge. None caught a glimpse of their quarry. They grumble it is easier to find gold.

Yet, Loklok has shown himself to Ryan's native workers. Sometimes, his face smiles in their direction from within a group of men. Often he is a lone figure perched on a hillock along a haulage route—always beyond pistol range.

Loklok has stopped killing and mutilating white shepherds and drovers. Weeyn suggests Loklok has made his point and now will avoid being hunted by angry hordes of white men. Ryan agrees but expects Loklok to strike again in a different manner.

"Polligerry," Ryan says to his foreman, "give every driver weekly target practice. I worry Loklok may start attacking our crews next."

"Yes, Warrain."

"I am surprised," Ryan continues, "that Officer Billy has not gone after Loklok."

"Warrain must ask Billy," Polligerry says.

"I'll keep yer advice in mind."

Ryan deliberates on the chair Ellen usually occupies, wondering if she might offer insights, if present. She rarely visits. When she does, Ryan never asks for an explanation. She doesn't offer one.

Partings

August 1854

A wail pierces Ryan's sleep. In the weird way the mind sometimes incorporates outside noises into the dream world, Ryan, for a moment, is in Ireland. He cowers under bed sheets while his mother relates old folk tales and moans like a banshee spirit.

He jerks from slumber into wakefulness. But the mournful lament continues. In the predawn twilight, he spies Alinga's dark form upright in bed. It is she emitting the anguished howl.

He reaches to embrace and comfort her. She dodges his arm and leaps from bed. With her arms hugging her chest, she paces in a circle, sobbing.

"Alinga, lass. 'Tis a nightmare. Come to bed."

"Amadeat know nothing!" She stomps out and into the main room.

It is the first time Alinga has applied that pejorative term to him in anger. Ryan slips his legs into a pair of trousers and follows her. She has plopped down on the divan and is pounding the padded seat with her fists. He reaches out to her.

"Stay away!" she shouts.

Ryan feeds wood into the fireplace and coaxes embers into flames to brighten the immediate area. He drops into a high-backed chair opposite, speechless. He's not witnessed this side of Alinga before.

Her anger dissipates into convulsive sobs. He now understands, it was no ordinary dark dream—it was a vision.

The rear door rattles open. Tarra arrives to start breakfast. She bolts to her friend's side and hugs Alinga's shoulders. They whisper in Wadawurrung.

"Can someone tell me—" Ryan begins.

"No!" Tarra barks. "Wait!" She helps Alinga to her feet and guides her to the bedroom.

"I need a shirt, if 'tis possible," Ryan bellows from his seat. His work shirt sails across the room and engulfs his head.

"Much obliged," he mutters.

Weeyn enters the room and glances towards the bedroom. "Why is my sister crying?"

Ryan relates the recent events.

"It must be a bad dream," Weeyn comments.

"Can ye find out what it is?"

"No," Weeyn replies. "Dawn arrives when it is ready."

"Damn. Ye be speaking in parables now."

Weeyn ignores him and begins making coffee. "Can you still fry eggs?"

"Aye."

"I'll take two, please."

Faced with his entire morning topsy-turvy, Ryan gives in. "Would ye like toast with yer eggs, brother?"

*****

Alinga and Tarra skip breakfast and ensconce themselves on a treed hillock a twenty-minute walk from the compound. Ryan dispatches Gellibrand to guard them. His orders are to protect but not interfere.

The teenage wives build a fire against late winter's damp chill. They shed their manufactured garments for two old possum shoulder wraps. Cross-legged and holding hands, they chat. For hours, they avoid the topic of conversation that drove them to the secluded grove of gum trees.

They recall the joys of bush life, the colorful birds, the fragrant flowers, and the savory tastes of various meat dishes, wild nuts and tubers. They speak of the tight family bonds and the sense of being safe in the care of their warrior siblings and cousins. In hushed tones, they try to describe the spiritual connection they have with the wild world, where Dreamtime governs the relationship humans have to the land and all creatures. Both young women tell stories about witnessing the spirits in storms, ravens and rainbows. They recount tales passed down from elders.

Sometime after midday, Alinga tells the story of her first visit to Dreamtime. «In my fourth summer, I dreamt myself surrounded by dingoes. The image was so vivid, I awoke screaming in the belief wild beasts had kidnapped me. Father soothed my fear and explained the gift of dreaming.»

Tarra, who never dreams to Alinga's level, in turn explains her connection to the spirit world.

«Good spirits walk across the lands invisible to us. Since a child, I could feel their presence and believed they protected me from danger and evil. The house of my white father cut me off from them. I felt alone and he scolded me when I cried.»

«Do they still visit you?» Alinga says.

«Yes, but never inside any building made by a white man. I walk under the sky and sleep under the stars as often as I can.»

«I pity Belongs-to-the-sea and other whites for being blind and deaf to the spirits,» Alinga says. «Their God does not serve them well, except Mr. Stephen.»

«We must return to our people,» Tarra begins, «to give our children a chance to connect to the Dreaming. Our unborn deserve to start life in a world where our ancestors will rejoice at their arrival.»

Alinga purses her lips.

«You do not agree?» Tarra says, letting go of Alinga's hand.

«The old ways are dying. We need to accept the white world and its ways.»

«You would prefer being a sheep to a dingo?» Tarra says, rolling her eyes.

«I will be content as a sheep for my husband. The spirits pushed us together. It must be their plan for me.»

Tarra wags a finger at Alinga. «Are we not confined by the white man's clothes, and houses and living always in one place?»

Alinga smiles. «Our home is warm and dry when the weather is cold and wet. We have curtains and rugs in rich colors and comfortable furniture. Your husband runs a business. He may become the wealthiest black man in this country. The white man's ways are not all bad.»

«But what about our children? Will we deny them their culture and grandparents?» Tarra asks. «I want to see my mother and son again. Fire promised to take me for a visit but that was a year ago.»

Alinga pokes a stick into the embers and ponders her friend's words. Tarra closes her eyes and waits. Clouds scud across the sun. A sprinkle of rain sweeps the swale and reaches into their leafy refuge. Neither woman shows annoyance or discomfort. Clouds, sun, and rain are favors from the spirits.

«I have made my decision,» Alinga says.

*****

The young women reappear in the house and prepare the evening meal, as if nothing happened. Unable to contain his curiosity, Ryan blurts, "Alinga, what did ye—"

Weeyn grips Ryan's shoulder. "Not yet."

Ryan groans and stomps outside to busy himself in the cooperage, scattering chickens as he strides across the compound.

Supper unfolds in near silence. Stephen, who is unaware of the storm Alinga's dream caused, attempts conversation. He makes remarks no one acknowledges and asks questions that elicit shrugs.

After the main course, he slaps his palm on the table. "Can someone please include me in whatever intrigue dominates this bloody household tonight?"

Stephen delivers the rare cuss with vehemence only a Scots burr can muster. It jars his four mates.

Tarra and Alinga exchange looks. Alinga shifts in her chair. "I am sorry kind Stephen," she says. "We," she points to Tarra, "made a decision. We must go back to our people—back to the land."

"Your home is here!" Weeyn says.

"Why?" Ryan demands.

"Last night," Alinga says, sucking in a ragged breath, "I had a vision. All my life, I appear as a dingo in Dreamtime. Last night, I was a…a sheep. My two children were lambs. The spirits mock me because I abandoned them. I will accept sheep dreams as the price for loving my husband. But I will take my son to discover his true spirit while he can."

"You dreamed two children?" Ryan asks.

"Yes, husband," Alinga says. "I am with child."

"I also," Tarra adds.

Weeyn reaches out and holds his wife's hand, "A son this time." Tarra shrugs.

"How long will you be gone?" Stephen says.

"Until our children are born," Alinga says.

"Maybe longer," Tarra adds.

Alinga shoots Tarra a questioning look but says nothing.

"Ye can't go. We can't protect ye afar. I forbid it," Ryan states, standing for emphasis.

"Alinga loves Warrain," she says, "but he cannot stop this thing."

"Then I'll come with ye," Ryan says.

"And me," Weeyn adds.

"It might ruin us," Stephen remarks, "but I understand the compulsion."

"Do not treat us like children or property," Tarra says, standing. "Our people will protect us. They always have. My husband should know this."

Weeyn slumps in his chair. "Yes. With Murrangurk dead, no one will harm you."

"This may be opportune," Stephen says. "Cholera be prevalent in the mining shanties. I expect it will spread with the warm weather. They may be safer away."

Alinga slips her arms around Ryan's neck. "My husband may journey with me but must not stay."

"I will stay with them," Weeyn offers. "Do not worry, Warrain."

"When do ye depart?"

"Within five days. Before our family walks to the sea," Alinga answers.

"'Twill be grand to visit Laarr and Mokborree for a few days, but lass, I'll miss ye and wee Yearn terribly after I leave."

*****

October 1854

Stephen hums in the kitchen as he prepares a special supper. Ryan whistles while he sets the main table. After a long absence, the table boasts a clean and ironed cover. China plates supplant the men's dented tin settings. With the women absent, Ryan and Stephen had canceled the formal Sunday meal and returned to old bachelor habits. But, they received a note yesterday saying Ellen plans to visit.

Ellen arrives alone in a buggy at midday adorned in a floral dress and shawl befitting the cozy spring weather. Ryan hangs back while Stephen helps her from the high seat. "Ellen, how we missed your delightful presence."

"You are so kind, Stephen. I missed your cheery manner."

Despite the upbeat tone of her voice, Ryan recognizes underlying tension. Hers is not a social visit. While Stephen finishes the last dinner preparations, Ryan shows her to the divan. "Do ye care for a sherry? Ye can drink solo. 'Tis only Stephen and me that'll know."

"Why, yes. Please."

He pours the amber liquor into a small crystal glass, passes it to Ellen and occupies the chair opposite. As she sips the sherry, he submits to her intoxicating allure. Her orange locks and green irises still dazzle him. She seems not to age. Her form is that of a younger woman.

She lifts her gaze to meet his. He spies worry lines under her eyes.

"Yer thoughts are heavy, I can see," Ryan says.

"How perceptive." She sips her sherry. "I fear for Henry and to a lesser extent for Charlie."

"Does the gold elude them?"

"Lady Fortune has blessed both with the luck to meet expenses and pay the exorbitant license fees. I am worried concerning their involvement in the rising political tensions."

"Is it getting out of hand?"

"The gold commissioner is behaving like a despot. He sends gangs of ruffians to collect the license fees. The commissioner's friends win lucrative contracts and literally get away with murder."

"Murder! Really?" Stephen says, folding himself into a chair next to the divan.

"Two days ago, James Bentley and his thugs beat a digger named James Scobie to death. Bentley was not charged. Neither were his accomplices. People say Bentley is a close friend of the police magistrate and a business partner. The diggers are furious and several are talking of aggressive direct action."

"'Tis like Canada afore the rebellion in 1837," Ryan says. "A few high and mighty families control the government for their own benefit. Is Henry involved in the opposition?"

"Sadly, he is in the inner circle. I hoped you could talk sense into him. You once paid a high price for being on the wrong side of a revolt."

Ryan recalls that distant event. He did suffer for his part in the Canadian rebellion but he never doubted his role. The fight was right even if the effort proved futile. A valiant cause can entrap an idealist like Ross. Once ensnared, dissuasion by a friend or loved one may have no effect.

"What are you thinking?" Stephen asks.

"What if when talking to Henry I get hit with my own boomerang?"

"The intent of your metaphor eludes me," Ellen says.

"What he means," Stephen says, "is instead of him pulling Ross free, Ross might pull our Ryan into the fight. Nothing excites an Irishman like a tussle with the Brit overlords."

"Please do not involve yourself if there is any such possibility. I could not bear having both of you in harms way," Ellen blurts.

Ellen's revealing outburst hangs in the air. Stephen returns to the kitchen. Ryan's love for Ellen stirs. He leans in her direction and places a hand over hers.

"Dear Ellen. I'll talk to Henry and keep myself out of the troubles. Trust me. I harbor no interest in dying at battle or being a prisoner in Van Diemen's Land agin."

A shimmering bead of water wells from one green eye and follows a crinkle to her cheek.

"Another sherry?" Ryan offers.

"No thank you." Ellen dabs her face with her handkerchief and changes the subject. "Any news of my three pupils?"

"Nay. They are on the south coast this time of year, sou'west of Geelong. The region is remote and little news travels from there."

"Supper," Stephen bellows, carrying a sizzling platter of lamb chops to the table.

*****

The next morning Ryan and Stephen wave to Ellen as she leaves in her buggy. An inbound wagon rattles past her towards the compound. Corrain yanks back on the reins and slams the wagon's brake lever. The vehicle squeals to a halt before the ranch house.

"Ye look troubled cousin," Ryan says.

The sullen Wathaurung teamster points to something in the wagon's box hidden by a canvas sheet.

Ryan lifts the cover.

Responding to the grimace on Ryan's face, Stephen says, "What be wrong?"

"'Tis our young Taungurong driver. He's dead and…his man parts are missing."

"Loklok!"

"Aye."

"Corrain, find Polligerry for me."

Not one for words, Corrain nods once.

"Why now?" Stephen says. "He has had ample opportunity."

Ryan pauses before answering. He feels guilt at the teamster's death. They should have done more to hunt Loklok. "I reckon he either feels he is stronger or we are weaker," he answers.

"What be our response?"

"We hunt him down," Ryan says.

"But he be a ghost. No one can locate him," Stephen says as he rubs the back of his head.

"He's not a ghost. He's a man and a man can find him."

Polligerry trots up. "Warrain need me?"

"I need yer opinion. Billy is the best tracker, right?"

"Yes-yes. Officer Billy see like eagle. Quiet like possum. Tough like wombat. Mean like dingo."

"Can ye take a message to Billy, please? Ask him to visit. I have a job for him."

"Yes, Warrain."

"And here," Ryan says, pulling five pounds from his pocket. "Take the poor lad's body to his family and give them this. Say Warrain mourns for their boy and will avenge him."

"Yes, Warrain."

*****

Four days after the killing of the young driver, Officer Billy appears in Ryan's compound. One second the expanse is empty. The next, there he stands, examining Warrain from one hundred yards. Billy makes no effort to come closer; so, Ryan walks to him.

"Billy," Ryan says, "Loklok killed one of my drivers, a member of yer clan."

214

"Yes, a cousin," Billy mutters.

"Ye know I posted a big reward for anyone who can kill or capture that renegade?"

Billy nods.

"No one but Billy can track down Loklok."

"Warrain getting smarter."

"I wish to hire ye to track Loklok. I'll pay ye twenty-five pounds a month in wages. Either find him or learn what he plans. If ye bring me his body, three hundred pounds will be yers."

"Billy happily kill Loklok for many less pounds, but accepts the generosity of Warrain." Grinning, Billy extends his hand. "Deal, boss."

"May the spirits guide ye," Ryan replies with his handshake.

*****

Nine days after promising Ellen to talk to Ross, Ryan makes good on it. He had instructed his drivers to report on any political activities involving miners and diggers, and to send news on Ross and Doudiet if possible. For a week, their accounts suggested peace had returned to Ballarat, but yesterday Gellibrand heard news of a planned protest for October 17 organized in part by Ross.

At dawn, Ryan departs from the station on trusty old Dan. His saddlebags hold spare clothes. His Colt rests by his right hip.

The spring morning chill retreats as the sun rises higher. Across the land, waves of grass bend and sway in a northern breeze. Armies of sheep munch methodically through the swale. On one highland, Ryan spots a single kangaroo. Once a common sight, the beasts are becoming rare as impoverished miners decimate their ranks for cheap food.

In Ballarat, Ryan leaves Dan at the stable and walks to the Café de l'Europe. The usual grating roar of digging is absent. The silence is a bad omen. Idle men make trouble.

Inside the cafe, James Sayers is on duty.

"Welcome Mr. Warrain. Breakfast today?"

"Aye. Whatever ye recommend."

"Very good, Mr. Warrain."

After a meal of poached eggs with ham and toast, Ryan slips into the adjoining hotel and encounters William Robinson at the hotel's front desk.

"Did you enjoy your breakfast, Mr. Warrain?"

"Indeed Mr. Robinson. Now, I'd appreciate a room and information."

"The room you enjoyed last time is available."

"Grand. I'll take it."

"Done," Robinson says, with a flourish of his quill pen. "And how else can I help you?"

"Are the miners meeting today?"

"Yes sir. Go to the Eureka Hotel at noon, down by the corner of Eureka and Otway."

"Thank ye, William. Another thing. I could use a haircut."

"Yes sir. Go a few blocks east on Main. Go right on Lydiard. There is a tent for a barber and dentist. I do not recommend the latter."

*****

By chance, the barber recognizes Ryan. "I know ye," says the middle-aged Irishman. "Ye are that kangaroo fella."

"Call me Ryan."

"Of course, of course. Wanna cut today, er a shave too?"

"Both," he says, slipping into the proffered chair. "And I'd be obliged for any news on the miners. I live on a station and rarely visit town."

Over the course of Ryan's haircut and shave, the barber recounts weeks of growing tension. A reform league formed by the miners to advocate for their rights has met continued resistance from local authorities and the state governor. The barber claims fifteen thousand miners and prospectors now reside in the immediate Ballarat area and most support the league.

"I am with 'em in spirit," says the barber. "They be taxed heavily, they be denied the vote and have none in gov'ment to speak for 'em."

"Do ye know a pair of Canadians, Henry Ross and Charles Doudiet?"

"Plenty of Canadians in these parts. We named a gold field after them."

"Aye, but have ye met Ross?"

"Nay. Not had the pleasure of his patronage yet; but his name rings a bell. Part of the miner's league, I expect. Are ye goin' to the big meeting at that bastard Bentley's hotel?"

"Aye. As soon as I'm done here."

*****

Ryan walks the six blocks to Bentley's hotel. Several thousand angry and sweating diggers already mill in the street. He spots Ross leaning on a wagon parked in the intersection.

At half-past noon, a well-dressed, stocky man Ryan doesn't recognize climbs onto the wagon and silences the men with a wave of his hand. He begins speaking in an Irish accent, retelling the murder of Scobie. He lashes out at the police for refusing to charge Bentley. With long-winded detail, he replays every connected event, building an unassailable case in the public mind. He promises his committee will petition the government to prosecute Bentley for Scobie's death. He insists such a move from the authorities is necessary to impress upon the minds of people the importance of peace and order for all. Ryan relaxes at the call for peace. He hopes the speaker has calmed the throng.

When the speech ends, people drift away. Ryan climbs on the now abandoned wagon and surveys the street.

The majority of protesting prospectors swarm in front of Bentley's hotel. A rock shatters a second-story window. The mob scoops up all projectiles within reach. Every window lies in glittering shards within seconds. A group of men break in the front door. Others climb through empty window frames. Someone in the horde hollers, "Burn it!" Dozens pick up the chant.

"*Damnú ort!*" Ryan curses in Gaelic.

A troop of British regulars appears from around the corner. Though a mere ten in number, everyone respects the redcoats and their bayonets. The mass of angry diggers shifts back from the hotel. The soldiers flush out the men inside.

From his vantage point, Ryan notices four men slip into a narrow storage shed next to the hotel. They emerge within half a minute and blend into the crowd. Smoke tendrils curl from the shed's smashed windows. Within a minute, a smoke fog pours forth, followed by tongues of fire.

Fanned by the wind, flames soon render the tinder-dry wooden structure into a raging inferno. The conflagration spreads to the Eureka Hotel. To the cheers of thousands, Bentley's hotel is soon a two-story bonfire. After an hour, the hotel collapses in an eruption of sparks and smoke. Volunteer firefighters, aided by bucket brigades manned by the now civic-minded miners, prevent the fire spreading further.

Ryan grunts and kicks the wagon's side. From his experience in the Canadian rebellion and from stories told by his grandfather about ill-fated Irish rebellions, he expects a peaceful resolution to the dispute is now unlikely. Unless one side capitulates, volatile passions will escalate. Arson is always the last step before murder and mayhem.

Ryan wants a word with Ross. He follows the greater mass of departing miners drifting along Eureka Street. A man sitting on the raised sidewalk with a large pad catches his attention.

"Charlie. What are ye up to?"

Doudiet swivels the pad for Ryan. The watercolor shows a mob surrounding the burning hotel. Ten redcoats line the foreground, as mesmerized by the flames as the miners.

"We are witnesses to an extraordinary period in this nation's history. My duty is to chronicle events."

"'Tis a fine piece. Have ye seen Henry?"

"You may locate him at the Charlie Napier Hotel."

Ryan hurries to the center of Ballarat East. The front door of Gibb's hotel leads into a hallway bisecting the ground floor from front to rear. To his left are separate parlors for men and women decorated with wallpaper and furnished with a brocaded settee, dining tables and desks for letter writing. To his right is the saloon. An ornate bar of carved, dark wood spans the room's twenty-five foot length. No tables or chairs are present.

Not finding Ross in any public room, he approaches the bartender. "Have ye seen Henry Ross?"

"He's up in the meeting room. Take the stairs at the end of the hall."

Upstairs, Ryan follows the sound of conversation and enters a room with a Masonic sign above the door. The room has an attic-style slanted ceiling and a large dormer window. Chairs and divans line the walls.

Ross recognizes Ryan and breaks from a knot of men. "Ryan, how very good to see you; though I am surprised you are in town."

"Aye. I came to talk to ye."

"On what subject?"

"Step into the hall for a bit," Ryan says, clutching Ross' elbow and guiding him from the gathering. "Ye know my rebel history."

"Yes, but what has that to do with me?"

"Ye are walking down the same path. Gatherings like today are the first step to rebellion. 'Tis how it began in Canada in 1837 and how it began each time in Ireland."

"Respectfully Ryan, you are mistaken. We advocate for a fair deal and justice."

"'Tis how ye started, no doubt. But the fire today tells me ye've gone too far."

"It was the action of a few hotheads and does not represent the majority," Ross says, crossing his arms.

"'Tis the hotheads who always start the trouble. 'Twill be a hothead on yer side or t'other who fires the first shot, then they'll be a war."

"Nonsense, Ryan. No one wants a battle."

"Ye are wrong. The miners burned a hotel today and took pleasure in it. They've a taste for fighting now. I urge ye to go to yer claim and stay away from the politics. 'Tis not yer country. Do not risk yer life for it, like I once did in Canada."

Ross squints at Ryan like someone trying to read small print in a book. After a moment, he squares his shoulders. "I'll give your advice due regard. But for the moment, I resolve to complete this matter. Our committee must decide the next step."

"Ye do not need to be part of it."

"Yes, I do. I made a commitment. In a few days I may find opportunity to disengage. I must return immediately. Good-day to you, Ryan."

*****

A week after arriving in Ballarat, Ryan prepares to return home. Every overheard conversation hails the arrest of James Bentley and two employees for the murder of Scobie. People believe the riot at

Bentley's hotel forced authorities to undertake a thorough investigation. To Ryan, justice has triumphed.

For the previous five days, Ryan has visited customers in Ballarat, Bendigo and surrounding areas. He rarely meets the people who made him wealthy. Stephen and Ellen court and manage customers. The warm welcomes and camaraderie convince him to spend less time at his isolated station in the years ahead.

On his travels, Ryan witnesses a legion of miners and diggers living in squalor—men who blame their poverty on the high license fees. Ryan also notes a build-up of British troops and police detachments in the Ballarat area. He has no doubt the government will deploy the army to enforce its crippling taxation regime.

Ryan lingers an hour over his breakfast, reading local newspapers, content in his belief that Bentley's arrest might bring peace to the goldfields. At the hotel desk, Ryan settles up for his lodging and food bills.

"Sorry to have you leave us, Mr. Warrain. It is always a pleasure."

"Thank ye Mr. Robinson. 'Tis my longest stay in Ballarat."

"Will you be attending the meeting before you leave town?"

"What meeting?" Ryan croaks.

"The miners are protesting the arrest of three men for burning the Eureka Hotel. They will be assembling at Bakery Hill across from the police detachment."

On Dan, Ryan trots to the edge of town. A crowd of diggers numbering in the thousands has gathered on the hill. Armed policemen stand in rows inside the low-fenced compound across the street. From his mounted vantage point Ryan spots Ross and Doudiet near the summit. Unconcerned about the groups of restless men, Ryan guides Dan through the throng. Most diggers recognize Ryan and move aside. A few newcomers curse him for riding a horse into the gathering. Wiser men call them fools and order them to shut their gobs. "Don't you know who that is?" they whisper.

Ryan halts Dan ten feet from his friends. He glowers at Ross like a cross parent at a misbehaving lad. The young Canadian shows no sign of intimidation as he looks up at Ryan on his horse.

"What are ye doing, Henry?"

"We are protesting the arrest of our brothers."

"Are ye not content Bentley and his two thugs were arrested? Are ye not willing to accept the victory and go about yer business?"

"We must make a case for the arrested men."

"They burned a bloody hotel," Ryan shouts. "What'd ye expect—a bouquet of roses?"

"All we want is their release, nothing else."

"Are ye blind or stupid?" Ryan bellows. All men within hearing distance go silent. "The law is working as it should. Ye can nary expect them to arrest murderers and pardon arsonists. Let the courts do their job."

Ryan glares at the men closest to him, but addresses his next remarks to all. "Unless ye all want war, return to yer claims. Let yer leaders send petitions to keep the gov'ment's feet to the fire, but ye can't win by showing force. It gets the commissioner's back up. Go back to yer diggings."

A faint murmur rolls through the assemblage but no one moves to leave. Ryan concludes the single-minded purpose that brought four thousand men together leaves them with no more self-determination than a herd of sheep. And he expects they believe their numbers accord the reform league an illusion of invincibility.

"Yer cause be noble," he shouts. "I wish ye all luck."

Ryan rides home in defeat. He slumps in the saddle, dragged down by a mental burden that manifests as a physical weight. His efforts failed to prevent Ross and Doudiet from spiraling into folly and danger. Ryan fears facing Ellen.

Rebellion

November-December 1854

Leaving Ross behind on Bakery Hill does not permit Ryan to park his worries in Ballarat. For four weeks, Ryan's drivers continue to report news on the miners' activities. Ryan reads every newspaper his men can find for him. Bentley and his henchmen receive three years at hard labor for Scobie's death. The arsonist diggers also get jail time, albeit less than a year each. To Ryan, the courts have fairly apportioned blame.

But, today's newspaper reports the miners' demands now include the right to vote and an end to the license fees. "Damn foolish impatient bastards," Ryan mutters.

"Pardon me," Stephen says from across the table.

"The miners' reform league has a few smart leaders, including Henry. They've the means to fix their problems but they're in a hurry. If they don't give the gov'ner a chance to retreat with honor, he'll nary give an inch. I can't understand—"

A knock on the door interrupts Ryan. Polligerry steps inside. "Warrain. Big-big trouble with them diggers today."

"Tell us."

"Thousand-thousand digger fellows had big meeting and burned licenses. Say no pay gold tax."

Ryan slaps the table. "See what I mean, Stephen. They are forcing the hands of the gov'ner and gold commissioner."

"It be not your fight, Ryan," Stephen cautions. "Let Ross and the rest make their own mistakes."

"I can't, Stephen. In my heart, I'm with them. This is the kind of cause my ancestors have fought for six hundred years. I'm smart enough to stay out of the fracas, but I can't sit here and wait."

"You are returning to Ballarat?" Stephen asks.

"Aye."

"There be more," Polligerry says. "Mrs. Ellen want see you."

*****

Within an hour, Ryan is on Dan trotting towards Ballarat. On the last day of November, the late spring sun is oppressive. Despite the heat, Ryan keeps the horse at a fast pace. He knows the steed can keep it up for the short journey.

At the boarding stable, Ryan makes sure Dan has a long drink of water, and orders a rubdown as well as stable and board. With his horse cared for, Ryan hurries uptown to the Duchess of Kent Hotel and finds William Robinson at his station.

"Ah, Mr. Warrain. I was expecting you. Your usual room, sir?"

"Aye."

"We have a lady staying here who asked me to alert her when you appeared. Shall I grant her request," he says, with a questioning tilt of his head.

"'Tis Mrs. O'Sullivan?"

"It is she, yes."

"I'll have tea for two in the café, if ye please."

The tea arrives seconds before Ellen. Ryan admires her low-cut summer dress. White with pale green at the collar and hem, it contrasts with her flaming hair. He pulls out her chair.

"Thank you," she mutters.

Ryan notices the red rims of her eyes. He pours her a cup of tea. He settles in the opposite chair and gives her time to compose herself. "I take it by yer look ye've tried and failed to talk sense into Henry."

"Yesterday," she says, "several thousand miners protested by burning gold licenses. This morn, the gold commissioner ordered a squadron of police to respond. They fired warning shots and arrested eight men. The diggers became furious. A company of soldiers saved the constables from mob violence. Oh Ryan, I am so frightened for Henry and Charlie. The atmosphere reminds me of dry range waiting for the first bolt of lightening to kindle an inferno."

"Ellen, I tried to reason with Ross. He insists they can win their cause peacefully."

"What is your opinion?" she asks.

"The line between peace and war is already behind them. I reckon two hundred redcoats are camped nigh Ballarat. They were ordered here for one reason."

"Why do they wait?"

"If 'twas me in the gov'ner's shoes, I'd wait for a tad more provocation. Burning licenses is not grounds to kill men."

Ellen gasps and dabs her face with her napkin.

"What do ye know, Ellen?"

"Henry had a flag made to represent a new republic. The reform league leaders will present it this afternoon. Might that be sufficient motive for the governor?"

"Where?"

"They will march with it from Bakery Hill to Eureka Flats."

Ryan rises. "Excuse me. I must go."

*****

Ryan arrives at Bakery Hill in a sweat from running. Thousands of restless men roam the hill, grinding the spring grass into pulp. Near the hill's summit, Ryan spies Ross chatting with several men. He winds his way through the human obstacle course towards his friend. He encounters Ross and a bearded, stocky man in his late twenties. Together they work to attach a piece of cloth to a makeshift pole.

"What've ye there, Henry?" Ryan calls out.

Ross turns to the voice, startled at first. "Ryan. I did not notice you approaching." He pauses, and points to the man holding the flagpole, the same man Ryan saw speaking from the wagon the day the diggers burned Bentley's hotel. "Ryan, this is Peter Lalor, the president of our reform league. Peter, this is Ryan Warrain."

"The man with all the fighting kangaroo wagons," Lalor says, extending a hand. "Did you come to join us?"

Ryan does not accept the handshake. "I came to talk ye out of yer foolishness."

Lalor runs his fingers through his wavy hair. His eyes narrow and his lips compress. Ryan ignores the man's demeanor and presses on. "Is that a flag of some sort?" he asks, pointing.

"Yes," says Ross. "Let me show you." He unfolds the cloth. On a deep blue background, a thick white cross stretches to the flag's four sides. At the cross' center and at each of the four points, a seamstress has sewn an eight-pointed star. "We call it the Southern Cross."

"It will be a symbol of an independent Australia," Lalor adds.

"'Twill be the shroud on yer coffins is more like it," Ryan states. "'Tis the provocation the gold commissioner and gov'ner need to bring the army down on ye all."

"We can call on fourteen thousand men," Lalor says. "We have nothing to fear."

"The British have the best professional soldiers in the world. I've met them in battle, have ye?"

Lalor and Ross do not answer. Lalor fidgets, uncomfortable with Ryan's interference.

"Ye may have several regiments of volunteers, but how many have guns? How many can ye truly bring to battle? Can they shoot straight? Will they stand their ground when the lead is flying?"

"What is your point?" Lalor demands.

"My point is yer numbers mean nothing. The two hundred redcoats bivouacked nearby can rout thousands of civilians, especially if they choose the place and time of attack."

"I wonder if we have not already gone too far," Ross says.

"Ye could end the certainty of bloodshed if ye truly wished it."

"How?" Lalor asks, crossing his arms.

Ryan ignores Lalor's sneer. "See that mounted British officer at the police barracks," Ryan says, pointing. "I expect he commands the soldiers. Walk down and surrender yer flag to him. Tell him ye mean it as a symbol of freedom and not a sign of rebellion. And then go back to work and win by negotiating."

"Never," Lalor says, spitting. "I'd rather die."

From Lalor's stance and grimace, Ryan concludes he means it. He faces Ross. "Abandon this madness while ye can. Ellen is in tears worrying for ye."

The mention of Ellen's name elicits a change in Ross' expression. Ryan detects a hint of doubt.

Lalor hoists the flag in the air. "It is time, Ross. Will you march with nation builders or slink away with that wagon builder?"

"Come with me Henry and let's sup with Ellen," Ryan implores. "Yer a Canadian. 'Tis not yer fight."

Lalor climbs atop a tree stump and waves the flag. The mass of men, as if trained for the event, encircle him. Lalor holds up his left hand. The multitude goes silent.

"Please kneel for a pledge of allegiance."

To Ryan's amazement, the mob does as requested. He alone refuses to kneel.

"We swear by the Southern Cross," Lalor shouts, "to stand truly by each other." He pauses for effect. "And fight to defend our rights and liberties. Amen."

The crowd repeats "amen" in one voice and rises. Lalor marches down the hill, the flag held aloft. The rebellious diggers swirl like a school of fish and fall in behind.

"It grieves me Ellen worries so," Ross says to Ryan, "but I have a duty to these men." He hurries after the departing throng.

The last human on the deserted hillside, Ryan meanders amid the debris—cigar butts, empty pottery bottles and newspaper pages. He scuffles with his inner rebel, fighting to detach himself from Ross' cause and his foolishness. Part of him wants to follow.

At the foot of the hill, Ryan notices Doudiet painting. "Did ye capture that madness?" he asks the young artist.

"Do not call it madness, my sardonic friend. It is the bright light of brotherhood, the valiant spirit that moves men and nations to better themselves."

Ryan smiles, recognizing something of his younger self in the speaker. "Promise me Charlie, when the shooting starts, ye will be out of harms way."

"I came as a witness, not as a combatant. Do not worry for my skin."

*****

During a candlelight supper at the Café de l'Europe with Ellen, they have little to say beyond weather and business small talk. They avoid the obvious issue of Ross. The one subject that brings any joy is speculation concerning Stephen's prospects of ever finding a spouse.

"I fail to understand why he has not found a wife," Ellen says, when Ryan mentions Stephen's growing frustration with bachelorhood. "He is a handsome man, smart and wealthy. I'd consider him myself in different circumstances."

"'Tis arithmetic. Thirty thousand men and a few thousand women. Stephen is particular. He wants a young woman built for birthing babies and running a farm and household. Stephen tends to fancy woman on the large size. I expect, if she can't hold up the back end of a wagon, she'd not pass muster."

"In that case, I would not qualify," Ellen remarks, smiling.

Ryan forms a question. He ponders it from various angles before speaking. "Ye seem to qualify with Henry." Ryan probes Ellen's face for clues of how his comment affected her.

Ellen folds and unfolds her napkin, and adjusts the position of her knife and fork on her dinner plate.

"Do you miss Alinga?" she says.

It is not the reply he expects. "I miss my wife, yes."

"If she was not your wife, would you still miss her?"

"Aye."

"So, the marriage has little to do with you feelings for her?"

"Aye."

"So, you agree societal formalities can be irrelevant in relationships?"

"Aye."

A smug smile crosses her face. She has deflected his probing question.

He refuses to let her off easily. "But I clearly recall how yer past marriage was highly relevant to our relationship."

Ellen blanches, which is uncommon for a woman of her skin color. She begins to fuss with her napkin again. Moisture glistens in the corners of her red-rimmed, green eyes. For a second, Ryan hates himself for attacking when she is so vulnerable.

"Forget what I said. 'Twas not fair."

Ellen twists her napkin into a rope and ties it into a knot, all the while staring at the candle's flame. She struggles to untie the knot. Failing, she throws the napkin to the floor and drags her eyes back to Ryan.

"You and I…we…I admit an attraction," she says. "I may have staked too much on my marriage." She pauses and lets her gaze drift to the room's ornaments and pictures. "Henry is charming and handsome. He loves me madly…but he is a boy. All his talk of honor and the great cause is the prattle of an immature intellect."

She signals James Sayers. "James, a port please. And a pot of tea with a side of maple syrup," she adds, with a nod towards Ryan.

"Very good, Mrs. O'Sullivan."

"Did you hear what he called me?"

"Aye. 'Twas yer name."

"I'd much rather it be Mrs. Warrain."

All his repressed affection for Ellen expands from his core like a surging fever. He extends his hand across the table to touch her fingers but she withdraws beyond his reach.

"But I should avoid the siren call of romantic speculation," she says.

"Ellen, dear Ellen. A moment ago, ye spake as honestly as ye've ever to me. Can we agree to be honest with t'other and stop hiding our feelings?"

"Honesty presents great risks, dear Ryan. If we shed our emotional armor, it makes one so severely vulnerable."

"'Tis true. So, I'll remove my armor first." Ryan pauses while Sayers sets down the tea service and removes the supper dishes. With privacy restored, Ryan continues. "I've loved ye, Ellen, from the day we met."

Ellen reaches forward and takes Ryan's extended hand. "I love you, Ryan. I have from the day we met."

"But I also love Alinga," he says.

"And I may love Henry. And I also love Alinga, in my fashion."

"What do we do now?" Ryan mutters.

"We take care of a minor unfinished matter," she says.

Ryan cocks his brows.

"Go to your room. I shall follow presently. Years ago you tried to kiss me. Tonight I shall permit such an intimacy."

"Just a kiss?"

"Yes. Though I often picture myself ravaging you from toes to curls, I shall not...due to my affection for Alinga and Henry."

"I can grow to like this type of honesty."

*****

On the traditional first day of Australia's summer, Ryan and Ellen enjoy an early breakfast in the café, knowing the day's heat may become unbearable before midday. Conversation is limited but winks and coy smiles are plentiful.

The sun is still low in the sky when they ride out from the boarding stable towards the gold digging area called Eureka Lead.

Once again, the gold fields are silent, meaning the diggers are up to mischief.

Their mission is to locate Ross and use their combined persuasive force to pry him from the fatal embrace of the reform league. What they discover confuses Ellen and raises the hairs on Ryan's nape.

"What is that rambling structure on the hill?" Ellen says. She points to a crude wooden fence in the approximate shape of a square with rounded corners. Someone has erected a dozen canvas tents inside the makeshift walls. The new flag hangs limp on a rough-cut flagpole. Four gum trees provide blotches of shade from the summer sun.

"'Tis similar to forts me and my brothers built as children using old logs and lumber," Ryan says. "We imagined we were defending our position agin a battalion of the King's soldiers. Our feeble plaything matched what ye see here, except in size. 'Tis nothing more than a flimsy stockade. 'Twill enflame the British, not stop them."

"You mean they fortified the hill?" she says.

"'Tis so."

"Are they not asking for trouble?"

"Aye."

"We must find Henry," Ellen says, spurring her mount into motion.

At a gap in the stockade wall, an armed guard hails them.

"Two friends of Henry Ross," Ryan calls back.

"Go fetch Captain Ross," the sentry says to another man.

Ross emerges from the largest tent and saunters their way, smiling.

"Captain Ross?" Ryan queries. "Ye've a military rank now, eh!"

"I command ten Canadians," Ross counters. "Diggers from the same country are arranged into companies. Imagine, we have people from twenty-one countries engaged in this protest—every nationality in the area except the Blacks and the Chinese."

"It appears they are the smart ones, Captain!" Ellen snaps.

"The rank is a mere formality," Ross says, ignoring her. "Our show of force will persuade the authorities to meet our demands."

"Ye are falling into a trap of the gold commissioner's design," Ryan says.

Ellen tosses her reins to Ryan and dismounts. She hurries to Ross and grabs his wrists. "Henry, come with us. You face grave danger."

"I have a responsibility, Ellen. Surely you can see that," he says, thrusting his chin towards the stockade and gathered men.

"You also bear a responsibility to your parents and eleven siblings. They expect you to return, not end up in a foreign grave."

"Do not get hysterical Ellen," Ross says.

Ryan observes Ellen bristle at his statement, but calm herself in a blink.

She releases Ross' his wrists. "What of your responsibility to me," she adds in a low voice.

"Do not worry. There will be no fighting," Ross replies, reaching for her chin like one would a frightened child.

"Then why are those British officers watching every move?" she demands, slapping his hand aside.

Ross glances past Ellen to a distant knot of soldiers and policemen. He does not answer.

"I'll tell ye why," Ryan says. "Cause they are planning their best route of attack. Ye are being willfully blind."

The gate sentry approaches. "Captain Ross, Colonel Lalor wants you in the command tent."

"I will join him momentarily," he replies. Turning to his friends, he adds, "I appreciate your concern but I committed to this enterprise. Only a coward would leave now."

"And only a fool would stay," Ryan says. "Have ye forgotten what I've told ye about my past crusade?"

"You were in a losing battle. Do not assume we will fail if it comes to battle. Good day to you both."

Ellen exhales a frustrated grunt and shouts, "Young men love risks and adventure more than wives and sweethearts. Damn you all."

*****

Ryan and Ellen ride to the hotel in silence. She has wrapped herself in anger. Her emotional struggle manifests as twitching fingers and the occasional stifled sniffle. Ryan wants to comfort her but caution restrains him. She teeters on a precipice between frustration and sorrow. Any consoling touch might engulf them in an embrace they would regret when passions cool. At the hotel, Ryan asks if she wants to meet after he returns the horses to the stable.

"No, thank you. I intend to return to Buninyong on the next stage. I shall not stay here a moment longer. I wash my hands of that foolish boy."

"I'll send word if anything happens," he calls to her retreating back. She does not acknowledge him.

At the stable, Ryan brushes Dan himself. The repetitive physical activity calms him. He checks the time on his pocket watch. He cusses and trots to the corner of Main and Barkly. A familiar rig maneuvers through the wagon and buggy traffic. He flags it down.

"Hey boss," says Gellibrand.

"Gidday. Can ye give Mr. McNichol a message, please? Tell him I'm joining the diggers at Eureka."

"Warrain be in big danger," his driver says.

"I will not join the fight. My goal is to protect Ross as best I can. Ask Mr. McNichol to collect a load of bandages and blankets. Ask him to let all the local doctors know their skills will soon be required."

"Be careful, boss. The spirits not have power to protect you there."

"Thank ye, my friend."

Ryan marches the distance from midtown to the diggers' stockade. On his way, he stops at the police station and interrupts a conversation between the British infantry captain and a police sergeant.

"Gidday captain. Can I've a word?"

"Who are you, sir?" the officer replies, giving a tug to the bottom of his red jacket.

"This is Ryan Warrain, captain, one of our leading citizens," the sergeant offers. "He's not a digger, sir."

"What is your interest here, Mr. Warrain? This is not a safe area."

"I aim to join those men at the stockade. Not as a combatant. I'll try to convince them to lay down their arms and abandon their position."

"I am pleased to see loyalty to the Queen," says the captain, "but I cannot guarantee your safety in the event of an armed uprising."

"'Tis naught to do with loyalty to the current tenant of Buckingham Palace," Ryan says, almost spitting the last words. "I'm here to lessen the carnage when yer regiment storms that stockade."

"We have no attack plan, Mr. Warrain."

"Why are yer soldiers sharpening bayonets and stockpiling powder?"

"It is merely everyday readiness, sir," the captain replies, with a wink to the police sergeant.

"Assurance from a British officer is as useful as money stashed in a kangaroo's pouch." While the captain puzzles for the meaning of his final remark, Ryan strides towards the stockade. He spies Ross and Doudiet seated near a fire pit sipping tea from tin cups.

Ross spots Ryan. "If you returned to renew your assault on my intelligence, save your words," the young Canadian says, rising to his full height.

Doudiet, surprised by Ross's tone, leaps in front of his friend to prevent a fight.

"Nary worry, Charlie," Ryan says. "I came to join ye."

"You have embraced our glorious cause finally," Ross says, smiling.

"Nay. Yer cause may be in the right but yer methods are wrong. I came hoping to prevent yer death when the shooting starts."

"They will not attack," Ross assures him. "We have fifteen hundred armed men at this location. Two hundred Californians on horseback patrol the immediate area to warn of any approach by the soldiers or police."

"Superior numbers don't promise victory," Ryan says.

"But they provide a deterrent."

"Maybe."

"Sit, Ryan. Enjoy some tea. I even have maple syrup in my kit."

"Aye."

Ryan sits on a camp chair while Ross' orderly serves tea.

"By the way, if you wish to come and go, I must impart the password," Ross says.

"It is Vinegar Hill," Doudiet adds.

Ryan gags on his tea. After a brief coughing spell, he barks at companions, "What fool chose that?"

"Colonel Lalor."

"Do ye know what it refers to, either of ye?"

Ross and Doudiet return blank stares.

"Vinegar Hill is where the English slaughtered the Irish rebels in the 1798 rebellion."

*****

For the remainder of Friday and most of Saturday, Ryan shadows Ross. Ryan observes armed diggers in drills and men adding boards and fence sections to the walls. He has to admit, despite the flimsy defense, the diggers enjoy a positional advantage. The stockade encompasses an acre of land atop a modest rise with a clear view in all directions. While Ryan is certain the two companies of soldiers he'd encountered nearby could overrun the diggers despite their numerical superiority, he doubts the British are willing to accept the massive casualties such an assault would bring. He suspects the captain is waiting and ascertaining the digger's weaknesses.

Late on the long summer afternoon of Saturday, Ross attends a meeting with the officers in the command tent. Lalor refuses Ryan entry; so he waits nearby with Doudiet.

"Did ye make more paintings, Charlie?"

"Indeed. I captured the stockade's likeness."

Ryan scans the stockade area. "Charlie, does it seem to ye the ranks are a wee bit thinner hereabouts?"

"Indeed. The officers gave the majority twenty-four hours leave."

Ryan rolls his eyes skyward. "Why in God's name?"

"Well. Tomorrow is the Sabbath and tonight is the usual night for celebration. General Lalor insists we are in no danger of attack on Sunday."

"So the men are leaving to get drunk afore a battle," Ryan says. "Why does the pudgy colonel think we are safe on Sunday?"

Doudiet winces at the insult to the commander. He continues in a quiet tone. "The gold commissioner has insisted diggers not work on the Holy Day. He has fined men for doing so. Given that—"

"Lalor is a fool!" Ryan blurts. "No war in history paused for prayer." He hooks the young man by his lapels. "Charlie, join the men in the bars tonight. Go while ye can."

"Unhand me, sir."

Ryan complies.

"It so happens I have arrangements off the hill this evening." He gathers his duffle bag and departs without another word.

Ross exits the meeting tent and meanders to Ryan, chatting with various men as he makes his way.

"Where are the mounted California diggers?" Ryan asks.

"A scout said a British regiment was marching from Melbourne. They went to intercept them."

"How many men are ye keeping here tonight?" Ryan asks.

"We have two companies of Irishmen and my Canadians," Ross says, pointing to some men, "plus assorted units. I estimate one hundred and twenty."

"Tell them to be ready for an attack at dawn," Ryan says.

"What makes you so sure?"

"Don't be blind," Ryan says, placing his hands on his hips. "They mean to crush yer uprising. They waited for a moment of weakness. Ye provided it by thinning yer ranks and sending yer cavalry afar. They'll move troops close overnight and attack afore sunrise."

"How did you reach that conclusion?" Ross yells.

"If I was the commander, that'd be what I'd do."

Ross contemplates that response. Ryan witnesses skepticism evolve into acceptance and then into worry. "I will talk with the colonel," Ross says.

Alone, Ryan treads around the stockade's inside perimeter. For every point of possible attack, Ryan appraises the best escape route in the opposite direction. He can do nothing else in the long wait for the inevitable.

*****

Ryan sleeps under the stars. He awakens in darkness. By the glow of a cooking fire's dying embers, he reads his watch—4:30.

The moon has set and the heralding bloom of dawn is due in fifteen minutes.

He treads to the wooden wall and attempts to probe the inky dark. Unable to see, he listens. Snoring men in the compound mask sounds beyond the barrier. He leaves the stockade's limited safety. Twenty paces out, he cups his palms behind his ears to increase his aural sense. He pivots his head, seeking any out-of-place squeak or clink. The warm night air carries indistinct sounds: a hint of creaking leather now and then; a nearly inaudible deep sigh, rising and falling; and, a faint metallic clanking once or twice. All the disconnected sounds add up to danger. He returns to the stockade and shakes Ross' tent pole.

"Wake up Henry. The army is here."

Ross emerges without his coat and rubs his eyes. "It is too dark to see anything."

"Trust me. They are nigh and waiting for a bit of light. Wake up yer men."

At the barricade, Ross peers into the Stygian dark. "You are imagining it," he concludes.

Ryan fights an impulse to punch Ross in the nose. "Wait. Morn is coming."

The interlude is brief. A pale line of deep blue edges the eastern rim of land like the hem of a dark frock. The color shifts up the light scale to pale blue on the horizon. Above, the sky is no longer uniformly black.

"Look," Ryan says, pointing north to a row of pale diagonal lines. "The white bandoleers on the soldier's uniforms are picking up the faint light."

"Damn," Ross exclaims. He pulls a Colt from his holster and fires a shot into the air. "Arise! Arise!"

In one coordinated action, every man in the British force pulls his seventeen-inch bayonet from a scabbard and clicks it into place on his musket. The metallic clang washes over the stockade. Goosebumps roll up Ryan's spine. One never forgets that ominous sound.

"Ye bloody fool. Ye just told the British we've seen them. Ye forfeited a chance to prepare."

Ross ignores Ryan and tries to rally his Canadian company. The sleepy diggers tumble from tents and blankets. They fumble with belt buckles and weapons, oblivious to Ross' orders to form into a line.

Ranks of British soldiers, shoulder to shoulder, converge on the stockade from three directions while a drummer beats double-quick time. Ryan calculates he has thirty seconds to somehow entice Ross to flee.

"Follow me, now—for Ellen's sake," he shouts. For once, Ross seems to obey. Ryan begins a sprint to the south wall, one direction free of soldiers.

At the barricade, Ryan looks back for Ross and cusses. The tall Canadian is on a stump, scrambling to raise the flag. Ross will be the most obvious target when the soldiers open fire.

Mayhem surrounds Ryan. Diggers are hitching up trousers and cursing while they scramble for their guns, powder and shot. Lalor emerges from a tent. He waves his arms and shouts orders, trying to direct the armed men to the stockade wall. "Hold your fire until they shoot first," he hollers.

Ryan peeks over the four-foot high barricade. The army has covered half the distance. Fifty more yards and they'll be in musket range.

Some men either did not hear Lalor's order or ignore it. Muskets boom on the north side. Two puffs of smoke rise in the morning air. Then a third shot. Two hundred British muskets return fire. The booming wall of sound assaults Ryan's ears. Splinters explode off the stockade where the lead balls make contact with wood. Men scream as slugs rend their flesh. Ross and Lalor both fall. Clutching his shoulder, Lalor crawls behind a pile of wood slabs. Ross lies motionless.

With two senior officers shot, half the diggers drop their weapons and disappear over the stockade's south wall. A hard core of defenders, mostly Irish based on their accents and Gaelic cussing, stand firm and fire on the approaching lines of soldiers.

The taint of gunpowder smoke is heavy in Ryan's nostrils. He casts a longing glance at the clear escape route through a gravel pit beckoning him. "Fool!" he barks, this time addressing himself.

He rushes to Ross and kneels beside him. A musket ball has ripped open his bowels above his groin. Ryan pulls off his shirt, folds it and presses it to the wound. In seconds, blood soaks the garment. Ross blinks and grinds his teeth but says nothing.

"Don't die ye bastard. Ellen will nary forgive me."

Ryan waves over men from Ross' company. "Get a blanket for a stretcher." He shouts above the din of hollering and gunfire.

Amidst the chaos of battle, Ryan and three men each heft up a blanket corner and hustle Ross from the flagpole. The sun is not yet up and the musket smoke conceals their movement.

Another volley of musket balls rips through the stockade from multiple directions in a deadly crossfire. More screaming men join the chorus of pain.

Ryan falters when one leg gives way. He drops to one knee. "Sorry gents," he says. "I seem to have stumbled." The moment he completes that remark, his brain registers pain. Something has torn a hole as wide as a man's thumb in his calf and fractured his fibula.

A familiar man runs to his aid. Charles Doudiet relieves Ryan of his burden and helps lower Ross to the ground. The young man pulls two handkerchiefs from pockets to bandage Ryan's wound.

"Get Ross to a doctor," Ryan orders. "He's worse than me. I'll live."

"Are you certain?" Doudiet asks.

"Aye."

A deep voice shouts "charge" from outside the stockade. A wave of red-uniformed soldiers bursts over the flimsy barrier. Bayonets rip into the dozen brave men holding their position.

"Go! Now!" Ryan shouts.

Doudiet needs no further encouragement.

Ryan curls up to make the smallest target possible. He keeps pressure on the bandage, and waits. He has no other option. He cannot stand or run.

Over two hundred attackers pour into the stockade. The dark blue of police uniforms mixes with the red of soldiers. The last fighting diggers die or surrender. One constable tears down the Southern Cross and stomps on it. Ryan passes out.

*****

Ryan awakens on a blanket shaded by a tree. He raises his head, fighting the immediate vertigo the effort causes, and looks right and left. Dozens of wounded lie near by. Someone has applied a proper bandage and splint to his leg.

He notices a big man working his way along the row of damaged and dying men. "Ah, there you are," says Stephen. He whistles and waves to a person beyond Ryan's view.

"Gellibrand will be here in a minute with a wagon. We will take you home. The authorities released you and all noncombatants found at the stockade."

"Where's Ross?"

"He's in a room at the Star Hotel."

"He's alive?"

"A doctor is in attendance, but—" Stephen shrugs.

"I must see him."

"No. You fainted from blood loss. I am taking you home to convalesce. That is an order and I will have my way."

"Stephen, please send a message to Charlie. I want updates on Ross' progress."

"Aye, but dunnae get your hopes up."

*****

Four days after the battle, Ryan lurches from bed and hobbles into the main room on crutches Polligerry built for him.

From the kitchen, Stephen hears his thumping progress. "Take a seat. I have tea on and fresh scones.

"What news have ye today?" Ryan shouts. After a pause, he bellows. "Did ye not hear me?"

"Stop your bloody yelling," Stephen growls. He places a ceramic teapot and plate of steaming scones to Ryan's right. He transfers two mugs, spoons and a pot of maple syrup from the tray to the table, and returns to the kitchen.

"'Tis bad news, I wager—since ye ain't talking much."

Stephen returns. He pours tea into both mugs, stirs syrup into one, and offers it to Ryan.

"The news is sad on all fronts. Twenty-four diggers died at the battle or soon after. Six soldiers also perished. Lalor survived, though he lost an arm. Nearly a hundred men are in jail on treason charges."

"Ye are avoiding news of Ross."

Stephen sighs. "Mercifully, the Lord ended his suffering. Charlie told me two hundred and sixty people followed his body to the mass grave site the army set up and held a service for him and the other dead."

"Does Ellen know?"

"Aye," Stephen says. "She is in seclusion in Geelong. I assumed her business duties until she recovers. I sent Benboo to locate Weeyn. We require him here, with you and Ellen out of sorts."

"How is business?" Ryan asks. Elbows on the table, he holds his cup in two hands and blows on the hot tea.

"Half our wagons are idle and the import firm is at ten percent of the usual revenues. I predict we will be back to normal in a few weeks when people regain confidence in law and order."

"Unless some event or person interferes," Ryan mutters.

Dingoes and Whirlwinds

January 1855

Alinga holds Yearn close and rests one hand on her bulging belly. She gazes from the shade of a familiar thicket of gum trees to the beach below. Beside her, Tarra stands in silence, with Maya tight in her arms. The shadows cast by the spear-like leaves dapple their dark bodies. Immobile beside the multi-toned bark of the trunks, they are invisible.

«Here I first saw your father,» Alinga tells the boy. «Your Uncle Fire thought he was dead, but I knew he was alive and was important to my future.»

«How did you know?» asks the boy.

«My dreams told me.»

«Grandfather says you are the best dreamer in our family,» Yearn states, looking up in awe at his mother.

She smiles at the flattery but does not reply. Her mind drifts though recollections of the past five months with her family. Dreamtime has welcomed her return and recast her as a dingo. But the dream quality has diminished. Where once the spirits offered clear warnings of obstacles and dangers, recent visions present cryptic messages.

Last night was a repeat of previous dreams. She is a young dingo resting alone on a rocky hill overlooking a waterhole. The scene includes no other beasts. Dark clouds billow across the horizon as if a storm approaches. She searches the area for shelter—a hollow tree or cave or rocky overhang. Nothing. She begins to panic and awakens.

«When will Uncle Fire come back?» Yearn says.

«We will see him when we return to your father's house.»

«Father promised me a pony when I return. Why did we not go home with Uncle Fire? He wanted us to leave.»

«White and I want our new children to be born here.»

Alinga unties the white cotton bandana from her neck. She steps from the gum thicket and ties it to the barren top of a dead cedar bush. It flutters in the shoreward breeze.

«Why?» asks Tarra.

«I saw it in a dream.»

«You are fortunate to still dream. My spirits no longer visit,» Tarra says, kissing Maya's forehead. «I am frightened.»

«Me too,» Alinga answers.

*****

Walter Fraser steps off his porch into the midnight darkness hoping for relief from the heat. An intermittent breeze teases him with a cooling caress that promises more than it delivers. He locates the Southern Cross in the night sky, and recalls the flag of the digger's failed rebellion. *Unrest is bad for business.* He hopes the authorities hang the prisoners to restore confidence in Australia as a place to buy wool and invest. His haulage firm may be defunct but other endeavors keep him prosperous.

He turns. A man stands in silhouette before the window. The lamps inside cannot illuminate his face. The stranger carries a pistol in his hand—a black hand. Fraser has no Aboriginal employees. Just one black man would dare such boldness.

"Loklok, dear boy. To what do I owe the pleasure?"

"The only pleasure you offer is a chance to split your skull—but that is not why I came. We share a mutual enemy."

"You refer to Ryan, I assume."

"Yes. The time for revenge has come. He is weak. If we strike now, together, we can restore our honor."

Scott Healey steps outside at the sound of conversation. A puppy sleeps in the crook of his right arm. He gasps on recognizing Loklok.

"Relax Scott," Fraser says, "Loklok has a scheme to repay Ryan for his arrogance and bullying."

"Why should we trust 'im?" Healey asks.

"Because any enemy of our enemy is our friend."

"What's his plan?" Healey asks.

"It is like this," Loklok begins. While he lays out the broad details of his campaign of vengeance, Fraser rubs his chin with his forefinger. He analyzes each step in the plot. Healey strokes the puppy's downy fur and smiles.

"We will need more men," Fraser says when Loklok finishes.

"I know several hard cases who'll ask no questions if the money is right," Healey offers.

"Good," Fraser says.

Healey's smug grin vanishes. He steps close to Fraser and uses him as a shield to conceal his left hand while he readies his pistol. Fraser's eyebrows arch in a questioning gesture. Still holding the puppy, Healey leaps to his left and fires two shots into the shadows. An unseen man grunts and a weight thumps to the ground.

The dog whimpers. Healey whispers in its ear and strokes its tiny nose.

"Bring a light," Fraser orders.

Healey retrieves a lantern from inside the house. Holding it high, he treads into the wall of darkness until the circle of light reveals the inert body of a black man in a faded uniform.

"How could you possibly have seen him?" Fraser asks.

"Saw light shinin' off them buttons of his."

"What is Billy doing here?" Loklok asks.

"Spying is my guess," Fraser replies. "Put that damn dog down, Scott, and bring a wagon. I want this useless pile of meat dumped in the bush for the dingoes to feast on."

To Loklok, he says, "When do we start?"

"Can the men be ready and mounted by morning?"

"Yes."

"I will need a horse too," Loklok adds.

*****

Ryan is sipping tea and reading a newspaper when Stephen calls from outside. "Ryan. Please come out here, now!"

Ryan limps onto the porch. Stephen points up the hill beside the lane. "Look, something moving."

In the low afternoon sun, rocks and trees cast long shadows. One blob of shade shifts position.

"What manner of beast is that?" says Stephen.

The shadow jerks to life, crawls inches and collapses.

"'Tis no beast."

Ryan half runs, half limps towards the object. Stephen's heavy footsteps follow close behind. Well before he reaches the body, Ryan recognizes Officer Billy. A trail of blood-splattered sand and crushed grass snakes uphill.

"Turn him on his side—slow and easy," Ryan says to Stephen. They kneel beside Billy on opposite sides. Ryan lifts Billy's shoulder. Stephen pulls the man's hip.

"There are two bloody holes," Ryan remarks. "One in the chest and one in the gut." He puts his ears to Billy's face. "His breathing is shallow and bubbly. One bullet must've hit a lung."

Billy's lids flutter and half open. "Warrain?"

"Yes, Billy. I'm here."

"Billy warn…" His voice falters.

"Warn about what?" Ryan says, bringing his ear close to Billy's dry-lipped mouth.

"Two bunyip…"

An old scene leaps into Ryan's mind—the time when he first heard that title applied. "Fraser?"

"Yes…"

"And Healey?"

"No…black."

"Loklok?" Ryan guesses.

"Yes…"

"What are Fraser and Loklok up to?"

"Revenge…kill."

"I have ten armed men. We can fight them off, Billy."

"Not…here."

Ryan strains to hear Billy, so little power remains in the dying man's voice.

"Where Billy? Where will they attack?"

Billy gasps. One callused paw snags Ryan's longish hair. His mouth moves. He struggles to form and expel a word. He pulls Ryan close until his lips touch the white man's ear. "Laarr."

His big body goes limp.

"He's dead." Stephen says. "I wonder how far he crawled to give you that message. Too bad he died before he—" Stephen pauses at the transformation in Ryan. Every muscle in his body shakes as he gapes at Billy.

"Ryan," Stephen shouts, prodding his friend's shoulder. "What did he say that has got you so flummoxed?"

Ryan cannot reply. His intellect rejects the obvious meaning.

"For God's sake, Ryan, snap out of it," Stephen bellows.

Alerted by the yelling, Polligerry and Weeyn run from the stable.

Ryan looks up, trembling. "Fraser and Loklok are headed to Laarr's camp bent on revenge."

In mere seconds, Stephen analyzes the message and forms a plan. "Then, we must get there first." Weeyn and Polligerry arrive. "Listen lads. Fraser, Loklok and maybe Healey are riding to Laarr's camp with bloodthirsty intent."

Weeyn gasps.

"My life is yours," says the old Wurundjeri.

"Thank you, Polligerry. Prepare horses for Ryan and me. We will ride to Geelong and hire a steamer to ferry us along the coast. You will be in charge while we are gone. Send a message to Mrs. O'Sullivan. And contact Billy's people to fetch his corpse. Tell them Warrain and I honor him as a brave and noble friend. Aye?"

"Yes. You count on Polligerry."

"Weeyn," Stephen says, "how much time by horse to the south camp?"

"One long day if you know the trails and have a good horse."

"We may gain additional hours if they cannot locate Laarr," Stephen says.

"Loklok leaves nothing to chance," Ryan mutters, on his knees beside Billy's corpse. "He'll know where they are."

"Round up all our Wathaurung men," Stephen says. "Issue everyone a horse and a gun. Ride like the wind to the south coast to Laarr's camp. God willing, you will overtake Fraser's men."

"Someday, I will cut Loklok's heart out," Weeyn promises.

With Weeyn gone, Stephen strides to Ryan and jerks him to his feet. "Stop imagining the worst. I want you clear-headed. Alinga needs you."

Her name acts like a slap. "Aye."

"I assume Billy got his wounds sometime early today—he could not survive longer in his condition—and Fraser's gang departed soon after, they are eight to ten hours ahead of us. If we hire a boat, we can arrive first, if you can guide us to the camp?"

"Weeyn told me they are at the same place I stayed ten years ago," Ryan says.

"We can be on our way in ten minutes. Collect your gun, a coat, and lots of pound notes."

"Make it five minutes."

*****

Ryan and Stephen rein in their sweating steeds at Geelong Harbor as the clocks near midnight. They prowl the lantern-lit docks searching for a shallow-draft steamer to hire. After several frustrating hours, Stephen locates a rugged little freight ferry whose captain is willing to take them. They lead the horses onto the deck.

"How long until we are underway?" asks Stephen.

"We require an hour to get the steam up." The captain enunciates each syllable with pauses separating every word. He reminds Ryan of a schoolmaster.

"This ship is made for the bay, ain't it?" Ryan asks.

"Yes," the skipper replies.

"How's it handle once we clear the bay and hit the open ocean?"

"She'll manage any normal sea," claims the captain.

"What speed can we expect from her, sir?" Stephen asks.

"In the bay, we can count on four knots. Might be slower outside. Where exactly am I going?"

Ryan shrugs. "Sail close to the shore heading west. I'll recognize the place when I see it."

Ryan and Stephen delve into their supply of bread and cheese. The ship's mate supplies mugs of weak tea.

"I calculate we will leave the bay in five or six hours," Stephen says. "After that, I cannot ascertain since the destination is indistinct."

Ryan bites his lip. "I hope I can find the spot."

Stephen ignores Ryan's doubts. "We should rub down the horses and try for a nap."

*****

Dawn finds the sidewheeler leaving the calm waters of Port Phillip Bay. Ryan leans on the rail by the bow. In the open ocean ahead, great rollers cross the ship's path and crash on the distant beach. The height from the trough to the summit of each swell

Ryan estimates at eight feet. In the cloudless morning, the surface of the indigo combers is glassy in the motionless air.

Moments before the ferry encounters the open ocean, it slows with a lurch. It chugs onward at a pace so slow the passing shore seems frozen in place. Ryan runs to the bridge and yanks open the door. Stephen stands behind Ryan and peers over his head.

"This is too slow. Ye must go faster. 'Tis a matter of live and death."

"This is a safe speed in these swells," the captain explains in his slow-talking style. Reacting to Ryan's baffled expression, he continues. "This ship has a paddlewheel port and starboard, you may have noticed. If any wave rolls this ship to a point where a paddlewheel loses contact with the water, that wheel would have no resistance. It would speed up and destroy the engines. We would be dead in the water. At one knot, we can prevent it." He regards both men with disdain and adds, "Please leave my bridge or I will turn this ship around."

They back out.

*****

Alinga is a young dingo. She crouches alone on a rocky hill overlooking a waterhole. Familiar dark clouds billow across the horizon as if a storm approaches, but this time a pack of black dingoes emerge from the storm and gallop across the swale towards her. They mean her harm. Far behind are a red and a gray dingo. They mean to help her. She searches the area for a place to hide—a hollow tree or cave or old wombat hole. Nothing. She begins to panic.

She awakens. This time the dread does not dissipate. She crawls from her hut, sweating with anxiety. Under the silver moonlight, she recognizes the stout form of her father, his face turned to the stars.

«You dreamed, my daughter?» Laarr says without looking at Alinga.

«Yes. Five evil dingoes are coming. Why are you awake?»

«I too visited Dreamtime.»

«Did you see dingoes?»

«No. Every dreamer interprets messages in their own way. I see whirlwinds. The five coming are the largest I ever dreamed.»

«I saw other dingoes racing to our aid.»

«Yes daughter. Fire travels by land and your husband travels by sea.»

«Will they arrive in time?»

«I do not know, daughter.»

«Let us awaken everyone and flee into the forest,» Alinga says. Her fingers dig into her father's bicep.

«There is no place to hide from our fate,» Laarr says as he strokes Alinga's trembling fingers.

«We can ask Spark to help us,» she suggests.

«No. We must not endanger our friends with our problem.»

«Call out our warriors.»

«Let them sleep. The sun will rise before the evil arrives. We will prepare a welcome for our uninvited guests and conceal the women and children.»

Alinga rests her head on Laarr's chest and takes strength from his steady heartbeat.

«I love you, Stone.»

«I love you, Sun.»

*****

The ferry follows the coast four hundred yards offshore. For hours, Ryan leans on the starboard rail staring at the forest-clad hills passing by at a turtle's pace. He surveys every new vista for a valley from which a river flows. To his chagrin, valleys and freshwater creeks and rivers are not uncommon. He wracks his memory for clues. An afternoon on the beach with young Weeyn ten years earlier comes to mind. They camped beside a river ten paces wide at the mouth, without rapids or obstacle for as far as a man could see from the beach. Ryan recalls a fuzzy image of steeper than normal valley walls covered in towering trees. And dunes. A wall of sand dunes topped with wind-bent cedars. But dunes and cedars are as common as river outlets.

By midday, Ryan is cursing and pounding the rail with his palm at the ferry's sluggish progress. That, and his growing inner doubt, makes him feel helpless and useless.

"Damn it. We are way behind. They could be there by now."

Stephen leans on the rail, examining the same coastline. He shows no emotion. "I contemplated putting a gun to the skipper's head to encourage greater speed," Stephen says, "but I calculate he be correct. When the waves roll under us, the ship tips from starboard to port, almost exposing the entire paddlewheel."

The ship chugs past a new headland, revealing another long stretch of beach. Stephen points to shore. "What be that distant white thing?"

Ryan fixes on the bit of fluttering cloth caught in a cedar growing from the summit of a dune. The mouth of a river slides into view framed by overhanging trees. Ryan recalls another piece of white cloth that once guided his way across a grassy plain.

"'Tis here. Alinga has marked the spot. Captain! Captain!" He runs to the pilothouse and accosts the captain as he emerges.

"Is this the place?" the mariner asks.

"Yes sir. Run us ashore," Ryan says.

"Impossible. I'd smash the ship to kindling," the captain says.

"What do you propose?" Stephen asks.

"She's got a shallow draft. I can bring you within fifty feet of the breakers but you swim to shore."

"That'll do," Ryan yells. "Take her in."

The helmsman turns the ship ninety degrees and drops the speed to a bug crawl. The ferry inches closer to the breaking white foam. "Full stop," yells the captain. The paddle wheels slow to a halt and reverse a few rotations to stop the ship's momentum.

Ryan climbs on Dan, digs in his heels, and hollers, "Away Dan my boy." The fearless and loyal steed lunges across the ship's deck, leaps the rail like a steeplechase and plunges into the foaming sea. Ryan surfaces with a firm grip on the saddle horn. He floats on his side while Dan swims to shore through the surf.

Stephen is still on the ship. His big horse has balked at leaping overboard. Two crewmen open the stern gate and drive the protesting beast into the water with whips. Stephen shakes the captain's hand and jumps for his horse.

Dan's hooves contact the sandy bottom and the horse struggles out of the surf. Ryan pulls himself into the saddle and guides Dan to the river mouth for a drink. He waits for Stephen.

"Where to now?" his friend asks.

Ryan points ahead. "There should be a faint path by the river. The camp will be upstream were the hills start."

"Lead the way."

Ryan finds a trail on the river's west side. In mere minutes, the forest has closed in. The path winds between trunks. Low boughs make horseback riding impossible. They dismount and walk. Ryan leads.

Fifteen minutes later, Ryan says, "I hear voices."

They enter a glade of giant gums with all underbrush removed. Clusters of Wathaurung mia-mia lie among the trunks. Several appeared damaged—knocked asunder. No one greets them. Ryan follows the murmur of conversation to a clearing. He recognizes Dyeelaga and several of his men dragging wood from the bush and adding it too a large pile. Ryan assumes he has found Dyeelaga's camp not Laarr's. All women and children are absent. *Where are they?*

«Greetings Spark.»

Dyeelaga's glazed eyes acknowledge Ryan and Stephen. Gray has crept into his mop of hair and whiskers since their last meeting. His cheeks twitch with concealed emotions.

«Where is the camp of Stone?»

«It is here.»

Ryan tilts his head. His eyes narrow. «Where are his people?»

Dyeelaga motions to the pile of firewood. Silver droplets roll down his dark cheeks.

"Oh, damn the devil, Stephen! We're too late," Ryan cries out.

He slides off the saddle. The bodies of Wathaurung men, women and children—every one familiar—lie face up on the funeral pyre. Laarr's body, showing four bullet wounds in his torso, lies next to Mokborree. She has a gaping gash in her chest—an exit wound Ryan knows from experience. His teamster and friend Benboo and the beautiful-even-in-death Tarra lie next in the grisly row. Ryan drops to his knees with a cry of anguish. His guts twist into painful knots. The next corpse is Yearn. His pale, perfect form seems unscathed until Ryan notices the blood matted hair at the back of his head.

Stephen nudges Ryan's quivering shoulders. "Ryan. Alinga is not here. Pull yourself together for now. You alone can talk to these people. We need answers."

Ryan kisses Yearn's cold lips and wipes his tears with a sleeve. "Aye. Thank ye, Stephen. Ye are a rock."

To Dyeelaga, Ryan says, «Where is my wife, Sun?»

«Tracks show a man captured her.» He points west. «And another man took two boys that way.» He points north. «My son followed them. I said going alone is too dangerous. I could not stop him.»

«Did you see who did the killing?» Ryan asks.

«No. We heard shooting. All my warriors ran to help. Everyone was dead or taken.» He pauses. «Laarr seemed prepared for battle. Many spears were thrown. The women and children were hiding in the dense forest. Someone tracked them. Mokborree tried to shield Yearn. The bullet passed through her into the boy.»

The details of Yearn's dramatic death wrack Ryan. He fills his lungs several times to regain composure. He forces his mouth to speak. «How many killers came?»

«Tracks show five horses. All gone but two dead whites. I guess Benboo killed them. He had a gun. One rider who fled is bleeding. One horse still here. That is all we know.»

Ryan translates for Stephen.

"Where be the white men's bodies?" Stephen asks.

Ryan poses the question to Dyeelaga. He points to towards the river.

"I'll take a look," Stephen says.

«We think one attacker was Eagle,» Ryan says.

«Then he is certain to be the man who took Sun, his once betrothed.» Dyeelaga says, wringing his hands. «Eagle was a fine young man until he worked for that white man.» Dyeelaga grabs Ryan's forearm. «Find Eagle. You must send his spirit to Dreamtime, so it can heal. And you must kill that white devil.»

«I swear to the spirits of Stone, my son Moon, my wife Sun and all of the dead here I will do these things you ask.»

«The spirits walk with you, Belongs-to-the-sea. To us, you are the great white Wathaurung. May Dreamtime bless your path.»

Stephen returns. "The bodies are of two whites I do not recognize. Hired thugs, I expect. I assume Fraser or Healey took the boys."

"Forget Fraser for now. We need to follow Loklok. Can ye tell when the murders occurred?"

"The corpses are beginning to stiffen; so, three to four hours ago. Can you track him?"

"I wager my life on it."

Ryan addresses Dyeelaga. «Fire and his cousins will arrive soon. Please do not burn until they arrive and can bless their dead.»

Ryan hurries to the camp's west side. Clear boot prints show in the granular soil. "Look Stephen. Loklok is on foot now. Horses are too big for this dense brush. The boot print depth means he is carrying Alinga. And see here. These odd scuffs in the dirt are where she drags her foot. The brave girl is leaving a trail for me."

"The weight will slow him," Stephen says. "We may catch up."

"Follow me."

*****

For an hour, Ryan and Stephen follow Loklok's tracks in dense and pathless forest. Ryan's leg, not yet healed, aches. Ryan wants to run but the spoor is faint and he knows he'd miss a change of direction.

They reach a shallow stream. The tracks do not continue on the far side.

"Wait there," Ryan orders Stephen.

Ryan meanders upstream studying the rocks lining the creek bottom. After twenty paces, he reverses and walks downstream. He spies a flat rock with its coating of moss and algae facing down. A footfall has flipped the stone.

"Stephen, walk on the west side ahead of me. Search for tracks coming out. Let's hope he exited on that bank."

Ryan continues with the current. Tracking underwater is a tedious, slow process. The signs of Loklok's passage are the occasional misplaced rock or depression in a group of pebbles. Loklok, as skilled at hiding his trail as he is at tracking, choose the water route to slow any pursuer.

Something shiny glints in the drab river gravel. Ryan bends to brush sand from the object. "Stephen! I found Alinga's wedding ring. 'Tis a sign."

On the east bank, Ryan spots a two-inch red fiber on the tip of a shrub. He recognizes it as a thread from Alinga's skirt, a strand of a gift given years earlier.

"This way," Ryan yells.

The pursuit continues east and south towards the sea through a continuous forest of gum trees in dozens of varieties and innumerable sizes. Parrots announce their coming. In the thick brush, diminutive mammals and marsupials rustle and scoot off.

Loklok's tracks lead to a high bluff overlooking the seashore. Wind has scoured the limestone ledge free of sand. Loklok's trail disappears. Ryan cannot determine if he went left or right.

Stephen peeks over the cliff edge to waves crashing below. "No one went that way unless he jumped."

"He'd nary choose suicide if he had a choice. He wants a warrior's death," Ryan says.

"In that case, you go west and I'll go east," Stephen begins. "We will both walk one hour. If we do not locate Loklok's trail, we return here. If either of us finds something stay on it."

Ryan examines his pocket watch, amazed it still ticks after the seawater bath. "Aye. 'Tis a good plan. Keep yer wits about ye. Loklok may lurk in hiding."

*****

Ryan follows the cliff edge westward. On his right, cedars and gum trees with entwined branches provide an impenetrable barrier. To be certain, Ryan checks every gap, however minor, for footprints or broken branches—any indication Loklok moved inland. The relentless onshore wind sweeps the sand granules, meaning no tracks in the open remain visible for long. Ryan cannot determine if the trail is true or false.

The cliff top curves north and descends to a sandy beach. He finds no boot prints in the sand. Beach footprints last longer. Maybe Loklok came this way, maybe not. The tide has peaked and is just going out. Loklok could have walked in shallow water and left no trace.

Ryan spies a movement in the shadow of the beach trees. He draws his colt. A stooped old woman of indeterminate age yells at him. «Do you plan to shot an old woman, you white devil? »

«What are ye doing here, mother?» Ryan uses a formal voice to lessen her fears. «What is your name and your clan?»

«My mia-mia is close by. My name is Orana. I am Wathaurung but live alone.»

«Has anyone come by?» Ryan asked.

«You look for something. What have you lost?» she asks.

«A man has stolen my wife.»

Why would anyone steal a white man's wife, she wonders. «No one has come by in many days, and I see everyone.»

«Thank you, Orana.»

Ryan has traveled more than an hour. He swears in Gaelic and retraces his steps, this time at a brisk pace. He returns to where he and Stephen split up. He waits five minutes for Stephen and begins to hike east, scrutinizing every gap in the wall of brush for Loklok's or Stephen's tracks.

He spots Stephen standing on the cliff looking down. Ryan waves. His friend does not respond. Ryan trots up and peers over. Two hundred feet below, surf crashes on boulders shed by the cliff.

"What happened, Stephen?"

Stephen chews his lip and sighs. "I nearly caught up to Loklok. He saw me coming. I drew my gun." He swallows and sucks in a deep breath. "Loklok…he raised up dear Alinga and…hurled her over the cliff. I ran to this spot. Alinga's tied wrists caught on a dead tree limb part way down, but…it snapped. She…plunged…into the sea and disappeared."

Ryan stares at the pounding waves. He wanted to believe she survived but knew she could not with her hands tied.

"She uttered a cry of despair as she fell but did not scream. She be the bravest woman I have ever met."

Ryan shed silent tears, the drips falling towards the sea. His entire family gone in an afternoon. He began subconsciously to lean seaward into the wind.

Stephen clamped a massive hand on Ryan's shoulder. "Let's find a way to the beach and look for her body."

Ryan nods, incapable of words.

They head east until the cliffs dip to a sandy cove. The walk on the beach as the tide recedes examining grottos and rock ledges for Alinga.

Darkness puts an end to the search. Ryan collapses on the sand above the high tide line. Stephen gathers drift wood and starts a fire. His work done, the big man collapses and begins to sob. "I was so close."

Ryan suppresses his grief at the finality of Alinga's fate—that can wait. His friend needs comforting. Ryan puts an arm around Stephen's broad shoulders, and whispers, "Ye did your best."

Stephen tries to reply but emits a faint sob.

"I know ye cared for her nigh as much as I. 'Twas like losing a dear sister, for ye."

Stephen blinks and wipes wetness from his face.

"We'll find that bunyip and avenge Alinga," Ryan says.

Stephen inhales in ragged spurts.

"Tell me, what happened to Loklok?"

"He laughed at me and dove into the forest. I couldn't follow because of Alinga."

Stephen, now unburdened, blubbers without restraint. His sobs cut through Ryan's veil of self-pity. He pulls his friend close. "Poor Stephen."

The agony is contagious. Water courses from stinging sockets. Arms draped across heaving shoulders, the two men cry with abandon.

*****

To Orana, the sea is her larder. Too old to hunt, she beachcombs twice daily at low tide to survive. She pries blue mussels off exposed rocks and drops them into her basket. In the gloom, a dark bundle rolls lazily back and forth at the water line as little waves push up the sand and retreat. She dismisses it as a conglomerate of seaweeds, a common sight.

Orana focuses on her task as the tide turns. Her food source will soon be under water. The seaweed bundle bumps against the back of her leg. She ignores the slimy wetness.

A black foot pokes her ankle.

Orana screams.

*****

Ryan and Stephen spend half the next day in a laborious trek to the dead group's camp. They exchange not a single word. Dark, morbid, self-pitying thoughts whirl in Ryan's mind. Three times or more Alinga had saved his life and the one time her life depended on him, he failed her.

He failed her too when he accepted Ellen's offer to kiss when they stayed in Ballarat. To his anguish, Ryan adds guilt.

This horrible day coincides with is his birthday. Can he ever celebrate that event again? He is thirty-seven and a widower. Is there any chance he could start another family, or dare love?

He struggles to fight off the heaviest layer of grief—the layer than can make a person weak and indecisive. He accepts he will grieve for his lovely young wife and son for his lifetime. Alinga's fierce loyalty and love, her kind heart, captivating eyes and warm smile are a loss he will take to his grave. He will cherish the memory of Yearn giggling in her arms.

He pledges to not dwell on her death nor the loss of so many people dear to him. To do so would be self-indulgent—he is not the sole person injured by the terrible deed of Loklok and Fraser. Weeyn lost his parents, sister, wife and daughter. Corrain lost his parents, wife, a daughter and his brother Benboo. His son is missing. Ryan's two youngest Wathaurung drivers lost their parents.

And everyone will soon want bloody revenge. Left alone, the Wathaurung will track and kill Fraser and all his men. It will be suicide—no white jury would judge such actions justified. The rules are brutally simple. Whites can kill blacks with near impunity; no black can kill a white for any reason and expect a fair trial. Ryan needs to channel the Wathaurung lust for justice in such a way as to achieve their goal without exposing them to retribution. Ryan vows no one close to him will suffer for his action or inaction.

*****

Smoke rises from the large pyre when Ryan and Stephen arrive. Dyeelaga's entire group now inhabits Laarr's former camp. Sad-faced women thrust bowls of cooked meat and roots into their hands. After thirty hours without food, Ryan and Stephen accept with weak smiles and gobble the nourishment in silence.

Ryan spies Weeyn reclining at the base of a tree, eyes closed. He pads over and slides down the trunk beside him. He holds his tongue and waits for his friend to speak.

"We rode hard," Weeyn says in a voice ragged from sorrow. "So hard, the horses almost went lame. We found a dead white man on the trail coming here," he recounts. "He had a spear through him belonging to my father. Then, I knew we were too late."

"The ship we hired was too slow in the ocean," Ryan says. "A different ship or calm water might have made the difference." Ryan looks around the camp. "What of the missing boys?"

"The trail is cold—we tried to follow. I trust Nalong to track them." Weeyn runs his eyes across the throng of tired, sorrowful people. "Soon anger will be stronger than sadness. What then?"

"Are ye expecting trouble too?"

"If blacks kill whites, many more blacks die."

"Aye. Ye and I must prevent that happening."

"How? Our people want revenge," Weeyn replies.

"Whites do not care if a black kills a black. Loklok led the whites here. The Wathaurung can hunt him. Stephen and I can take care of Fraser and Healey."

"No," replies Weeyn. "Our people must be part of killing Fraser too."

"I accept that. Let me think this through. Can ye keep yer people calm until tomorrow?"

"If Warrain asks, they will wait."

*****

Several senior men build a fire in the camp center. Dyeelaga's people and the remnants of Laarr's family gather without a verbal summons. Pots of white clay appear. Men and women paint traditional symbols on their skin. In darkness, the firelight accents the white until the shapes glow and grow from the dark bodies.

The men tell stories. They relive brave deeds of Laarr, his brothers and their sons. Next is the women's turn. They recall generations of friendship between the two families and the filial bonds created through intermarriage.

After hours of storytelling, Dyeelaga holds his arms to the stars. All assembled gaze upwards.

«Bunjil, our creator who lives among us as the all-seeing eagle in the sky, please accept the spirits of our family and friends so they may return to the Dreaming and watch over us.»

Dyeelaga addresses the assembled group. «From this day forward, any kin of Stone has a home among the family of Spark.» He extends an upturned palm to the somber knot of four men, the last adults of Laarr's family. «Among my people are young widows and maidens. Join us and keep the seed of your clan alive.»

Dyeelaga says to Ryan, «I know our white brother soon leaves us for camps of the white man. His spirit will live on among us as long as we are alive to tell his stories.»

Throughout the storytelling and the opening lines of Dyeelaga's offer, Ryan has fought a stabbing irritation in his sockets and blinked away moments of mistiness. Dyeelaga's generous offer—coming after hours of testimonials for the dead—is his undoing. While he contains his sobs, his tears have free run of his face.

Ryan unhooks his tomahawk and extends the weapon on open palms to Dyeelaga. In a halting but strong voice, he responds. «Please accept this offering as my pledge to you and your family. I, Belongs-to-the-sea, offer my brotherhood, friendship, support and protection, as I once did to Stone.»

Dyeelaga accepts the gift, with a slight bow. He reaches for a pot of white clay. With a finger, he draws on Ryan's chest and abdomen. The symbols do not show well on his pale skin but in time, the pictograph is clear. Between upper and lower wavy lines, several shapes suggest mountains and creatures.

«I drew your life: past, present and future. You came from the sea. You live and hunt amongst us. Someday soon, you will return to the sea. Dreamtime has told me so.»

A collective low moan ripples through the assemblage. Ryan, now a believer in Wathaurung visions and Dreamtime, does not argue, though he cannot foresee an ocean voyage in his future.

By unspoken consensus, No one eats until sunrise.

*****

Few of the grieving that night find temporary refuge in sleep. Like Ryan, most do not even try. Ryan picks up mumbled fragments of conversations around the fire on two topics: revenge and restoring honor.

"We should clean our pistols in case they are needed, what with the salt water and sand," Stephen mutters.

Ryan grunts his agreement. Both men open their pistol magazines, empty the cartridges and rinse all parts in fresh water. With a handkerchief, they dry the moving parts and apply gun oil to the inside of the barrel and the trigger mechanism. The habitual labor takes their minds off sorrow for a few precious minutes.

Ryan's mind proceeds to churn and flit between subjects. At times, he ruminates on Dyeelaga's prediction he will soon return to the sea. Did he mean he will leave Australia? Or did he conjure up a death by drowning or a watery mishap? At other moments, he frets about how to avenge their dead without incurring white retribution. Logic and deduction foil every plot line. Stick in hand, Ryan pokes the gritty sand at his feet. The rapidity and force of each jab increases with his anxiety—without a plan soon, the Wathaurung will act on their own.

Raw skin develops on his right palm from the repetitive prodding. Ryan tosses the stick in the fire. With that quieting of activity, the fatigue he'd kept at bay creeps over him. His eyelids close. In a second, he drifts into a surreal oneiric state, the brain's neutral zone where the conscious mind freely associates with its unconscious counterpart.

Instead of passing through this zone as most sleepers do, he lingers. He remains sitting upright—his voluntary muscles stay active. A parade of images rolls past his mind's eye like an hour of theater compressed into a moment—yet he consumes every scene. Another play commences; the actors and sets flashing by with the urgency of lightning.

His eyes pop open and his sagging shoulders snap upright. Beside him Weeyn, asks, "Did Warrain almost fall off the log?"

The question sweeps aside the lingering mist of Ryan's dreams. He pivots his head and regards the speaker. His brain registers his friend, Weeyn. A conversation from ten years previous rises to the surface of his foggy mind.

"Ye once said Dreamtime wasn't for an amadeat. Do ye recall?"

Weeyn nods his acknowledgment, his body tense with anticipation of what Ryan might say next.

"Ye were wrong."

"Did you have visions?"

"Aye, Weeyn."

"What did you see?"

"I was shown the way forward. I'll explain later. Now I sleep. Wake me for the morning hunt." Ryan lies next to the log and falls into deep slumber, not noticing the scattered rain showers.

*****

Dyeelaga assembles all hunters before dawn. They must replenish the meat supply after feeding extra mouths and missing two days of hunting. Ryan joins the hunt party—glad to do something other than mourn.

The summer morning retains heat from the previous day, even with the damp air. Dyeelaga's womenfolk giggle at Ryan's nakedness. He hears "white like a dead fish" to describe his butt.

Stephen joins the hunting party. His muscled and shirtless torso flexing in the firelight elicit compliments from the women, though he is oblivious to it.

"I always cherished your tales of hunting with the blacks," he says. "I be keen to try it but my Presbyterian privates stay that way."

"Yer trousers will get soaked from raindrops on the undergrowth."

"Better that than soil my soul."

Dyeelaga leads the men along a riverside trail to the beach. «Many times, we see kangaroos here. They nibble the grass and new plants at the forest edge,» he explains to Ryan.

«I don't see any now.»

«Too dark. Wait.»

The pre-sunrise light expands. Every second, more of the beach unfolds. Dark forms loom in the dwindling dusk. Kangaroos. Dyeelaga directs two men to sneak inland away from the forested shore. Their task is to get behind the kangaroos and herd the troop towards the hunting party.

Ten minutes later, the pair emerges from cover behind the roos. With an even and unhurried pace, they tread on the sand behind the big beasts. Cautious but not afraid, the ten animals shuffle west on the beach. Hemmed in by the brush-covered dunes and the sea, they maintain a safe distance from the two humans.

Ryan, Stephen and eight hunters crouch and wait. Sinewy, muscled arms hold spears at the ready. Stephen alone carries a pistol.

The troop passes in a long line. With no obvious group of beasts to target, Dyeelaga waits until four kangaroos drift within spear range. He emits a low, two-note whistle. Nine men rise as one and fling long spears. Three beasts drop to the sand, each pierced with multiple spears. The seven survivors bound down the strand faster than a galloping horse. Two roos lie dead. One squirms and squeals. Stephen bolts across the sand and puts a kill shot in the brain of the suffering roo.

Dyeelaga and his men laugh and shout with joy. The hunt has proven quick and bountiful. The Laarr family survivors force muted smiles. In the midst of great sorrow, a successful hunt symbolizes continued life.

The sun rises through a gap in the eastern clouds. Its yellow light pours through a thin veil of airborne droplets. A vivid rainbow arches from the coast hills to the sea.

«Behold,» Dyeelaga cries, «Binbeal says the spirits of our friends reached their destination.»

In answer to Stephen's questioning expression, Ryan explains, "Binbeal, son of Bunjil, is the god of rainbows. Dyeelaga says the rainbow means all our dead are in Dreamtime, their Heaven."

Stephen shakes his head in wonder. "The Lord moves in mysterious ways."

*****

Stephen carries one kangaroo. Pairs of hunters take turns carrying the other two. When they enter the camp, Ryan spies two children encircled by singing women. Corrain yelps, drops his end of a dead roo and pushes past Ryan. The gruff clansman drops to his knees and hugs a child—his abducted son. Weeyn grasps the significance. He too drops his burden and surges ahead seeking Tarra's son, Lakorra.

Ryan singles out Nalong, noticing how much the eighteen-year-old resembles Weeyn at that age. "Ye've grown to a man since last we met," he says by way of greeting.

"I not thank Warrain for freeing me from Fraser's stable many years ago. I apologize for bad manners." He extends his hand, being well trained in white man's etiquette.

"Ye are the hero for saving those boys. What happened?"

"I followed the trail. Mr. Healey had boys tied to a tree. He ready to hurt them. I killed him," he relates in a clinical, detached manner. "I let boys ride on his horse back here."

"Ye do not look happy. Does his death bother ye?"

"His death brings me peace. For that, I thank the spirits. I hold sadness because I failed Warrain, the man who once saved me." Before Ryan can ask for an explanation, Nalong continues. "I saved boys, but not Alinga. My choice haunts me."

Ryan seizes Nalong's shoulders and pulls his forehead within inches. "Ye couldn't do both," he says in a quavering voice. "Either choice was proper. I'll not hold it agin ye. 'Tis Loklok who bears all the guilt."

"I will help Warrain find Loklok. When my cousin is dead, then I truly rest."

"I welcome such a fine warrior. We will talk of next steps soon."

Ryan scans the camp to locate his lieutenants, Weeyn and Stephen. Chattering Wathaurung women surround the big Scotsman, who nods and smiles, deaf to the meaning of their words. Weeyn is engaged in a pointed conversation with Lakorra.

*****

Weeyn kneels to be even with Lakorra's height. «For White's sake, I thank the spirits you are safe.»

The six-year-old boy shrugs and looks away.

«When I return to the white man's place, you must come with me.»

«Why?» asks the boy.

«I am your father's cousin, and your mother's husband.»

«You did not stop my father from dying. You took my mother. I hate you,» the boy shouts. He turns to run, but Weeyn holds him back.

«You have seen too much death in your few years. Live with me. I will keep you safe.»

«Smoke is my mother's uncle. His people are cousins. I will live with my grandmother. Go away!»

Weeyn releases Lakorra's arm. He believes in his heart the boy has chosen the route Tarra would advise if alive. He will honor her wishes.

*****

Ryan approaches the gaggle of women surrounding Stephen. He grins at the goings-on, glad to have something to smile about.

"Ryan," his friend bellows. "Thank God you are here. I dunnae ken a word they be saying."

"They are speculating on the length and girth of yer manhood." Ryan laughs when Stephen blushes. "Some wager ye be hung like a stallion, 'cause of yer stature. T'others bet ye be tiny 'cause ye wear pants to hide the embarrassment."

"Help me," Stephen pleads.

"There's more. That lass tugging yer arm has not seen her husband for a year. She offered to share her bed, and ye nodded at her twice."

"Oh my Lord! She thinks I said yes."

"I can chase them off, if that is what ye want," Ryan says, winking at his friend.

Stephen ponders his suitor. The Wathaurung temptress is past her prime—bush life and multiple babies age women before they are thirty—but she exudes a confident and unabashed sexuality. From Stephen's shifting expressions, Ryan discerns the moral battle underway inside the devout churchgoer. *Poor Stephen has forsaken the comfort of women for too long.*

"Ryan. Help me. Either choice leads to regrets."

"Stephen, if ye lie with her and she becomes with child, her family will punish her and the bairn severely. Does that help yer decision?"

"Aye. Much obliged." Stephen scoops the full-figured, naked woman into his brawny arms, and holds her close, reveling in her breasts pushed against his bare chest. He plants a big kiss on the giggling lady's forehead, sets her down and escapes. "Of all possibilities, that be the best resolution," he confides with a smile.

The women follow. Ryan sends them away with terse words in Wadawurrung. He nabs Stephen's elbow. "We've much to discuss."

"Go on."

"Wait. We need Weeyn too."

The two white men cross the camp and observe Weeyn by himself, engrossed in a dark reverie.

"Weeyn, my friend. We must talk."

The warrior rubs his eyes to clear his mind fog, and replies, "Does Warrain have a plan now?"

"I do," Ryan says, pausing to ensure no one else is close. Satisfied, he continues. "Dyeelaga said five men attacked. One was Loklok. The four whites are dead. But, what of Fraser?"

"Assuming Billy was correct, and I do," Stephen says, "Fraser planned the atrocity but dinna soil his hands."

"I agree," Ryan says. "As I see it, we have two separate missions. Find and punish Loklok. And deal with Fraser without attracting blame to ourselves or the blacks."

"I am with you as far as circumstances require," Stephen pledges, "even if I abuse a commandment or two."

"I stand with my brother," Weeyn adds.

"Thank ye, both. My plan can't succeed without ye."

"What do you have in mind?" Stephen asks.

"I'll call the men together after the midday meal. To most I'll explain only what they need to know. We must guard our secrets— any leak and we'll fail. I'll confide every detail to ye two. Walk with me."

Under a canopy of gum trees on rocks by rapids, with the roiling water masking their voices, Ryan relates his visions. The road laid out before him requires he abandon his impractical ideals. He must resort to subterfuge and homicide. While both his friends agree with the broad details and specific tactics, neither accedes the final step without qualifications.

"The last is hard, I grant ye," Ryan says, his expression somber, "but 'tis the only way to be certain naught bad happens to anyone dear to me."

"I will wait to the last scene of the last act to make my decision," Stephen says.

"I pray we find another way," Weeyn adds.

*****

Ryan finds Dyeelaga alone. «Spark, my friend, I cannot thank you enough for your help and sympathy in this time of our greatest need.»

«Belongs-to-the-sea is the husband of my niece, he is family. I do what the rules of Dreamtime require. Also, I do what my heart tells me.»

«All the white raiders are dead. We are avenged in part. We will leave you this day and go to the white world.»

«What of Eagle and his wickedness?» Dyeelaga asks.

«For that I request your help.»

«How may we serve justice?»

«Eagle cannot be tracked and found if he chooses to stay hidden. So, we make him come to me. I know this from a dream.»

Dyeelaga gasps. «Dreamtime came to you?»

«Yes. My dream instructed me to spread a message among all clans from the sea to the great hills in the north. Your family must start the message on its journey.»

«Tell me,» Dyeelaga says.

«The once great warrior Eagle is now a cowardly old dingo who survives on carrion. He kills those who cannot defend themselves and is afraid to meet Belongs-to-the-sea in combat.»

«This will anger him deeply.»

«Yes. And it will drive him to me.»

«I will do this for Belongs-to-the-sea, my parting tribute to you, for I know we will not meet again in this life.»

*****

Before leaving Laarr's camp, Ryan and his men incinerate the two white killers' remains in a bonfire. Onto the flames they toss the saddles from the horses used by Loklok and Fraser's men. Ryan instructs Spark to grind any surviving bones to dust and bury the ashes. Ryan wants no evidence whites were here. Any hint of a dead or missing white in a tribal area could bring trouble.

In mid-afternoon, Ryan, Stephen, and Weeyn ride from camp with Fraser's horses and their spare mounts on leads. Ryan's two youngest drivers decide to stay with Dyeelaga's family and take wives. Corrain remains behind for his son's sake.

Two hours out from camp, they discover the third dead white man. They strip the corpse, bury the clothes and drag the body deep into the woods.

Several hours later, they locate Healey's remains following Nalong's instructions. Ravens have pecked out his eyes and dingoes have devoured his liver. Weeyn cuts off and buries Healey's garments. They leave the decomposing body for the carrion feeders.

They camp overnight where the coastal gum forest gives way to the interior plains. Ryan removes the bridles from the Fraser-branded horses and sets them loose. If any whites catch them, they will be miles from the coast. The killers' fates will remain a mystery, and given their mission, Ryan wagers Fraser will never report his thugs missing.

*****

In the late afternoon next day, Ryan and his companions halt in sight of his station. None speak. Ryan cringes at the prospect of entering the home he once shared with Alinga and Yearn—a dwelling that will seem lifeless and empty. He hopes he does not break into tears when he tells his employees the terrible news. He wants the crying behind him.

And Ellen. How will she take it? Can he be stoic in her presence or is he asking too much of himself.

"How much of our plan do we tell Polligerry and the others?" Stephen asks.

"Polligerry already knows Billy's accusation of Fraser and Loklok. I assume he told t'others. We'll ask them to spread the message about Loklok. Tell them we found no proof Fraser was involved. We'll investigate. We'll get justice." Ryan leans towards Weeyn. "Can we count on them to play their parts and keep secrets?"

"Yes," Weeyn replies. "For Warrain, our men will stay loyal and silent."

Ryan clucks to Dan and the big gelding begins an eager trot towards his stable. Only the steeds are happy to be home.

A distant figure spots the horsemen and runs to various buildings. Ryan's gut churns. People spill from every dwelling, barn and workshop into the wide compound, everyone anticipating news from the approaching riders. Six men departed and now three sad-faced men return. Ryan's employees can read the signs.

Ellen steps onto the porch. Her optimist smile fades.

Ryan reins in Dan. His remaining drivers, his stable boys, carpenters, coopers, blacksmiths and wheelwrights, and cook crew form a semi-circle. No one speaks.

Ryan recognizes Taungurong and Wurundjeri. Other than Weeyn, not a single Wathaurung remains in his employ. His ten years as a member of a roaming Aboriginal clan have ended in blood and anguish. He sucks in several deep breaths to fend off the remorse threatening to strangle his resolve.

"There is a great sadness in my heart this day that I share with Weeyn and Mr. McNichol. My friends, I must now burden ye with the same sorrow. For that I apologize."

Ellen gasps and clasps her hands to her bosom. Her chin quivers.

"We arrived at the camp of Laarr too late. The only survivors are the sons of Corrain and Tarra. Alas, our family members Tarra, Maya, Alinga, and Yearn have joined their ancestors." Ryan pauses. He swallows twice, trying to lubricate his dry throat.

Ellen collapses on a porch chair and doubles over in silent grief.

"Our warrior brother Benboo killed two attackers afore he died in defense of his family. Laarr killed another. A warrior from a neighboring group tracked and executed a fourth man. Of the five devils, Loklok alone escaped death."

He continues. "Corrain and the two lads are well. They joined the family of Dyeelaga. We rejoice they have found new homes among fine and welcoming people."

Ryan pulls his Colt and points it to the sky. "We are not yet fully avenged. For that, I need the help of each of ye."

Ryan waits for his request to sink in. The younger men seem startled but eager to join the quest. The mature hands—seasoned warriors all—nod with acceptance.

"None shall speak the details of our revenge. Nary mention the four dead murderers. Erase their passage through yer lands from yer thoughts. Tell anyone who asks ye know nothing about who did the killing. One slip of yer tongue and many blacks could be massacred. Pledge me that on the name of yer creator."

Eyes skyward, scores of lips mouth a silent promise.

"Loklok now hides from me and the justice I'll bring him. Any of ye who travel from this station speak to yer kin and brethren wherever ye go. Pass on my challenge: Loklok is now a lame old dingo who survives on carrion—a child-killer and a coward who is afraid to meet me in combat."

"Tell me any sign of Loklok you see or hear," Weeyn adds. "The spirits of my family ask this."

The men and youths nod almost as one.

"Be there any questions," Stephen says.

Polligerry steps forward and asks in a low voice, "Did not Billy speak name of bunyip Fraser?"

"Fraser did not take part in the killing," Ryan bellows for all to hear.

"I will investigate," Stephen adds. "If Fraser be involved, we will deal with him."

"For now," Weeyn replies, "none speak of Fraser. Let the white men punish the white man. The black men will punish the black man."

Polligerry accepts the statement's wisdom.

"Another thing," Ryan begins, addressing his crew. "People may say bad things about me in the coming weeks. Ye may be asked what I'm doing. Don't believe the stories and say naught. Ye'll understand what I mean later. Trust me on this."

Polligerry senses Warrain has finished. With waves of his arms, he sends the men back to their tasks.

"I will see what I can do to get our enterprise on course," Stephen says, dismounting.

"Don't hire drivers. Work with what we have," Ryan says.

"Why?"

"We need to appear damaged by our loss. 'Tis part of the plan. Ye'll see."

"All our businesses?" asks Weeyn.

"Nay. Just the haulage. 'Tis the part most people know us for." Ryan dismounts and offers Dan's reins to Stephen and Weeyn. "Can ye two please see to Dan, while I speak with Ellen."

"Aye," Stephen says. He and Weeyn give Ryan privacy.

Short, tentative steps pull Ryan towards the house. Dust puffs follow his heels. The two wooden step treads creak from his weight. The porch boards echo hollow thuds from his footfalls.

Ellen remains folded—her head in her palms and her chest on her thighs. He bends on one knee, drapes his hands on her heaving shoulders, and presses his lips to her scalp at the part in her orange locks. He holds the kiss—trying in some magical way to pass strength to her through that gentle contact.

Her shuddering body begins to calm. A normal rhythm supplants spasmodic breathing. Her hands peel from her face. Like the petals of a flower opening in morning sun, she unfolds and sits erect. Her eyes, at first unfocused, alight on Ryan.

"I wish I had never met you," she mutters, raising a hand to his cheek. "So many people I knew through you and cared for have died."

Ryan takes her hand, at a loss for words.

Her attention drifts across the compound and flits over the roofs of buildings to distant hills. Ryan indulges her dreamy meditation. Her focus snaps back to Ryan. Her fingers darts out and grasp Ryan's chin. "Fraser must be punished!" she hisses.

"He will be. What Stephen, Weeyn and I have planned can land us all in prison. Ye should leave here to be safe. The less ye know, the better."

With the reflexes of a cat, Ellen slaps Ryan. Knocked off balance, he drops to his backside on the porch. "How dare you! I am no brittle vase to be put on a mantle. They were my friends too. Either I join you or I kill Fraser myself."

*****

Orana is changing the bandage on the girl's head when she notices her eyelids flutter. After four days of delirium and restless sleep, she awakens.

«Lie easy child.»

«Where am I? » asks Alinga.

«In my mia-mia by the sea.»

«How did I get here? What happened?»

«I found you on the beach. You were partly wrapped in seaweed,» Orana says. «Do you remember how you came to be in the ocean?»

Alinga closes her eyes trying to remember. «No.»

«Think! Did someone push you?

«Why do you ask that?»

«Your hands were tied behind your back.»

«If someone threw me into the sea, how did I survive?»

«A branch was wedged up against your back. I think the wood and seaweed kept your head above the water. The spirits count you among the blessed.»

Alinga tries to sit up. Her head pounds. Her loins ache. She nearly faints.

«Easy child. You have a deep gash on your head. »

Alinga touches her belly and notices it seems deflated compared to her last memory. Her eyes ask a question.

Orana takes Alinga's hand. «A child came out. It was stillborn. I am sorry.»

Alinga sobs deeply. Her head throbs with pain and dizziness.

She forces herself to be strong and fights off her grief. «What is your name, kind mother?»

«Orana. What is yours?»

Alinga blinks hard twice. She shudders. «I don't know.»

Plans and Plots

February 1855

Walter Fraser peruses the street traffic from the sidewalk by the Charlie Napier Hotel in Ballarat. He and hotel proprietor John Gibbs exchange pleasantries and remark on the summer finery of people passing by on foot, horseback or carriage. Fraser could not give an ounce of wallaby dung for the crowd's sartorial quality. He chats with the portly publican to disguise his real purpose. He inspects every face in the human parade for the three thugs he hired to deal with Laarr's group. Scott Healey is overdue. Fraser has begun to worry.

"I say," Gibbs says, "this town has recovered handily from that bothersome digger affair two months ago."

"Their vile *lèse majesté* was harshly and properly dealt with," Fraser replies, without looking at Gibbs.

"Business confidence is better now too," Gibbs adds.

"Indeed," Fraser mutters, hoping Gibbs will shut up. Gibbs doesn't.

"Have you noticed, Walter, all drivers on Mr. Warrain's wagons are wearing black arm bands? Why do you think?"

"I am at a loss, John," Fraser replies deadpan. "Perhaps a black chieftain has passed away."

"Say," Gibbs says, pointing, "is that not Stephen McNichol. He would know."

Coming down the street is a large man riding a tall horse. Fraser stiffens with concealed anger when the fool Gibbs waves over Ryan's Scottish henchman.

"Stephen, can you please enlighten us as to why all your drivers wear symbols of mourning."

Stephen dismounts, his shoulders slumping. "Aye John, our family and our firm suffered a terrible loss," he says. "It makes a man question one's faith in the Lord."

His words and tone catch the ear of men loitering nearby in the glorious summer morning. A group forms around to listen.

"You know my partner Ryan lived with some Wathaurung and married one of their maidens." He pauses and sucks in a noisy breath. "Four days ago, someone massacred the entire family."

Frowns on multiple faces indicate a general displeasure with the news but, as expected, Fraser detects no strong expression of grief.

Stephen continues. "Among the murdered are Ryan's wife and son."

"Oh no," Gibbs exclaims, "not that charming lass! What a shame!"

Fraser bristles at the heartfelt sympathy for the dead black whore. He restrains his temper and says, "Have you any idea who is behind the killing?"

"I hoped you might know, Walter. Black massacres are your specialty."

Fraser shrugs off the insult. "I have not knowingly killed a Wathaurung. We were on good terms. I used to school their boys. Besides, I was in Geelong four days ago. Are you certain other blacks did not murder them? Those people are always fighting amongst themselves."

"I viewed the corpses myself when word of the shootings arrived through others," Stephen explains. "They died from gunfire. I found shod hoof prints in the soil."

"Any sign of the perpetrators?" Gibbs says.

"No. The trail was cold."

"And how is Mr. Warrain taking the tragic loss?" Gibbs says.

Stephen chews his lower lip. "Sadly, my teetotaler friend has taken to the bottle. He has not drawn a sober breath in the four days since I confirmed the deaths. I now attend to our enterprises myself. And we lost several experienced drivers. Hiring replacements is proving difficult."

A warm glow tingles Fraser's chest. He struggles not to smile.

The next instant, Fraser's joy scatters like scared birds and his gut flips when Stephen steps closer and growls, "Where be your man, Scott?"

"Ah! Um! I sent him to Melbourne…on company business. Why do you ask?"

"I believe he might have information to help in my investigation."

"I will relay your message when he returns," Fraser mumbles.

"Please, do," Stephen says.

While Stephen rides away, Fraser cannot help wondering what he knows.

*****

When Stephen enters the ranch house, Ryan and Ellen pounce on him.

"Did ye locate Fraser?" Ryan asks.

"Aye. He was where Polligerry told us."

"What did he say?" Ellen says.

"He said he sent Healey on business to Melbourne. He pretended he knew nothing and claims he was in Geelong when the killing happened."

"That much is true," Ellen says. "I made discreet inquiries as to his whereabouts."

"Tomorrow I'll pay a visit to Ballarat," Ryan says.

"Are you certain it is essential to sully your reputation," Ellen says.

"Aye. 'Tis the only way."

*****

For his vigil the next day, Fraser picks a bench next to the Cobb & Company Coach office. From the welcome shade of the covered wooden sidewalk, he can view everyone arriving and leaving by stage. He also has a clear line-of-sight to the town's largest stable.

Co-owner Freeman Cobb steps out from the cool, wainscoted interior. "Are you waiting for a coach, Walter?" he says.

The young man's American accent and uncalled-for familiarity grate on Fraser's nerves. But today, politeness is necessary.

"Freeman, it is a rare treat to see you. What brings you up from Melbourne?"

"This is my week to tour our facilities in the goldfields."

Fraser points. "Here comes one of your conveyances now." The burgundy coach body perched above canary yellow wheels identify it as a Cobb stagecoach. "Maybe my friend is on board. He was unclear on his arrival time."

Four draft horses halt with the clang and jangle of metal harness fittings. The handbrake squealing against the iron-rimmed front wheels rents the morning peace. The American-built stagecoach sways on its leather-strap suspension system. Fraser can attest from experience that Cobb offers the smoothest ride in Australia. Four people disembark.

Fraser rises in annoyance. "He is not here. I will try later. Good day, Freeman." He had not intended to depart but Cobb's presence irritates him.

Fraser strides down Main Road. His frustration heightens as he passes the Duchess of Kent Hotel. He had entered the hotel's café earlier, intending on breakfast. The sentimental saps Robinson and Sayers were wearing black armbands in misguided respect for Ryan's dead bitch. Fraser had stomped out.

He seeks out another location to continue his surveillance. Near the Star Hotel, he spots a rider slumped on a familiar horse. The horse halts. The man slips off the saddle and flops onto the dusty street. With effort, he pushes himself to his feet and wambles into the hotel's bar. Fraser's intellect at first denies the clear reality. Even though Stephen had prepared him, the image of the high-and-mighty moralist Ryan Warrain publicly intoxicated astounds him. The truth and implications of what he witnessed fill his thoughts. After days of scowling, Fraser smiles at the reality before him. Unable to resist further spectacle, he follows Ryan into the hotel's wood paneled bar.

This early in the day, Ryan is the lone customer. The slim, blond-bearded, twenty-three-year-old co-owner, William Irwin, is defending his bar. Fraser chuckles while the two Irishmen—one sober and the other pickled—joust with the arcane cant of homeland slums.

Ryan turns at Fraser's footsteps. "Aw-w-w-w Walter. Grand to see ye. Tell this miserable, worthless ale-draper to pass me a bit of bingo."

Fraser raises his brows in a silent query to Irwin. The barkeeper slaps the bar and says, "There'll be naught for this swill-tub. I'll be fetching a bus-napper to haul his arse to jail none too soon."

Fraser bends to Ryan's ear, ignoring the stench of whisky on him. "Let us step out back. I have a flask in my inside pocket."

Ryan brightens and steadies himself on the bar.

"Mr. Irwin," Fraser says, "I will escort Mr. Warrain out the rear door."

"Aye. 'Tis the proper way out for the likes of him."

Fraser guides Ryan down the hall and exits into the courtyard separating the hotel and its stable. He maneuvers the drunk into shade cast by the building. Fraser imagines how he could kill Ryan this moment and claim self-defense after an unprovoked attack. With no witnesses, it would be his word against a drunkard's.

Not now. There is a bigger prize to be had.

Fraser hands over his polished silver flask. Ryan slumps on the wall and holds the slim container in both hands.

"I topped this up last night with brandy."

Ryan takes a swig, grimaces, and grins. "Thank ye." He tips the flask and chugs. Fraser retrieves the flask before the sot empties it. "Easy, friend. You need to stay awake, at least."

"'Twill not matter," Ryan slurs. "Asleep…awake…dead…'tis all the same."

"I heard you have been in your cups for many days now. Who is managing the business?"

"Hell if I care. S'pose it be Stephen. He's always a sober prig." Ryan slides along the wall, upsetting his tentative balance.

Fraser checks Ryan's fall. "Maybe I can help lighten your load."

"Naught can relieve this burden," Ryan says, sniffling.

Fraser smiles, rejoicing in Ryan's grief. "Please ask Stephen to look me up next time he is in Ballarat."

"Bloody Stephen in bloody Ballarat." Ryan pushes himself off from the wall. "Where's my bloody horse?"

"You abandoned him out front. See that passageway to the right. It leads to the street."

Ryan staggers through the courtyard and into the alley, holding a wall for balance. Fraser follows the gormless drunk, forcing himself not to skip with joy.

In the street, he spots a familiar woman seated on a buckboard. Ryan's gelding is tied to the rear.

"Hello Ellen," Fraser says. "It has been a long time."

"Hello Walter. It is a pity these are not better times and we could chat," she replies. "I ought to take his highness home before he drinks himself to death. Could you please force him into the wagon? Strike him if you must."

Fraser clutches Ryan by his shirt collar and the belt of his trousers and marches him to the wagon's rear. He pushes Ryan's head and torso onto the platform. With a heave, he rolls the bedraggled lump of humanity until Ryan lies on his back inside the box with his feet poking out the open tailgate.

That is the most fun I have had in days, he muses. "Take care, Ellen," he says, tipping his bowler hat.

"Thank you, Walter. I truly appreciate the assistance," Ellen says. She shakes the reins to start the wagon moving, its embarrassing cargo on display for all to witness.

Fraser chuckles. *Too bad Scott is not here to see this.*

*****

"Are we clear yet?" Ryan mutters from the wagon's deck.

"Yes."

A green-faced Ryan hoists himself up and hangs over the sideboard. To Ellen's peels of laughter, he spews the boozy contents of his guts onto the roadway. After a final sputtering dry heave, he says, "I can nary understand why anyone drinks that vile stuff."

"You poor thing. Like a young man on his first binge."

"'Tis not fair to be laughing at me in my state. I've not had hard liquor afore today."

"I put a jug of water in the wicker basket."

Ryan twists out the cork and guzzles the cool, clean liquid. "Aye. That feels better." He lies with his head on his arms.

"Did Fraser take the bait?" Ellen asks over her shoulder.

"He asked to see Stephen."

*****

Two days later, a plate of scrambled eggs in hand, Stephen joins Ryan at breakfast. "I miss Ellen already," he says.

"She claims the guest room bed hurts her back," Ryan replies. "I suppose there is no point in buying another."

"Nay," Stephen says.

"Where is Fraser today?"

"Gellibrand says he watched a show at the Montezuma Hotel Theater last evening and roomed there overnight. I propose to visit customers on Main Road today to hear complaints about our service. I admit, it pains me deeply to disappoint them."

"We need a few complaints. 'Twill not be much longer."

*****

Walter Fraser leaves the hotel in mid-morning and steps into the blazing street. The summer sun is already uncomfortable. It promises to be another scorcher. A dry wind is raising wisps of dust, adding an alkaline tang to the air.

After a week in Ballarat, Fraser decides he will return to his lonely sheep station today, Scott or no Scott. His ramblings in town have been futile and have set the local gossips speculating on reasons for his long visit. As a middle-aged bachelor, he is unwise to encourage wagging tongues.

Fraser now admits an event unfortunate and unexpected has occurred. Scott may be lying injured somewhere, wounded again like he so often is in fights. None of the men he sent with Scott returned for their pay. Perhaps the blacks fought better than Loklok predicted. He must accept Scott could be dead. He dabs his eyes with a handkerchief.

Two passing women stop and gauge his condition with compassionate inquiring expressions. "A spot of grit," he says with a smile. *Mind your own damn business.*

Stephen may have information about Scott but Fraser cannot ask, not since he claimed Scott was away. Any hint Scott helped massacre Laarr's group would sober up Ryan in a heartbeat and bring wraith and ruin upon him. Loklok might have answers, but Fraser knows he is impossible to locate. He has no contacts in the black community, not even a servant he can ask. Fraser admits Loklok has no reason to help Scott. He may be Scott's killer given how he suffered as a boy under Scott's supervision.

Fraser struts along Main Road on his way to retrieve his horse at the stable. Ahead, Stephen McNichol steps from the Criterion Store in an argument with the diminutive proprietor, David Jones.

The textile merchant cranes his head to look up at Stephen. "This will not do. I must have shipments on time. I cannot sell empty shelves."

"Aye, I am terribly sorry. I promise we will solve our problems very soon."

"And tell that partner of yours to sober up and find his backbone. Everyone has troubles but you don't see us all staggering in the streets." Jones dismisses Stephen with a flip of his hand and returns to his shop.

"That bloody cockalorum was always a quick-tempered fellow," Fraser says.

Stephen jerks his attention towards the voice. "I regret you had to witness that."

"His is not the only voice of discontent I have overheard from your haulage customers."

"We will get our house in order soon," Stephen counters.

"That would be prudent. I know from experience how fast another company can woo unhappy customers," Fraser says. "I take it you have problems with your black teamsters."

"Aye. They interpret the death of Ryan's wife as a bad omen and a signal the spirits no longer favor Ryan. At least, Weeyn tells me so."

"Why not hire whites?"

"Ryan refuses. He maintains loyalty to his blacks even as they begin to desert him."

"Maybe you should sell out before your reputation collapses, while you can command a reasonable price."

"Are you making me an offer?" Stephen asks, his voice low and conspiratorial.

"I miss the haulage business. By buying you out, I become the top hauler without serious competition. Plenty of down-on-their luck miners will accept teamster jobs now."

"Ryan will not agree."

"Insist," Fraser barks. "He is weak and degenerate. He will bend to your superior moral suasion."

"Aye. But it will cost you dear."

"Do you still own fourteen wagons?"

"Aye. I would keep two buckboards for the station."

"For twelve of your biggest and best wagons, two dozen healthy draft horses and all their tack, my offer is eight hundred pounds."

"Nay. Nay. The wagons and horses be worth two thousand pounds at auction. And there still be value in the firm's reputation and customer list. I will not let the haulage go for less than three thousand…and we keep the cooperage, smithy, wheelwright and luxury goods import."

"I expect a Scot to bargain well," Fraser says, "but your price far exceeds the value. My final offer is two thousand."

"Add five hundred more and you have a deal," Stephen adds.

Fraser twists the end of his blonde mustache. "Agreed, but Ryan must sign an agreement to refrain from the transport business for life. Do we have a deal?"

Stephen's face screws up while he considers the offer. Resignation crosses the big man's features. Fraser knows he has won.

"I will ask our lawyer in Buninyong to draw up an agreement and deliver a copy, if that suits you."

"Come to my sheep station in four days," Fraser replies. "I will examine it and contact you concerning the transfer details."

"Do you want a copy for Scott too?"

Fraser frowns. "No. One will be sufficient."

*****

"Twenty-five hundred is a bargain," Ryan states. He plops into a seat in Stephen's office.

"Aye."

"Fraser knows to pay with gold or sterling, no credit."

"Aye. It be a huge sum, even for Fraser. He will borrow most of it against his station."

"Where do I sign?" Ryan says.

Stephen unfolds a contract and passes it. "Sign by the X under Fraser's name."

Ryan accepts the pen Stephen hands him. He dips the nib in the ink well and scrawls his signature. "Do ye have the other paper from our lawyer?"

Stephen slides the requested document across the desk. Ryan notices his partner's frown as he signs. "I accept ye are not happy with dissolving our partnership but 'tis the only way. Perhaps if I'd killed Loklok or Fraser when I had a chance, our future would be different."

"Remember what I said about the Lord dictating our paths in life?"

"Aye. But I can't believe we've no choice," Ryan says.

"You have a choice between good and evil. From my observations, you stay close to the former."

"Thank ye."

Stephen shifts in his chair and drapes his arms over the armrests. He watches Ryan sign the document describing how they will split up their entwined enterprises among the four partners. "I dunnae like it but I be committed. So be Weeyn and Ellen. It saddens me. I cannot imagine a finer set of business partners. Together, we made a respectable fortune."

"Aye, and a better set of friends there nary was," Ryan says.

The conversation tugs at Ryan's heart. By dissolving the partnership, Ryan marks the end of years of love, friendship and prosperity. It adds to the unabating sorrow of losing Alinga and Yearn. "Ye can make new arrangements with Weeyn and Ellen after, if ye sees fit."

"It be too early to ask. They be on tenterhooks. And both have sufficient wealth to make other choices."

"Who's watching Fraser?" Ryan says.

"Weeyn and Polligerry."

"Polligerry is privy to the entire plan now, I take it?" Ryan asks.

"Aye. I saw no alternative. Weeyn requires assistance. Do not worry. Polligerry would die before betraying you."

"I know. I'll miss him," Ryan says, sighing. "When is Fraser expecting his loan money to arrive?"

"Tomorrow."

"Then ye had better be off to Geelong today to establish yer alibi."

"Aye." A trace of a smile crosses Stephens face. "I be leaving shortly."

"'Tis a queer look. What are ye not telling me?"

"I will have a perfect alibi," Stephen says. "I be meeting a new partner of sorts in Geelong."

"Already!"

"Aye. My eldest brother in Scotland has found me a bride. The lady and I corresponded. I join her tomorrow. We be married the next day."

"Ye've been keeping that hand of cards close to yer chest, Stephen."

"Aye. I dinna want to jinx it by speaking prematurely." He reaches into a drawer. "Here be a daguerreotype of the lass, Sarah."

The grainy photograph displays a stout but comely woman in her early twenties, with light hair and freckles. "It is true then as the proverb goes—every cloud does have a silver lining."

"Aye. This station will hear the sound of children again."

"'Tis a pity her first experience here will be of a disaster," Ryan says.

"We will all recover in time, God willing."

Ryan stands and extends his hand. Stephen rises and envelops it with both of his mighty paws.

"I'll miss ye, my friend."

"And I you. I have not…" Stephen cannot finish his remark.

"Promise to hire as many natives as ye can," Ryan says to change the subject.

"Aye. I ken their value and count Polligerry and others as friends."

"And Dan. Take care of him. He's a mighty fine animal."

"Aye. He will have a home for life with me."

"And make sure ye sell out the haulage firm afore the railroad arrives," Ryan says. "There is a line already running between Geelong and Melbourne.

"Aye."

"One part of the plan worries me," Stephen says as he folds the business documents. "Loklok has not played his hand."

"He is nearby," Ryan replies. "He will make his move soon."

"How do you know?"

"I've dreamed it," Ryan says.

"Another vision?"

"Aye. I nary had one when Alinga lived. Now I do. 'Tis like she opened a door to Dreamtime for me."

"The Lord works in mysterious ways."

*****

Ryan's gut cramps as Stephen leaves on his blond horse. No person in his life, except his grandfather, gave Ryan such consistent and useful advice; yet, Ryan must forsake him. Their paths will never cross. Their parting is one more loss to rip at his heart.

In the distance, Stephen pauses to chat with a second rider on his way in. Ryan tenses. No one is supposed to visit during his period of faked drunkenness.

He darts into his house and exchanges his clean shirt for a filthy one. He uncorks a whisky bottle and dribbles the amber liquid on his lapels. He swills a sip in his mouth and spits into a chamber pot.

He lurches out the front door and collapses into a chair, feigning insobriety yet again. The rider is Charles Doudiet.

The young man, his once fancy clothes faded and mended, dismounts. He approaches the porch, his gait hesitant. "I am sorry to disturb you during this time of ill health, but I felt compelled to make one last visit."

"I'm glad to see ye Charlie, ill or healthy." Ryan hates having to lie to the sincere and polite young man. "Are ye going somewhere?"

"My adventures here are at an end. I have funds remaining to buy passage to Canada and little else."

Ryan rises from his chair, forgetting for a moment to play the drunk. He retrieves several pound notes from a trouser pocket and hands them to Doudiet. "I didn't pay ye for yer sketches. An artist of yer caliber shouldn't work for free."

Doudiet balks but his resolve wavers. "I am grateful. I could use a little extra."

"Ross is often on my mind," Ryan says.

"Such a tragedy. I lost a brother that day," Doudiet says. He shifts his feet and clears his throat. "I was terribly saddened too by the death of Alinga. You noticed, I am certain, I was quite smitten by her. I mean no offense!"

"None taken," Ryan answers. "'Twas many who were smitten."

"And how is Mrs. O'Sullivan? Has she recovered from the loss of Henry?"

"The wound is fresh but healing," Ryan says.

"Poor woman. She and Henry had such grand plans to run off to Canada."

"Pardon," Ryan says. "What of her marriage vows?"

"Henry told me the church granted her a separation several years ago. They hoped to have her husband declared dead once in California."

Ryan's legs begin to wobble and he seeks safety in the nearest chair.

"I apologize if my impromptu visit has strained your strength," Doudiet says. "I bid you farewell and a speedy recovery."

"Aye, Charlie," Ryan replies, trying to regain his composure. "Have a safe journey."

*****

Ryan remains in the chair for an hour staring at the porch floorboards. He rubs his small, half finger. His right boot toe taps non-stop while he wrestles disappointment and jealousy. His rational mind insists Ellen was free to make her own choices once Ryan married Alinga. But his emotions do not accept that reality—not at first. Anger, like clouds, conceals the light. Why did she not mention the separation?

The darkness in his thoughts dissipates. A thin beam of hope illuminates his path. A smile cracks his sorrow-aged face.

Ryan ends his sulk and stands. Ellen will arrive soon to sign the partnership dissolution agreement. In the parlor, he pauses next to the framed sketch of Alinga above the mantel. *I hope ye will understand.*

*****

Washed, shaven and sporting clean clothes, Ryan greets Ellen when she arrives in her carriage. "Hello dear Ellen. 'Tis grand to see ye."

Ellen's expression confirms she has caught the calculated nuance in Ryan's voice. "You seem unusually chipper."

"Charles Doudiet visited earlier bearing interesting news."

"I passed him on the road. He told me he returns home. Is that the news of which you speak?"

"Nay. Charlie mentioned ye were granted a separation some years ago." Ryan picks his words and tone. He does not want to scold or accuse. "It came as quite a surprise."

Ellen folds her gloved hands at her waist and fixes Ryan with her best schoolmistress glare. "I did try to tell you once."

"When?"

"Do you recall the day I met Alinga? I arrived and said I had good news."

The forgotten vignette unfurls in Ryan's memory. "Aye. I do now."

"I had come to inform you that I acted on your suggestion to ask for a separation, and that my parish priest had sent a recommendation to the bishop in Sydney that he grant my request. Alinga's presence made my news meaningless. Six months later, I received official notice. I remain married but have greater social freedom."

"'Twas right of ye not to tell me. Marriage to Alinga shut the door to anything other than friendship between us," Ryan says. "But…"

The hard edge of Ellen's features softens as she interprets the meaning of Ryan's dangling remark. "But what?"

"I nary stopped loving ye." Ryan steps towards her and extends his right hand.

Ellen balks at meeting him half way. Her hands remain folded. "I tried very hard to erase my feelings for you," she begins. "I felt betrayed by your choice of Alinga—though I agree I had no right, since I rebuffed all your advances. I indulged myself with Henry to forget you."

"Charlie said ye were going to leave Australia together."

She smiles, as if for a poor joke. "That was Henry's fancy. I played my role." She frowns. "The sober and sane part of my mind always knew I was too old for him—that I was a plaything he would not invite to meet his parents."

"So, is honesty the rule agin?"

"I perceive no other road to take at this juncture," she replies. Her right hand unfolds from its twin. With a halting, tentative movement, like someone testing the temperature of bathwater, she extends a finger and touches Ryan's outstretched palm.

Ryan encloses that single digit and pulls Ellen into his arms. He touches his nose to hers. "Let's make Henry's idea our own," he whispers.

Ellen leans into him, spreading her arms in a body hug.

"Our plans for Fraser," Ryan says, "call for ye to leave soon to establish yer alibi. Instead of visiting Melbourne for a few days, prepare to leave Australia."

She kisses his chin. "Go on."

"Pack yer belongings. Withdraw yer funds from the bank and ship out to Sydney. Take a room at a hotel on Macquarie Street nigh the harbor and I'll find ye. Listen for the name Mr. Pine."

"And then what, Mr. Pine?" she says, nibbling his earlobe.

"We'll go to America as husband and wife. If we can make it legal, we will. If not, we'll live in sin and ask the Lord for forgiveness."

"I could use a little sin right now," she whispers, "that is, unless you want to wait."

"I've waited eight years. 'Tis enough."

*****

The little dingo rests on a hillside. In the distance, she spots the red dingo walking away with a white dingo.

Alinga's eyes snap open and she sits up crying.

«What is it, child?» Orana kneels beside her on the possum skin bed.

«I remember. Everything.» She looks at the old woman. «White devils killed my father, mother…my little son, my entire clan. A black traitor carried me away and threw me off a cliff. »

«You are Wathaurung? Who was your father?»

«Stone?»

Orana emits a piercing cry.

Alinga understands immediately. «You must be my father's first wife. I am Alinga, his only daughter.» Alinga lays a hand on Orana's shoulder. «I saw father kill one amadeat before they shot him. He died a warrior's death.»

Alinga stands up. «I cannot grieve for the dead. I must go find my brother. And my husband. He thinks I am dead.»

«Stay a bit longer. You are not well enough.»

«I must go. My husband is making plans to leave this land.»

«Why would a Wathaurung leave this place?»

«He is white. He came from far away and will return there.»

Orana gasps. «White? With red hair?»

«Yes. Why?»

«I met him. He came looking for you the day before I found you.» Orana sobs. «I am sorry. Had I known, I would have sent word through my cousin Spark.»

«Do not fret, sweet mother. The spirits have decided my path and place obstacles to test my worthiness.»

*****

From the loft of Fraser's stable, Weeyn peeks between the horizontal barn boards at three men. Fraser, his young stable hand and his aged cook—all armed—wait in the shade of Fraser's porch. To Weeyn's left, Polligerry snoozes on the old hay, unaffected by the oppressive midday heat.

A black stagecoach drawn by four horses rattles into the compound amid a plume of dust. Polligerry awakens. The guard beside the driver holds a shotgun. Two men wearing pistols exit the coach and approach Fraser. One carries a leather pouch.

Fraser steps from the porch. They exchange words Weeyn cannot discern. Fraser assays the satchel contents, signs a document presented to him, and returns to his house. The stage leaves. The entire handover lasts less than two minutes.

"Many hours until dark," Polligerry says. "Busy-busy later. Time sleep now." The old Wurundjeri returns to slumber.

Weeyn lies awake. Swirling images of recent tragic events and the intertwined details of Ryan's plot prevent his mind from resting. For most of his twenty-three years, he lived a life supported emotionally and often materially by his family or his white business partners. That is now dust in the wind. In a day, maybe two, he must choose a new road to travel.

*****

Polligerry nudges Weeyn awake. He jerks to a sitting position, having no recollection of falling asleep. Narrow, parallel lines of moonlight illuminate the mow and etch Polligerry's face.

"Bad man sleep now," says Polligerry. "He lock doors. He on chair in parlor. Big gun on lap."

"Are you sure he sleeps?"

"Yes. Polligerry sneak out. Hear bad man snore."

"Where are Fraser's guards?"

"Guards no good. Young one sleep now on porch. Old one drink whisky. Sleep soon."

"Did Fraser leave any windows open for a cross-breeze?"

"Yes. One front. One back in kitchen."

Weeyn and Polligerry descend the ladder into the stable. The horses shift in their stalls from the sound and scent of humans, but make no fuss. Weeyn shows Polligerry which horse to steal. A big black mare with a white blaze is Fraser's favorite mount.

Polligerry whispers to the docile beast while he saddles her. From a duffle bag, Polligerry extracts strips of dark cloth. He ties a piece to the saddle's dee rings and every buckle to prevent metallic jangling and reflection of moonlight. To each hoof, Polligerry fastens a thick wad of folded blanket to muffle its steps. Instead of a standard bridle, with all its metal connectors, Polligerry settles for a simple rope halter and rope lead.

"Polligerry ready," he whispers to Weeyn.

"Meet me behind the kitchen," he replies.

Polligerry leads the horse out the rear on his way to a predetermined thicket of gums to the east. Weeyn exits through a side door. Thin, scattered clouds stream past the moon. A waxing and waning breeze raises and settles dust and loose leaves. Weeyn imagines the spirits inhaling and exhaling in contented slumber.

Weeyn passes close to the house, staying in the shadows cast by structures and trees. Both of Fraser's men—fellows not trained to be proper guards—snooze in chairs on the front porch. Moonlight illuminates half of the main room and reflects off Fraser's polished boots. It will not be easy to approach Fraser without alerting his slumbering sentries.

Weeyn pads around the house to the rear, deep in night's dark shelter. A block of wood holds one window open two inches. Entry appears too easy. Weeyn slips his hand through the gap and caresses the window frame's lower edge like someone smoothing the feathers of a wounded songbird. He finds nothing suspicious.

He pushes his arm in past his elbow and moves his hand in a slow arc up one side of the window, across the glass to the opposite side. His forefinger brushes a textile or piece of string. Something metallic clinks the glass. Weeyn dismisses the sound as too faint to awake Fraser.

He slips a fingertip down the fabric until it encounters a metal object. With force no greater than a beating moth wing, his fingers explore its roundish contours. The data feeding to his brain conjures up a picture. It is a bell used for sheep or goats. Weeyn clasps the bell's clapper with his thumb and forefinger and waits for Polligerry. He cannot both hold the bell and disconnect it in his physical position.

Polligerry finds him kneeling in the dark by the window. Weeyn explains the simple alarm Fraser has rigged. Knife in hand, Polligerry slips his slim arm through the window gap and severs the string. Weeyn withdraws the bell and hides it nearby.

Weeyn and Polligerry place their hands under the window and wait. When the next gust of wind makes the dwellings' board siding creak, they apply gradual pressure. The windows begins to slide up with a soft squeal.

Weeyn enters the dark kitchen. Polligerry follows. They pause and listen. The house is quiet. Fraser snores. They ease down the hall. The parlor is well lit by the moon, at least to men whose pupils have adjusted to darkness. With their dark skin and clothing, they are the spawn of shadows, invisible should anyone look in from outside.

Their footfalls force a squeak from the floorboards. They freeze and listen. Fraser does not stir. With simple hand gestures, they agree to employ an old stalking technique. Gusts of wind tease the house. Each time the building groans with the wind, they take one step together. They pause varying lengths between steps to avoid creating a pattern. This way, any noise they do make seems innocent.

Twenty paces consume ten minutes. They halt inches behind Fraser's high-backed, stuffed chair. Weeyn studies the furniture closest to Fraser, ascertaining what he might dislodge in a struggle. Fraser's feet are a safe distance from a low parlor table, but to his right an oil lamp rests on a pedestal stand.

At the speed of a lazy koala, Weeyn lifts the lamp and sets it on the mantle. Next he lifts the stand and places it well to the side. Weeyn inspects the shotgun on Fraser's lap. The sleeper's relaxed fingers are well away from the trigger. The hammer is not cocked. Weeyn concludes the gun is impotent in its current state.

Polligerry pulls a length of braided cloth from his pocket. He grasps both ends and positions the garrote near Fraser's throat and waits for Weeyn.

Weeyn pulls a wad of cloth from one pocket. His task is to hold Fraser and stop him from yelling. In a synchronized movement, Polligerry loops the cloth band under Fraser's chin, yanks and twists. Fraser's eyes bug out and his lips spring open. Weeyn shoves the wad into Fraser's mouth and grabs both wrists. He lays his considerable weight over Fraser to pin him.

Fraser twists and arches his back, fighting for breath and life. He cannot flail his arms or legs because of Weeyn's weight. His knee connects once with Weeyn's exposed groin. The Wathaurung warrior absorbs the stinging blow without a sound.

With his air cut off, the intense struggle soon exhausts Fraser's oxygen supply. He slips into unconsciousness on the way to death. But death has to wait.

When Polligerry feels the body slump, he relaxes pressure and Fraser resumes breathing. Weeyn picks up the shotgun and pads barefoot to the front door. He peeks out the window. Both guards remain at slumber.

The two natives lay Fraser on the floor. With ropes they bind his ankles, knees and wrists. For good measure they rope his arms to his torso. They tie a proper gag across his mouth and slip a hood over his head.

Weeyn returns the stand to its former position and places the lamp on it. He rests the shotgun on the parlor table. One more task and they can leave.

"Find the money satchel," Weeyn whispers in Polligerry's ear.

Polligerry's toothy grin glows in the gray room light. "Mother goose always sit on eggs," Polligerry says. The fabric on Fraser's chair extends to the floor. Polligerry kneels and reaches beneath and slides out a pouch.

Weeyn opens the clasp to make certain it indeed contains the money. He ties the satchel to Fraser's trussed up body, and heaves up the man's front end. Polligerry lifts Fraser at his knees. They exit out through the kitchen. Weeyn sets his burden down to reattach the bell to the string. He closes the window to the original height. Nothing is amiss. The rear door remains unlocked as it would be if Fraser let himself out.

They hustle Fraser to a nearby gum glade and dump him in a blackened buckboard pulled by a single draft horse with muffled hooves. Polligerry has tied Fraser's horse astern. Unseen and unheard, they follow narrow sheep tracks northward.

The Last Act

February-March 1855

Fraser awakens with a cough that sears his throat. He tries swallowing but receives another painful hack for his efforts. He is hooded and seated on a chair. Someone has tied his hands behind him, and his torso and feet to the chair. He tugs to test his bounds. Nothing gives. Nearby people shift in squeaky chairs.

"Water," he croaks.

Heavy steps cross a wooden floor. Ryan yanks off the hood and holds a cup to his parched lips. Fraser guzzles the cold liquid, soaking his chin and shirt with the overflow. He drains the cup and surveys the room—a parlor in what appears to be a ranch house. His clothes are gone, replaced with unfamiliar working garb. The low yellowish light outside tells him it is shortly after sunrise. Beside Ryan are three glum black men—two he recognizes: Nalong and Weeyn. He shudders at what their presence implies.

"Why am I here?" he says.

"To stand trial for murder," a very sober Ryan answers.

A chill of fear crawls up Fraser's spine. "I have not killed anyone," Fraser exclaims. He wants to shout but his damaged larynx forbids it.

"By yer own admission, ye have killed dozens of blacks."

"Nearly one hundred, but blacks do not count."

"They do to their friends and families."

"Nonsense," Fraser snarls. "Besides, unless you can name names, you have no case."

"Ye want names? Let's start with my father-in-law Laarr." Ryan proceeds to name every man, women and child massacred by Fraser's men, ending with Yearn and Alinga.

"I played no role. I was in Geelong."

"Ye sent yer man Scott in the company of three bushrangers and that accursed Loklok to do yer killing."

"Scott is off on business. You are inventing this. You have no evidence."

"Aye we do. One day last month, Officer Billy crawled on his belly to my station and with his dying breath said ye and Loklok planned to attack Laarr's family. That is evidence."

"It is the ravings of a delusional man. You need to do better than that."

"Yer lie about Scott is evidence yer hiding the truth."

Something on Ryan's smug expression makes Fraser shiver. "Where is Scott? What do you know?"

"I'll let Nalong testify on that subject," Ryan replies. "Tell him what ye saw and did."

"My family camped close to Laarr," Nalong begins. "We hear guns. When we arrive, all blacks dead. Two whites also dead. Two trails lead away. I follow one trail because I found feet marks of boys among boot marks. I guessed who took them." Nalong says, staring at Fraser.

"What did you do with Scott?" Fraser hisses.

"I follow the trail. I see Mr. Healey. He wears no trousers. He did tie two boys to tree. Before he can hurt boys, I thrust my spear up that bunyip's shite hole."

Fraser gasps. A bolt of sympathetic pain runs from his anus to his gut.

Nalong continues. "The spear come out his belly. He scream like wounded wombat. I watch him in pain. I want him to know how I did feel. Then I slit his throat."

"Murderer," Fraser screams, ignoring his ragged larynx. "You killed my Scott. The devil take you, you ungrateful heathen."

*****

Fraser's outburst confirms for Ryan what he always suspected—Fraser loved Healey more than as a friend. Still, Ryan finds no sympathy for him in his heart. He reaches for a cup of water and dashes it in Fraser's face.

"Have ye anything to say in yer defense, Mr. Fraser?"

Fraser leans forward as far as his trussed body will allow. "This is entirely your fault," he says, his voice full of contempt. "You! Mr. Kangaroo Fighter. Mr. Tough Guy. Mr. High and Mighty. All the death is on you. You bloody bastard. You!"

Weeyn steps forward, raising a hand to slap Fraser.

"Nay, Weeyn. Let him speak. I grant him that one right."

Fraser draws a deep breath. "You never gave anyone opposed to you an inch of ground to call their own. You used cutthroat business tactics to ruin my haulage business."

"I nary did," Ryan says. "Yer drivers left for the goldfields and ye had too much pride to hire blacks."

Fraser ignores the interruption. "You inflicted horrible damage on poor Scott when less would have sufficed. You ridiculed and emasculated Loklok. And you called me a kiddy bugger before half the town."

"Well, ain't ye?"

"I never touched those boys. Ask Nalong and Weeyn. It was Scott. I begged him to stop but he couldn't. He is…was sick."

Ryan glances at Nalong and Weeyn. They both shrug, confirming Fraser's statement.

"Why didn't ye stop Healey's abuse?"

Fraser sighs. "I tried," he mutters. "Scott threatened to leave. I gave in. I opened a school to try in some small way to make up for the damage."

"But yer school became the source of boys for Healey."

Fraser sucks in a ragged breath. "Many boys graduated without any interference. I did some good."

"Ye could've done better."

A twisted smile crosses Fraser's face. "Are you not being a hypocrite?"

"Pardon?"

"You profess disgust regarding Scott's attraction to underage black boys, yet you dallied with a black girl hardly much older."

Before Ryan can respond, Weeyn leaps forward and snags Fraser's neck in one hand. "I should rip out your throat for that blasphemy. My sister chose Warrain. I never consented to Healey, nor did Nalong, Loklok or the others."

Ryan lays his hand on Weeyn's shoulder. Weeyn understands the wordless message and releases Fraser.

"I suppose," Ryan says, "I should apologize for accusing ye in public."

"Too bloody late," Fraser hollers. "You destroyed my social status. I vowed that day to get even. Your bullying ways left a trail of death and sorrow behind you."

Fraser's accusation hits Ryan like a punch in the gut—Fraser killed Alinga and her family as retribution for Ryan's alleged bullying. He wobbles and plops into his armchair. All his life he has resisted bullies. Fraser is the last person he'd ever expect to accept criticism from—yet the vile man succeeds in casting doubt where Ryan foresaw no vulnerability.

His mind races to rationalize the facts. He tugs at his half-finger, while he reruns every violent encounter. Yes, perhaps he bullied Fraser the day he insulted Alinga in Ballarat, but never Loklok and Healey. Those men aimed to kill him. It was self-defense, not bullying. Ryan composes himself and leaves his chair.

"Basic justice does not permit a public insult or a business thrashing to be an excuse for murdering women and children."

"What do you intend to do with me?" Fraser mutters to his feet, his anger and energy now spent.

"Why, hang ye of course."

Ryan motions to his companions and points to the door. The four move outside.

"Lads," Ryan says, after closing the door, "the last scenes in this bit of theater are ready to be staged." He steps close to Nalong and grips the youth's muscular shoulders. "Now, we must say farewell. Go home. Get married. Have children. Keep the secrets we share."

"Yes Warrain, though it will injure me to hear the false tales."

"Tell and retell the stories of Warrain in the better days. The truth is powerful."

"I must help avenge Loklok's crimes."

"Go home. Ye have had a fair helping of revenge already. I'll settle with Loklok. He is mine to kill."

Nalong shakes Ryan's hand, says farewell in Wadawurrung to Weeyn and in Woiwurrung to Polligerry. With a salute, he begins the long trek home.

"He make good arweat someday," Polligerry remarks.

"Aye. He knows the white world and language. It may help his people." Ryan answers. "And now friend Polligerry, ye must play yer last role in our little drama. Hitch up the twelve wagons we selected. Gather all the teamsters and anyone else ye require to manage the horses for a few days."

The old Wurundjeri chews his lower lip throughout Ryan's instructions. "The wagons ready," he says. "We hitched before sunrise."

"Good. The better to not delay. Please, drive the wagons to Fraser's station. Wait there until Mr. McNichol comes for ye."

At Ryan's last word, Polligerry steps forward and hugs him. "May spirits always walk with Warrain," he whispers.

With a slight bow of the head, Polligerry faces about and strides to the stable. At each final parting, the weight of another loss accumulates on Ryan's already sorrow-riddled soul. He punches his open palm with his fist to regain his focus. Much still needs to be done.

"Are ye ready for the last act?" Ryan says to Weeyn.

"Yes. The spirits of my dead family are eager."

Fraser's head jerks up when Ryan and Weeyn return. Ryan draws the curtains. Weeyn fetches a coil of hemp cord already fashioned into a hangman's noose. He fixes the rope over a roof beam. Beads of sweat form on Fraser's forehead.

"I do not suppose a plea for mercy will be welcomed," Fraser mutters.

"Ye deserve as much mercy as ye showed our family," Ryan answers.

Fraser licks his dry lips. His gaze roves the room and settles on Ryan. "You once stated in public you did not wish to soil your soul with my death. Remember?"

Ryan smirks at Fraser's feeble gambit. "I regret I did not kill ye that day. 'Tis a mistake I can't undo. But, Weeyn and I'll bring justice to our dead kin now."

"The rope is ready," Weeyn says.

"Let's shift him," Ryan replies.

Weeyn pins Fraser to his chair with his mighty arms while Ryan unties Fraser's restraints, except his hands. Weeyn lifts Fraser. Ryan positions the chair below the noose. Weeyn lowers Fraser's feet onto the chair and holds him upright. Standing on a chair, Ryan fits the noose over Fraser's head and slides the braided knot to tighten it around the left side of Fraser's neck. Weeyn and Ryan step back. Fraser, his hands still tied behind, fights for balance on the wobbly chair.

"You will not get away with this. Your guile will be punished. Constables will investigate. The evidence will doom you both."

"Aye, Stephen will insist the constables investigate," Ryan says. He opens a closet and retrieves Fraser's missing clothes. He removes his shirt and trousers and dons Fraser's better quality garments, finishing with Fraser's signature dark blazer and derby.

Weeyn hauls in a ten-gallon keg of coal oil from the kitchen.

"The police will discover this house burned to the ground." Ryan lights a candle and places it in a holder on a nearby table.

"Inside will be a body matching my description with traces of rope around the neck and an empty whisky flask near by. The constables will conclude a despondent drunkard torched his house and committed suicide."

Fraser's brow knots and his teeth grind as the web of his demise becomes clear. "I take some solace in knowing your reputation will be as ruined as mine."

Ryan ignores that blunt truth. "In two days, Stephen'll complain that Walter Fraser has disappeared with the money he promised to pay for our wagons. He'll inform the constables he expects to take his property home until the transaction can be completed. The police will investigate yer disappearance. Yer guards likely won't admit they fell asleep but will testify ye did not leave by the front door. The police will follow the horse's trail and will locate a few witnesses who saw a man matching yer description riding yer horse on the plain east of here. The law will conclude ye absconded with the borrowed money. The men who loaned ye the money will repossess yer station. Kangaroo Fighter haulage will continue in business without its founder."

"You conniving dishonorable fiend," Fraser croaks.

"Walter," Ryan says in a subdued tone, "ye killed my wife and child. For years ye executed black men because they slew yer family. Ye of all people should understand why ye must die today."

"No! You married outside your race against all societal norms."

"Walter," Ryan says, "ye had an attraction to Scott that society calls unnatural, did ye not?"

Fraser looks away. Ryan grabs his chin and lifts his head to force eye contact. "Walter, rules of society change. Love does not.

If ye had accepted Alinga in my life like ye wished society accepted yer love for Scott, our fight in Ballarat would nary have happened. We'd not be here today, both of us losers."

Ryan releases Fraser's chin.

"Have ye any last words, Walter?"

Fraser whispers, "May the Lord forgive my trespasses." Resignation softens his tense features.

Ryan nods at Weeyn and begins counting, "Three. Two. One!"

Both men kick aside the chair. Fraser drops two inches. The rope stiffens and creaks. His boots flail the air, while his body rotates. Over the space of a long minute, a purple hue darkens his features. His tongue lolls out and drips with saliva. A urine stain spreads across the crotch of his pants. One last body spasm jerks the rope and he goes limp.

"Our family is avenged," Weeyn says.

"As are the family's of a hundred dead clansmen," Ryan adds.

They fixate on the dangling corpse; through procrastination, not morbid curiosity. Neither wants to hurry to the next and last step. The ticks of the mantel clock echo in the silent room. Fraser's body swings in a narrow arc from the force of his final struggle. The width of the arc diminishes as each second passes.

The jangle and rumble of twelve wagons leaving the compound reanimates Ryan and Weeyn.

"Of all the friends I leave behind, ye are the one I'll miss the most," Ryan says.

Weeyn places his right palm over Ryan's heart. He pulls Ryan's right hand and holds it to his bare chest. "The bond of friends, the kinship of warriors, they go with us all our days."

"'Tis a pity we'll miss the chance to grow old together and help our children take our places."

"We will all come together in Dreamtime."

"Farewell, Weeyn."

"Farewell, Warrain." Weeyn departs and closes the door behind him.

From the closet, Ryan pulls out packed saddles bags. He reviews the contents: a change of clothes, his tomahawk, his copy of *Romeo and Juliet*, and both of Doudiet's sketches rolled in a protective tube of paper and oilskin. In a hidden pocket lies three thousand pounds of his savings plus two thousand pounds confiscated from Fraser—five hundred went to Weeyn and Polligerry.

Ryan walks one last time through his doomed house. Each room holds a happy memory—camaraderie in the dining room, good conversations by the fire, hours of reading pleasure in the library nook, and many nights of love and passion in the bedroom.

Ryan discards his sentimental musings and gets to work. He spreads the coal oil so it contacts walls, carpets and furniture. He pours several quarts on Fraser, soaking the clothes.

Ryan tips the candle onto the pool of oil. He pauses for a dozen heartbeats while a wave of flame engulfs the floor and climbs up the late Mr. Fraser.

His catharsis by fire underway, Ryan exits the rear door and hurries into the cover of gum trees behind the house. One hundred yards in, Polligerry has tied Fraser's saddled mare to a tree. Two jugs of water hang on the saddle horn. He refuses to look back at his station, his old life, as he starts the six-hundred-mile overland ride to Sydney.

*****

Weeyn appraises every tool and feature in his soot-darkened smithy. The room that once filled him with pride brings no joy today and offers no refuge. The forge is as cold as his mood. He caresses the big anvil. He pumps the bellows a dozen times, though there are no hot coals to excite. He marvels at the hoops of iron he'd made, now waiting for wagon wheels. They represent the skill that has set him free.

The expected shout of 'fire' interrupts his dreary reminiscence. He steps into the sunshine. Smoke pours from open windows in the main house. Flames already lick the outside wall of the porch. Most ranch hands are away with the wagons. Four men run with water buckets. Weeyn knows they are too late. He waits until the men exhaust themselves with their futile efforts.

"Stop," he shouts. "We are too few. Protect the other buildings from sparks. Stop brush fires."

The men hesitate. Weeyn knows the men believe Ryan is inside.

"It is too late," Weeyn says. "No one could survive."

The men relinquish to the flames the grand house that Ryan built for Alinga and their children. To Weeyn, the conflagration is another in a long list of recent funeral pyres.

Within half an hour the house collapses into itself, sending a geyser of sparks and embers into the air. Weeyn and the remaining crew dose every kindled offspring of the mother fire. Soon the blaze subsides to a jumble of smoldering beams.

In his shanty—the original farmhouse—Weeyn puts on fresh trousers and a shirt. In a saddlebag, he packs spare bullets and mementos. His past consists of a bracelet belonging to Tarra, a handkerchief embroidered by Alinga, a wooden bowl favored by Mokborree, and Laarr's knife, the gift from Warrain years ago. He slips five shells into his Colt. He straps on his hunting knife and holster. From under a loose floorboard, he retrieves his money— six hundred and twenty-four pounds he accumulated through wages and profits, and three hundred pounds from Fraser's loot.

Weeyn wanders once through the house of ghosts. Eyes closed, he calls forth memories of when it once was a place of love and laughter. He slaps his forehead, pushes back his shoulders, and marches out the front door. He leaves it ajar—an open door will welcome someone new.

At the stable, Weeyn saddles a gray gelding he knows from experience has great endurance. The horse is new to the stable and not yet marked with Ryan's brand. He guides the horse to the group guarding the charred and smoldering beams.

"I will ride to Buninyong to report the fire."

He does not wait for a reply. And he has no intention of riding to Buninyong.

Once beyond sight of the station, Weeyn leaves the Geelong Road and follows a cross-country trail leading to Fraser's place. He arrives at midday and arranges a private meeting with Polligerry.

"It is done," Weeyn says, "as Warrain planned."

Polligerry squints at Weeyn. "Why you here? Warrain plan not say you come here."

"Old friend, tell Mr. Stephen I have gone to search for a new life," he says.

"No hurry? Boss home soon. You wait and tell. It better way."

"I cannot wait."

Polligerry's expression changes. "A-h-h. You follow him."

Weeyn smiles at his astute companion. "Yes. He should not have to go alone."

"If I younger man, I follow too." He lays his palm on Weeyn's heart. "I pray peace find you on the road ahead. Go now. I tell truth to Mr. Stephen. For other people, I say you return to Wathaurung clan."

"Thank you. Take care of Mr. Stephen. He needs a good man like you."

Weeyn remounts and rides at a gallop northeastward. He hopes to cross Ryan's trail before dark.

*****

Ryan follows local trails and avoids roads and settlements. He steers close enough to lonely shepherd outposts to be seen but not so close as to reveal his facial features. Men wave. He ignores them.

Ryan rides until sunset. He picks a treed hilltop for his camp. The trees and brush provide concealment. The rise commands a view of the surrounding range. He unsaddles the mare and tethers her on a long lead to graze. Supper is strips of dried beef and water. For security reasons, he makes no fire. Ryan is certain Loklok follows him at a distance. He cannot spot his stalker—he senses his malignant energy.

Reclining with a tree as a back prop, he reflects on his night with Ellen, the slaking of an eight-year thirst. His mind fills with images of her long slim body, with her small breasts, white skin and orange hair. Such a contrast to the raven skin and mounded roundness of Alinga. As a lover, Ellen is a slow burning fire—intense but not showy—the opposite of Alinga's raging sexual energy. What both women had in common was their ability to satisfy Ryan and to inspire life-long love.

Ryan brings the horse deeper into the trees. He crawls under a thicket of low-hanging shrubs to sleep. No one can approach him in such a location without making noise, even if they discover his hideout in the dark. His last thoughts are of Ellen and future nights together.

*****

Sarah McNichol opens the curtain of the shanty to admire the setting sun on the strange landscape. New to Australia, she is still adjusting to the round hills and the strange trees. The golden light bathes a black person kneeling in the ashes of the destroyed ranch house.

"Husband. Come quickly."

Stephen steps up behind his new wife, gentle holds her shoulders and rests his chin on her red curls. "Yes, wife?"

"Look! Who is that?"

Stephen squints. "Impossible!

"What?" Sarah calls as Stephen moves her aside and bolts out the door.

"Alinga," he shouts, as he strides across the compound. "Dear Alinga."

She rises and buries herself in his brawny embrace. He feels her sobbing.

"Nice Mr. Stephen. Where is my husband? People told me he died in a fire but I have seen him."

"Aye, he is alive. He had to fake his death in order to cover up the execution of Fraser when he avenged the murder of your family. Healey is dead too. The evil is gone."

Alinga closes her eyes and leans into Stephen searching for strength to deal with this new revelation.

"Their deaths do not bring my family and Tarra back, but may sooth their spirits," she whispers.

Stephen finds nothing to say. He gently pats her back.

"And my brother?"

"He travels with Ryan."

"Where do they go?'

"Sydney. On the east coast."

"Then I must go to that place. I must find him before he returns to the sea. How do I get there?"

Sarah joins them. "I assume this young lass is Alinga back from the dead?"

"Aye."

Sarah extracts Alinga from Stephen's embrace. "Come inside. You need food and a cleanup."

"But I must go to my husband."

"You need nourishment and a plan first. I insist."

Alinga gazed into the larger woman's blue eyes. She smiled. "Thank you kind Mrs. Stephen."

She kissed Alinga's forehead. "Call me Sarah."

*****

Ryan is a red dingo crouched under cover on a hill. All is peaceful until a black dingo with a limp creeps up the hillside. He searches for someone. He seeks a battle to the death.

Ryan's lids snap open. He remains motionless and scans his immediate surroundings. What woke him up? Faint blue dawn light softens the darkness but limits visible objects to a few yards. The ears compensate for sight's limitations. He hears a swish of leaves nearby followed by a hard stomp of a horse. Why is the mare uneasy? Someone or something has crept into his treed refuge.

With minor, incremental movements his rolls from his side to his belly, a position that provides a wider scope. Confident he remains unseen, Ryan waits for the light to increase. He pulls his Colt from its holster. He waits to cock the pistol. The metallic click could reveal his position.

Light in the forest intensifies at a predictable pace, doubling Ryan's field of view every minute. Through the weave of bush stems surrounding him, a human silhouette takes shape in the vanishing gloom. Though in shadow, the broad shoulders and thick torso give the form a name.

Now with a clear target, Ryan cocks the pistol. "If ye move, ye die," he yells.

Loklok faces the voice. "Yes. I see you now." He lays his hands on his scalp, as if in surrender, and says, "Come out. I will wait."

A rational man would shoot the bastard without hesitation, Ryan concludes; but Loklok's passive stance collides with Ryan's notion of fair play. With his pistol pointed at his adversary, he crawls from under the low brush cover and stands. Loklok wears a handgun in a holster and a long knife in a sheath hanging on his trouser belt. His feet and chest are bare. Ryan notices a slight paunch.

"Ye put on weight."

"Too many days in hiding. No time for running and hunting."

"Did ye come to talk," Ryan says, clenching his teeth, "or to die?"

"I came to fight. Our opposing destinies have walked side-by-side for ten years. Today, we end that. We will battle like warriors until one or both are dead. No guns. Traditional weapons."

"Ye bear the nail scratches of my dead wife on yer cheek. I should shoot ye now for killing Alinga."

"Warrain has much honor. You will fight. The spirits demand it."

Billy's advice from two years past replays in his head: *Kangaroo Fighter has too much honor. Sometimes kill is best.*

Ryan dips the Colt's barrel and squeezes the trigger. Loklok's knee explodes and he drops to the ground, hollering with rage. He fumbles for his gun. Ryan fires again. The large caliber slug amputates his opponent's thumb. Ryan bolts to Loklok's side and kicks the firearm aside.

Ryan sits on his haunches, watching blood pour from Loklok's leg wound. The bullet must have nicked an artery.

"Ye are a killer of children and girls," Ryan says. "Ye don't deserve a warrior's death."

"How the great Warrain has fallen," Loklok chants. "Kangaroo Fighter betrays the warrior's bond. The spirits will desert him now."

Ryan raises the pistol to put a bullet through Loklok's skull to end his irritating babble. He hesitates. *No. I will not kill in anger.*

"My honor stopped me from killing ye that time we fought. My honor prevented me from killing Healey when he attacked me with a knife. My honor held me back in Ballarat when I had justifiable cause to kill Fraser. The spirits repaid that honor by letting ye, Healey and Fraser butcher my family. Honor is a myth created by men."

Loklok rolls his head side-to-side in earnest disagreement.

"Don't dictate rules of honor to me," Ryan continues. "Ye were the top Wathaurung warrior of yer generation. Ye became a murderer of the defenseless and the innocent."

"You also kill," Loklok murmurs, his voice weakened by loss of blood.

"Aye. I've Fraser's blood on my hands. My soul may be soiled. But it doesn't make us equal. I punished a fiend. Ye are too full of hate to see the difference. I blame Healey and Fraser for that."

Loklok raises his head. A wordless question poised on his face.

"Dyeelaga told me ye were a fine boy with great promise until ye returned from Fraser's station," Ryan says. "I guess ye couldn't rid yerself of the shame, like Nalong and Weeyn. It ate yer soul."

Loklok lays back, eyes skyward. After half a minute, Ryan notices ragged breathing and wetness on his cheeks. His legendary opponent weeps.

The mare fidgets and inclines her head to the west. Ryan detects a familiar rhythm and rises to investigate. A mounted, gray horse gallops his way. Gun in hand Ryan follows the stranger's progress. Long before the man reaches the base of Ryan's hill, he holsters the pistol. He recognizes the rider, a man unexpected but always welcome.

"Weeyn, lad. What are ye doing here?"

"I did not want Warrain to fight Loklok alone. Have you seen him?"

"Aye. He is inside this copse," he says, pointing.

"What is he doing?"

"Dying."

They pass through the thirty feet of thick brush and halt. "I'll be damned,' says Ryan.

In Ryan's absence, Loklok extracted the knife Ryan had not confiscated and, with both hands, plunged it into his heart. His lifeless orbs stare at his nemesis.

"Loklok cheats me of my last revenge," Weeyn growls.

"He is gone. 'Tis what matters. Help me gather firewood."

"Why honor him?" Weeyn says. "That bunyip deserves to be fed to the dingoes and ravens."

"No. We send him to his ancestors and pray they can heal his tortured soul."

"I pledged to cut his heart out," Weeyn says.

"He's done it himself. Let him be. The hate ends now."

Weeyn sighs. "Warrain is wise."

*****

They pull branches and logs from the forest to cover Loklok's corpse. Creating a pyre is solemn, silent work. For twenty minutes, Weeyn stifles the questions gnawing at his gut. He has not yet told Ryan the true purpose for following him.

"Do blacks live in North America?" Weeyn says.

"Aye. Blacks from Africa. Why do ye ask?"

"Is life better for blacks there than here?" Weeyn says. He piles wood, his back to Ryan.

"'Tis terrible in the Southern States. Whites enslave blacks and whip them for all manner of trivial reasons. The Northern States have no slaves but people treat blacks as second-class, though they have more opportunity than here. In British Canada, 'tis better than America but blacks still aren't equal."

Weeyn weighs the new information. He has no geographical reference for any place Ryan mentions. He warms to the idea of general opportunity. In Australia, chances to prosper in the white world exist solely with fair employers like Warrain and Stephen. Charity from a few cannot erase unfair treatment for all.

Ryan tosses a log on the pile and places his hands on his hips. "These are curious questions ye ask. What are ye not telling me?"

Weeyn piles bark, twigs and tinder on the woodpile's edge. He cannot look at Ryan. He replies, "Loklok is not the only reason I came. You do not have to travel away alone. Weeyn has no close family except his brother Warrain."

Ryan hesitates to answer. Weeyn assesses Ryan's expression and detects hints of surprise and confusion. "Does this displease my friend?" he says.

"Nay. It pleases me more than ye may know. But...I'm not going alone. Ellen will travel with me."

Weeyn concentrates on the woodpile. The only visible sign of his reaction to the news of Ellen is how fiercely he rubs sticks to start the fire.

"Ellen and I decided to live as husband and wife. I'll meet her in Sydney."

"You did not tell me," Weeyn says.

"'Twas a quick decision. I told none 'cause telling had no purpose and secrecy was better."

He accepts the honesty and wisdom in Ryan's words. The fire sticks begin to smother. He bends low and close, and blows on the nascent ember. A thread of smoke rewards his effort. A feeble flame appears and grows as it feeds.

"We are friends and brothers," Weeyn says, "but Warrain needs a wife and children."

"Ye can journey with us, if 'tis what ye wish. I'd nary turn ye away. We can be business partners agin."

Weeyn respects Ryan's sincerity, but cannot imagine an equitable partnership with Ellen. She is his former teacher who will never treat him as an equal. And he will always be the brother and constant reminder of Ryan's first wife.

Weeyn inserts thicker sticks into the growing flames. He has decided to leave his birth land. Ellen's appearance will not change that. His money will take him anywhere in the world. He can read and write. He can start his own business. Most important—he remains a warrior. He can hunt alone.

"I will ride with Warrain to Sydney. I make no promises for after that."

Weeyn rises and retreats from the growing heat. The fire spreads through the dry wood and the scent of burning flesh taints the air.

Ryan removes Fraser's clothing and tosses them on the flames.

"What about Fraser's horse?" Weeyn asks.

"I'll ride the beast Loklok used. We'll turn Fraser's mare free. She'll wander to a stable in a few days."

"People will recognize Fraser's brand but his end will remain a mystery," Weeyn adds.

"Aye. We ruined his reputation, stripped him of his wealth, took his life and denied him a place for anyone to erect a tombstone."

Weeyn feels Ryan's hand on his shoulder. "Ye know, friend," Ryan says, "the plan would have failed without ye. We are stronger together than apart."

Weeyn holds back what is on his tongue. *No matter how strong our friendship, Ellen can always come between us.*

*****

"A black lass cannot travel alone, Alinga," Stephen says. "You must have an escort," he adds, pushing aside his empty dinner plate.

Alinga shrugs. "I must go in the morning."

"I'll send word to Ellen. Maybe she can accompany you."

"Ellen is far away. She travels to meet my husband." Seeing the shocked expression on Sarah, Alinga adds, "I dreamed it."

Sarah's eyebrows arch in disbelief. Stephen chimes in, "Alinga is famous for seeing the near feature. She has a gift. Believe what she says."

"You seem calm about it," Sarah says.

Alinga smiles. "My husband believes me dead. I am not angry that he seeks comfort in another."

Sarah clears the dinner plates and returns with a pot of tea. "I must accompany you. 'Tis the only choice." Stephen begins to rise from his seat. She shoves him back. "Sit husband, and listen."

She pours Alinga a cup, then herself. Facing her guest, she says, "My husband loves you like a sister, but he cannot go to Sydney. He must act normally to keep up the deception he is party to. You need a white person to ensure your safety. So, I should be your travel mate."

"Very sensible, wife" says Stephen. "Polligerry can take you by wagon the Geelong. There are packets that sail to Sydney daily."

"Then, 'tis settled," Sarah says. "I seems strange to leave here so soon, but I welcome a chance to see more of this country."

"How many days travel to Sydney," Alinga asks.

"One day to Geelong. Four days to Sydney in fair winds. More in foul weather or if the packet makes stops at extra ports."

*****

After eight days of riding, Ryan and Weeyn notice an increasing density of white habitation. Farms become frequent. Hamlets rise from the dusty sward. Ahead a blue line of distant hills looms higher every hour.

"Somewhere in those hills is a road. It leads to the coastal plain and Sydney," Ryan says. "We be bound to encounter people soon."

"None will recognize us here. We are safe."

"Remember to use the names we agreed on, if asked," Ryan says.

Next day, on the outskirts of Sydney, Ryan and Weeyn sell their horses to a boarding stable and hike into the sprawling city in the late afternoon.

"I did not know this land had so many white people," Weeyn whispers.

"I hear fifty thousand folks live here now, but 'tis naught compared to many American cities."

Ryan ponders every shop as they march into ever-denser habitation.

"What are you looking for?" Weeyn asks.

"The time has come to change our appearance and leave the frontier behind. We need a barber, a bath and a haberdashery. And then an inn. 'Tis too late to reach the harbor today."

"Will a white barber cut a black man's hair?"

"Aye. If ye offer enough shillings and pounds they will forget yer skin color. 'Tis the way of money in the white world."

At sunset, Ryan and Weeyn rest in the dining lounge of a modest inn. Clean-shaven and with close-cropped hair, they are now attired like successful merchants. Each wears a white cotton shirt under a silk vest, with matching jackets and trousers.

Weeyn, once skeptical of Ryan's faith in wealth's power, is now a convert to the rule of money. A few pound notes and well-spoken English can erase the color bar, a least for the purchase of products and services.

When Weeyn places his supper order and the waiter responds, "Yes sir," he admits he has turned a corner. His days as a bushman are gone forever.

"Money brings privilege, my friend," Ryan says, sensing his friend's musings, "but nary be lulled into false beliefs. None of these polite white folks would ever let ye marry their daughter. And in this country, blacks can't vote or enjoy many things whites do."

"That is why I am leaving the land of my birth," Weeyn says. "No one remains to hold me here."

"Then ye will travel with Ellen and me to America?"

"Warrain is my friend and brother. For that reason, I say no."

"Why?" Ryan says, shifting back in his chair.

"Three is not a sound number. Your hopes for a happy triumvirate are optimistic. Let's part as friends now rather than risk hard feelings later."

"I can't say farewell to ye agin," Ryan says.

"You must. I will stay until I escort you and Ellen to a ship, then we part."

"Where will ye go?"

"I will hunt until I find a land where I am welcome."

* * * * *

The next morning after breakfast, Ryan and Weeyn hire a cab for the final leg of the journey to the docks at the foot of Macquarie Street. Ocean-going sailing vessels are roped hull-to-hull in the large natural harbor. With their backs to the artificial forest of masts and spars, the two men meander up the street.

At two hotels, the desk clerks do not recognize the name Ellen O'Sullivan. At the third, the clerk responds, "Are you Mr. Pine?"

"Yes. Ryan Pine and Wayne Laarson."

"Very good, sir. The lady asks that you to meet her in the tea parlor. It is around the corner on your left. I will alert Mrs. O'Sullivan."

"Thank ye."

Weeyn admires the parlor's opulence: brocaded settees, dark paneled walls, a chandelier, and china on white linen table clothes. Ryan orders tea.

"'Tis a happy and sad day," he says, "gaining Ellen but losing ye."

Weeyn shrugs. "We must accept the paths the spirits guide us on, as Mr. Stephen always said."

Ryan drinks his tea in silence, drumming his fingers on the table and monitoring the door. People enter and leave. One man attracts Ryan's notice. His features suggest youth but he has white hair and walks with a cane. He reminds Ryan of a sea captain or man of maritime occupation. The stranger takes a seat and coughs into a handkerchief.

After ten nervous minutes, Weeyn whispers, "She is here."

They both rise and face the door. Ellen enters the parlor with hesitant steps. A bonnet hides her curls. Darkened eyes peer from below her furrowed brow.

Pressure builds in Ryan's chest. He expected joy, not sullenness. "Ellen!" He steps towards her with his arms open.

Ellen halts his embrace with a gloved hand on his chest. "Please be seated." Turning to Weeyn she adds, "I am pleasantly surprised to see you, especially so handsomely attired, but I need a moment alone with Ryan. Would you be so kind as to wait in the lobby?"

"Yes, Mrs. O'Sullivan," Weeyn says.

Ryan remains standing, caring naught that strangers occupy many tables. "Ellen, my love, what—"

"Please," Ellen interrupts, "do not call me that. I cannot be your love."

"Ellen! What changed?"

"Do you see that white-haired man at the table behind me near the wall?"

"Aye," Ryan replies in a low voice.

"That is my husband Seamus." Ellen pauses, letting the weight of her words sink in. "He spent a decade shipwrecked on a cold and uninhabited island southwest of New Zealand. When he returned, he searched for me in Sydney for weeks. We met by chance four days ago at church. He wants me. He forgives me for any past dalliance in my long wait for his return."

Ryan swallows to keep calm amidst a volatile mixture of anger and sorrow. "But who do ye love?" he asks in a voice only she can hear.

Ellen forces shut her eyes. A single wet pearl rolls from one corner when next she looks at him. "Seamus is my husband. He returned ill with consumption. My duty is to care for him."

"Ye did not answer my question?"

She leans closer to Ryan and whispers. "You should not have to ask that question."

"Come with me, then. We have money to hire him the best doctors and a room in the best sanatorium. That is duty plenty."

"No! I made vows. The church granted a separation, not a divorce. I loved Seamus once. I may again."

Ryan reaches out to touch her hand. She pulls it back. "Do not make this harder than it is," she whispers.

Ryan withdraws his hand. "What will ye do now?"

"I shall return to Buninyong where the dry air will be restorative for Seamus. I may engage in business with Stephen."

Ryan's posture stiffens and his hands retract into fists. "I told Stephen I'd write him when I settle in America, using the name Mr. Pine; so he can send me final payments. Should ye ever need to contact me," he says, a cold edge to his words, "ask Stephen."

"I am sorry, Ryan," Ellen says. "I had counted on seeing forests like living sunsets. But, honor requires me to stay."

"Ye and I suffer from too much honor."

"How can there be too much honor?" Ellen asks.

"When it costs more than it's worth." Ryan says, picking up his hat. "Good-bye, Ellen." With a nod to Seamus, Ryan returns to the lobby.

"Something wrong with Mrs. O'Sullivan?" Weeyn asks.

"Aye, a surplus of husbands." To acknowledge Weeyn's quizzical look, Ryan adds, "I'll tell ye later."

Ryan walks beside Weeyn down Macquarie Street towards the harbor.

"Ye know something, my friend?"

"What, Warrain?"

"Ellen would be a poor substitute for Alinga. I should just accept that 'tis not my fate to find another like her."

"We both have deep wounds to heal," Weeyn adds.

Ryan pointed towards the masts towering above buildings a few blocks away. "Let's get on the next ship out of here. This land has too many ghosts."

*****

Mid-morning two days later, Mr. Pine and Mr. Laarson board a barque loading merchandise and passengers bound for Aukland, Honolulu and San Francisco. They carry new carpet bags of personal belongings. Porters wheel two trunks up the ramp behind them. Each wears a loose-fitting overcoat. The day before, they paid a tailor to sew multiple hidden pockets in each, which now hold bundles of pound notes.

The ship's purser greets Ryan with a side glance at Weeyn. "Welcome aboard. We get underway at noon as soon as the tide turns."

"Thank ye. Can ye show us to our staterooms, please?"

The purser looks at Weeyn, shrugs and says, "Follow me, please."

As a bell in Sydney chimes twelve times, the barque's crew casts off the lines and a steam-powered tug pulls the three-masted ship from its slip. The tug moves them forward at a pace slower than walking, a necessity in the narrow confines of the inner harbor. Once the ship clears South Head, they see the Tasman Sea shimmer in the distance.

Ryan and Weeyn watch the crew detach the vessel from the tug and ran up a pair of foresails. With wind off the land, the ship moves seaward under its own power. Ryan stands close to the helm and watches the harbor pilot steer the ship through hidden reefs.

Weeyn nudges him with his elbow and points to a small sidewheeler steaming toward them from North Head, the last finger of land. "What is that ship doing?"

The pilot hears the question. "That is my ride back."

As the little steamer pulls along side the massive barque, the sailors drop the sails and toss the steamer a line. Once both ships are lashed together, the steamer captain climbs aboard and waves over the purser.

"I have an additional passenger."

"Impossible. I have no empty berths."

"She paid the company a small fortune. You must make room."

As they speak, an uncommonly large but pretty young woman climbs the rope ladder onto the barque and asks the purser a question.

Ryan nudges Weeyn. "She looks familiar."

"Not to me," Weeyn replies, as the purser points the woman in their direction.

As tall as Ryan, the woman walks over and asks, "Are you Mr. Pine?"

Ryan's eyebrows shoot up. "Few people know to call me that. I know you from a picture. Ye be Stephen's bride."

"Yes. His new wife." She takes his hand and looks at him sadly.

"Are ye bearing bad news, ye look forlorn? Be Stephen in trouble?"

"No, no. He is well. I am saddened to meet a man I have heard so much about only to say farewell."

"Then why are ye here?"

Sarah smiles and points to another woman who has just climbed on deck.

"I have a surprise."

###

Series

Counter Currents and *Dark Southern Sun* are the first two parts of a series called Ryan's Journey. Others in the series are pending.

This is the second version of *Dark Southern Sun*. The original had a different ending.

About the Author

Besides this novel, Shaun J. McLaughlin published history books on the Patriot War of 1838 and the novel *Counter Currents*, the award-winning prequel to *Dark Southern Sun*. *Counter Currents* and *Dark Southern Sun* are the first two parts of a series called *Ryan's Journey*. Others in the series are pending.

Shaun maintains two history blogs: Raiders and Rebels, about a nineteenth-century Canadian/American border clash; and, Pirate Bill Johnston, which covers the exploits of William Johnston, the Thousand Islands legend. A researcher, journalist and technical writer for over thirty years, with a master's degree in journalism, Shaun lives on a hobby farm in Eastern Ontario, Canada.

For information on Shaun's other writing, including his science fiction novelettes, visit http://www.raidersandrebelspress.com.

Author and Historical Notes

While a work of fiction, *Dark Southern Sun* respects the history it borrows. The major events portrayed in this book—displacement of the Aboriginal people, the world's largest alluvial gold rush and Australia's only armed uprising—are historical and accurate. The names of towns and places are those that existed in 1845 to 1855.

This book is a sequel to *Counter Currents* and its family-friendly twin, *Islands of Love and War*. This book stands alone and no prior reading is required to fully appreciate the story.

This story includes several fictional characters belonging to the Wathaurung clan. I owe a debt to former transported convict William Buckley (1780-1856). Under the name Murrangurk, he spent thirty-two years (1803-1835) living with the indigenous Wathaurung people in what is now Victoria State. His biography provides the best description of what life was like for the natives before colonists disrupted their world.

Besides Buckley's work, I consulted other primary and secondary sources. *Letters from Victoria Pioneers* is a collection of fifty-eight letters by early settlers gathered in 1853 by Lieutenant-Governor Charles Joseph La Trobe. The collection provides useful details on pioneer life and describes a wide range of Aboriginal reactions to colonists—from assimilation to warlike hostilities. *Black Gold* by Fred Cahir is a modern account of the Aboriginal people in the Victoria gold fields.

All main characters in this novel are fictional; however, I base the quest for bloody revenge by Walter Fraser on that of William Fraser. History credits him with leading the extermination of an entire Aboriginal clan of some 300 people as revenge for the killing of nine members of his family in 1857.

Two secondary characters, Henry Ross (a.k.a. Charles Ross) and Charles Alphonse Doudiet, closely follow their historical roles. Ross did serve as a rebellion leader and met his fate as described. His prospecting partner, Doudiet, documented the gold rush and brief rebellion before returning to Canada. His sketchbook lay in an attic for generations until discovered in 1996 and sold to a Ballarat art gallery.

Actual historical characters in the gold rush play many minor and cameo roles. The novel presents them as accurately as possible, at their correct location, time and occupation. They are: James Bentley, Freeman Cobb, James Dunlop, William Gates, John Gibbs, Thomas Hiscock, William Irwin, David Jones, Peter Lalor, William Mumby, William Robinson, James Reagan, James Sayer, James Scobie and William Willis. The character of Officer Billy loosely reflects Billibellary, an early member of the Native Police Corps.

A few terms may need explaining to a non-Australian audience. A gum tree is a member of the eucalyptus family. Australia has seven hundred species of eucalyptus, which account for eighty percent of the tree cover. Van Diemen's Land is now Tasmania. A station is the equivalent of an American ranch. Readers will find a glossary of words spoken by the Wathaurung characters at the end of this book.

To make it easier to know what language characters are speaking, conversation in a native language is indicated by angle quotes or guillemets, instead of standard English double quotation marks.

The novel benefitted greatly by feedback from my volunteer beta-readers: in Canada, Patricia Bradley-White, George Hill, and Jill McCubbin; United States, James Graff; and Australia, T. D. McKinnon and Barry Sullivan.

Special thanks to Wathaurung elder Marlene Gilson and her daughter Deanne Gilson for reviewing the manuscript for cultural and linguistic authenticity.

Glossary of Wadawurrung Words Used in this Story

When presenting indigenous words, this novel attempts to use the language spoken by the Wathaurung. The spellings are phonetic and thus may vary with the source.

amadeat: white man

arweat: chief, headman

boolgana: sheep

boort: smoke

bunyip: the name for a mythical devil creature used by some southeastern Australian clans but not necessarily the Wathaurung

darr: hunting spear

dyeelaga: spark

goeem: kangaroo

kadak: large snake

karnweel: long spear with a jagged end

kaweerr: emu

keerram: long shield

koorr: battle club, waddy

laarr: stone

lakorra: sky

lanapoon: wife

loklok: eagle

lubra: native girl, woman or wife (a word of Tasmanian origin and introduced by colonists)

maya: wind

mokborree: peace

nganaboon: husband

ngoorr-ngoorr: wombat

tarrarrapeel: white

walert: bushtail possum

wardoong: elder brother

weeyn: fire

woorrak: blossom of the banksia plant

yakka: grasstree plant

yearn: moon

Notes: Alinga means sun in a clan language other than Wadawurrung. I used this name rather than the correct word mirri. Warrain does mean belongs-to-the-sea among some southeastern Australian clans but not necessarily the Wathaurung.